BLESSED

THE LEGACY SERIES

MARIANNE MAGUIRE

ISBN: 978-0-9959303-7-7

ALSO BY MARIANNE MAGUIRE

The Legacy Series

Born

Inheritance

Bequeath

Blessed

DEDICATION

For Buddy, Merlin, Rupert, and Winston.
The paw-prints of the past, present, and future- forever in my heart.

CHAPTER 1

We all have moments that will mark our lives. Moments in which we realize nothing will ever be the same and our lives will forever be divided into two parts, before this moment, and after this moment. Sometimes these moments are the markings of a loved one passing; I have experienced more than a few of these. Sometimes they are of an event of great change or discovery.

As I walk the girl out of the old barn into the dry Nevada night, I realize I have just experienced such a life-altering event and nothing will ever be as it was before, but as it will be from this moment on.

"What kind of fuckery is this?"

The brunette's tongue is sharp, laced with attitude, her brand of feisty snaps me from my thoughts, rushing the blood from my brain right to my cock and making it twitch.

"There's a fucking guy with wings in my barn and a chick who shoots rainbows out her ass. Not to mention I just bit a dead human to bring him back to life as a werewolf. This has to be a horrible dream because I know I haven't been slipped any peyote recently."

I stifle a chuckle, no need to laugh at the poor she-wolf for her ignorance, not when I'm digging the rough edge to her, "The guy is an angel, and the girl is a witch in transition. She's just become one of the most powerful goddesses on Earth, and she will need the angel and human to build her strength."

I explain this with pride I feel for Lilith, the chick with the rainbow shooting ass, because she is my sister after all.

This surprising discovery I found out only hours ago. One look at the desert landscape transforming into a grove before me, tells me she is indeed as powerful as our mother had once been.

"I don't care if she's a goddamn unicorn, this isn't natural. Do you not see the forest sprouting in *my* desert?"

Little miss prissy throws her hand out to the air towards the trees growing up in the pasture outside the old barn. Despite her anger, a hint of her arousal drifts back to my nose on the gentle breeze. I take in her sweet scent with interest, while her sexy smoke tone lures me in, and I listen to her rant.

"I don't know who you people are. Why this is happening here or what it's even all about. But, you have to get off my land. Go back to the magical make believe you came from, and leave me the hell out of whatever bullshit you're selling. I'm not interested."

Her frustration is understandable, it's not every day a goddess is born, almost never, and the side effects can be difficult to take. Although, over the last few months, I've witnessed two of these transformations. This one is nowhere near as intense as Queen September's had been in Toronto. The Queen's magic was insane in comparison, and it left the crowd in a state of sexual frenzy because of it. The brunette has every right to be a little upset, but there's no way we can leave. Not until I get my hands on the fucking warlock who tried to kill Lilith. The bastard will pay for what he's done, and karma is just the revenge-seeking bitch to get the job done right.

"Look, Paige, is it?"

I turn from watching the new forest blooming up with life to face the female, hoping to calm the situation, but she doesn't answer. She seems to be preoccupied with thought. Her brow is creased behind her dark wavy locks, eyes shielded in the night's shadows as she stares down at the grass growing around her feet. I notice her chewing on her bottom lip, it's sexy as hell. I watch her with attentive curiosity, also picking up on the sway of her hips, ever so slight, as her hands ball up the thin skirting of her tiny black dress.

I'm not sure if this is her nervous tick. Hell, maybe she just needs to urinate. I step towards her, placing my hand on her shoulder to inquire.

"Hey, you alright?"

She jumps with a gasp at my touch and whips her head up, as though she's just realizing she's not alone. This is when I get my first real look at her, and it stops my world in mid-rotation.

She is simply stunning. Her gorgeous dark features hinting to a Native American heritage. Sharply cut eyebrows show off her almond-shaped eyes of a cognac color, captivating me with what I can only describe as a gaze of deep hunger. Her mouth is open in the shape of her gasp. It allows her to run her wet tongue along the thickness of her bottom lip before sucking it in with a moan.

The she-wolf has been all rough-around-the-edge attitude since showing up tonight and it matches her exterior well. Scantily clothed, making up for the loss of fabric with loads of ink. I'm not usually into chicks with this much color on their body, but I'm starting to form a new appreciation for the art. She does have a lot of exposed canvas to look at.

A canvas with just the right amount of curves and perfectly shaped hips. Some would call them child-bearing. I prefer doggie-style grip handles. And as I stand completely still, mesmerized by her beauty and magnetically drawn to her, I think of how amazing she would look in that position underneath me. With her tits swaying, more than a handful to hold while she's being drilled from behind.

There's just something intoxicating about her, she's a syringe full of sin I crave to plunge deep into my veins. I wet my own dry lips, shaking my head to clear out the impure thoughts racing through my mind.

When I try again to check in with the female my voice cracks, "Are you okay?"

I'm speaking to her, but the words are meant for me. Her answer is not what I expect when she grabs one side of my open jacket to pull me to her.

"I'm fucking horny," she states, as one would say they need a drink to quench a desperate thirst. "Please tell me you have a big cock because if you don't, I'm about to go attack that fence post."

She nods at the remains of a cedar post at the edge of the pasture, which I turn to inspect. Hiding my increased interest in her by explaining her sudden hormone shift, "Yeah, I know what you're feeling, it's from the magic Lilith and Lazarus are throwing around in the barn. It can be difficult to manage."

"Difficult?" She snorts. "More like insane fuck-lust. I want to rip your pants off and suck you hard. If that gives you any indication."

Christ, the girl is vocal and my dick swells with anticipation of her idea. I'm not one to turn down such a bold offer, especially when I'm digging her groove. Except, we're in the MC territory and I don't know her. She might be someone's old lady, and I sure as shit don't want a nine in the head for helping her get her funk on.

"I know what you mean. When our Queen got her powers, the lingering effects of her magic were so strong, I couldn't stop jacking-off for a week."

"A week," she groans deep in her throat, the sound stimulating me even further and I have to shift my hips to adjust my cock. "I don't have time to be laying around diddling myself for a fucking week. I need something hard between my legs, now."

She stops with wide eyes, seeming to come to some conclusion, and her lips part to offer an incredible mischievous grin. Her statement, coupled with the smile, are visual and auditory porn that I could replay on repeat all day.

"Unless you're gay, then I totally get the hesitation. We can work around it. I'll let you do me in the ass to make it more familiar for you."

I choke at her accusation, "Wh-what?"

The erotic fantasy of her in my head scatters, while my hard-on softens.

"I'm not gay," I stumble with a defensive tone that I don't understand. The mix of feelings over her suggestion confuses me.

I don't get time to digest it as she grabs with desperation at my shirt, crumpling the material in her grip. "Then help me, I feel I'm going crazy, like I'm in heat. Lend me your dick and give me some relief from the insanity."

Jesus, she's relentless, similar to a she-wolf in heat. Not easy to ignore when just her touch has me barely hanging on to my own lust.

"I'm trying to be considerate here. I don't mow the grass on some else's lawn. You get me?"

She rolls her eyes. "Great, of all the times to be stuck with the gentleman." She blows out her breath and throws her hands up. "Never mind, I'll go to my brothel. I'm sure one of my clients will be happy to help me out."

A frustrated growl escapes my throat as she starts walking out of the pasture, off towards her brothel in the distance. I'm overcome with an urge to protect this sultry vixen. It is somewhat our fault she feels the way she does. I also don't know why, but the thought of some slimy asshat touching her gets my hackles up. I leap forward to grab her arm, spinning her around and pulling her to me until we collide with each other.

When I look down into her face, her eyes are hooded with a dangerous desire. The kind of danger that will make you pray for forgiveness after the amazing sex. Something clicks, somewhere deep in my head, and I suddenly have a need to pray, hard, and on my knees.

"I know exactly what you crave, and being the

gentleman that I am, I'm going to give it to you until the physical ache goes away."

I hear her gasp with excitement when I lift her from under her arms. Carrying her, I walk us both back against the barn. Off to the side and tucked away from the door.

Being this close to her, the heavy scent of her arousal gets my motor revving. My cock begins to strain against the seam of my denim as I pin her against the faded wood wall, as the masterpiece that she is. Stretching her out, arms above her head, while nudging her knees apart.

She's picture fucking perfect.

She's putty in my hands, willfully allowing me to have my way with her and manhandle her goods. A voice somewhere in the back of my head nags with wonder, to know if she's like this with all males. In which case, it's a bit of a turn-off. I shake this off, though. I have no right to judge her when she's not the first female I've rocked and rolled off of. Nor do I expect her to be the last.

Once I have her pinned and under my control, I press my weight against her surprisingly toned body, holding her in place. I'm met with a nose full of the fragrance drifting up from her satin smooth skin. She has a natural scent, free from chemical enhancements, but with just a light hint of animal. Horse to be exact. An odd combination, yet I'm compelled to nuzzle into her neck to breathe her in. It's such an intoxicating stimulant. The kind that causes one's sub-conscience to send out warning bells because I'm about to become addicted.

"If you kiss my neck, we're going to fuck, hard and dirty. But if you try to bite me, I swear I'll kick your ass." She warns in a breathy, yet serious, tone and adds, "I'm nobody's bitch, got that cowboy?"

Wolves are dominant beasts by nature, they are predisposed to fight to their death over territory, family and especially their females. When an Alpha is crowned, he will publicly mate with his Beta and mark her with his bite to show his ownership and seal their bond. Gage did this with September in Toronto and from their mating, he became the one True Alpha to all the wolves.

It also put a target on his back. Lesser Alphas will forever be challenging him for the top spot. One of the reasons I chose to join the court is to help protect him and our Queen from these threats, and not just from the wolves. It's why I'm in Nevada now, protecting my sister and the threat to our Queen from Cale the warlock. Although, at the moment, I seem to be failing at my duty because I don't wish to think about them.

I'm more interested in Paige; she's hinting at being unattached. A relief on many levels, except she's also saying she has no use for a mate. This is not normal behavior for a she-wolf. I'm beginning to suspect Paige isn't a typical female wolf.

She's the chick you friend not just for the benefits. She's strong and independent, a smart choice of an ally to have in our corner. I'll work on the friendship later. Right now, I plan on taking advantage of the benefits package. By the sound of her racing heart, she's anticipating much of the same.

She gave me her warning, but in this position, she's mine to control, and I play dirty. I lick at her collarbone and up the side of her neck, stopping every few inches to nip her skin with my teeth. She tenses against me but doesn't fight, and as a reward, I suck at her flesh until she's moaning. I'm asking her to trust me with every nip, and by the time I reach the sensitive spot behind her ear, she seems all in, grinding herself against my erection... Unapologetically.

I'm digging how responsive she is to my touch. Just trailing my left hand up the side of her body has her panting out little approving moans. Then I discover she's not wearing a bra, and I'm all about taking advantage of the fullness of this breast, caressing what I can through the thin material of the dress.

When I grab for an ample amount of her right tit, to lift and squeeze, the nipple peeks aggressively against the fabric, begging to be tasted.

Who am I to deny the little bud of such joy?

I dip my head down, placing my mouth over the dress and her nipple. Rolling the tiny gem with my lips, then holding the bud with my teeth to flutter my tongue against it.

"Mmm," she whimpers. "Harder," she begs.

I moan at her directness. Yanking down the stretchy fabric, I free this same breast to devour it with my mouth. I put all my attention into it, spoiling it with licks and sucks around her areola until it is puckering with anticipation. This is my cue to attack. Sucking her whole areola and hardened nipple in my mouth, to lick, chew, and slurp the goods until she is crying out for relief. When I hear the quick hitch in her breath before she stops breathing altogether, I know she's close to orgasming.

I smile with satisfaction against her breast, knowing I could easily make her cum. But she won't be satiated. The magic we experienced has a lasting effect, and a nipple orgasm will only scratch the surface of what she needs.

I know because I need it too. But this isn't for me. I'll take care of myself later. This is all about her pleasure, and I have a sudden craving to appease her completely.

I continue to mouth fuck her breast, softer, and with less aggression, while sliding my hand down her back to grip her sweet round ass. I moan from the firmness which I fully grasp in my hand. I could bounce a quarter off her cheek, it's just that hard.

She groans from the vibration of my moan on her breast. This prompts me to continue my hand scan of her body. I'm digging all the soft parts and the smooth indents. But I really heat up once I discover a garter belt, absent of underwear beneath the dress.

My cock pulsates inside my pants from the sensory

overload. It's painful but in the best possible way. As I bring my hand around to her thigh and down the crease towards her pussy, the warmth coming from her helps to grow the excessive wet spot at the front of my jeans. I can't help myself, I turn my hips into her right thigh, holding her leg between both of mine, to rub my covered cock against her garter. I could easily pump myself off like this and be done. But, there's no need to rush my own joy, not with so much more of her to appreciate.

I still my hips, pressing my groin against her for one last thrust before pulling away from the temptation. She takes this opportunity to slide down the wall. Digging her cowboy boot heels into the dirt as a brace, she opens her thighs wide, inviting me in. I groan again, getting one last suckle on her breast before moving away, anxious to take in my first views of her forbidden forest.

I want to see it, her, exposed and vulnerable. I lift her skirt to tuck it up between her breasts. Then, taking a step back, I finally get an eyeful of the splendor before me.

She's presenting the package well. She's unwrapped and shaved smooth over the pelvic bone, and all the way down to her glistening folds, sprinkled with a mouth-watering dew.

"Stunning," I whisper. "A beautiful fucking cunt."

I don't even think, I just drop to my knees in front of her to give my salivating mouth a taste of her pussy honey.

She whimpers as I clamp my mouth over her cunt lips and use the full width of my tongue to swipe through her slit.

I'm greeted by the taste of her sweet juice. It's velvet against my tongue. I savor the unique flavor while playing a game of hide-and-seek with her clit. I'm in no hurry to find it, exploring her folds down to her wet opening for more sampling of her cream. I want to tongue fuck every inch of her until she's drowning me in her essence.

Her hands, no longer pinned above her, are free to roam in my hair. She uses her fingernail grip to my skull, directing me to the sweet spot, and when I flick my tongue against her nub, it pearls up to greet me.

That's right, say hello to Daddy.

I wash the sin from her pussy with my tongue, swirling, sucking, and slurping my way around her clit, until it is as hard as her nipple had been right before her breath hitched. I hear the same telling sound, music to my ears, and I know she's at the edge of her release. I enjoy learning these little triggers. I'm obsessed to know what will get her dripping wet, and how far I can take her before she's at her limit, begging me to make her cum.

Ideas flicker in my head as I suck her nub hard, biting down on it between my teeth to give her jolts of pain.

"Oh God, yes, like that," she coos above me.

When I glance up, her beautiful eyes are blazing with the heat of her desire. She's staring down at me, watching the erotic show as I eat her out. It's enough to make my cock throb with discomfort inside the confines of my pants.

I choose to ignore it. I want the gift of her pleasure more than I want my own. I'm a madman as I dive in. Plunging my tongue up inside of her, feeling her cunt shudder as her sweetness seeps out, dripping down my chin. She's moaning out little sounds as I build the momentum.

I'd much rather have her screaming my name when the orgasm hits, too bad she doesn't know it, yet.

I concentrate on licking her slit, up towards her clit, circling the nub with the flat of my tongue to work over the sensitive nerves. It gives me the chance to bring my hand between her legs. She did say she wanted something deep in this spot.

I wipe my fingers across her opening to lubricate her with pre-cum before plunging two in, and up, inside her tight hole, working the back side of her clit from within. She seems to like this as she grips a fistful of my hair to hold my face in place, over her clit.

I counter her move with one of my own. Using my index

and ring fingers in a curling motion to hit her g-spot, I slide them in and out of her pussy. Her muscles flutter in response. I pick up the pace until her cunt tightens, and she's milking my fingers in return.

I add a third digit and stretch out my fingers. A selfish move on my part, to see if she could take my cock inside of her. She gasps and stills from the sudden fullness, but it doesn't take long before her hips begin to rock, pushing against me as she fucks my mouth and hand.

"I need it deep," she pants her commands, "Hard and really fast."

"Fuck," I muffle moan against her pussy, plunging my fingers inside of her to a fast but steady beat that soon has my hand coated with her cream.

I hear the hitching of her breath. This time, I want her to let go. The reward for our efforts.

I help her along, reaching up with my other hand to seek out her exposed breast with my fingers. Pinching down around her nipple, I pull at the little bud while twisting it hard with my thumb and index finger. That little bit of pain is all it takes.

Her cunt tightens, squeezing my fingers right before the release soaks her hole, and causes an adorable mousey squeak to escape her mouth. The sound doesn't match her aggression as she grinds her pussy against my face. I suspect she might be holding back some. It's enough to intrigue me for more. I try to keep up, licking her until she's dry, and savoring every drop of dew from her cunt until her body is convulsing.

"Oh God," she sighs, sliding further down the wall when her legs give out.

I'm quick on my knees, catching her mid-fall in my arms, and standing us both up so she doesn't land in the dirt. Her body is Jell-O as she lazily wraps one arm around my neck, the other around my waist, to hold me while she catches her breath. It takes some time before her legs are stable enough to carry her again. I find myself not minding the wait.

I take the opportunity to continue to get to know her more intimately. I listen to her heart thumping wildly in her chest, strong and bold just like her. Her scent drifts up, encompassing me, from her essence being all over my face. I don't bother to wipe it off, I like having it there. It adds to the taste of her still on my tongue, and the images of her spread wide for me, in my head. Even the weight of her against my body is welcoming. Not too heavy or tall, and not too light or short, the perfect combination to fit me.

The longer we stand in this cuddled position I find myself having some deep feeling for this chick. Something more than just an attraction. Something I never thought I'd be allowed to feel.

Something has changed. Maybe the magic is playing with my head or maybe, it's from what we just did and my still raging hard-on talking, but this, with her, is more than just a passing fancy.

"Oh God, I can't believe I just did that." She stirs against me, standing up straight and pushing away from me with a wobble as she adjusts her clothing to cover up.

Such a shame.

"Christ, you must think I'm a sheep. I swear I'm not. I don't pull train, I don't do any of the shit the club expects from a mama, and I'm nobody's old lady," she babbles out while avoiding any eye contact, interrupting my own thinking.

I step forward, bridging the sudden cold gap between us. I'm far too comfortable already with her warmth against me. I place my left hand under her chin, cupping it as I lift her head so she can see, in my eyes, I'll never judge her in such a degrading context.

"I think nothing of the sort of you, it's the magic. Believe me, I get it."

She blinks a couple of times, registering me for the first

time.

"Oh," she sighs with the kind of smile that causes another flicker of feeling I don't understand.

Her eyes blink a couple of times when she steps away. Breaking our intimate connection with a little stumble as her words ramble out. "Yeah, you did say something about magic, before I lost my goddamn mind, and apparently my dignity. Jesus, I don't even know your name. I'm Paige Sky, by the way. I guess I should say it's a pleasure to meet you."

She nervously giggles while confidently extending her right hand for a formal greeting. I chuckle, knowing, like my face, my right hand is also covered in her essence. I lift it to my mouth, licking the remnants of her from each of my fingers before offering it up for a shake.

With a smirking grin to her wide-eyed shock, I also introduce myself. "I'm Zander Paine, and your sweet pleasure is all mine."

CHAPTER 2

"Christ, obviously modesty isn't your strong suit," Paige snaps in a sarcastic tone, whipping her hand back for a quick retreat to avoid touching me.

The tiny glimpse of embarrassment I had seen, evaporates in the second it takes her to flick her fingers over the skirting of her dress, bringing the attitude back in full force.

"Thanks for the mediocre fingering and all, but it's time for you and your people to get off my property. I'm not interested in being a part of this fucked up mess, and neither is the MC. So y'all need to leave, now."

I watch her desires, shyness, and lust, fade into business-bitch, in a heartbeat. The flip is both impressive and infuriating, and I tell her as much, "Wow, nice attitude. Where did you get it, Abercrombie and Bitch?"

Her eyebrow pops up and her face stills with anger, bringing out the yellow flecks in her icy stare. I can tell she's not used to having someone talk back to her. I'm enjoying being the one to give her the challenge.

"Listen up cowboy, I'm no cactus expert, but I know a prick when I see one and it's standing in front of me."

I snort at her attempt to jab me. I've never been much for the true love aspect. I've seen that blow up for too many people in my life. However, this annoyance at first sight thing is turning me on with possibility.

I'm eager to playback and I cup my erection to emphasize my point. "Sure is, hard and impressive, but I take it we're not talking about my mammoth appendage. Are we, cupcake?"

She grunts with frustration while coming at me with her finger, the claw extended to poke sharply at my chest. "You're an arrogant asshole. I can't believe I let you touch me. You're just like the rest of the one percent, a dirty fucking pig."

I cup her hand in both of mine. Bringing her long talon up to my mouth, I nip at her finger with my teeth then I suck away the sting. A shiver comes over her as we touch and I like having this effect on her.

"From what I saw, you enjoyed every minute of the dirtiest part," I growl out in a low seductive tone.

Her gasp comes out as a whimper, she's still turned on, too. She might be back to her dominant self after the orgasm, but it will be short-lived. The magic around us is powerful, and before long, another craving will hit her. I secretly hope she comes to me when it does.

Until she's begging for more, while still being difficult, I'll just play as dirty as she suggests, and use the magic to my advantage until she sees things my way. She'll be putty in my hands, or rather, at the end of my cock. Meaning, I'll make her see that we're not leaving, even if I have to use the powers of magic, and my dick, to convince her.

"Understand, the Queen sent us to solve the murder of the witch your people found in the quarry. We know the warlock killed the girl. He's been siphoning powers from the magical beings. He almost killed the goddess in your barn to collect hers. If we don't catch him, it could mean bad news. Not just for our Queen, but for us all. So, I'm asking you nicely, Paige, let us stay. Help us find this asshole before he has time to play out whatever plan he's got cooked up."

She pulls her hand away with her step back, glaring at me as she listens. Her jaw clenched, teeth grinding back and forth, she thinks it over.

"What difference does it make to me? We've always stayed away from the royals and the otherworld crap. We live in our own world, out here, and as far away from that drama as possible. Unless you make it worth our while, we care nothing about this shit."

I sigh, knowing this is her MC upbringing talking. Every

motorcycle club I've met, human or otherwise, thinks they are more superior in every way. They don't think the laws of human government or royal courts pertain to them. They play their own games by their own rules, with honor, loyalty, and respect to their own club, and it never gets any of them, anywhere.

It's this bubble I intend to burst, and I lay it out for her. "If Cale escapes Nevada, he won't stop until he brings our Queen down, by whatever means he can. He's a shifty fucker, he kills to extend his life and to become strong enough to take the Queen on. If he's willing to do that, I bet he'd be willing to let the humans know we exist too, so that only his magical kin will be left to rule. If news of our existence gets out, the MC can't protect you, and you know it."

I stop to wave my hand at her land, to make a visual point. "All this you built means nothing, when the humans have you captured in some testing facility, doing God only knows what to you. There's a bigger picture now, one outside of the club, and you have to stop being so fucking naive about it."

She rolls her eyes at me, an impatient gesture that makes me want to pin her across my knee, so my hand and her ass can have a meeting.

"How do you know all this? I heard you're just some nomad. You don't even have a pack."

Her thick lips curl into a smirk and it's clear what she's doing. She's trying to get under my skin to get rid of me, but I'm not easily provoked.

"It's true, I belong to no pack. No one owns me or tells me what to do. Something, I'm sure, you can appreciate. However, when it comes to loyalties, mine have always been for our Queen. I believe she will be the one to guide us to a better future. A future that will include all races equally, and not just this every wolf for himself motto you've grown accustomed to."

My slight dig drops her smirk in a heartbeat, creating a deep frown on her brow that my hand itches to sooth away. It doesn't make me lower my tone any, she needs truths, no matter how blunt they are.

"I'm from the original pack. Long before your grandad's daddy was a swimming sperm in a bitch's cunt. You ask how I know all this? It's from roaming this world a long time. Living in the shadows, listening, watching and learning, so when the choice of paths presented itself to me, I could choose the right one. I recommend you seek out the same path unless you want the blowback to land in your lap. If that's the case, go ahead, continue to be a clueless bitch."

I see her wheels turning as she processes this information. Questions flicker in her eyes, about my lineage, I'm sure. There are a few hostile glares from my insults too, but she doesn't ask anymore.

Instead, she places her hand on the amazing curve of her hip and cocks her head up in defiance. "Fine, stay. It's not like you give me much choice in the matter. And I'll be happy to lend a hand to your cause if it means getting rid of you sooner."

I grin, knowing I have won this round, but I doubt this will be the end of the argument from her.

"Thank you," I offer with a bow of my head.

I hear her bark with laughter, making me lift my head in time to see her cross her arms over her ample breasts. Her dress stretches in protest, grabbing my full attention when the tops of her areoles are exposed, and what appears to be a jewel on her left nipple, pops out of hiding.

"Anyone ever tell you, you're a dick? A polite one, but a dick, nonetheless."

I should be shooting back some smart-ass reply as I listen to her chuckle away, but my fascination has the best of me. I'm drawn in by the sight of her pierced nipple. I swear it's begging to be pulled and played with. Ideas of ice and wax play start to form in my head. She did almost get off on having her nipples sucked hard, the mere thought of adding a little hot or cold pain with that pleasure is making my heart pound and my dick swell. I don't know how I missed this earlier. I could have had so much fun with that sparkly gem.

Damn, do I ever want to turn back the clock and explore her all over again.

"Uh, hello, cowboy? I think your pants are buzzing."

I shake my head just as my phone vibrates again in my pocket. I laugh when I realize it was turning me on.

No, she is.

Either way, I'm off my game, distracted by this wicked vixen, and her glittering tit. I scramble to dig the phone from my pants and hit the answer button hard.

"Paine," I snap with annoyance for being interrupted, before the phone even reaches my ear.

"Where the fuck is the angel?" The deep, gruff voice barks at me from the other end of the connection.

I don't take kindly to his tone and answer back with sarcasm, "Well, hello to you, too, Alpha. I'm fine and thanks for asking. Always a pleasure to hear from you, even though we do have a bit of a situation here. Don't worry, I assure you we are handling it like fucking pros."

"Fuck you, Zee, this isn't a social call. September's sick. She stopped breathing; we thought she was dead. It was brief and there's been a significant improvement, but there's no telling if this will happen again. I won't take risks with my mate and unborn child. So, put the fucking angel on the phone before I reach through this receiver and rip your goddamn head off."

I watch Paige's eyebrows pop up with curiosity as she listens in on the conversation. The problem with wolves is they hear everything, even if you don't want them to. More blowback I'll have to deal with after I calm down the Alpha. A mediator and peacemaker is not quite the job I signed on to do. It's more fitting to my sister, and it makes me question why I've been bothering to do it.

I mentally switch gears. "Laz is a bit indisposed at the moment..." I begin to explain but Gage doesn't give me a chance to finish.

"I don't give a rat's ass which skank-ho is blowing him, just put him on the goddamn phone, now."

I pull the phone away to prevent my eardrum from bursting and wait until he's silent, before unleashing my own assault. "Calm the fuck down, G, and let me explain. I can't get the angel because he's just bound himself to the Queen's witch.

But not before Cale tried to kill her, and she had to fight her way back from the fade to be reborn as a goddess, which is why our Queen got sick. The court is connected magically, and when Sunshine tried to fight off the warlock, she began draining magic from the Queen through the connection. She's on the mend now, thanks to her mating with the angel, which means the Queen is out of danger.

In the meantime, Cale got away after he siphoned Sunshine's powers. Now I have to find the asshole before he makes his way back to your mate. So, shut your damn yap, and let me get back to my own situation."

"Fuck." It's really the only answer he can give to my ramble. "I'm grabbing Sab, we'll jump on a plane to red-eye it down. You're going to need trackers, and those desert dogs couldn't smell their way out of an outhouse."

He has no idea, although I say nothing in front of the she-wolf. I can already see she's not taking kindly to the insult. There's no need to add salt to the wound.

"Happy to have the extra help, but I'm hoping to catch the bastard before you even get here."

"I'm not taking any chances. See you in a few hours." The line clicks, ending the call.

Gage is on his way.

I blow out a tired sigh, relieved to have reliable backup on the way for a situation that's getting much more complicated than I initially expected. The day has been a long one, and I've already blown off an hour to be with this she-wolf. I need to get Cale dealt with, so I can get back to the solitude I've grown accustomed to over the last few thousand or more centuries.

"Wow, the Alpha's a bigger jack-off than you." Paige's comment brings me out of my mind shuffle. "Does he treat all his subjects like that or just you?"

Her insults are starting to dig a little deep. You can attack me, but not my friends, and I've about had enough. "Who lit the fuse on your fucking tampon? The Alpha is concerned for his family and has a right to be a douche. You? Not so much."

The full width of her beautiful cock-sucking mouth drops open. The mere sight has me so overwhelmed with need that I have to concentrate hard on keeping myself from going over to her, to plug her hole with a big dripping load from my sac. There is this irksome quality about Paige that makes me want to fuck her hard. Right to the point of her getting off, but not allowing her the joyous satisfaction, just to teach her a lesson.

She reminds me of a spoiled child who has had it easy for far too long. Sure, she's done well for herself. One look at the miles of property she owns tells me as much. I do wonder how much is her own doing, and how much is the MC letting her have her way because her Daddy was their original Alpha. They have allowed her to reach Princess status for a reason, and now, no one wants to knock her off her pedestal.

Oh, how I would love to try if only I didn't have to save the fucking world first.

As if right on cue, gunfire echoes out across the hills off in the distance. It's a clear and quick double-tap from a handgun. I'm guessing some type of Glock. They seem to be what I noticed the wolves toting back in the bar. A loud boom answers from someone firing back with a rifle.

And we got ourselves a standoff.

"Shit," I curse, knowing I sent Ducky out after the warlock, and I've been too preoccupied with my prick's desires, to lend the guy a hand.

There's no time to wallow in guilt, though. I shrug it off, and beeline it to the barn, barking out at my cock tease as I go. "If you really want to help, get back to the bar, call up some of Ducky's boys and send them out. Just tell them to wear colors so I know who not to shoot."

I don't wait to hear Paige's rebuttal. I know she'll have one, but I don't have any more time to waste on her spoiled, yet spectacular, ass.

And what a shame that is.

I hit the ground running, as fast as I can. However, the raging hard-on between my legs isn't helping, and I almost regret not finishing myself off on her thigh earlier, when I had the chance. Almost being the optimistic word, I'm holding out to sample that fine drink of water again.

I enter the old building to find, then follow, Ducky's scent out the back exit. As I go, I call out to Lazarus, "We got trouble in the hills. I could use some back-up."

As I pass through, the inside of the barn is nothing but a blur. Flashes of the chaos that happened a few hours ago whip by in my rush. A pool of blood from the human Sunshine asked me to turn for her is now a dark drying stain. The human, Sam, stands alone beside it. He's beaten up and naked, but alive. He's a wolf in transition now, thanks to Paige siring him because I couldn't.

He'll become part of a pack soon. Whether it be with the she-wolf or Gage, will be up to him to decide. A choice I never got, but then again, I'm not really a wolf, either. These thoughts I push away for another time. After I take out the warlock or after the Queen and my sister are safe.

Maybe just much later, or possibly never.

I reach the field out behind the back exit, just as the sound of wings whoosh in the air somewhere above me. Lazarus, the angel, has taken flight.

I hit the open field stretching out before me. My feet pound the desert floor hard as I run, full-tilt, towards the gunfire echoing down the hills. My thoughts go to my own wings touching the sky, but I'm brought to reality by this curse, where my feet are chained to the dusty ground for eternity. Something I'll never really get used to or over.

More discharging weapons ring out, not just the handgun and rifle. This is something quicker, a semi-automatic, and I hear a lot of them. I dig deeper, pumping my legs to sprint onward, towards the mouth of the hills.

Ducky's scent trails left into a shanty town made up of older Airstreamers, rusted and worn past their age. They are stuffed in between rickety, weathered wood cabins with bowing roofs from the sinking foundations. It's the shit-hole he had described earlier to me, where the witches have been living.

I slow, checking out the other direction. On my right, in the east, is a wrecking yard with a wall made from row-on-row of mangled cars. Before the entrance to the metal burial ground is a service station, complete with antique gas pumps that don't appear to have had a customer in decades.

The Wicked Ones MC clubhouse hides deep within the flattened car fortress. I haven't been to it for many years, and the walls have grown in that time, making it appear like the junkyard version of Fort Knox.

This is but a quick assessment my mind registers to judge my surroundings. I know the fight is beyond the two locations, where the field narrows. It's apparent the gunfire is being exchanged on either side, perhaps by each club or just the wolves against Cale. It's hard to tell in the darkness, but I'll find out soon enough. For right in front of me, behind two barriers of concrete placed at the base of the hill to prevent cars from entering, covering his own ass in the crossfire, is my man Ducky.

I slide in like a ballplayer stealing home base. Gravel rolls up my pant leg and the back of my shirt; it's going to leave a mark of road-rash. I try to dig in my heels to slow myself. My legs tangle, causing me to roll like a rag doll across the dirt until I stop hard against the barrier beside the biker.

The liquid ooze of perspiration leaking down my face gets mixed with the settling dust. It leaves me cough-gagging when a rush of air escaping my lungs from the abrupt halt mixes with the silt.

"About time you showed up," Ducky dryly comments, firing a couple of shots over the concrete before turning to glare down at me hacking dirt from my mouth.

His nostrils flare as he takes in my scent, and Paige's. "All hell is breaking loose, and you stopped for what? A blowjob?"

He takes another sniff when I offer an innocent glance, and he corrects himself. "No, I can smell the cunt on your breath- you dined out. So not cool leaving a brother alone, man. You know the code is always bros before the hos."

I also know the biker's overprotective nature for the she-wolf. He won't be happy to know she's the one I dined on, but he is right. I brush off the sex like I wipe off my brow, making it a non-issue. "Yeah, well, I had no choice. It was a magic thing, totally out of my control. Besides, I'm here now, that's what matters. So, tell me, who we aiming at?"

Ducky seems to take my brush off in stride and we both take a position, back to back, behind the barrier. I peer up and around the concrete, in the direction of the returning gunfire. With the sky black above us, we must rely on our supernatural night vision to see out into the shadows cast across the desert.

"I'm not sure," he begins with a pause, thinking over his response.

He continues slowly, filling me in so we are able to make up our next move. "I did what you asked. I followed the warlock into the trailer park where he picked up a few friends. They headed up into the hills, I assume, to get over the west ridge to the highway, then to the protection of his MC. But about halfway up, my area patrol tried to stop him, and he did some magic mumbo-jumbo to get away. I started firing to stop them. His buddies returned the gesture, which gained attention. I don't know if it's from us or them at this point. I ran back for you and got pinned here in the crossfire. I think he's still in the hills with my guys on his tail, just don't quote me on that."

A bullet pings the barrier in front of us and pieces of cement fly in several directions. We both crouch low to avoid getting hit.

"Shit, we'll never find him if he makes it over any of these ridges. We need to get up the hill to flush him out."

Ducky peers low to the ground on his side to confirm. "Yup, but we also can't find him stuck behind this damn wall, either. What do you want to do?"

He fires a shot out towards the west side. There's no telling if it hits a target or if he's just unloading his clip. Reaching inside my jacket to the sling harness on my left side, I pull out my Sig Sauer P228. It has a shorter slide and barrel than his Glock 19, making it lighter in weight to hold, and smoother for firing. It also houses more rounds in the magazine, which makes the difference between living or dying in this battle.

"We need to figure out who's out there so we don't get shot or kill one of our own," I tell him, while trying to get a look out at our surroundings to aim my firearm appropriately.

Another shot is fired further up the hill, I see the flare coming off the gun, from someone on the east side. I can't tell if they are friend or foe, witch or wolf.

"Damn it," I curse in frustration and hear Ducky grunt in agreement as he fires blindly on his side until his clip is empty.

I hear a click from him jamming in a new clip just as the air swirls, whipping up some of the dirt with the flapping of feathers. I roll back against the barrier in time to see Lazarus come down in a smooth walk-in landing.

The disturbance has Ducky jerking, then shuffling his feet and legs back and forth on the ground to get away. In his panic, he aims his weapon up at the angel and squeezes off a shot. The bullet sparks from the gun then suddenly slows, turning with a wide berth, avoiding Lazarus altogether. A neat magic trick.

"What the…" Ducky gasps in shock, watching a pure white feather float down from Lazarus retracting his wings.

I grab the wolf's leg, trying to stop his panicked thrash before he shuffles himself away from the protective concrete wall. "Easy brother, Laz is on our side."

Ducky bats my hand away and he fumbles his weapon in his hand. I fling back, and thankfully, it doesn't go off in his haste to hang on to it.

"I don't care whose side he's on. What the fuck is he?"

Lazarus is full of humor tonight as he smirks down at the guy. "I'm evil incarnated, asshole. Shoot at me again, I'll kill you once, then bring you back from the dead to watch you die a second time, just for fun."

I bite my tongue as not to laugh at the expression on Ducky's face. It's a cross somewhere between confusion and pants-shitting terror. From the smell of fear drifting off of the poor guy, I imagine my buddy is going to need a change of shorts soon.

"Never mind him Duck-man." I pat my buddy on the legs. "Laz thinks he's a wise-ass comedian, but he doesn't realize angels just aren't that funny. His wings, on the other hand, those will be useful in helping us locate the warlock."

Ducky's confusion deepens his brow. Like most young pups, he's never heard of real angels before. They've only been a myth over the years; a character in religious stories for some, a make-believe fantasy for another.

He doesn't comment, though. He remains quiet while watching Lazarus flick me his middle finger before offering a grin with his news. "I've already located the warlock. He's taken a defensive position over the ridge to the east just before the peak."

"Quick scouting." I'm impressed by Laz's retrieval of Intel, especially when he's still weak from the earlier battle. "It means he's heading back to Vegas. We're screwed if he gets there before we get him. How many are with him and how many chasing?"

A shot strikes the front of the concrete again. I instinctively duck while it ricochets up into the air to wing right past Lazarus's head. The angel doesn't crouch, nor does he flinch from the bullet's close encounter. Then again, he is an immortal angel with the powers of a god. While a gunshot wound would hurt like a bastard, it won't kill him. Ducky and I wouldn't be as lucky if we got shot in the right spot.

"I saw five with him, all armed and firing unsuccessfully at a handful in pursuit. The wolves have him pegged in a valley below the peak. The warlock's only escape is up and over. He should be captured before that happens."

Ducky, finally over his initial shock of meeting the angel, jumps in with some important information of his own. "It sounds like my guys are running the warlock to our territory cutoff. Once he's up Charleston Peak, he's in Clark County and the Vegas chapter's problem."

Lazarus turns on Ducky with a snarl of disapproval. "You mean, they are avoiding the conflict, being cowards by letting him get away."

His statement does not bode well for Ducky, who points his gun barrel up at Lazarus. "Back off fucker, my boys aren't cowards. They're only playing it safe. Better to get rid of the problem than to have it cause us blowback with another MC. No one even knows who this warlock is, not to mention what he did. Hell, I don't even know why I'm chasing the witch."

I interrupt with a hard glare up at Lazarus. "Alright, enough with the pissing contest. Let's focus on our main priority, getting to Cale."

I turn my head to the biker. "The only way to do that is to get past this ambush, and I'm hoping you got another way around it."

Ducky's eyes are locked on Lazarus with menace. There's still a bit of fear in his stare, but mostly, he seems to be studying the giant man and waiting for any sudden moves as an excuse to shoot him. I don't blame him. If I didn't know Lazarus like I do and what his capabilities were, I wouldn't be taking my eyes off him, either. We are on a mission however, and I tap the guy to get his attention.

Ducky blinks a couple of times, running his free hand through his long greasy locks before focusing on me and lowering his weapon. "Of course, there are hundreds of hiking trails on these ridges. What are you thinking?"

I roll myself back to the edge of the barrier and pop my head around the side to study the landscape. As I take in the surroundings, a few more flares from gunshots spark up the main trail, about a half mile in the distance. There are a few bunches of trees dotting that incline, where I suspect the shooters are bunkered down.

"We break off. Ducky can head up on the west side through the trailer park, cutting north across this main trail about a mile up. I'll go east, along the perimeter of the scrapyard to meet you on the other side."

Facing Lazarus, I continue with directions, "While we make our way into position, you babysit Cale. Make sure he doesn't get over that peak. I know you're still recovering, but use what you have magically to keep him in the valley until I get there."

Lazarus shakes his head. "And then what? Do you think you can take on the warlock, as who you are now? He siphoned Lilith's powers before her rebirth, he is strong with her magic. Stronger than even I am at the moment, you wouldn't even stand a chance."

"Not strong enough for one lucky shot to the head." I wave my gun at him.

He makes a disgusted grunt while crossing his arms over his massive chest. "Will you make the shot or will you end up dead like the last time? I think you're out of second chances, and Livia didn't give you this one to waste. Pull your pride out of it, and rethink the plan. We both know there are only two people who can stop the warlock. One of them isn't here, and the other needs some time to recharge her magic."

A wave of anger hits me as Lazarus brings up my past and the events that landed me in this world. No longer a god with powers, thanks to my dear old dad, and not quite a supernatural. Blessed, in this current form, by my mother's oldest friend so I could have a second chance at life.

Blessing, my ass. No, this has been a curse. A life that has spanned thousands of years without purpose. I've wandered lost and alone, until today. Being reunited with my mother and learning of the existence of a sister has renewed me, giving me a new outlook. That is, until I realize my sister and our Queen are the only ones with the eminence power to stop the warlock for good.

This knowledge stings more than I thought. It's a sledgehammer to the face, knowing I can't protect my family. Not something either my god side nor my male side wants to admit.

Lazarus is right. I must pull my pride out of it, but I don't know how to say I'm not good enough or step aside to let them protect me.

The last part is what my mind latches onto and it festers, making me lash out. "So what- we just let him go? Fuck that! You can pussy out if you want, but I won't allow him to best me, not when he's trapped. No, we're bringing him down. With one lucky bullet, your half-assed powers, whatever it takes. He's my kill."

The eyes of the angel darken until I'm staring at myself in the refection of his inky irises. For the briefest second, this stare reminds me, he is not just a fallen god. He's one that has been to the pits of the Underworld. Lazarus is good and evil in eternal opposition, and right now, he scares me.

"I'm not a pussy. I'm realistic. There's nothing wrong with waiting for help. You'd see that if you'd get your head out of your ass," he snarls at me.

From the shadows behind Lazarus, an authoritative sounding female is demanding with her question, "Who has their head up their ass?"

A second female chimes in with spunk, "The jerk calling my man a pussy, that's who."

I also hear a snort that freezes me with an anticipation to what will follow it. Equal to an obsession with anything, I'm eager to hear what this third voice has to say.

"Oh, cowboy, by the looks of these two, you done pissed off the wrong chicks. I'm not bailing you out of this one. I will watch them kick your sorry ass, though, and thoroughly enjoy the show."

The throaty comment is dripping with sarcasm, seductive music to my ears. Instantly, it relaxes my body, which has been tense from the situation and my mood. On some natural instinct, my head jerks up so my eyes can seek out the person who owns the voice. We've only just met, but I'm tuned in to recognize it immediately as Paige's.

Lazarus takes this exact moment to step sideways and twist around to meet the newcomers, who I see walking with his mate and his niece, as they come across the field. The eyeful I take in is a wet dream fantasy coming true. Three stunning beauties, all different in every way imaginable. Each with their own amazing traits, together they are enough to make any male fall to their knees to worship.

As the three slowly stride up to our protective wall of concrete, an overwhelming sense of dèjá vu hits me. It's as though the ghosts of my past are revisiting me; I've been in this exact spot before. Except, it's not the women before me I see, it is of their mothers. Well, at least the two of them. And the resemblance is uncanny. I'm not sure how I didn't piece it together earlier, months ago when I first met them.

Because I've been in denial and not wanting to relive a past I worked so hard to put behind me.

When the females stop beside Lazarus, I notice a sudden silence around us. The guns are quiet in the distance. I wonder if the fighting has ceased from the arrival of the Queen or if, somehow, she has put a spell on the land.

Ducky scrambles beside me, he hesitates in a half crouch before landing on his knees in an awkward bow of respect. Lazarus moves just as fast, following the wolf into position. I'm so distracted by my haunting thoughts it takes me longer to join them in the greeting.

Once I'm there on bended knee, however, I'm all too aware of who I kneel before and the repercussions that could follow when her men realize she isn't at home. I pride myself on being honest in every situation in life. Sometimes it helps me, most times, it does not. And even knowing this, I don't bother to control my tongue.

"My Queen, what the fuck are you doing here?"

CHAPTER 3

A wave of shocked gasps rolls through the group at my somewhat disrespectful greeting. But one loud burst of laughter rings up into the air.

"Keep digging that hole, cowboy, I think you'll be needing it very soon," Paige snickers out.

As fortune would have it, September is only similar to her mother in appearance. Her temperament seems more laid back when she too offers a chuckle. "Please, everyone, stand. This is not the time, nor the situation for a formal greeting."

Ducky, Lazarus and I stand quickly in front of the Queen and as I lift my head to meet her eyes, she offers me a wink. "Zander's question, though bold, is one of concern and I appreciate you asking. I am here, simply to help, in whatever way I can. I sought out Lilith's signature and traveled to her, as I thought she would be the one needing me most."

Her unique heritage provides her with gifts, like the ability to travel to anywhere she wishes, just by thinking of the place or person. Lazarus and his sister Livia, September's mother, were once gods from the heavens and this gift is from their heritage.

"And as it turns out, she arrived just as Paige came into the barn with her pack, looking to help you. I guess we're all here for you, Zander." Sunshine adds with a beaming smile that reaches all the way up to her brilliant green eyes.

I take a moment to study my sister. She's been to hell and back, almost literally. The battle she endured with Cale, and the struggle she took on to stay out of the fade, appears to have taken a bit of a toll. Her usual cream-colored skin seems more alabaster, and the dusting of pink normally in her cheeks is clearly absent. Her short black mane has a few streaks of white in the front. A brush stroke of painted color to remind her of this horrible day every time she looks in the mirror.

Even her eyes, though they shine with a glistening of unshed tears that I suspect comes from knowing our connection, are circled with a ring of purplish-blue. I can't tell if the color is from bruises left over from Cale hitting her or if she is simply exhausted. I imagine it might be both, and that tugs at my heartstring and makes me want to lash out even more at Cale, for her.

When I return her smile with a kinder one of my own, she bounds forward to wrap her slender arms around my waist. She hugs her tiny body close to mine with a whispered sob in my chest, "Mo deartháir."

I welcome her embrace with one of my own, a lump forming in my throat as she acknowledges me as her brother. Looking down at her dollish frame in my arms, I'm quite aware of my gentle grip, as not to hurt her. I know she's not fragile, she is a powerful high-priestess and the Moon Goddess. Those titles alone come with great strengths. Yet, I have the overwhelming sense to care for her, protect her, as any big brother would.

The thought is both foreign and appealing, that I don't know what to say back. I'm almost never left speechless, yet here I am, not knowing what to answer. Instead of speaking, I just hug her tighter. Hoping, somehow, by holding her, it will make up for everything I've missed out on in her life. I also hope it will explain who I am and apologize for any disappointments she finds in me. But mostly, I hope it tells her I love her and I'll always be here for her, no matter what.

"Tá an-chion agam ort Zander," she tells me she loves me too.

My eyes go wide when I realize she has read my thoughts, just like Lazarus sometimes does. I don't get to process how I feel about the mental invasion because we get interrupted.

"Ah-em," Paige loudly clears her throat with impatience. "I hate to break up this touching love fest, but don't you people have someone to catch?"

I blink away my amazement for Sunshine's abilities and settle on a frown at Paige's tone. It's laced with enough snark to push her agenda home and sounds ruder than normal. My eyes jump straight to her face to offer a scolding and catch her glaring back with a hint of possessiveness. It's only there for a second, maybe not even at all. After another blink, I catch her making a dramatic eye roll so impressive, I swear she probably checked out her own ass.

Sunshine stirs in my arms, taking a step back so she can tilt her head up at me. "Paige is right, Cale must be caught and punished before he does any more harm to our kind."

I had been distracted yet again, about to laugh at Paige's antics when Sunshine's words hit home and I'm snapped back into our mission. "Ducky and I were about to head out. I thought we could go around the crossfire and meet up about a mile north. That should take us to the path leading to the peak, where Lazarus last spotted Cale. From there, it's an easy shot at the guy, now that we have you and Queen September here to help."

Lilith nods at my plan, then turns to September with a question, "Do you know if we need to go around or has the pack secured the area?"

The Queen glances toward the east with a smile. "I believe it has been secured, but we can ask Mac Tìre. I see he's running this way."

I perk up. I once knew a Norseman by this name, back in the late seven-hundred. He had been a part of history during the Viking Age, traveling on a ship off the coast of Antrim to be one of the first to raid Rathin Island.

When some of the Norseman stayed in Ireland to put down roots, the werewolves that were there first didn't take kindly to the new intruders pillaging and raping their way through the villages. They retaliated and Mac Tìre had been bitten, turning on the first of many full moons thereafter.

I met him a year after he turned, he still hadn't fully grasped the local tongue. His original name, Maciej, sounded similar to Mac Tìre, the Celtic word for wolf. To an untrained ear, the phonetic pronunciation of the two names, the original Mah-chay and local interpretation Moc-chee-da, caused much confusion. In time, he adopted Mac Tìre, to fit who he had become- a lone, bastard wolf.

We have often crossed paths over the centuries, as many rogue wolves do. It hasn't been since the Great Depression that I've seen the man, when we were running moonshine into Canada during prohibition. It was during those trips I fell in love with the country, it had much to offer. I decided to set up shop to take advantage, while Mac Tìre carried on his own way. We soon lost touch and I haven't thought of the wolf since.

As the long-ago memories flood back to me, I turn in the direction the Queen is staring, taking in the familiar image of the beast jogging down the hiking trail towards us. My old friend hasn't changed much. He's still a brute in size with a shaggy, chest-length, reddish-brown goatee and similar colored long hair, shaved on the sides of his head and pulled back in braided dreadlocks.

He has added some tribe ink on the shaved bits of his head, which may pay homage to his ancestry. The ink doesn't stop at his head; it continues to run down his neck and under the leather vest he's wearing. I notice the vest sports the Wicked Ones full patch colors and member title stitched on his breast pocket. The Norse-Gael seems to have finally found himself a pack, after all these years. A pack that fits right into his ruthless criminal nature.

"Bloody hell," Mac Tìre puffs, winded from his run. "It's a good bit yer th'ee Queen, love, it'd be the only time I beat th'ee ground for anyone. I'd be needing a fag about now."

The wolf digs his ring and tat-covered hand into his dirty

jean pants pocket to pull out a mangled pack of cigarettes. He taps the small box to release one of the slender sticks and pinches it between his index and middle fingers to bring it up to his lips, before patting his vest down in search of a lighter.

The Queen steps forward. I see her lips move as she lifts her hand. The words to the spell are silent, but I feel the air around me stir just as a bright orange flame flickers to life upon her fingertips.

She smiles at the wolf and extends the flame towards him to light his smoke. "I appreciate your hurry, Mac Tìre, but if you get this winded with a short jog, you should consider quitting smoking. You can always take up something healthier to replace the habit."

Mac Tìre draws on the filter a few times, generating coils of smoke until the cigarette is finally lit. He then inhales a deep lungful of nicotine before answering, "Aye, that I should, but I dare say, a healthy shag in the sac wit ye, be just as hazardous to me health, ya? I think I be sticking to me fags, love, it be keepin' me outta trouble."

The Queen laughs, and again I'm reminded of how different she is from our first ruler. Livia would have backhanded the bastard from the word go. She ruled with an iron-clad fist and did not take kindly to insubordination. September is softer, in a kind approachable way that makes her more personable. Always quick to laugh while being genuine with everyone. She listens with interest to her subjects and in doing so, is able to make well thought out decisions for her kingdom.

Yet I also know, when forced into action, she'll rip the hide from any one of her enemies and not think twice about it. I've seen her demon in action, and when it comes out, she holds no mercy for anyone that crosses her. She can be far more ruthless than her mother when she needs to be, but her humanity is more grounded.

The more I see of this Queen before me, the more I think

how much better she will be for our world. I am becoming less angered by the cursed life her mother gave me. I now have something to be proud of. To be a part of this Queen's rule, a part of her history. No matter what race I am or how I get to play in this world, she accepts me for who I am as a person. She makes me want to stop being a lone wolf, to be a part of her pack, and to do better for myself.

In my seconds of life reflection, I miss the beginning of the conversation our group is engaged in and only catch the last part of Mac Tìre ranting, "...The bastards were shooting at each other."

Ducky swears and shakes his head. "We've been shooting at our own this whole time, like a bunch of idiots. For fuck's sake."

"Yer words lad, naught mine."

While the Irish wolf laughs, his Sergeant in Arms continues to curse his pack's stupidity. September is the one who clears her throat, getting us all back on track. "It doesn't matter who was accidentally shooting at whom, mistakes happen. It matters that none of you got hurt. And the good news is we can now coordinate the wolves to surround Cale in the valley, so we can continue with Zander's plan."

"Zander, you mean Zander bloody Paine in me arse, that fecker?" Mac Tìre questions with surprise, pitching the last of his smoke while swinging around to check out our group, and landing an ugly smirk in my direction. "Well, shite, tis you. Don't ye look like a big mug o' piss to me sore eyes."

He walks over to extend his arm for us to clasp each other's elbows before we pull ourselves together for a man hug. "And you still have a face like a bulldog chewing a wasp, you dirty old dog."

"Ye still as mad as ditch with words like them, I see," he comments on my sanity then cocks his thumb behind him with a laugh. "If ye runnin' with this lot, I suspect ye are."

I laugh along for a whole other reason. I just thought of how proud I was to be a part of this history when I would have never done such a thing in my past. Perhaps I'm as crazy as Mac Tìre suggests, or maybe I finally entered some type of adulthood.

When we finish our greeting, Mac Tìre steps back to clap me on the back. "Ah, we must be havin' a good o'chin wag, yu and me."

"When this is over, my friend, there are a couple of cold beers down at the bar waiting for us." I turn to my left to make sure Paige heard my offer and I'm quite happy to see her smile with a nod that she had. The day is looking better by the minute, especially if she joins us for that drink.

"Right then, if there be pints involved, let's get to it." The wolf gets serious and turns back to the Queen, "What's th'ee plan then, love?"

September smiles at the wolf but makes a gesture towards me. "As I said, Zander has a plan."

It takes me a few minutes to explain what I had in mind and a few minutes more for our group to polish the plan to perfection. Then another half hour to organize the troops. Paige had done what I asked and got some wolves from the bar, but it was September that had them go out into the hills to control the gunfire.

As Mac Tìre had said, the pack had been firing at each other this whole time. I'm sure Cale had wrapped a spell around the pack to make them think they were fighting with another MC. With this sorted, we should be smooth sailing all the way into the valley. Cale is smart though, intelligent enough to confuse the pack and cunning enough to kidnap Sunshine to siphon her powers, so we will need to be on our guard.

I have been on raids, in battles in many different wars at many different times in history, and never have my nerves been more wrecked than right now. I'm not fighting alone anymore, nor am I fighting for the sake of fighting or to prove that I am capable. This is no longer just about me. This is about all the people jogging up the hill with me and those back in Canada, relying on me to eliminate the threat to our world, while keeping our Queen safe. I've never been this responsible for such precious cargo in my life, and if I'm honest with myself, I'm not sure I ever want to be again. The stress alone is enough to make me nauseated.

Our large group jogs up the ridge to a well-worn path cutting east, where a few veins of lesser traveled trails trickle off the main path. I stop to reassess, sniffing the air to discover the thick stench of gunpowder wafting at us. I take a knee to the ground to try to scent out the warlock. There's been so much foot traffic, from the men Cale's with and the wolves following him, that I can't get a good enough whiff to tell which of the paths the warlock took.

"Okay, let's break off here to go over the ridge and secure the escape routes. Ducky, you take half the pack north and circle back down the peak, block Cale from going into Clark County." Ducky is quick to respond to my command and gathers up about a dozen wolves to him for the trek up the ridge to my left.

Satisfied that Ducky will secure the peak and prevent Cale's escape, I turn to point to the right of me. "Mac Tire, you take the rest of the pack south, span out to keep the other exit routes covered. Don't let him get out of the valley, and remember, nobody fire unless you are fired upon or magic is being used on you. Got it?"

The wolf's lips crack wide open into an evil grin as he strokes the length of his bushy goatee. "Aye, but ye didn't say I can't be using me axe."

The bastard cackles like a madman at the mention of his beloved Danish axe. A treasure he has carried, strapped to his back, since before landing on the Irish shores long ago. I've seen him wield the wide curved blade on a shorter two-foot wooden handle, carved by his own hand and bound in leather thread. From what I remember, he made it look effortless to strike a man straight through the skull with it. I know the heavy weight is anything but easy to swing with accuracy, which makes it much more impressive when he does it.

"This is not that kind of a fight, wolf," Lazarus warns the biker. "We let the Queen decide who lives and dies today, not your blade. Am I clear?"

"Aye, but where be th'ee fun in th'at, then," Mac Tire grumbles with a wink at me, while he rounds up the rest of his crew. "Pea, you be with me, on me six, yeah?"

Paige glances from Mac Tire to September to Lilith then over to me with a frown. She doesn't hesitate when she turns down his order, "No, you go on without me. I'm staying with this lot to ensure nothing goes wrong. The quicker we get this done, the faster they leave us be."

Mac Tire's brow pops up as he and Ducky share some eye gestures back and forth before they both shrug and bow a nod to the she-wolf. Never in the history of the werewolf have I ever seen a male give a female direction and have her counter with her own orders. Only the Queen has the power to rule the packs, but even she relinquishes that rule to her True Alpha, Gage. It proves my initial thoughts that Paige is not the typical she-wolf. She's somehow in control of this pack, not as their Alpha, but maybe a Beta-Alpha.

I'm intrigued by the dynamics of this pack and how Paige plays a part in it. If she has this much control over two high ranking wolves and members of this MC, it means she has proven herself in a fight, and perhaps the attitude she sports has merit. Just the idea of her being an aggressor, a dominant bitch, sparks a whole new level of interest, deep in my loins, for this female. The thought of her giving as good as she gets, has me visualizing the possibilities of being tied up and whipped and liking it. I'm not saying sex is all I want with her, but I sure would love to fuck her to find out.

"And the rest of us, where do we go, Zee?" Sunshine's sweet sounding voice crashes through my fantasy, making me feel like a dirty old perv.

I clear my throat a couple of times to clear my head,

avoiding any eye contact in Paige's direction, looking only at my sister to keep me on track. "The rest of us stay east on this main trail right into the valley. We'll have the advantage if Laz, you and the Queen stay out of sight, until Cale plays his cards. Once he shows himself, we stick to the plan and take him by surprise."

"Copy that," Ducky confirms, swirling his hand up in the air above his head to direct his half of the pack up the hill. "Let's roll out."

"Aye." Mac Tìre does the same with his people, giving some encouragement to his wolves as he heads up the ridge, "No one but th'ee warlock be dying on me watch, yeah."

As the pack breaks off and disappears into the darkness, I'm brought back to my feelings of responsibility. The plan is sound, but there is always room for error when dealing with this many people. I hope I'm not sending any of my friends into the fade today, and for the first time ever, I whisper a bit of a prayer, "Peace be with you, brothers."

Once the last wolf has completely vanished from my nocturnal sight, I turn to the court to prepare for our part. When I meet September's eyes though, the deep amber color flickers to a brilliant red and back into a bright yellow. I've seen her demon nature in action before and it was impressive, in a scary as shit, sort of way. This part of her is very much Livia but on steroids. Knowing it can take all four of her mates to pull her from the deep clutches of her dark side worries me. Especially with Gage and Sabre still a few hours away.

I can't help but send my apprehension out in thoughts towards Lazarus, *"Is the Queen able to handle this alone and in her condition?"*

It isn't Lazarus that answers, though he does turn in my direction with a worried frown as September offers the straightforward reply. "I assure you, Zander, I'm in full control and would never do anything reckless to bring harm to my child."

I take immediate action to bow my head in respect. "Yes, my Queen. I'm sorry to have doubted you."

"No need to apologize. I know you're just looking out for me in Gage's absence. This isn't the first time you showed your loyalty with blunt honesty, and why I am glad I recommended you as a member of this court."

I bow deeper this time, for my respect for her and to hide my emotions over what she said. I've never been welcomed into a pack, court, or club because my secret keeps me distant. Being different in the supernatural world means being shunned. The Queen's own lover, Sabre, was kept away for being a white wolf hybrid. If they knew my secret, I wonder if the Queen would be as trusting of me as she became of him. I want to believe she will welcome me with open arms, but the reality of my history keeps me guarded. It's just better that way.

"Thank you, my Queen," I acknowledge her kindness.

"No thanks necessary, just keep being you. I appreciate that more than you know. Now you and Paige better get moving before the pack arrives and spoils our surprise." She smiles, then adds with a wink, "And don't worry about our part, Cale wouldn't think about guarding the skies."

All I get in is a nod that I understand what she means, before she turns her back to join Lazarus and Lilith. They don't look back at us, they just start walking out, distancing themselves a few feet from each other to allow some space for their wings to come out from their backs and not tangle with each other. It only takes a few seconds for the wingspan display to stretch out before they lift off into the heavens, but the wall of feathers is quite impressive. I haven't seen this much plumage since my own time in the heavens and it makes me sort of miss home.

"Whoa, butter my butt and call me a biscuit." Paige's shocked but comical comment chases away my homesick blues. "Holy shit, they can freaking fly, like birds and shit."

She whips her body around to look at me, her expression

is one of awe and surprise, but oddly, she doesn't seem scared. "Are you sporting a set of feathers too, cowboy? I don't know how I feel about letting a bird creature eat my vagina. There's something just not right about that."

I snort at her candor. "I try not to wear my wings every day, I get too tempted to take them off and beat the stupid people with them."

Her eyebrow slowly goes up in question and she purses her lips in thought. "You're pulling my leg, right?"

I answer with a shrug then bob my head up towards the hill. "We better head out."

As I turn to move towards the path, she grabs my jacket and pulls me back around to face her. "Hold up, I haven't digested this whole flying thing. Do you or don't you have wings? If so, why aren't you up there with them? And don't tell me it's to babysit me, I sure as shit don't need a babysitter. But if not, I have a list of questions you need to answer before we go anywhere."

"It will take too long to tell you the story and we don't have the time right now," I snap.

That claw-like finger of hers is back in my face, wagging at me as she goes off. "Watch your tone, cowboy. I wish I had a condom to give you. If you're going to keep acting like a dick you should probably start dressing the part."

I sigh, knowing she's right, and this time I take her hand in mine to offer a squeeze. "I'm sorry. I'm taking something out on you that isn't your fault, nor is it fair to you. I know you must be curious, it's not every day you meet an angel and a couple of goddesses, never mind seeing them fly. I promise to answer all the questions in that pretty head of yours after this is over. If you still want to know."

She pauses with a rapid blink when I call her pretty, like no one's ever called her this before. As I speak, her posture relaxes and her head tilts a little; she seems actually interested in what I have to say.

When I'm done, she squeezes my hand back and offers the sweetest smile. "When this is over, I want all the down low on them, about the parts of our world I seemed to have ignored for far too long. But most importantly, I want you to tell me about the dark tangled secrets you keep hidden away, deep inside, if you'll be willing to share them with me."

Her request acts as a riding crop, jolting the thumping wild creature in my chest to life. Her crude mouth and wild eyes are enough to invite me in, sparking my desire for her with a raging hard-on that won't go away. Her observant and brilliant mind, though, lights a fire straight to my soul. One so fierce, I fear she will become the weakness to my strength, and in turn, become the strength for those weaknesses.

I have no answer for her. I just stand, staring, trying to figure out how to decipher the odd emotions I have over her words. I chalk it up to seeing my mother, again. Drudging up my past must be what has made me transparent, enough for some simple she-wolf to see right through me.

Yeah, she's simple alright, like quantum physics. If I'm not careful, I'm about to give my heart completely over to her science.

CHAPTER 4

I somehow manage to get my shit together enough to get us up the ridge to the edge of the valley, without any promise of answers to Paige's request.

The quick run does wonders for my head, clearing the deep fog of emotions that have been swirling since earlier today when Sunshine sealed me in a room inside Paige's brothel with my mother. I'm more than ready to settle the score with Cale, get this situation dealt with so the Queen and Sunshine can get home safely, and I can begin to drown myself in a vat of liquor and pussy.

I bury my thoughts deep in mind and hope they stay lost in there forever, as I move us into a spot overlooking the valley floor. We stop to stand amongst a sparse grouping of trees, far enough out so Cale won't sense us, and the wolves that have been tracking him won't scent us. All while keeping our distance so Ducky and Mac Tire can move into position around the warlock.

Then we wait and wait some more. Watching the darkness as two frozen statues, rigid and ready to pounce at the first sign of chaos. But, nothing happens.

In the distance, I can just make out head-shaped bumps behind some rocks about a hundred paces to the east. They bob up from the rocks every so often, reminding me of gophers coming out of a hole in the ground looking for predators before making an escape. At this distance, with the right rifle, I could pick them off one by one with ease, like target practice at the range. Too bad I didn't come prepared.

The wind has picked up, whistling sharply around my head and flicking up the dust at our feet to make cool little dirt funnels. At first they provide amusement as I watch them rise up, implode, and sink back down into the ground. Over and over again, they come up from the packed desert floor and fall, until I'm about to start screaming from the boredom.

Paige shifts on her feet, shuffling from one foot to the other, showing her impatience. It is so quiet, I can hear the grains of sand crushing against the sole of her boot as each one touches down. When she crouches low, the movement jerks my head up to seek out any sign from the darkness that Cale's buddies might have noticed our location. Still nothing.

"Ducky and Mac Tire have to be in position by now. Can't we move forward?" She mumbles softly, lower than a whisper so our enemy doesn't hear.

I lower myself to a couch beside her and lean against her warm curves to remind her of the plan. "Not until Lazarus tells me to."

Being this close, I become too aware of who I'm with as her amazing scent hits my nostrils. Before I can catch my tongue, the thoughts in my head just spew out my mouth, "You smell like you want to get fucked."

My chest is pressed against her side, giving me a full view of her profile when the smirk breeches her lips. "Maybe, but the only piece of ass you'll be getting will be next time your hand slips through the toilet paper as you wipe."

I instantly bite down on my tongue to stop a burst of laughter from shooting out and calling us to the attention of the warlock.

"Jesus," I hiss from the pain and spit out the taste of the blood starting to fill my mouth.

Her head turns so her lips graze my ear, making the tiny hairs on my lobe stand straight up, and it isn't the only thing trying to stand up. "What, did you think we had something special because I let you touch my vagina?" She stops to cluck her tongue in judgment. "Trust me, it takes a lot more than tickling my g-spot before I allow a man in my life. A little word to the wise, I can touch my own vagina. What I want is someone that will reach out and capture my soul."

"Fair point," I mutter and shift on the balls of my toes to inch away.

I hear her huff, "Typical," while her head shakes.

"And what exactly does that mean?" I snap back a little louder than the rest of the conversation, but she's starting to prick at my last nerve.

"Shh!" She cups her hand over my mouth, pulling herself up to my chest with her own, to balance herself enough to check on the bobbing heads behind the rock.

She holds on to me for a minute, watching the darkness for any movement. I place my hand on her back and drop a knee to keep us from moving until I feel her body relax, then I know Cale's guys didn't hear us.

It hasn't changed the subject though, when she turns back to offer me a nasty scowl. "I meant, you and the rest of the men around here are like pantyhose. Either you run, cling, or just don't fit right in the crotch. I give you a bone, you get a boner. Then I say something heartfelt about what I expect and you inch away like I have fleas, it's so typical."

I lick the palm of her hand that still cups my mouth, to force her to pull it away. When she does, her nose crinkles with distaste, but her mouth opens like she's about to offer a moan. I don't get this game; her words are crystal clear rejection. Her actions, though, speak loud for her desires. She's an enigma of contradiction that frustrates me.

"I'm not running, but give me a break. I've had a raging hard-on for you for hours, and it doesn't help that you smell like sex. I'm a guy; I can't help thinking a vagina is like the weather- when it's wet, I want to go inside."

Her eyes start to roll, but stop and go wide, just as a giggle erupts from her lips. The hand she had cupping my mouth is suddenly slapping over her own to stop herself from busting out a loud laugh. Her other hand comes up to act as a fan on her face. I've seen women do this often but never understood why. It seems to do the trick, though, as the giggle fit subsides and she gains back her tight inner control with slow even breaths.

"Sorry," she mouths, leaning into the side of my face to finish the apology, I don't get to hear it.

Instead, my posture straightens with a jerk and I clutch Paige in my arms, stopping her as Lazarus's voice breaks into my head, *"Zander, the pack is ready. Time to move in."*

My eyes search out Paige's and I give her a nod. "It's time."

We both help each other up, it's clumsy given our embrace. Paige dusts off her knees then looks around with confusion, searching for someone not here. "How do you know? I didn't hear the big bird, or see him, for that matter."

I reach in my jacket for my Sig and hand it to her. "Later. I'll tell you how I heard him, later. Now take this and cover me."

I see her struggle with this, I know she wants to understand. I'll give her credit though, she brushes it off quick with a frown that turns into a head nod. She grips the gun, checking to see if the clip is full, then aims it out towards the rocks.

"Go, I got your back."

I step back a few paces and start to jog on the spot to create a loud foot thumping on the ground. The heads behind the rock pop up at the sound, and I know I have their attention. I run to my left, far enough from Paige to conceal her cover, hitting the branches of a tree to show my location.

A pot shot is taken, low at the ground and a few feet ahead of me. The boom sound echoes up the hill in front of me as someone shouts, "Stop right there or the next one hits your head."

I come out from the shadows of the trees, my arms up, hands out in surrender. "This isn't your fight, I'm here for Cale. Send him out and you'll get to leave unharmed."

There's a lengthy pause and I imagine them trying to

communicate their next move. These guys are rookies, though, because they don't even notice when I move up a couple more feet to get a better view. Only two of them guard this path entrance, leaving another four spread out around the valley and Cale somewhere behind them. But if the rest are half as dimwitted as these two, the pack will be able to ambush them with ease.

"We outnumber you wolf, maybe you should go before you get a shot to the head." The guy is overconfident, standing up with his rifle loosely aimed in my direction.

I step even closer, bridging the distance between us, testing the waters. As I walk, the young warlock raises the weapon to his shoulder, pointing it at my head, but his finger isn't on the trigger. Not a threatening pose from my side.

I'm about ten feet from him, close enough to notice his arms are shaking. Another two steps lets me see the trickle of sweat dripping from his brow.

Even his voice is shaky as he warns me off, "Stop, final warning."

I hold in my laugh at the lackluster show, and try to defuse this with a calm chat, "You and I both know you aren't going to actually shoot me, so let's work this out. Lower the rifle and walk away. I won't tell if you don't. All I want is Cale."

The guys both shake their heads. "No," The one still sitting says in a softer tone. "Cale hasn't done anything."

"Are you sure about that?" I ask, taking the last few steps to stand in front of the two warlocks between the big rocks.

"Cale said he's here on official OSU business for the Queen, she wants him to shut down the MC. He's only following her orders and the pack came after him for it."

This time a small snort comes out my mouth, and I hide it with a cough. No point making them feel stupid for believing Cale's line of shit. "Cale isn't following any orders from the Queen. He's using you as part of his plan to escape so he can take out the Queen."

The first guy frowns at me then turns to his buddy, who is about as equally stunned, but asks the question, "How do you know?"

While the two take that brief glance at each other, it opens up the opportunity I've been waiting for. I reach up to grab the barrel of the rifle and wrench it from the first guy's hand. Once it is free, I push the butt end forward into his stomach. He lets out a whooshing grunt from the blow, teeters off balance, and falls back on the ground.

The second guy is slow to react, shocked by my quick assault. It takes him a minute to realize I just disarmed his friend. By the time I hit his buddy, he's finally clued in enough to aim some old-looking pistol at me, as he screams, "Stop or I'll shoot you."

"Not if I shoot you first, magic boy," Paige announces herself as she comes from behind the guy, placing the barrel of my Sig to the back of the guy's head.

His eyes spring wide open when he realizes he's up shit creek without a paddle. He throws the pistol down and his hands way up above his head. "I surrender."

Paige huffs, grabbing the guy's shoulder to push him forward towards the path. "Well, that was no fun."

I chuckle at her enthusiastic participation and tragic disappointment in the outcome, while I help the first guy to his feet. I understand what she's feeling, I thought there would have been more bloodshed or struggle getting past this checkpoint. These two were easier to catch than a bucket full of snails.

Two quick, sharp whistles sound from down the path Paige and I are leading the two warlocks. Ducky and another wolf jog towards us. "You guys clear?" Ducky asks, seeing me and Paige with our catch.

I push my guy forward for the wolf to secure. "All clear on this end. And you?"

Ducky nods his head at the other wolf, pointing to the

two warlocks and gestures to take them back up the path they just came from. "Yeah, we caught two more coming down the ridge. They didn't even try to fight. When I heard a shot come from this way, we headed over to give you a hand. Doesn't appear you need it though."

Paige comments, "Hardly, these two were easy pickings."

She hands off her prisoner then turns to me. When our eyes meet, I know she's having the same thoughts of concern and we both make the same statement together, "Too easy."

We both agree with a nod and I gesture with my hands, pointing two fingers at my eyes then back across the terrain. Signaling for us to keep a sharp eye on our surroundings. If these two were easy to catch, I have to wonder why the other wolves seemed to be having such a difficult time earlier. The situation feels off but I can't quite figure out how.

Ducky and Paige spread out beside me, each taking a side of the path to monitor while I keep to the middle of it, guarding our backside. As we walk, the path curves to the left. Our eyes are glued to the landscape, noses sniffing the downdraft trying to scent any sign of the last two guards with Cale, and the warlock himself.

The scenery begins to change the higher in elevation we go. The sparse tree groupings lower on the path, seem to double, then triple, in size the closer we get to the peak, turning the ridge into a forest. The extra trees provide more obstacles for us to clear, what with their different odd shapes and sizes. It makes us slow our pace and spread out even further from each other as we comb the area, seeking out our prey.

The path begins to bend again, this time yielding to Paige on the right. As we move past the wide curve, a clearing appears to open up ahead of us. Ducky's curled fist rises above his head, signaling for us to stop, and as we do, we take cover behind the closest tree to where we stand. I'm not a botanist by any stretch, but I do know there are many different pine trees in the area, and the tree I stand in front is definitely a bristlecone.

It's wide but stunted gnarly shape provides great cover at my back, and the twisted, bottle brush branches are sparse enough to not block my view. I can make out the open space before us as a viewpoint pit stop along the trail. It has cliffs jutting out of the rocky incline of the mountain on one side, which makes the path no longer passable. We either keep going up or turn to go back down, which is the perfect location to contain Cale. Yet, I don't see anyone in the clearing.

Ducky falls back from his hidden spot to make a crisscrossed, round-about-way back towards me. His movements resemble a drunk man trying to do the sobriety straight-line test, and he seems to be failing miserably at it.

At first, I wonder what the hell he's doing, but then I catch a scent in the air and start to pay closer attention. On each pivot turn he makes, he passes a person hidden well amongst the shrubbery. The pack is here, covered by the landscape and darkness. Still figures awaiting direction on the next move in our plan. Except without the bad guy present, there is no next move.

Ducky finishes his staggered walk at my pine, coming in beside me to crouch down so we can talk. "We're in position on both sides of the lookout. Mac Tire has his group guarding the other end. He found the last two guards, but nobody has seen the warlock. What do you want us to do?"

I rub my face in a frustrated gesture, wondering that same question. Without Cale, this is pointless. I stand and start walking towards the lookout area, Ducky at my heels and Paige pulling in behind him. As we get to the clearing, I don't notice an obvious place for the warlock to hide but he has to be close. The pack has run all through this vast area, capturing Cale's guards along the way, and with every sign that the warlock would be here. Even Lazarus had said Cale was pinned in the valley.

I turn myself around and around, examining both exits of the path, even looking over the edges to see if he's hanging off one of the cliffs. Still, I don't see anything to indicate Cale was or is here. I'm beginning to think we somehow botched the plan and Cale made his escape. Then, before the thought can settle into my brain, another crosses it.

This has been too easy, the capture of Cale's men without a struggle, and the ease to which we entered the valley undetected. "It doesn't make sense, something is off."

As I verbalize my thoughts, something catches my eye, over by the viewpoint in my peripheral vision. My head jerks in that direction and I scan the open area. I can't explain what I see, it might just be movement, a shadow of a shrub or tree. Except there isn't either in the clearing. I close my eyes and rub them with my fingers, giving myself a second to relax before reopening them. When I do, I focus on a spot on some rocks and concentrate, putting my energy and will into the stare.

As I remain honed in on the light-colored rock, something I haven't felt in millennia begins to stir inside of me. I thought I lost these powers long ago, before Livia blessed me with her magic and I became who I am now. My god powers are weak, barely there, but surprisingly still alive inside of me. The discovery makes me jump.

"What is it?" Paige grips my arm with a gentle grasp of concern. "You look like you saw a ghost."

I turn to her, not sure what to say. I'm delighted by this sudden awareness but confused as to why I've never felt it before now.

You never had a need for it, before now. My subconscious screams loud and clear inside my head.

When my eyes meet Paige's, it breaks the spark of energy I just felt. It causes the aura of green around her to dull considerably until just her normal shadow outline surrounds her body. I stare at her, her face, her shoulders, watching the shadow disappear until I'm shrugging my own shoulders as a way to explain what I can't.

"You look weird, are you okay? Is the warlock putting a spell on you?" Paige asks while tugging at my jacket sleeve.

Ducky reacts, taking up a fighting stance with his gun aimed out in front of me. Paige releases my arm and swings the opposite way from Ducky to cover us from behind. And as they move, her words ding onto a new thought, Cale putting a spell on me. It isn't me the spell is on. It's on Cale. And that's what the shadowy shape is, that I saw by the rock.

"Invisible spell," I whisper lower than what could be audible for the warlock, but loud enough for Ducky and Paige to brace themselves for an attack.

I turn back to the rocks and stare at the spot. Again, relaxing myself to try to get back in the headspace I had moments ago. Trying to find the lingering power in me to bring it forward. It comes quicker this time, but not stronger, it's still just barely above a whisper.

I work with what I've got, moving my eyes slowly, inch by inch, allowing my body to turn even slower as I scan the air. I'm looking for any abnormality, similar to a missing pixel on a computer screen. Except this screen is the world, and the pixel will be the spell cloaking Cale.

I'm half turned back towards Paige, about to start thinking I imagined all of this, when the view of the canyon, out beyond our position, has an oddly shaped blur in front of it. As soon as I see it, I panic. Cale is there alright, and he's standing right beside Paige.

I don't even think, I just act. Lunging forward, I grab for Paige's hands, gripping my own around hers. Then I use my forward momentum, cradling her into my side as I turn our arms to point the gun barrel up.

"Pull the trigger. Shoot, shoot!" I bark out the command, knowing we have a sliver of time to surprise the warlock and make this shot.

As Paige is knocked off balance, she rolls into me with a low squeal. I feel her tense, then go limp, allowing herself to be directed by me. Her trust, in this moment, gives us the perfect aim we need. As the gun goes off, three quick shots ring loud in my ears, but I don't get a chance to see if they hit our intended target.

Our bodies continue their movement, mine rolling around, hers moving forward. It takes a couple of seconds for our impact with the ground to happen. In that blink of time, I'm able to twist to land on my back with Paige landing face first into my chest.

I'm a big enough male that hitting the ground makes a dent. Add Paige's weight, and we start to slide towards the edge of the cliff. I know we are close as I watch her eyes open wider the further we go, all I can do is put my hands in the dirt to slow us down, and try to roll.

Paige reads my actions and kicks the toes of her boots into the ground to help us stop. Then she clutches the open halves of my jacket and pulls me up and to her left, steering me sideways away from the edge to our stop. As we come to a halt, I embrace her to flip her onto her back with me on top, making sure she is cleared from the cliff.

Our panicked glances meet as we both exhale a breath of relief and offer each other a small smile of thanks. The front of her body is wrapped snug around mine and I get a quick visual of how she'd look under me during sex. The thought doesn't go farther than that, as chaos erupts behind us, and I'm forced to detach myself from her beautiful body.

I hear a sharp yelp and a couple of howls as I help Paige to her feet before turning towards the viewpoint area. Ducky is on his knees. His gun is on the ground beside him as his hands press into the sides of his head, fingernails digging into the skin. I know the look well, having been in the position a few hours ago in the barn. Ducky, and a few of the other wolves who had come out from the trees, are experiencing the swelling of the brain into the skull. The pressure and pain are excruciating and there is no relief until the magic is stopped by the user.

The magical user, in this case, is Cale, finally visible by the rocks where I first noticed his invisible spell. He's bleeding heavily in the shoulder. I'm happy Paige hit him with at least one shot. It didn't kill him and it hasn't made him any less dangerous, since he has a handful of wolves wishing for death from his brain swelling trick.

To our luck, he hasn't noticed me standing with Paige, yet. I quickly scan the ground for my gun that we lost in the tumble. I spot it close to Cale's feet, not a great option. The only other gun close to us is Ducky's and to get to it we have to make ourselves known to Cale. I get Paige's attention. She's been staring at the scene with a deep frown of anger and when she looks at me, there's a serial killer trying to get out from behind her eyes.

I shake my head and push my hands in a downward motion, telling her to calm down. Her jaw flexes as she grits her teeth and her eyes narrow into tiny slits from her annoyance. When I point to Ducky's gun, then gesture for her to go to it, I see her register with confusion and she points at me with a shoulder shrug.

She's asking what I plan on doing, and I really don't know. I need to distract Cale enough for Paige to get the gun, and hopefully, get another shot. It's our only option, and I have no time to explain it to her. Instead, I trust in her to get the job done while I start moving. I run full out towards Cale, like a bear charging to protect its clubs.

I don't get as far as I hoped. My charge is good, but the magical invisible wall Cale's placed around him stops me in my tracks, hard and painful. I'm like a train hitting another head-on. I crash head first into the force field and as my weight pushes in behind me, my head cracks between my ears. It's so loud, it leaves a ringing in its wake, while my vision blurs and I land with a flop to the ground. I just broke my own neck.

By some miracle, I don't pass out but I also won't be dancing anytime soon. Not until the bones heal. I feel disconnected from my own body, trying to move, push myself up, only I can't. I'm left to lay in a limp blob aware of what's happening but unable to do much about it.

"Oh God, Zander." I hear Paige scream out and my heart jerks from hearing her use my name.

Then my heart speeds to a wild pace, as she screeches from Cale shooting some form of magic torture at her too, and there's nothing I can do to help her.

"Stop!" This yelling demand comes from September. "Cale, let the wolves go, it's me you want to fight, not them."

In my paralyzed state, I can only groan with disappointment at myself. I failed in capturing Cale, leaving the Queen to expose herself to protect me and the wolves. I've put her and her young in harm's way. When Gage finds out, I'm going to be praying for a deal with a demon to take me to the Underworld because he's going to kill me slow, and not so gentle.

"Queen September, how…" Cale trails off his question of how September could be here. He must not know of her traveling ability through mind connection since he's shocked by her appearance.

"Cale, I warned you. I told you to stay away from Lilith, me, and my court, and if you didn't, you would have to deal with me. You obviously didn't take my warning seriously," September reminds Cale of her promise at the OSU meeting before I came to Nevada with Lilith.

As they talk, bits of feeling begin to return in some parts of my body, as the bones and nerves knit themselves back together. I hope September continues to calmly speak with Cale until I am able to help her in this fight.

"I did, my Queen. I came to visit friends and discovered the witches here were the ones siphoning powers. They attacked Lilith and the poor dear couldn't fight them off before she went to the fade. When I discovered the tragedy,

I tried to take them down on my own. By then, the wolves got involved and through their misunderstanding of the whole thing, I fear our murderers have escaped."

I mentally roll my eyes at the creative tale he weaves, but it's Sunshine that says, "You better wipe your mouth Cale, there's a bit of bull-crap on your lips from that line of shit."

Cale gasps, probably from seeing Lilith. "You were dead, I felt your energy disconnect. How is it possible..."

Lilith doesn't allow him to finish. "It's possible because I have more powers in my little finger than you could ever hope to have. What you did to me and all those other witches is immoral, and against everything the coven stands for. You've been standing on a soapbox preaching loud and proud the rules of our kind. Meanwhile, it has been you who disgraced us. You hypocrite."

"I've only protected what should have been ours. By Livia's hand, she created us first, from her own magic. The strength of our people comes from her higher power and it should be us that rule the kingdom, not some evil abomination."

I hear the venom in his voice, his hatred for the other creatures, and it makes my blood boil listening to his arrogant racism. His delusion for why Livia created the supernatural is one of ignorance. I know because I was one of the gods who played with the human race as though they were toy figurines, bending them to our will, torturing them by vial methods for our own amusement. She feared us enough to make beings capable of fighting us off and to help her keep this world a safe one.

Her idea was not always sound and some of her creatures became extinct, like the elven population. But she did manage to keep this world going, until the beliefs of the humans became the power which many of the remaining gods now fear. The birth of modern religion is how the humans claimed this realm as their own. It weakened many in the heavens and the rest knew to leave this world well enough alone.

What Livia did was a sacrifice not many would ever give. After the battle between gods and angels, where she thought the war was won and she was the last standing, she cursed herself to a human state to birth a daughter. She knew there would be a time in the distant future where this world would need someone better than her to guide them.

It will be September and her court that brings back the peace, not Cale. I'd wish anything to be the one to tell the fucker this, but my body isn't healed. The only thing I can do is lie here, staring at the ground.

As the thoughts race through my head, the air around me stirs with an energy of snapping static jolts from deep in the earth. The fight is on and I don't know which side is firing first.

My wonder isn't for long when I hear September snap, "You dirty bastard," Right before the ground quakes underneath me from her and Lilith tapping into the ley lines below.

The force they use to do so shakes this part of Nevada with a small tremor. It won't be noticeable to anyone in the area but if there happens to be a seismometer anywhere close, the needles will be flicking away recording the motion. It might lead to a few scientists scratching their heads, but that's for them to figure out.

A whirl of dirt is kicked up and sand particles fly into my face. I close my eyes and wait for it to settle while I listen to what sounds like a swarm of bees zipping by my head. The sound has to be the magic shots being bounced back and forth, volleying little energy balls.

I feel a pop in my shoulder that brings pain to the part of my neck that's broken. The bones are mending and the healing must almost be complete if I can sense the pain. My body twitches on its own in a convulsion of nerves being reconnected to the system. Every muscle does a dance, from eyebrow to toe knuckle, as it does the air pockets trapped in some of my joints pop to release the buildup.

I've never changed into wolf form. Livia's blessing had given me the form, but I could choose to not change if I wanted, and I never had the balls to try. If I did, I imagine this current sensation must be how it feels, the regrowth of bones, shifting and moving, until one last jump, and I'm back together.

I test the waters, moving my toes and fingers then lifting my head to look around me. I'm right in front of Cale, about five feet away. On my right Ducky and Paige are laying on their backs breathing heavy, trying to recover from the massive headaches they received from Cale.

I roll myself over on my back to see behind me. Lilith and Lazarus stand with September. There's a bright light drawn in the air around them, showing their magical link and that they fight as one. Tilting my head up, I notice Cale is starting to pale from the overuse of the magic, but he's still a threat.

He shoots an iridescent shot of energy. I follow the shot that's aimed at Lilith, but she's shooting her own energy bomb and doesn't have time to bat his away. It hits her square in the chest and sends her flying back, breaking their linked connection. Lazarus goes with her, as they are now one magical force from their bonding, which leaves September on her own.

I'm on my knees now, facing sideways to see both sides. I try not to worry about Sunshine as I watch September lobby a ball at Cale with some serious force. It whips by me so fast, I don't even see it but hear the high-pitched whistle trailing behind it, piercing my eardrum. The Queen can pitch better than any major leaguer out there.

Cale is prepared for the ball though. He waves his palm in a circle creating a giant invisible mitt made of rubber, to catch and then fling the energy back. September isn't as prepared and by the time she sees it, the ball drops low enough to hit her knees, making her fall forward.

"Oh, shit," the words fly out of my mouth as fast as my body jumps into action.

The lucky shot Cale got in has disabled our dream team. When I turn towards the warlock, he knows it too, if the gloating grin on his lips is any indication. My mind is racing, frustration turns to anger, which turns to rage as I leap forward, running at Cale with everything I've got. I'm so focused on hitting him, I don't even notice my arm punching at the air in front of me until it makes contact with the male's body.

I'm screaming as the blow lands flat against his chest, "Die you fucker!"

I'm so over this whole day, over Cale, over this damn place, that I miss what happens next. It's only when I don't catch myself from the momentum of the punch that I end up tripping. All I see is the aftermath of Cale slamming up against the rocks, limp as a rag doll. His arms and legs twist in every direction as his body flops forward and down, hard enough to cause the dirt around him to rise and fall, creating a cloud of dust.

There is a rush of motion behind me. I hear Lilith checking on September and Lazarus checking on Lilith. Paige and Ducky check on Cale by rolling him over, and that's when I see the large gaping hole burned into Cale's dress shirt and carrying on into his body and out the other side. When I look up at the rocks behind him, the surface of the cliff is also scorched.

I frown in confusion. I know Cale is dead. There's nothing left of his heart and even a magical being can't come back from that, but I don't understand how it happened. Ducky and Paige turn towards me with slow cautious movements. Ducky's mouth is wide open in surprise, while Paige is staring at me with some form of awe, contradictory to the fear playing havoc in her eyes.

"That was taking your rage to a whole other level,

cowboy. You fucking channeled Thor for Christ sake."

Her statement makes me click back in and I realize what did just happen. "Thor has nothing on me. I don't need the hammer to throw the god bolt, obviously."

No one laughs, not even me. We can't, when what I just said isn't even a joke. The proof is in front of us. I just killed Cale with a bolt of lightning from my hand. I'm not the Norse god Thor. I'm Ruadan, the god of mystery, and though I might not have the full strength of my powers, I'm still very much alive.

CHAPTER 5

"Hey there, Sugar," the bartender greets me by placing a cardboard coaster in front of me at the bar. "To which *F* are you drinking to tonight, the fun kind, the forgetting kind, or the fucking kind?"

I saddle myself into the metal bar stool with a heavy flop, allowing my exhausted body to speak for me. The tattooed beauty, with hair the color of a white sand beach, notices my actions and adds to her speech.

"Looks like you might need to drink away some frustration and fatigue, my friend."

She's nailed that on the head, more than she'll ever know. Since I'm feeling sorry for myself, I add, "I think you left a few other *F's* off your list, like fatheaded and failure."

Her eyebrows pop up in understanding, making the ring in her right brow more noticeable. It reminds me of someone else's piercing. Someone who scattered pretty quick with the rest of the pack, after I killed Cale. A thought that brings out an irritated sigh of frustration from my lips.

The blond notices and makes a quick hop, beginning the bartending dance of turns and stretches. She produces a full bottle of bourbon and a glass, into which she pours a few ounces of the liquor.

"I'll leave the bottle for you, sounds like you'll be needing it."

I bow my head in thanks then take a deep pull from the glass. I suck back most of the dark liquid in one large gulp, trying to wash away what happened on the mountain ridge. Setting the glass down when I finish the last drop, I exhale from the burn the drink leaves in my throat. As the liquor blazes a trail down into my belly, the blond picks up the bottle by the long neck. Flipping it with her wrist, she refills my cup. When it's about as full as the last shot, she flips the bottle in the air before returning it to the bar top.

I lean in to watch her circus tricks of flaring the bottle. It gives me time to sip the drink slower, until the Kentucky blend of high octane paralyzers my taste buds. She fills my glass once more as though she knows I'm trying to also numb the rest of me. When she's done, she offers a sympathetic smile before heading a few paces, to where the redhead that served my group earlier in the day, is talking to some patrons of the wolf variety.

"So, whose turn is it to deal?" I hear the redhead ask.

The two females are entertaining a couple of males, sitting at the bar, with a game of cards. When I check out the redhead again with a more lingering glance, she offers me a wink of recognition in return.

Waving the deck at me she asks, "You want to play?"

I wave a hand. "Nah, I'm good. I'd rather watch."

She licks her lips then produces a sexy grin. "Suit yourself, we don't mind an audience."

I swear my words are the challenge this female needed tonight. Before she even finishes speaking, she's stretching herself across the bar, leaning over to hand the cards to one of the patrons to shuffle. The move has her ample cleavage front and center for us to view, and her ass up in the air, looking tight and teasing. I take more than an eyeful as she plays it up, putting on a flirtatious show.

The card game goes on, and I watch for a few minutes more while sipping my drink to try to relax. The bartenders are a beautiful distraction with Red projecting some interest in my direction. Though the landscape is lovely, they just aren't doing anything for me, and I don't understand it. I had been hard most of the night, to the point of exploding in my pants. Yet, here I am watching the girls fondle each other, and I don't even have a tingle in my trousers.

It isn't long before I'm somewhat bored and start swiveling around in my chair. I peruse the crowd, looking for something that will hold my attention. The bar is fuller than it had been during the day, with an equal mix of clientele from human tourist to werewolf, and even a couple of vamps down by the stage. I'm not recognizing anyone in the room and it bums me out. Not that I'm looking for anyone in particular.

Yeah, right.

I had been disappointed when Paige took off with the pack after Cale was dead, but who could blame her? No one mentioned what had happened, but I could tell it was on their minds. Hell, it was on my own mind, and scaring the pants off me. Yet, I had been too shocked by the discovery to bring it up to September and Lilith, or even Lazarus, for answers to why it happened to me, now.

They had their own issues to worry about, like deciding to give Cale a witch burial in the hills. Which was fine with me, since I didn't have to think too much to get that prepared. We placed his body on a bed of dried pine limbs to light on fire, turning him back to the earth where he should have gone long ago. Lilith prepared the spell and brought the magic, while September said some final words as he began to burn.

The fight and events of the day had tired the Queen and her High Priestess to the point of exhaustion. Lazarus had seemed worried when he got them to fly back to the hotel with him. Our leader would need plenty of rest, and to be checked over, to make sure nothing happened to the young one she carries. I'm sure my mother, being the saint and protector of childbirth, will take care of that.

They left me alone to finish watching Cale's remains turn to ash before scattering them around the desert floor. After, I took the long walk back to the hotel. It gave me time to ponder my churning thoughts, and instead of coming to some conclusion, it brought about more questions I wanted to seek answers for. Sitting with the Queen to wait for Gage and Sabre while she slept felt intrusive, and I didn't want to disturb Sunshine either. She's still getting to know Lazarus and Samuel. So I came down to the bar to get, as its name suggests, to get elegantly wasted.

I want one night to blend anonymously with the wilder crowd. Pretending for a while that I'm no one of importance, and the events of today happened in someone else's life. In my past, whenever life got hard and I was faced with difficult decisions, I used to run from the responsibility. Tonight, that feeling is creeping back in. The urge to get on my bike and get the hell out of here is strong. Yet I'm still here and I don't have to wonder why. There are plenty of new emotions holding me to this place and that's scarier still.

"Okay, here's a question."

The redhead's voice, thankfully, breaks my thoughts. I turn back to the group, with an eager anticipation of distraction.

"If there was no sub world, what do y'all think you'd have become?" Red asks.

The blond picks a card off the top of the deck and shuffles it into her hand. Discarding another card to the growing pile on the bar top before answering.

"That's easy, Kingsley, I would be a nipple model. I do have fabulous nipples, you know."

Her answer is not at all what I expect and I choke on my drink when she says it. I cough hard enough for the wolf closest to me to turn and pound my back with his fist. "You alright, my man?"

I wave my hand at the guy, to tell him I am. Kingsley grabs a glass of water and places it on the bar in front of me.

"Do we need to get you a baby bottle to drink that bourbon, big guy?" She teases me with a wink and the rest laugh at her joke.

"No, I'm good. I just didn't expect the comment is all."

She giggles then answers, "Yeah, Bean's nipples will do that to a fellow."

The wolf closest to me adds to the conversation, "Except, knowing Bean, she wouldn't be happy just showing off her tits, and would eventually end up in porn."

The blond, Bean, laughs this off. "You know me so well. I mean my clam is even more outstanding than my nipples."

"A real man-eater," the wolf says while collecting the cards back into a pile.

The guy next to him adds crudely, "Don't you mean an easy sheep?"

Kingsley furrows her brow and comes to her friend's defense, "Hey, Bean's no slut. She's just friendlier with her vagina than others, is all."

Bean laughs, picking up the pile of cards to shuffle and deal a new game. "No worries, Kings. I don't take offense because I would never think of myself as a slut. I prefer the term sperm connoisseur, it's classier."

There is another round of laughter before the conversation moves on to other sexual topics that have the wolves eating out of the girl's hands. I've seen this game played worldwide in every bar, by every bartender, both male and female alike, in an attempt to make as much money as possible. These two have it down to an art, and I sit back in awe and appreciation of their talent. Before long the bartenders have captured the attention of a large group of admirers that fill their tip jars until they overflow with green.

By then, the bourbon starts to relax my body from the tension it has held all day, and my mind starts to wander as I take in the entertaining show of the two bartenders. Their borderline porn antics are just what I need to forget for a while.

As Bean prepares a line of drinks for the growing crowd in front of the bar, Kingsley comes behind her to plump and tease the blond's ample breasts. Seeing just how spectacular her nipples really are, the crowd of mostly male bikers, cheer and shout out perverse comments. The two bartenders shut them down fast with the dirtiest of comebacks, proving this isn't their first rodeo. It doesn't seem to bother the crowd any either, the dirtier the girls get, the more cash is left behind.

I'm over the halfway mark in my bottle, at the point where my lips are feeling numb and my vision is just starting to get fuzzy. That's when I notice the noise level has increased, thanks to ae band. Down at the far end of the room, high up on a stage, Samuel has joined a vampire group. They play a perfect mixed sound of swampy-blues with a gritty rockabilly beat. The music is catchy, contagious, and has the crowd on their feet. Before long there's a New Orleans Fat Tuesday party all around me, complete with exposed breasts, but minus the beads.

"How you doing, down here, Sugar?" Bean appears, studying me for a minute before pouring some more liquor into my glass and topping up my water.

"All good, thanks." I offer a wink with my air toast, realizing at the last second I raised my fist without the glass.

"Feeling no pain, I see," she laughs. "I'd say my work here is done, but just in case, you need anything else?"

I grin, trying to add some swagger by arching my eyebrow. "I'd love to wear your lipstick on my dipstick."

This time she explodes into a belly laugh. It brightens up her gray eyes until they are glistening with humor. "I was thinking maybe a cab home or some coffee, lover boy."

I pout my lips. "Home is Canada, that's one long-ass cab ride."

She makes a surprised face. "Sheesh, really long. Are you staying at the hotel then?"

I think about that question for a minute. I had asked Ducky for a room earlier for Sunshine but never bothered to get one for myself. I laugh at my mistake. "I don't think I am, I forgot to get a room."

She frowns. "Do you at least have somewhere to crash?"

My answer is simple, "Nope." Then I realize I'm passing on an opportunity, and add, with charm, "Unless you're offering."

Her eyes linger on mine for a minute, and I just start to wonder if maybe she's thinking it over, when she nails me with the rejection. "Not going to happen, Sugar, sorry. I do my best to stay away from bad ideas. No matter how tempting they are, and believe me, you are tempting." She lets out a regretful sigh then adds, "How about I check with the front desk to see if I can snag you a room? If you're interested?"

I shrug, not at all disappointed it won't go anywhere with the blond. "Sure," I tell her and offer a flirty wink for good measure, except I end up blinking both eyes instead.

Thankfully, she doesn't seem to notice my inebriated blunder, before heading down the length of the bar and towards a phone at the other end. I watch her backside as she goes, checking out what she made clear I can't have.

The tiny female makes up for her lack of height with big heels, big hair, and a great bra to enhance her big breasts. Add the simple splattering of ink, not too overdone for her beautiful features, and she's the perfect example of my usual one nighter. Yet, as I appreciate the gorgeous beauty, there isn't even a twinge in my dick for her.

I just start to wrap my mind around why I'm not turned on by the blond when out of the corner of my eye, someone far more appealing gives my dick a reason to jolt to life. I hone in on perfection as she breezes in through the front entrance. My eyes can't help but be glued to her. It's like they are her personal, invisible spotlights, following her around the room. This vision of loveliness doesn't even compare to the bartender, and is nothing like my usual hook up. Yet, I can't get her out of my head.

Paige glides through the bar, with an air of confidence so commanding, that everyone she passes stops to appreciate, even worship her as she goes by. I'm sure it helps that she's gift wrapped in a thin layer of black latex- a cat suit so snug, it leaves little to the imagination.

As she works the room, checking on the customers'

satisfaction, monitoring her staff's performance, adjusting sound levels for the band, and tweaking lighting for perfect ambiance, it doesn't take much to realize she's more than just a pretty face. Paige is in control and everyone in this room knows it. Only an assertive woman can project this kind of power to gain respect, and Paige is a fucking master.

"Hate to be the bringer of bad news, but you might want to set your sights on someone more available." Kingsley leans over the bar to whisper in my ear. "The boss lady is hands-off."

I swing my seat to face the red-head beauty. Cursing myself for being too obvious in my attraction, but still needing to ask the important question. "She *is* taken, then?"

Kingsley's eyes flicker over to Paige, talking with Bean down at the far end of the bar.

"No, not taken." She stops to look back at me with a warning glare. "She's just married to what she does and has no time for a steady companion. She's also not interested in finding a mate, so don't go there either."

Kingsley's tone is not unlike Ducky's had been earlier, protective of their boss. This pack consistently regards this she-wolf with the high status usually saved for an Alpha, and through him, to his mate. Being a single female wolf, of great wealth and connection, makes Paige a target for a suitor looking to add to their portfolio and gain a trophy wife. The fact that she is not only uninterested, but is also protected from it, makes me more intrigued than ever. To find out why this pack treats Paige more like the Queen than our actual Queen.

"Never said I was looking for a mate." I surrender my hands to defend myself.

"No, I guess you didn't." Kingsley's cheeks turn a few shades darker than her hair. "My bad. Pea is like my sister, and I get a little protective of her is all."

I drop my hands to the bar and offer the girl a warm smile. "I get that. She's an attractive woman and I'm some

75

random stranger."

She smiles wider, her pale green eyes lighting up as she begins to babble out her reasoning. "Exactly. Pea isn't some sheep. If that's what you're looking for, there are plenty around for the taking. And if you just want to jerk the chain, the Pearl Brothel is just down the road. It's just, some guys come in here acting like they have some right to Pea, just because they have a set of balls and she's single, you know?"

I can only nod as Kingsley verbalizes her distaste for male chauvinists, and how our world needs to change its view of the female. What she doesn't realize, it's her race that was the first to adopt the male ruler and implemented these barbaric caveman ways. I don't tell her, of course. I believe one day there will be a change in this way of thinking. The Queen has already started the conversations by becoming our ruler, it can only create more change from here.

"I guess I just put you in the same category with every other pig walking in here. Take these two, coming in the door now." She jerks her head to the front entrance as she goes on, "It's obvious they have money. Hell, they probably shit hundreds. I'd entertain a piece of that action. I mean look at them, they're damn sexy. But, I also know the type, and I'd just be another piece of property for them to acquire. For the right price, I might be interested, but I have nothing to lose. Pea, on the other hand, wouldn't even give them the time of day. Not when she's worth a hell of a lot herself. Yet, there is a double standard. She can't go around acquiring any fine piece of ass she wants, just because she can afford it. So I just don't get why they can."

As Kingsley rambles out her point of view, I have a mild case of curiosity and want to see what I'm up against- my competition. Not that I would ever think to buy Paige's affection, she's not some business arrangement. A woman like Paige isn't bought, nor is she controlled. She's far too wild of spirit. It's no wonder she had such a jaded attitude towards me earlier.

But, my thoughts of Paige and her attitude are pushed to the side when I realize who Kingsley is referring to. She's right, the two walking through the door do ooze money and power, for good reason.

"That's the True Alpha and the Queen's King. Trust me, they don't need to buy a mate. Not when they have the most powerful one there is, the Queen." I swing back around just in time to watch Kingsley's mouth drop open.

"No shit!" She explodes her shock so loud, it gets heard over the music by most of the bar patrons around us, who look our way.

Her surprise dissolves as her face pales, and while I watch the color drain, Bean appears on her right with a discreet announcement. "Papa Bear just walked in the door, something's up."

"This can't be good, he never comes in here," Kingsley explains.

As she does, her hand grips the bar top and she takes a step back. Her wide eyes jump down to meet mine, where I read her fear. "They're coming this way. What did you do?"

My first reaction is to smirk at the assumption I've done something horrendous. I might as well be saying I think I'm ten feet tall and bulletproof. Not today I'm not. I wear blood on my hands, and I have a feeling I'm about to get my dick slapped for it.

"Zander," I hear Gage's deep growl snap out my name. "You better tell me you caught Cale, or I am going to rip your head off for slacking on the job."

I'm looking at the girls as Gage demands answers. Bean does a quick about-face, heading with purpose down to the service area, acting like the orders are piling up. Kingsley offers me an apologetic shrug before grabbing my almost empty bottle and busying herself with wiping down the bar on her way over to her friend. The tension slides back into my shoulders as my drunk buzz slowly fizzles away. Even taking the last swig of my drink seems pointless, and when I'm done, I place my glass upside down, signaling the end of what I came in here for.

I wipe the remnants of drink off my lips with the back of my hand, then turn to face the Alpha. He doesn't appear to be in a spirited mindset and he isn't alone. Sabre stands rigid beside him, his jaw clenched as his blue eyes pierce me with his icy stare. The local Alpha, Papa Bear, stops just to their left with Ducky, Mac Tìre, and a couple other high ranking members of the club trailing in behind them. The words, "firing squad", enter my mind as I face the wall of pissed off beasts in front of me.

No matter what I say, someone in this group will not be happy. I keep my response as simple and to the point as possible, "Cale's dead."

"No thanks to you," snaps a surly Papa Bear, and like a beast waking from hibernation, he attacks.

The aggressive move comes out of nowhere, catching me off guard. His giant paws shove me with such force, I fly backward. I stumble against the bar and knock over the chair with my attempt to balance myself.

"What the fuck?" I curse loud enough for the band to miss a few beats, bringing more attention to our group than the original shove had.

"Hold it." Paige rushes in, stepping in front of her Alpha to place her palm to his chest and one in the air towards me. Her warning is laced with a venomous hiss, "Don't you dare start a fight in this bar."

Gage tilts his head towards the she-wolf, an amused cock to his lips. "And just whose balls did you steal to become boss?"

Paige swings herself around, hands on hips, to go face to face with Gage. A pose I know intimately, having been introduced to it earlier. She's either unaware as to his status or as he said, acquired a set because her answer isn't at all respectful.

"Not that it's any of your business, ass-wad, but this is my bar. Which kind of makes *me,* the boss. Big brassy balls and all."

Gage steps forward, towering over the she-wolf. Considering she's a tall drink of water herself, speaks to his giant size. A low warning growl rumbles from his throat as he stares down at her, with his unbreakable Alpha stare. To her credit, she doesn't back away. Instead, the poor clueless dear holds her commanding stance with an equally ruthless glare.

Ducky slips in behind Paige, placing his hand on her shoulder to lean against her ear with a whisper. My guess, he's telling her who Gage is. The newsflash, however, doesn't change her attitude any.

"I don't give a rat's ass, but I will suggest we move this to my office."

Gage grunts in agreement, gesturing with his hand for her to lead the way, but never unlocks his eyes from hers. Paige bows her head to his authority. Ever so slightly her eyes dart away, and she doesn't look happy about surrendering to him. With a jerk of her chin though, she pivots on her spiky heels, walking straight through the bar to a staircase on the far side, by the stage. Even though she's the subordinate, Paige takes ownership of this moment.

We all know it, too., as we follow her like a bunch of lost pups starved for her attention. Her perfectly round ass is our beacon in the dark. I watch it wiggle with a defiant purpose, begging for an attitude adjustment with a paddle. Jesus, she's got bigger balls than any of the men with me. A thought that has me not only wanting her with an aching need, but wishing for her to take that attitude and peg me with the same ownership.

While we wind our way up the metal spiral to the top of the stairs, I notice a great security feature. The meshed grid becomes a catwalk, continuing around the outside perimeter of the bar, for a bird's view of the club. At the top step, the walkway forks. On the right, it crosses high above the stage, in front of a large window that I presume is Paige's office. We head to the left, which jogs back to the outer wall, following the outline of the office. At the wide landing turn, at the back end, Paige stops to open a door, and begins waving us in.

Gage, Sabre, Bear, Ducky, and Mac Tìre enter the room single file ahead of me. The large bodies cause a jam up on the landing as we wait. A million thoughts race through my head over what lies on the other side of the door. I know they will have questions about today, about how Cale died, and I'm a little apprehensive, to tell the truth. I've kept my secrets so long that sometimes even I don't believe what is real anymore.

In the past, this situation would trigger the fight or flight response in me, and I'd be panicked, looking for any way to make my escape. One glance back tells me the other MC members are missing, a perfect time to bolt. Until checking below crushes the idea in a second. The two men stand as sentinels, guarding the exit, perhaps they suspect I'm a high risk ready to flee. I won't be running today, though, and maybe this is another sign I'm growing up.

I can't help but chuckle to myself over this. It gets me a hot glare from Paige, just before she turns to enter the room ahead of me. I realize she's making a statement by going ahead of me. Since the rest of the men entered by rank of position.

In wolf culture, no male is ever below a female. By allowing her to walk in front of me, she shows the Alpha, I'm not fit for the pack or even the court. Normally, this wouldn't bother me. I've never cared much for what the pack thinks of me. Considering I'm about to lay down some serious shit, though, I need to be accepted as an equal, to be trusted. And without pissing off Paige.

I'm not delicate as I react, bounding myself forward just as Paige steps into the threshold. Our bodies collide in the frame as I loop her arm through mine. She reacts, just not how I imagined she would.

Her beautiful eyes open wide and she puts a sideways smirk on her lips. The edges quiver just a bit, and I see she's trying to suppress a smile. The devilish vixen is testing me, she purposely walked ahead to see if I'd let her walk over me.

I halt our entrance in front of the partially closed door. "Not so fast, clever girl."

She turns to face me, her nose crinkles up as she tries to keep the smirk on her lips. It's futile though, she gives up and offers me a wide grin with her comment, "You're pretty skillful yourself, Flash."

Her grin is breathtaking, lighting up her whole face until it radiates from her eyes. I can't help but stare, wanting to cement this image to my memory bank for all time. I don't think I have ever seen a woman so stunning, and the picture I burn into my head makes me ache, knowing she is not mine. Whatever happens next, if the Alpha's decision is to cast me out or punish me for my actions today, my parting gift will be this smile.

I shake off my thoughts with a grin of my own and focus on a change of subject. "Flash? Really? That's what you came up with?"

The smile turns more mischievous with a cock of her eyebrow. "Now, don't go getting your panties bunched up. It's not an insult to your performance or anything. It's more of a compliment, for what you did on the hill, and I don't think anyone thanked you for it, is all."

Her speech throws me. She's showing me she has a softer side, a good heart, and I don't know how to respond. I watch her eyes roll and her switch flips back. "Don't get all touchy about it, sheesh. You're acting like no one has ever complimented you before. Toughen up, Flash, you're going to need a backbone if you plan on walking through this door."

She's right, on both counts. Being a nomad means being alone, which doesn't get me too many compliments. That I remember, anyway. Hers is one I will never forget. This tiny moment is but a blip in the greater picture of today, and because of her small gesture, I'm no longer anxious for what awaits me. With her on my arm, I feel an invincible strength to take on the world.

I wave my hand towards the door. "Shall we face the music together, then?"

Her brow pinches ever so slightly as she thinks this over. Her eyes never leave mine as she answers, "Yeah, I'll step up to bat with you. I think you earned that much respect in my eyes."

I bow my head, grateful to have her in my corner. I realize her respect is not easily earned, and to have her give it to me is something I don't take lightly. This shared moment is pinnacle for us. Not that I think there is an us, as a couple. More of an equal playing field for future meetings.

I don't even believe my own line of crap.

Who am I kidding? I want this chick more than I want my next meal.

I swear to myself, if I can smooth things over with the court and the pack, I'm going to do whatever it takes to quench my desires for Paige. Before this trip is over, I'll bed this vixen. It's the only way I can think to get over my obsession with her.

Here's hoping, the Alpha doesn't kill me, first.

CHAPTER 6

Walking into the spacious office with Paige has me thinking about old boxing matches I've seen in my past, in large arenas, with pumped up fighters ready to knock each other out. And how the crowd would feel the tension of the impending battle.

This room has a similar feel. It reeks of the heavy dousing of testosterone, so thick it could be cut with a butter knife. It's oozing from the Alpha males, who appear ready for confrontation.

And here I am without my gloves.

I'm not the only one who notices. Paige lets go of my arm and shivers as she moves off towards a desk by the back wall, standing behind it and beside her Alpha. I'm curious about her position, one that is usually held for the pack's second-in-command, who I had assumed to be either Ducky or Mac Tíre.

I'm also curious by Gage and Sabre's position, in front of a couch, in the middle of the room, standing as equals and not one before the other. It shows that both males consider themselves just as important to the crown as the other, and means Gage doesn't have a second in his command.

"So, now that we're all here, does anyone care to explain what the fuck has been going for the last fifteen hours?" Gage opens the floor with his question and makes my observations seem invalid.

I step further into the room and make my way to stand between Sabre and the desk. Facing the far side wall to angle myself to either Bear on my left, or Gage to my right. I take a deep breath and begin to weave the tale of the day, from the moment Sunshine and I got off the plane.

I explain how we were met by Lazarus, and then enlisted

Ducky, to help us find who had been siphoning and then killing other witches. Only to discover it had been Cale. I guess at how he had kidnapped Lilith and proceeded to drain her. I pick back up at the part where he had escaped to the hills, because no one needs to know about my encounter with Paige. I finish with how I got the lucky shot to take the warlock out.

"So, what happened to this warlock?" Bear asks.

"He's dead," I answer.

"I know you said that, but is he really dead or will he come back from the fade like the other witch, Lilith, that you mentioned?"

"Aye, Bear, he'd be deader than a doornail," Mac Tìre snorts a reply. "Ye can't come back from having yer chest blasted out."

Bear turns to Mac Tìre to clarify, "So, Zee shot him in the heart?"

Mac Tìre nods. "Aye, he did."

As he finishes, Ducky adds with disagreement, "Not quite, no."

Gage makes an annoyed huff. "Which is it, yes or no? Is Cale dead or not?"

Sabre steps in to clarify the situation, "I'm hearing, Zander shot Cale in the chest, and it may or may not, have pierced his heart. But, he is dead, right?"

"There be no doubt he got 'is heart, he got 'is lungs and most 'is ribcage, too. Th'ee damn hole be the size of me own head. Fecker ain't be coming back from that, no matter what power he stole." Mac Tìre explains in his Irish brogue, so thick that some of the words are hard to make sense of.

Gage, obviously well versed in the Irish accent from the Queen's other mate Magennis, moves on to other questions. "What the hell kind of gun blows a chest cavity open in that way?"

Ducky shakes his head. "It wasn't a gun. Zander shot some sort of light from his hand, and it burnt this huge hole right through the warlock. I've never seen anything like it."

Sabre and Gage both turn to me with puzzled expressions, and I brace myself for the avalanche of questions. However, it's Bear who breaks the silence. "I don't care if he used a rocket launcher. The problem is, he killed a powerful warlock, in our territory. The Warlock MC will see that as an act of war and they will be coming for us."

Paige has been quietly listening to the conversation, at her Alpha's side, until the declaration is announced. "I saw what the warlock did to the witch and he got what he deserved. Zander didn't do anything wrong. He did what any one of us would have done in the same situation."

Bear turns to Paige and I notice his eyes harden just a little as he gives her a stare. "It doesn't matter what you saw, Pea, the MC will still retaliate. You know that. This blowback is on Zee, and he needs to clean it up before we get stuck in the crossfire of this royal bullshit."

Paige shakes her head. "Not if we talk to them. Brigid was there, she saw the witch, too. With her ties to the coven, I know she'll talk to them. Zander isn't the bad guy here, he stepped up. The pack was under a spell, we couldn't move and when the witch and the big guy got knocked over, then the Queen got hit, it was Zander that saved our asses."

"Wait, did you just say the Queen got hit?" Gage turns his attention to Paige. His voice sounds even and calm but his eyes are burning right through the she-wolf. "As in *the Queen,* our mate?"

Paige pales under Gage's stare. "Yeah, but she said she was here to help us."

Gage's whole body starts to quake and a deep growl begins to build low in his throat. I step to the side to move away as he slowly swings in my direction. "You didn't say anything about *her* being here."

His voice is thick with anger, and I put my hand up in a gesture, that asks him to allow me to explain. He doesn't give me the chance when he blurts, "Where is she?"

My own eyes widen as I realize I'm not quite sure where September is. Thankfully, Paige jumps in, "I put her and the others in a suite upstairs. Brigid, our witch, went to check on her when we found out the Queen is with young."

I feel the blood drain from my face as Gage hears those words. Not only have I slipped the secret about the expecting Queen, but I was not with her when Gage and Sabre arrived, and I willingly accepted her help in the fight. In their mind, I failed at my job to protect the Queen. And by allowing this news to get out, I also put September in great danger by exposing her and the baby to more threats.

My eyes barely register the movement as Gage comes at me in a blur, knocking me on my backside on the top of the desk. His left fist clutches my jacket to hold me in place, so his right fist can nail me right in the nose. An explosion of pain bursts between my eyes, while the wet sound of flesh hitting flesh and the cracking of bone rings like a bell inside my brain.

It's so loud that I barely hear Paige scream, "Get off of him!"

Right before Sabre yells, "Gage, no!"

The beating continues when the next punch follows quickly behind the first, landing directly against my left eye socket with so much force, I actually see stars. When I try to shake it off, the room spins as a burning sting starts, telling me my eye is beginning to swell. It only gets worse when the third and fourth punch work together to sound like a shotgun pop in my ear as my jaw dislocates, and the bottom half swings down and over with a crunch like I just chewed on some broken glass.

The next blow releases what little air I have left in my lungs. A whoosh comes shooting out along with a spray of blood that has dripped down from my nose to pool in my mouth. As my blood and spit go flying, I vaguely see the outline through my impaired vision as it splatters against

Gage's white dress shirt and neck, reminding me of the mess a vampire leaves after a feeding.

I lose track of how many more blows Gage throws with his supernatural fast pace, and what damage his strength has caused. The blows just begin to blend into each other. Time seems to slow, and what feels like an hour, is maybe only a few minutes.

I'm also only marginally aware I'm moaning until I hear September's loud shout bring silence to the room. "Gage, stand down!"

Gage freezes mid-punch just inches away from my eye. The heat from his closed fist radiates down into my broken socket. A searing sting spreads out across my eyelid and cheek. I realize it isn't the heat from Gage's hand, but the pain of the left eye swelling shut.

"My Queen." I hear a collection of voices mingle together, and Gage lets go of his hold on my jacket.

My brain somehow manages to figure out that everyone has shown respect with a bow, and I'm the only one not doing so. Since I've just been beat up for my lack of protection to our Queen, I don't also want to add disrespect to the list.

I roll myself to the right to try to stand myself up. When I go to grab the desk beneath me, and there isn't anything there, my momentum keeps me moving forward until I hit the floor with a thud.

"Fuck," I moan from the throb in my head, most of the word is lost on the first syllable when my lips refuse to move.

"Oh, dear Goddess!" Lilith screeches somewhere above me.

I feel a warm touch on my hand at my side followed by a gentle squeeze. "Zander, it's September. I'm going to try to roll you over. Don't be scared, these are just my hands touching you."

She moves her hand, never taking it away from my body

as she slides it up my arm to my shoulder. Her actions are smooth, calming, and sweet. She's trying not to alarm me. I get it, if someone just grabbed me to roll me over, I might freak out. Only someone that might have been through something as traumatic would understand, and I just gained a little more respect for her. September doesn't have to tell me she's been through a lot, her kindness says it all.

"Back up, you've done enough," I hear her spit out, I assume she speaks to Gage.

"I'll help. If you don't mind, my Queen?" Paige's raspy whisper is music to my ears, as her hands warm a spot on my hip. I damn near swear the touch goes directly to my chest to wrap around my heart.

"Thank you, Paige. Zander, we are going roll you on three...two...one, and over." September orders the move before I'm ready.

As they bring me round to my back, I groan when my brain knocks from one side of my head to the other with a violent burst of light behind my eyes. I try to swear again, only a hiss makes it out my mouth.

"Oh, shit, Flash, this might improve your game. All these blood clots and mangled bits are damn sexy. I bet the sheep will be all over you tonight." Paige is going for the tease to help take my mind off the pain, but I detect a small tremble in her voice.

I reach for her hand, still on my hip and offer a squeeze. She takes my fingers with hers and holds them in a firm grip. I know she's worried, but it's nothing that won't heal. I know, I've been here before, only worse.

"Here, I got some towels from the bar and some ice. Is he okay?" Lilith's voice is much higher in pitch from her worry.

"He'll heal, it might take a few hours, but he'll be fine," Gage snaps somewhere to my left. When I try to look in that direction, I only make out blurred shapes.

"He shouldn't have to heal. What the hell is wrong with

you?" September snarls back.

"My Queen," Sabre butts in with his calm tone. "This is just a misunderstanding. We heard you were in a fight and got hit. Gage overreacted because he was just concerned for your safety; we are concerned for your safety."

"This is going to sting tough guy, brace yourself," Paige whispers over my head as someone, I assume Lilith, dabs a wet cold cloth against my cheek, making me hiss.

"Misunderstanding, my ass! Zander has done nothing wrong. It was *my* decision to come here, *my* decision to get involved, and *my* decision to fight. Are you going to beat my face in for that?" September is burning mad as she scolds her mate.

"No, of course not. How could you even ask that?" Gage throws back with hurt.

"Then why do it to him? Zander tried to argue with me, out there. I wouldn't hear it. Cale needed to be stopped by whatever means necessary. Unfortunately, because of what he did to Lilith, he weakened us and got some lucky shots. I did not get hit. Zander made sure of that when he stepped in front of me to kill Cale. Today, he showed his worth, and then some, and I'm more than grateful to him for what he has done."

I am so glad I'm not on the receiving end of September's temper. Damn, does she sound pissed, but it is touching to hear her have my back.

"Fine, so he took care of Cale. It doesn't explain why he left you unguarded with a stranger. If he's going to do the job, he does the whole job, not just the fun killing bits." Gage sounds equally as mad as his mate, but I know the anger is for me and not her.

"Zander didn't leave our Queen alone, I was with her." Lazarus's deep booming voice announces with Lilith's sweet chime adding, "And the witch isn't a stranger, she's mine and Zander's mom."

There is a long silence as I'm sure everyone soaks in

Lilith's revelation. I imagine heads turning to look at me and Lilith, but I can't see it happening, I only know how human nature works.

"You see, I was well protected, not that I can't take care of myself. I'm not a fragile human anymore, Gage. And your misunderstanding was uncalled for. Once Zander has a moment to heal, you will apologize." September seems to lose the bite in her words as she ends her lecture.

Once she finishes speaking, I hear a scuttle of movement off to the side before, "Yes, my Queen."

Gage's tone is a man defeated. He must realize he was wrong, although I believe it will take some time before he and I sit down for a friendly beer.

I jump when the icy cloth touches my eye again and another hissing sound escapes my mouth.

"Oh, sorry. I don't mean to hurt you, but there is a lot of blood to wipe off."

My sister is truly one in a million, but her effort is pointless. In a few hours, I'll clean my own face off when the swelling goes down.

"Let's not worry about the mess so much as the damage," Paige begins, going to what I had just been thinking. "We need to set a few of the bones back into place or they'll heal all wrong. We wouldn't want him too irresistible for the sheep."

I snort at her joke and shoot a blood-clot out my nose. "No need to worry, if he keeps shooting snot bubbles he'll drive the females crazy," Lilith adds to the tease but sounds disgusted.

"I hate to break up your lover's quarrel, Alpha," Bear interrupts the chaos with some of his own. "But what happened today has nothing to do with my club. Due to Zee's actions, the warlocks will be coming for us to get their payback, and I have my own family to protect. This incident is his doing and your mess, the least you, our Alpha, can do is smooth things over with the Warlock MC to keep it out of our territory."

"What the fuck?" I hear Gage swear and feel Paige jump a little at my side.

"Easy," September warns, but I'm not sure if it's to Gage for his outburst, or to Bear for his outright rude implication.

Sabre, once again, jumps in with reason, "I think what Gage meant to say is, pull your head out of your ass. The court does not negotiate for motorcycle clubs. We protect the races, and that is what Zander did today. He stopped more magical beings from getting killed. Something the coven will certainly be happy about when we send someone to speak to them later today. But don't imply we have to negotiate some truce between you and the other gang, we don't work for you."

I see more movement as Bear's large body moves closer to Sabre. "I'm not implying anything. The True Alpha should have our back on this, but you wouldn't understand since you aren't pure blood. This has nothing to do with you, hybrid, so keep your nose out of it."

Paige jumps to her feet beside me and steps over my torso. "Papa, don't, you'll only make matters worse."

I hear a snapping slap of flesh and Paige's hiss. "Don't tell me what to do, girl. You allowed this, and are just as much at fault as they are. I've told you to stay clear of the otherworld bullshit, but you never listen. You stupid idiot. This is why you'll never be anything without us." Bear barks at my she-wolf and I realize he just hit her.

Mother-fucker!

There is a loud roar in my head as my blood starts to boil. The sound is deafening and the pain it causes is volatile, but I don't care. I try to move, to roll to my side to get up and beat the life out of Bear, for what he did, what he said.

Someone with strength holds me down and all I can do is bat at the large arms in front of me like I'm swatting at a fly. *"Settle, she's fine. Sabre and Gage are throwing Bear out of the office, and September is with Paige, but she's fine."* Says the voice in my head.

I know this is Lazarus and he's holding me down. He's keeping me from getting hurt worse, keeping me from Paige. She has to be hurting, both physically and mentally. No one should have to endure such harshness from their own father. I know, mine had me killed, and I'm still not over it.

The door slams, following heavy footfall on the hardwood floor. "He's gone to the clubhouse for now. I'll go talk to him later, once he's had some time to cool down," Gage announces.

"Good," September answers, then asks, "Paige, are you okay?"

My heart picks up speed as I wait for her answer. "Yeah. I'm pissed, but I'll live." And with that, I breathe a sigh of relief.

"What a mess," Lilith states the obvious.

"That's saying a mouthful, Lil," September agrees with a sigh, then goes on, "There was a lot that happened today, and not all of us seem to be on the same page with it. I think we could use a cooling down period to let the dust settle, before we finish dealing with this in the morning."

As a collective group, everyone agrees, "As you wish, my Queen."

"Paige, before we go, I hate to ask, but since Gage and Sabre have arrived, I'm hoping we can get another room in the hotel." September has been staying with Lilith and Lazarus. With her mates showing up, I'm sure she'll want to have some privacy.

Oh, to be a fly on the wall in that room when she hammers Gage with another lecture.

"Sure, whatever you need, it's the least I can do. I'll have Bean take you up to my last suite." Paige agrees, and I hear the rustle of them moving towards the door.

"Thank you, and I hope you'll join us in the morning for the meeting?" September asks with an odd tone that makes me wonder what she's up to.

"Oh," Paige sounds surprised. "Um, yeah, I can be there. Thanks for including me."

The voices get lost when the door closes as Paige takes the Queen and the others downstairs.

"So, do you want the bones put back into place, or do you want to suck up some more attention from the she-wolf first?" Chuckling to himself, Lazarus pats my arm to let me know he's just ribbing.

If I could roll my eyes I would. Instead, I nod my head to tell him to fix my face. He grabs me by the arms and hoists me up to plop me on the couch. I must be healing because the jostle isn't nearly as painful. Once I'm seated, I lean back into the cool leather, with my head against the backrest to get comfortable. I suddenly feel the exhaustion of the day settle in and I sink into the plush cushions. If I could, I would just shut my mind off and go to sleep until this blows over.

"This is going to hurt, no way around it, so brace yourself," Lazarus warns, bringing me back from the drift.

I won't be enjoying the comfortable couch just yet. I shift myself over to be able to grip the arm of the sofa, nodding at the angel when I'm ready.

"I'll do the jaw first." He guides me through the process as he works, telling me what he's going to do.

One of his massive mitts cups my chin firmly and the other envelops the back of my head to hold me in place. He's swift in his movement of jamming my jaw sideways and then knocking it back against my skull. The worst part is the alignment, and with him holding my jaw closed, I can't even get in a scream for relief. I hear it click and pop as he manipulates the bone's position and the pain evaporates instantly.

He lets go of my face. "Try opening your mouth," he tells me and I wiggle it down and around. "Not too much or you'll knock it out again. I just need to make sure I got the head of the mandible back under the articular disk, or you'll have an annoying tick. I think I got it, though."

I know the jaw isn't completely fixed, I'll need to give it time to mend. It sucks that out of the twenty-eight bones in the skull, the jaw is the only one that moves and the one we use the most.

For talking, for instance, which I'm for when I have questions, "Who's here with us?"

"No one, they all went downstairs," he says then asks, "You need something?"

I shrug. "Just wanted to make sure Paige is okay."

I hear the angel chuckle. "Saw that one a mile away."

I'm about to ask what he means when his giant glove of a hand covers my mouth. He uses his thumb and index finger to press on the maxilla bone on either side of my nose, while the rest of his palm keeps my mouth closed. With his thumb and first two fingers on his other hand, he pinches the bridge of my nose then twists it. Working the upper nasal bone to line up with the perpendicular plate of the ethmoid. Again, I hear a click. This one sounds wet and pops in between my eyes, sparking another burst of light in my head, but thankfully, it doesn't stay.

There isn't as much pain with this adjustment and when I try to take a breath through my nose, though plugged, I can actually breathe.

"Thanks man, I think you got it."

"Glad I could help." Lazarus pats my shoulder, then hands me one of the ice wrapped towels Lilith had earlier. "You might want to put this back on that eye for a minute before I heal the rest."

The towel is dripping now that the ice is melting. Cold droplets dribble down my cheek and probably make the crusting blood patches smear worse. I could use a hot shower and a soft bed, but I'm thinking I'm not getting either tonight. The couch is as good as it's going to get.

"Feel better?" Laz asks from above me.

I move the ice away to look up, noticing I can make out

the outline of his face even his eyes, an improvement of sorts. "Yeah, my vision is coming back."

"That's good, but not what I meant."

I place the ice towel on my face. "Then say what you meant."

"I'm wondering how you feel about what happened."

The problem with Lazarus is you never know why he asks the things he does. He can see future events and knows before anyone what is coming. Sometimes, the questions are a foreshadowing to the events, but you never know it until the event happens. Without knowing how this will play out until it does, I can only shrug with indifference.

"Do you not have questions?" He tries coaxing me.

"I do, but I'm smart enough to know you will be little help in answering them."

"True," he chuckles. "But I can help with some of the answers you seek."

I snort. "Yeah, but figuring out which ones can be a long process. I'm too tired to play that game with you right now."

"Very well," he says. "Do you want me to heal the rest of your face or do you wish to continue to play the sympathy card with the wolf?"

"I'm not looking for sympathy from anyone," I snap at his observation, only because I hate that he's implying I have feelings for Paige.

"Suit yourself, I'm merely trying to help." He backs away, turning to head out the door.

I'm about to let him go but the nagging thoughts in my head won't let me. "Fine. Tell me why after all this time, my powers returned today?"

The angel swings back around with a satisfied grin on his face. "Your powers didn't just return, you have always had them."

I mentally roll my eyes as he approaches the couch. "Ah, no, I would have felt them before today and even right now, but I didn't and don't."

He extends his hands toward my face, and I lean my head back against the plush couch. "Think about what Livia told you that day, when she offered you this second chance."

His prompting makes me pause for a minute, trying to recall that day, so long ago. While I think, he sets to work on healing my mangled face. He spreads his thick fingertips out to press them against the side, from forehead to chin, surrounding the battered area. Once he's found the perfect placing, I start to feel a warming in my skin under each positioned finger. It heats up and eventually spreads out across my face through the nerve endings in my body until my whole head, even my neck and shoulders, feel flushed.

With the heat comes a tingling sensation, like laser beams zapping electric charges all at once, and a million times after. It overpowers the initial pain from the beating, making it dull, then disappears altogether. Leaving in its wake the sense of being wrapped in a warm towel, after a great straight razor shave.

As he continues with the healing, I get lost in my own head, and before long, I'm remembering my first moment here on Earth. What Lazarus is doing now to my face is essentially what Livia had done so many moons ago. She had pulled me from the Underworld, where my father had discarded me. She warmed me with her magic to heal my wounds before touching me with her blessing spell. Everyone calls it a blessing, but I have always seen it as my curse.

I walk this realm as no one of importance. I have no future and no real past. I was stripped of my glory, my pride, and my powers, to become this half shell of a person. I am no longer a god, but also not human. She put her mark on me, to deem me another species in her world of made up creatures. She called me a shifter, and then she left me to find my way.

"Once peace has been achieved, only then will thy true self be returned and regained whole again."

Her words from that day still confuse me. She was the one with the plan for peace, for a harmonious world between the realms. Yet, she chose to curse herself, and I never got to see what she meant. For Lazarus to bring it up now makes even less sense, and I'm not sure what it has to do with why my powers returned for a brief time.

"I told you, they have always been with you." Lazarus steps away, breaking his magic connection to answer my churning thoughts. "They have just been dormant, patiently waiting while you found the answers you seek."

The warming sensation melts away, leaving a feather tickle on my face. I rub my hands against my cheeks to get it to stop, feeling the grit of my own blood crusted to my skin. I open my eyes wide to discover the haze in my sight gone.

He has healed me back to new and confused me further still. "Thanks for the help, and the not so helpful conversation."

"You're welcome, on both counts." He chuckles to himself, then adds, "Your journey awaits, but it is up to you to decide which of the paths you wish to take."

"Whatever the hell that's supposed to mean," I snort back.

Lazarus doesn't get a chance to add any more, as the knob on the office door rattles following a thudding kick. When it doesn't open, Lazarus crosses the room to investigate while I get myself off the couch. He grabs the knob, turns it and opens the door just as Paige, arms loaded with supplies, kicks again at the bottom of the wood door. She goes flying forward and collides with the angel.

"Uh-oh," she grunts. "Shit, you're one solid dude."

Laz laughs, catching her and some type of bag from falling on the ground. "I shall take that as a compliment."

He helps her to balance, then hands her the square pack he's holding. She smiles and takes the bag to tuck it under her arm.

"Thanks, I thought I would bring up the first-aid kit." She turns to walk in the room, adding as she moves, "To help patch up Zander's face…"

She trails off, then gasps when she finally notices me standing in the middle of the room. "How did you heal…" She's staring at me in shock, then swings back to the angel.

Lazarus grins with amusement. "This is a question for Zander, he's full of answers." He chuckles at his own dig, then adds, "Besides, my little dove will be waiting. Enjoy your evening, or I guess early morning."

He bows slightly to Paige, then the bugger winks at me before he uses his powers and pulls his little vanishing trick. I hear Paige squeal as she stumbles a step back. She then turns herself to me with all kinds of eye-opening wonder on her face.

I curse the angel, he did this on purpose. Possibly to push me closer to the she-wolf, and to face her questions so that I can also reconcile my own.

The jack-ass!

CHAPTER 7

"Oh, shit! Where did he go?" Paige stammers out, twirling herself around as she looks for the angel.

"He's gone," I tell her, but she doesn't seem to take me at my word, moving towards the open door to peer out on the catwalk.

"Huh," I hear her grumble before she comes back in the office, kicking the door closed with the heel of her boot.

Her eyes burn with questions as I watch the previous shock resolve into confusion. She cocks her eyebrow as she studies my face, then drops her head to look down at her armload of goods. She snorts and shakes her head, then walks over to the front of the desk to unload the supplies. I notice the square canvas bag has a first-aid symbol on the front of the pack, and with it, she places a champagne bucket full of ice beside a load of hand towels.

"Guess you won't be needing these," she mumbles under her breath, then laughs.

As she unpacks her armload, my eyes drift to her backside. I'm not sure how she got into the latex cat suit, but I appreciate whatever effort she endured, to squeeze her hourglass curves into it. The tight wrapping perfectly outlines her shape, from her voluptuous hips to her slap-able round ass. And when she shifts on her spiky heels, I notice a seam to a zipper tucked between her ass cheeks at the base of her tailbone.

She pivots towards me just as I lick my dry lips, feeling the temperature in the room rise. As she moves, my eyes follow the seam of the zipper, from beneath her camel toe and up her body to her generous cleavage. The suit is cut in a circle at her chest to show off her amazing breasts... *that I wish to sink my face into and motorboat the shit out of.*

The suit picks back up at the shoulders, stretching to form a ringless collar around her neck. I cock my own eyebrow at this discovery. In the BDSM world, a ringless collar suggests a dominant person. I wonder if she's unaware of this sign or if she's blatantly announcing.

It doesn't matter, either way. The suggestive visual is enough to jolt my cock to life. The blood rushes to my organ, making it throb with urgency at the front of my pants.

She clears her throat just as I'm about to start drooling. I'm forced to pull my eyes from her incredible body to meet her amused expression.

"I'm happy to see your face doesn't look like it went through a meat grinder anymore. That image has turned me off of hamburgers for a while." She snickers and her eyes light up as she jokes. "You'll have to let me in on the secret of this miracle healing trick. I still have a bruise from Papa slapping me."

She's trying to tease me to keep our conversation light, but the mention of her father hitting her has me gritting my teeth in anger. A low deep growl bubbles up from my throat and I try to swallow it down as I examine her face for damage.

"Are you hurt?"

She waves a hand in the air. "Hardly. It was nothing."

I step in front of her to take her waving hand in mine. "Don't brush it off as nothing." I place my other hand on the side of her face and rub my thumb over her right cheek, where the yellowing bruise is faint. "That kind of disrespect isn't right."

She laughs. "So, it's okay for your Alpha to kick the shit out of you because he's got a hair-trigger temper, but my Alpha slapping me for not keeping my opinion to myself is disrespectful? I think you have your priorities messed up."

She pulls away from me, walking to the wall behind the couch, which has a two-way glass window, to look out over the club below. I watch her hips sway as she moves and grit my teeth again, this time, for a whole other reason.

I shake my dirty thoughts away to engage in our conversation, even though my cock wants otherwise. "I'm not saying what Gage did was right, but I understand why he did it. I shouldn't have left Queen September alone or accepted her help in the fight, not to mention letting her pregnancy slip. I'm still new to this game, and politics is not my strong suit. Yet, I know when I'm wrong, so I took the punishment." I try to explain Gage's actions to her to make her understand.

She turns with a frown denting her forehead. "Is that why you didn't fight back? Well, that's not right either, no matter what the circumstances."

I shrug. "It's water under the bridge now, and I know what not to do in the future."

She smirks, "And so do I, but it won't stop me."

I laugh at her stubbornness then frown from another thought. "Has Bear hit you before?"

It's her turn to shrug. "More than a few times."

This time the growl bursts from my lips as I clench my fists at my side. She reacts by raising her brows while placing her hands on her hips. I wait in the silence for her to unleash some lecture about her being able to take care of herself.

Instead, she tilts her head and offers my words back to me, "It's all water under the bridge, and nothing I can't handle."

I shake my head in disagreement and she grins up at me. "Thank you for caring, I can't say I've met many wolves who would defend me as you have. I also think I owe you an apology."

My anger subsides and I feel my own frown of confusion dent my forehead. "Whatever do you need to apologize to me about?"

She snorts, "Ah, maybe my attitude towards you and the Queen earlier. My ignorant opinions and rude comments. I didn't understand who you all were or why you came here, but now I do, and my eyes are a lot more open. I'm still a little freaked out by you all. Between that giant's disappearance, the insane magic, and whatever lightning bolt thing that came out of you earlier, I have to admit you're all a bit on the scary side."

While I listen, I'm not even sure how to answer her. After a minute of chewing on her confession and my own thoughts, I head over to the window to look out at the club. I'm not seeing what's down below, though. I'm wondering why her apology is giving me mixed feelings, and why her joking about it bothers me. If I get honest with myself, I know that answer too. She says she's on board and has no issue with what we all are.

Will she still feel the same way when she hears my story?

Will the Queen, the court, my sister, and my friends?

Minutes tick by where I'm in my head until she places her hand on my shoulder to offer a gentle squeeze. "Hey, I didn't mean to upset you, I'm only teasing. I'm not scared of you, never have been, especially not after you saved me from throwing my dignity out the window at the barn. I didn't thank you for that or for being discreet about it. You showed me you are different, then you went a step further and saved the Queen and the pack. Our own Alpha wouldn't have done that, not a chance."

I turn to face her as she explains, feeling new emotions tug deep in my mind and warm my chest. I want to wrap her in a tight hug against my chest for her acceptance, but I can't move. I'm frightened that if I do, this moment will be lost. I settle for brushing a strand of hair from her eyes so I can gaze upon her.

"Has anyone ever told you just how stunning you are?" I ask, then whisper, "Especially your eyes, they comfort me in ways I can't explain. They are so beautiful."

I'm watching her face as it starts to light up from one of

her incredible smiles. A soft pink dusts her cheek when she answers, "When you say my eyes are beautiful, it's because they are looking at you."

I'm frozen by her confession, though, manage to return the smile while my heart jerks in my chest and begins to thump. I ache to taste her lips, but I'm scared I won't be able to get enough. I want to ravage her until I'm so weak from a night of passion, that all I can do is hold her. It won't be enough. I know once I dip my toes, I'll get washed away in what I feel for her, and without her knowing who I am, I can't bear the thought of having her hate me for not telling her.

I step back with a deep sigh to collect myself, moving to the couch where I sit to the right side. I pat the cushion beside me and look back.

"We should talk."

Her back is to me and I watch her tense as she turns. "We should," she starts to say, "But I have a feeling this is going to get heavy and after the day we both had, I don't want heavy."

She begins to walk around the room behind me, stopping on my right to bend at the waist and whisper in my ear, "I want stress relief. With no thinking and enough kink to make us both forget our past for a night. We can talk after, tomorrow, or even a week from now. It won't matter when because the truth will still be there when we decide to face it."

She stands up to step back, allowing me room to turn towards her in my seat. I'm more than puzzled by her mood change, and unsure of where she's going or whether we should continue.

"Besides, I owe you one and I bet your cock could use a hug right about now, from my mouth."

Once she smiles down at me, the Earth could implode and I wouldn't care, because in this minute, I'm back in the heavens.

She steps in front of the couch with her hands on her hips, looking at me with eyes burning with her hunger. Yet, she's slow in her movement, telling me she's quite used to being in this controlling position. I sit back against the couch cushion and watch as she picks up her leg to place her foot on the cushion between my legs. The corners of her lips twitch as she nudges my balls with the toe of her shoe.

I moan as my cock swells beneath its denim trap, making her lips spread into an incredible mischievous grin. "You enjoy that, huh?"

She picks up her foot to place the toe point on my shaft, and the spike gently on the seam, where my balls are separated. This time, when I hiss it's because my cock throbs from the pain, in a good way.

"Hmm, excellent response. If you keep that up, you'll make me wet."

The low husky sound is back in her voice. The drop in frequency causes a rush of heat in my blood. I could cum in my pants from her dirty talk alone. Add a bit of that velvet rasp and I'm burning with lust for her.

She lifts her shoe to put it back on the floor before dropping down on all fours. I watch her crawl my way, her ass wiggling up in the air. It's begging for a slap and a hard fuck. I'm about to lean over to offer it my palm, when she puts her face in my lap and begins to rub her cheek, her chin, and her nose against my manhood.

I groan as she moans in approval, right before she uses her teeth at the top of my pants to tug open the first button. Her hands glide up my legs to my stomach, where she lifts my shirt to scrape her long fingernails down my ribs towards the top of the jeans. Holding the waistband, she uses her teeth to pop the next button, exposing the head of my cock. Once I feel her gasping breath on the tip, my shaft jerks, and a drop of pre-cum escapes.

She moans at the offering, "I like the first drop, it tells me I'm heading in the right direction to achieving my goal."

My dick jumps, weeping with glee as I hiss, "Christ, you're dirty."

She grabs the two halves of my fly to pull, releasing the beast before her. It jerks forward, and she's ready, mouth wide open, tongue sticking out to be slapped by my hard cock.

"And you're eager, but I love a good tongue spanking, especially when it comes from a cock this big."

"F-u-c-k," I moan and close my eyes, thinking about anything, but her, to hold myself off.

I take a deep breath and blow it out slow before opening my eyes. She's waiting patiently for me, giving me a moment to gain some control before leaning in to lick the drops of juice off my swollen hammerhead with an unapologetic greed. Her velvet tongue dips under to flick at the tip. Darting it back up and around, covering the area with a slippery layer of her spit, before she sucks me into her mouth with an audible slurp.

Her mouth is hot, wet, and as she gobbles up my cobra, she looks up at me with the eyes of someone devoted to the challenge. There is something so erotic about this look, about the way she's giving her mouth to me. I can't even begin to explain the emotions rolling through me. I've never been so turned on in my life, nor have I ever been this afraid.

I swallow hard, pushing down the latter to concentrate on her mouth inching lower on my shaft, lips pressing hard against the length. She breaks our eye contact to shift herself forward, gripping the waist of my pants to clench it into her fists to tug it down. I see where she's going with this and offer some help.

I bunch up her hair into one of my hands, holding it in a ponytail to keep out of her way. Then I lift my hips enough for her to whip my pants down below my knees. Once my pants are out of the way, I grip her ponytail tight and pull back her head to stand myself up. We are parted for only a second, but when I look down at this sultry vixen, she's holding her mouth open for me. Begging me with her eyes for more, as she juts her tongue forward in hopes of tasting the next bead of sin.

I grip my cock in my dominant hand and give it a long hard stroke. It's slick from our mixing fluids and my hand slides with ease down to the root, where I hold it tight and move towards her to slap her face. She shrieks with a gleeful giggle, then offers out her full tongue. I jerk her ponytail harder, holding her in place to slap my dick hard enough for the veins on my shaft to stand at attention. Only then do I sink myself deep into her hot hole.

Her lips are the best kind of sin, wrapping around my cock and glistening with a slick dew that's dripping down her chin. She slurps and sucks her way down my shaft, putting everything she has into this until I feel her throat gag a little around my dick. And still, she continues to mouth fuck me. Never once missing a beat from my hips as I watch her throat swell with every deep thrust.

A thought enters my mind that slows my pace. The irony of this blowjob- even though she's on her knees, she's the one that has me by the balls. In this moment, looking at her suck me with such passion and hunger, I know she's not only going to make me explode down her throat, but she's the one who will also make my heart cum.

As the thought forms in my head, it also begins to wrap itself deep into my soul. I can't hold on any longer. The need to mark is strong. I wonder if it is coming from whatever wolf instincts I've been given or my previous drake instinct that came back to me today. Whichever the case, I push myself down her throat, watching her eyes widen as I thrust forward.

"That's my *leannàn*, you earned it, now swallow," I command her, as my lover, as the explosion hits. It's a powerful release that has me screaming her name as she milks every last drop from me.

When the twitching jerks start, Paige pulls back from

my cock to lick her lips. Her face looks like she just ate a box of glazed donuts. There's saliva and ejaculate dripping off her chin. I don't even care that it's my own. I drop to my knees in front of her, taking her face in my hands to hold her as I devour her with my lips.

I lick her chin and taste my own bitter flavor. I swallow it down, and mentally promise, next time it will be mixed with her flavor as well. I continue my tasting, sucking her thick bottom lip into my mouth to nip it with my teeth.

"Harder," she moans and plunges her own tongue into my mouth, flicking it against mine like she's licking her own clit.

As we explore each other's mouths with suggestive tongue actions, my cock doesn't get much time to recover, and within seconds, I'm ready to go again. I knew once I started to taste her, to feel her aggression and passion against my tongue, I would never be able to stop. I want more, all of it, all of her, and whatever comes from that combination.

And to think, this is only our first kiss.

"Wa..." she mumbles. "Wait." She presses one hand to my chest, and grabs my cock for a hard squeeze with the other.

She takes a hard gasp to catch her breath before giving me bad news. "Even though I'm currently sexually destroying you in my head, we have to stop."

I drop my head back, looking up at the steel struts running across the ceiling, trying to compose myself. It's a futile exercise. I crave her now, deep in my bones. I settle for projecting my obsession for her, with a direct burning stare at her.

"You're killing me," I grumble, grabbing her fist to stroke it down the length of my shaft to the root, as I push, then hold down my arousal.

"Ah, don't look at me like that. I'm already breaking my own rules." She pouts in the most adorable fashion.

I groan at her delicious pushed out bottom lips, but

refrain from action by asking, "What look and what rules?"

She leans in an inch from my face, pulling her hand up my length with an incredibly controlled slow pace, matching the intensity of her pause. When her fist reaches the top of my head, she swirls it around with her fingers, slicking the swollen crown, until every last drop of my blood, seems to flow in only that one spot. Then with more disciplined control, she captures my lips. Her eyes never leave mine as she kisses me with the most unbridled passion I have ever felt in my life.

This kiss is methodical, patient, and passionate beyond anything I could ever imagine, and when she's done, I am but a mere shell of myself. A pile of goo at her feet to be molded into whatever she wishes. Hers to control and hers to have, fully and completely.

In her raspiest voice yet, she begins to explain, "You're looking at me like your cock is already inside of me. As though you can't get enough, and it is causing you deep, constant pain. Since you are already on your knees, it's like you are begging me for it. Wanting and needing to feel me from the inside out. You've been doing it all day." She leans in and gives me a shorter peck. "Thank you, no one has ever looked at me this way, with such loyalty, such willingness to please me."

She stands and holds her hand out to help me up. I take her fingers to turn her hand so I can plant a kiss on her palm. "Then you have not been hanging out with the right people, *mo àilleacht.*"

As I get to my feet I hear her giggle. "Such pretty words."

I pull my jeans up over my hips to close the front and secure the buttons. This time, I hear her sigh, "Such a shame to put that away."

I love both of her reactions and pull her to me to wrap my arms around her waist, savoring the way her luscious curves just seem to melt against me. "If it makes you smile,

I'll tell you every old story I know in my language, just to see your face light up. And if it makes you laugh, I'll do it more often, just to hear the sound."

"Jesus," she gasps. "With those type of words, you're going to make more than my clit throb. I'm already wet, and thankful I wore latex so no one will see it dripping down my legs. But the pretty words..." She trails off to lick her lips and choose what she'll say next, "You're going to give me feelings for you cowboy, and it goes against my number one rule of never getting involved with a pack member."

I nod. "Ah, your rules." I grin as she reluctantly pulls out of my arms. "It's not like they can't be broken."

She laughs and it sounds light, carefree. "Okay, you got me there. I have been known to break a rule or two in my day."

She pivots on her spikes and faces the desk, then rotates back to me, seeming confused. I can almost read the thoughts churning inside her head. They flicker in her eyes, changing the color of the brown and yellow hues, from light to dark. The thoughts continue to twitch across her face causing deep lines of indecision. She appears to be having a mental war, perhaps pertaining to our little affair.

I give her some space, tucking in my t-shirt and straightening my gun holster under my jacket. I don't doubt this is where she'll tell me to hit the road. Except, I hear her make a whining grunt sound that is, oh, so, adorable. When I glance up to find her pouting again, it makes me chuckle.

"I heard you don't have a place to crash tonight. Since my hotel has been inundated with the royal's, I'm all out of rooms." She starts off topic and makes me shake my head to try to catch where this is going.

I hear her heartbeat flutter and speed up, making my brow lift in question at her anxiety. "I hope I don't regret this later... if you give me a few minutes, I'll turn the room over to Bean and meet you out front. If you're interested, I have a place just down the road, and you are more than welcome to stay with me. I'll even grab some dinner; I'm sure you must be hungry."

She's being shy and even chewing on her lip as she waits for my answer. I sense this is a big offer she's presenting me, and I don't take it lightly. Paige doesn't strike me as a spontaneous person, in business, matters of the heart, or even her day-to-day routine. I can tell by the well-organized desk, the scheduling planner the only item on its surface, and the pristine tidiness of her office that she is regimented in her tasks, perhaps even a little obsessive compulsive about them. Coupling this discovery with Kingsley's statement from earlier, about her lack of interest in a mate and Paige's own confession of breaking her rules, I can see this is not an offer she gives out often, if ever.

I'm flattered, and like her; I'm also cautious. By saying yes, this could lead to new territory, for me too. It makes me wonder if the emotions starting to bubble inside of me are from deeper feelings, in which case, I need to confess my own sins first. Although, if I'm just having lustful cravings for this vixen, from the leftover effects of Lilith's magic, then a night with her will cleanse me of my obsession and tomorrow we can both start anew.

I weigh the pros, the cons, and all the ramifications of both. In the end, in true male fashion, once my eyes lock with hers, my dick swells in anticipation of another round with her, and makes up my mind for me.

"I appreciate, and accept the offer." I bow my head in respect.

She snorts, "Damn, you're so politely Canadian, it's hard not to fall for all that humble charm."

The tease breaks the tension of the decision and we both laugh. For me, however, it feels forced. I'm quite aware of the gentle undertones in her statement. A massive elephant has entered the room, and I'm glad when she guides me out the door. But once she takes my arm and we begin to walk down the stairs, I realize her hinted feelings aren't what scare me.

I find comfort being with Paige. Her confidence is freeing. It makes me want to pull off my mask and stop hiding in the dark shadows. Yet, the fear of judgment sits heavy, and I never want to see it cross her face when she's looking at me. I want to remain in this center of calm, the tranquil bliss before the vicious storm.

It's slowly becoming my favorite place and changing me, both physically and mentally. There's a low heat starting to grow deep inside me, burning deep in my chest as it simmers. It's making me stronger, transforming me. I wondered why my powers had come back to me on the hill. It doesn't take a rocket scientist to figure out it has something to do with my feelings for Paige or the fear I will never be enough for her.

I've dipped my toes and I'm becoming addicted, so much so, that I'm afraid it will destroy me for good. She is slowly becoming the weapon that will make me whole or kill me. I've experienced the latter before, it isn't a pretty ride, and this time, there won't be any second chances. I'm on the edge, teetering, and my willpower is weak.

God help me, but spending the night with Paige might just be my undoing.

CHAPTER 8

It didn't take us long to exit the bar and make our way down the dusty road on my bike, to where Paige hangs her hat every night. In my wildest dreams, I never expected she'd be taking me to another barn. Although, it does seem fitting for her.

"Clay, I saw your truck out front, you still here?" Paige shouts out a greeting as we enter a massive, state-of-the-art horse stable, with every bell and whistle one could imagine inside of a barn, and then some.

We walk through a side door into a brightly lit greeting area with a curved standing desk. There's no one behind it at this twilight hour, though I imagine someone must organize the neat paperwork stacks at some point during the day. Paige stops at the desk to pick up a clipboard on the top of the counter, flipping through a couple of the pages, before putting it back down.

"There's a few messages for you." The voice of a grumbly-sounding male calls out from our left.

When I turn towards the voice, a gentleman weathered beyond his aging years, sits hunched over on a stool in a tack shop. The supply area is of medium size, a retail store inside the stable. In front of him sits a row of saddles on specially made sawhorses, and it appears from the sheen that he has just spit-polished every last one of them.

The saddles aren't the only impressive part of this place. Standing by the desk, I'm in awe as I take in the enormous building. It's set up as an equestrian business. I'm not an expert, so it is unclear if the business is for riding lessons or breeding. However, there seems to have been no expense spared when this place got built. As they say, the devil is in the details.

Large steel beams hold some type of rigging for moving

the bales of hay to each hand-carved wooden gate stall. Each stall has its own sprayer, for the cleanliness of the horses, as well as for the building. Not to mention, an air exchange system so powerful, it's impossible to tell if horses even occupy the building. An outstanding feat when I consider my supernatural sense of smell.

Paige waves at me to follow her, and we head towards the saddle shiner. On approach, she leans over the Native American man to wrap her arms around him, for what I can only explain as a loving embrace.

"What are you still doing here?" She asks, but doesn't seem surprised.

"Margie's at her sister's." The grandfatherly human states with a grunt. I get the sense he isn't much of a talker.

"Ah," Paige giggles and kisses him on the cheek. "You know, if you'd learn to cook for yourself, you wouldn't have to stay in the stable quarters every time she goes to Rose's."

The man grumbles, "I can cook." He sounds defiant but then adds in a softer tone, "I like your special scrambled eggs, is all."

He finally glances up over his shoulder to give her a wide smile that mirrors the one on her face. I study the man, his features, the curve of his nose, the shape of his smile and eyes, though his appear to be a darker hazel to hers.

"Are you two related?" I blurt with curiosity.

Clay jumps off the stool, knocking it over. I'm amazed he's so spry for an older guy. He turns to face me, eyeing me up, as he jams a hand in the pocket of his well-worn leather duster. I've taken him by surprise, he sees me as a threat and he's reaching for a weapon, just to be safe. I put my hands up slow to show I'm unarmed. Paige places her hand on his trigger-happy arm to stop him.

"It's okay, Clay. This is Zander. He's with the Queen's people I told you about earlier. The hotel is full so I brought him here for the night." Paige talks fast to explain and as she does, Clay relaxes his shoulders but doesn't take his eyes off me.

I extend my right hand to make peace. "A pleasure to meet you, sir."

He gives me a double take with a raised eyebrow as he shakes my offered hand. "Cowboy does have some pretty words."

My brow pops up as I swing my eyes towards Paige. She's told this human about us, or me anyway, and I wonder why. The number one rule in our world is to live in peace, secretly. For her to share with this human who we are or even why we are here, makes no sense.

Unless she's somehow related to him.

As I chew on the thought, Paige laughs with a bit of nervous energy. "I thought so too, but as it turns out, he's Canadian."

The man grunts while nodding his head like this explains everything. Paige turns with a blush on her cheek to fire instructions at me, "I have to check on a few things, so go on up. My apartment is straight up the stairs behind the desk. Make yourself at home, I won't be long."

I grin at her blush and offer a wink that deepens the streak of red on her face. It reminds me of earlier, at the other barn, when she got flustered and embarrassed. I make my goodbyes to the man, then head for the stairs, while my mind tries to figure out how to exploit this discovery.

Paige is a tough nut to crack. One minute, she's up in my grill like some dominant Alpha bitch, and the next, she's timid and verging on submitting to me. My cock is already hard from having a sampling of the first in her office. It now springs to attention over the latter.

I'm eager with anticipation when I reach the door, noticing a slight nervous tremble in my hand as I turn the knob. I'm full of anxious energy when the door opens wide, until Paige's sillage trickles out on the air current to greet me. And with it, a gentle calm washes over me.

I stand before the threshold and deeply inhale her

perfumed fragrance. Sweet and intoxicating like a woman should be. Yet, with a hint of nature that reminds me of autumn in the forest. Even her scent is as conflicting as her personality. It's not a deterrent, if anything, I'm motivated to learn more.

I take another nose full, committing it to my memory, before stepping through the door frame into the dark. It doesn't stay that way for long, as lights begin to flicker with life above me, triggered by my movements. As I take more steps, my actions seem to trip off sensors that make the apartment come alive with sound.

A beautiful instrumental melody fills the room. I recognize the interpretation of Chopin's Nocturnes immediately. I know this isn't an original, I remember the man playing a bit faster in a live concert. However, this artist seems to enable me, the listener, to savor the musical piece in a way his more aggressive performance never did.

As I absorb the music, I'm fascinated by how well it pairs with the apartment. Much like a fine wine goes with the perfect meal. I'm once again in awe of Paige. For a female with such a bold and edgy appearance, this loft is a complete contrast, and proof you can't judge a book by the cover alone.

The detailing in this space is every bit as grand as it had been downstairs, just on a more elegant scale. As I walk across distressed wood flooring into the kitchen, I'm met by a large rectangular island with weathered wood drawers below, and a striking slab of granite on top. The stools around are made of old truck springs under tractor seats. The appliances are new, but the cupboards appear as though they came from another era, and I notice the handles are even made from carved sticks.

Everywhere I look, there's a mixing of old with new, modern chic with outdoor whimsy. A fieldstone wall on one side of the room showcases two reclaimed doors on roller slides. A stained-glass window on the other side frames a sliding garage-style door that goes out to a large modern-day patio.

The ceiling has massive wood beams with matching columns, lined all the way back to another stone wall. It gives the room a rustic log home feel. The designer has used the stone wall as a focal point for the fireplace, with a large television above, and decorated on both sides with stacks of pre-split logs. Even the floor before the fireplace has pieces of the logs cut into circles and placed like puzzle pieces in front of the hearth, drawing one's eyes to the area.

The brothel, the club, the stable, and this apartment, all have a similar elegance to them, showing a more cultured side to Paige. It's something I would never have guessed existed when we first met.

The fascinating part is the loft above the kitchen area. Quaint and cozy with an antique fainting couch that is under an umbrella lamp and in front of a plethora of books, stacked on shelves three and four high, until overflowing. I wonder how someone, with so many businesses to run, a pack to keep track of, and an MC to keep out of trouble, can find the time for so many books? I'm more curious as to what she might be reading. I don't doubt she is self-taught from the pages of knowledge above, and from what she absorbed, she was able to build her empire.

Paige is an impressive female who has no idea how much I find her accomplishments a turn on. Without her even knowing, she has seduced me with her mind. Add the sarcastic attitude, independence, confidence, and drop-dead gorgeous body and I'm addicted. I want to know everything about her, almost more than I want to have sex with her, and that speaks volumes.

Paige makes me want the full package before I've even seen the goods. It took less than a day, but she's managed to have my balls and heart wrapped up in a pretty little ribbon, and I want her to have it. Yet, there's a whispered warning deep inside me. Telling me this will not end well. I am, after all, cursed. Haunted desperately by a past that's bound to offer a bleak future.

Livia called it a blessing, yet, it has been nothing but torture. Every opportunity, hope, dream, even love I have ever encountered, has ended poorly, ripped away with violent force. I am not deserving of happiness or someone like Paige, and I fear what will happen if I get closer to her.

She will be my undoing.

"I come with gifts, dinner and a six-pack. I hope you're hungry."

Paige pushes through the door with a brown bag in one hand and a case of beer under her arm. She kicks the door closed with her foot and makes her way to the island to deposit the offering. She starts pulling one of the beers from the pack, twisting the top and turning to present me with the drink. The commotion, however, doesn't register as I'm deep in my thoughts. It isn't until she's standing in front of me that I realize she's even here.

She places her hand on my arm and gives it a squeeze. "Hey, everything okay? You kind of look... lost."

I blink a couple of times to clear my head and when I finally focus on her, I sigh with content as my anguish flutters away. "Uh, yeah, I was just thinking how impressive this place, and you, are."

Her lips twist sideways and she frowns for a minute. She shakes her head, trailing her hand down to mine where she places the beer.

"It would seem you need a drink because that was not the look of someone with compliments on the brain."

I take the refreshment with a laugh. "I guess you got me there, but I'm not lying. Seriously, this apartment, the businesses you built, it's remarkable and slightly unheard of in our corner of the world. I know it couldn't have been easy, and I'm impressed by how well you jumped the hurdles to get to where you are."

Her frown deepens and she steps back. "Normally, I'd

say you're blowing smoke up my ass, but I think you honestly mean what you say. You're really not like the rest. You don't look at me with dollar signs in your eyes or ownership on your lips. I'm not quite sure how to deal with that."

I step forward to take her in my arms, popping her chin up so she can see the truth on my face. "I don't want your money, nor do I want to own you, Paige. I only want to know you in every way. Something tells me, you aren't like the rest of the wolves either, and maybe we're more alike than either of us thought."

Her throat swallows under my fingers, and her eyes drop down from being embarrassed. I don't let her get away with it though, gripping her chin firmly for her to look right at me. "I'm aware you are not what people prefer you to be. But, those people don't know you're far more than what they will see. I want to see what they don't, and if you show me yours, I will show you mine."

"Damn, you and those pretty words." She sighs with a smile then steps back to cock her hip and place a hand on the curve. "There's a reason I don't have anyone lying next to me at night, it's so I don't have someone lying to me, come morning. I don't open up to just anyone because I don't want them to use it against me. For some reason, though, I want to with you. I, too, want to know you, just don't make me regret it."

I chew on this hard pill for a moment, swallowing it down with a few gulps of air. I'm asking her to trust me by opening up so I can get to know her, and in return, she wants the same from me. My heart speeds up, and my palms get clammy as I realize what this will mean. Truth and honesty.

I have never shared myself, my story, my secret with anyone, not even my own blood. We are at the crossroad, if we move forward this could end badly. Yet, if we open up with honesty, it could become something magical.

I take a small step forward and stop, thinking it over one

last time. From the moment I first met Paige, I knew she was special. The sparkling rare gem in a sea of dusty coal. I give in, taking the last step towards her when I realize, in these last few hours, she has shown me she is everything I have ever wanted.

I wrap my arms around her, pulling her tight against my chest as if at any minute someone could take her away from me. I try to tell her with this hug everything I feel. From my joy of knowing her to my fears of losing it all.

She melts against me until we become one continuous form. I hear her whisper, "You're making my heart smile."

I squeeze her a little tighter as I laugh at her quirky sentiment. "You have a unique vocabulary yourself."

She pats me on my back. "See, I've been sharing, even showing you how much of a smart-ass I am." She pulls back and gives me a sly smile. "I did kind of think it was sexy, earlier, when you kept putting me in my place while you treated me like *I* was the actual Queen. And the whole time, you had this look on your face that said you wanted to spend a weekend between my legs. Give me a few more of those pretty words and I just might make that dirty fantasy come true."

Her grin widens into a full beaming smile, lighting up her eyes until her beauty steals all my words away.

Shit, I'm a goner if just her smile sends me head over heels.

She begins to giggle as she takes my hand to pull me over to the island. "*Ven, niño bonito.*"

"You speak Spanish?" I answer her call for me, the pretty boy, to come.

"I speak many languages, and enough of yours, thanks to Mac Tire, to understand what you've been saying to me all day. Although I have to say, I do prefer your pretty words to his foul ones."

She gives me a wink as she begins to open the brown bag, pulling out take-out containers, and sliding them towards me with napkins and cutlery. I settle myself into one of the tractor seats in front of the island, and finally, take a long pull from the beer in my hand. It's a bit warm for my taste and doesn't quite hit the spot, but I have a feeling my craving thirst has nothing to do with a drink.

I watch Paige settle next to me and open the lid on her container, revealing a triple cheeseburger. I cock my eyebrow her way and chuckle. "Didn't you say something earlier about being turned off of burgers?"

Her hands wrap around the giant sandwich and she brings it up to her mouth, pausing with a grin to make her remarks, "You know I did. But, the more I thought about you, the more I realized- I love a thick and juicy slab of meat in my mouth."

Her jaw opens wide and she fills her sassy mouth with a large bite of the meat while wiggling her eyebrows at me. There is something quite erotic about watching a woman eat. It's a prelude to what they might be in bed, and Paige definitely has an appetite.

"Christ," I moan.

Someone needs a cocktail in her mouth, stat, hold the tail.

I quickly take another swig of my beer and move my attention to my own container. There is no way I can bear to watch her swallow, it will only remind me of how well she did that back in her office.

Just the thought makes me want to explode in my fucking pants.

I busy myself with a glance at my meal, finding a jumbo sirloin strip dripping with caramelized juices, surrounded by perfectly cut onion rings with a side of mayo. I get the hint, Paige wants my thick hot meat for a happy ending.

I burst out laughing, "Messaged received, loud and clear."

She turns with a sexy smirk as I dip an onion ring in the mayo, and extend my tongue around the coated curl, to suck it in my mouth. Making sure to exaggerate the slurping sounds to get her attention.

Her eyelashes flutter as she sets down her burger, leaning into me to grab the front of my jacket. "Come here and put that gorgeous mouth to use. Suck the grease from my lips like you want it, lover boy."

I don't need to be asked twice. I ditch the onion ring and reach for a handful of her wavy locks. I dig my fingers in until I have a good grasp of the roots, which I use to my advantage to tilt her head back, then I move in. I'm not gentle as I crush her wet pink mouth against mine and suck at both of her lips. I taste the beef, the ketchup, and the cheese, but I crave to taste her.

A sudden wildness takes over as I devour her, tonguing open her mouth so my lips can express my lust. She moans deep in her throat and I eagerly seek out her tongue. Once found, I suck on the tip how I want to suck on her clit. She gasps and plays back, taking my tongue into her mouth and bobbing her head in and out, showing me with her actions she wants my cock again.

The suggestion is a glimpse of what I hope is to come. With just this one kiss alone, it has my cock straining behind my zipper with tears of joy staining the fabric. I'm beyond breathless, gasping for air, but I don't care if I get any. I'm hungry for more, for this, for her.

She pushes me away, I move closer in. She mumbles and emits groans of ecstasy. I lick, suck and eat her lips harder until I'm out of breath. And just when I'm about to pass out, dizzy from the passion, only then do I finally move away, reluctantly and just a mere inch.

I give us just enough room to catch our breath. It takes a few minutes because I keep going back in. I can't get enough; her sweet taste is my cocaine bliss and I want to die from an overdose of her. But even the most raging rivers must quiet to a trickle sometime, and I slowly pull away, planting my lips one last time on her forehead before sitting back in my chair.

"Damn," she swears between pants then she adds with disbelief, "You made me orgasm, from a kiss."

I groan as I grab the front of my pants, squeezing myself before, I too, shoot my load.

"You're welcome." My voice sounds pained, so not what I want. I gaze upon her, trying to relay my yearning desires to her with my eyes.

"There's that look again, the one that says I'm going to be sore tomorrow." She gasps, "Jesus, my clit is throbbing. I know you said you wanted to talk, and you might want to hurry it along, before I come up with a not so polite way of asking you to slam me against the wall to make out again."

I think the idea over; her outfit does have a backdoor zipper. I could bend her over the island and take her here. *Tempting.*

Although, I do want to know her, and right now, it seems more important. Bad timing I know, but, hell, with foreplay like this, I'll happily talk all night, knowing the longer we wait the wetter she's going to get.

Leaning into the counter with a smile, I brush the long strands of hair from her face and tuck them behind her ear as she picks up the burger for another bite.

"I want to know all about you. I want you to weave me the colorful tale of the woman sitting before me. How she became the Empress of this desert, as well as the smart-ass warrior that drives me mad with desire? Who is this amazing beauty sitting before me?"

She rolls her eyes while finishing her last bite. Taking the napkin from the counter, she wipes the corners of her mouth. Plucking out a beer from the case, she cracks the top and chugs half the bottle. When she's done, she lets out a satisfying belch that makes me laugh. She's obviously quite comfortable, and I hope it allows her to speak freely.

"You make me sound so badass. I assure you, my story is quite dull. I'm just Paige Sky, a werewolf, businesswoman, and horse lover." She ends with a laugh, and wave of her hand as if to say she is nothing of significance.

I shake my head with a frown at her, for selling herself short. "Don't downplay who you are and what you have built. It is a remarkable accomplishment. One I know did not come without resistance or challenges. You should be proud of yourself. I, for one, find you inspirational."

She snorts, "Well, you're the first to notice. I thank you, but until now, I've never cared what others think."

She stops her confession short and wiggles a bit in her chair, seemingly uncomfortable to have told me she cares what I think. The blush of pink crosses her cheeks when she notices me watching her. This time, she shakes it off by beginning to speak.

"Fine, I'll start with my father, who came out this way long before Nevada was even a state. As a wolf, he found the desert provided a great open range to run and hunt without fear of being seen. It still does to a point, human population has made some areas off limits for us, now. But like my father, I too, love it out here."

She stops to take a sip of her beer to wet her lips before going on. "Back then, the only ones around were the indigenous people. Mainly the Southern Paiute, and to them the wolf-- *ye-oge*-- were sacred animals. It meant my father was able to run free, which appealed to him greatly, and was the deciding factor for why he settled here.

Of course, in his human form, he was able to interact with the local tribe, and they welcomed him in. That's where he met their shaman, the indigenous version of a witch. She was not as powerful as your sister, I might add, but to her people, she was of great importance."

"Your mother was human?" I ask with an eager interest as I begin to understand who she is.

"Yup, and somewhat magical, which makes me a hypocrite. You see, today I gave you grief about the Queen because, in our pack, hybrids are wrong. Bear has beat that in my brain since I was a child. This is why we keep to ourselves. We don't follow the royals because we don't believe they are worthy. Except, once I met her and then her King, the hybrid wolf, my past just started to come back to me, and I remembered my family wasn't as closed-minded once."

She pauses at this thought, then begins to explain, "My father bite my mother, not viciously or selfishly, but because they fell in love, and she wished to be with him forever. Once they informed the tribe of their supernatural secret, they were given protection and support. There was no fear on either side, and we all lived together in peace.

I realized today that I understand the Queen a little more, now. She is just trying to protect us supernatural. My father did the same with the tribe. He fought to keep our land, but once we separated from Mexico, and eventually became a state, tribe numbers began to dwindle. He didn't stop trying, though. He joined in on the silver rush in the late eighteen hundreds, making a small fortune so he could buy as much land as possible around the water rock, or Pahrump, as it is called today. Sadly, there aren't many of my mother's people left. Only a small group I employ here, and a band in the Ash Meadows area of the Amargosa Valley."

I remember Paige's conversation earlier with the saddle shiner. "Clay *is* related to you?"

"Yes, he's my twice great grandfather, but only Papa and Bean, and now you, know that. I was just in my tenth year of life, before my first shift, when my parents died. They left me with the tribe to hunt on the full moon, but they never returned.

Bear, an old friend of my father's, had been visiting at the time. Only he returned the next morning, saying he separated from my parents during the hunt, and didn't know what happened to them. My grandfather, the chief, had been the one to find them, not far from where we were in the hills today. They had both still been in wolf form when they got shot in the head then skinned of their fur. My grandfather assumed some human traveler got spooked by them as wolves and killed them, then they took the furs for the coming winter or to trade."

I notice her telling of the story is quite robotic, there is no emotion in her velvet voice, no shaky words or hitches in her breath. She sounds detached from the event like perhaps she no longer has any memory of it actually happening. Many of the supernatural become dismissive of their past lives, more so in older years because the memories fade. In time, the stories become fables we tell children at bedtime, and eventually, the tales change, the history is forgotten and our past is erased.

Putting down my fork to reach for her hand, I hold it for support. "I'm sad for your loss."

She cocks her head to the side with a confused glance. "Thank you, but I have had time to work through the grief, and I barely remember, it was a long time ago. I do recall Bear staking his claim on me, taking me from my people, saying he would raise me as his own. He never approved of my human roots, but he loved the money I inherited.

He brought me back here to live in my parent's old farmhouse, we passed it on the way in. It's just a foundation now, but pieces of it I used here in the apartment. The cupboards and sliding doors, they came from the old house. I tried to incorporate some of my past into this space when I built it, to honor my parents and where I came from.

I do the same with my name; my mother called me Sky and I use it to honor her and our heritage. My father wasn't as traditional, he named me Paige to be more modern, but he always called me his sweet pea. That name seems to have stuck with me, and later, once Bear established a pack and took a mate, he had a daughter of his own, Jill. He used to call her Jilly-Bean, which eventually just became Bean."

Her eyes light up and she giggles. "I just remembered

we used to call ourselves the vegetable sisters. This was long before Bear started the MC, and the nicknames became our road names."

Road names are nicknames the bikers use instead of real names to avoid being caught by the law. Her vegetable name has to be one of the most creative I've heard, and I join in on the laugh of her childhood whimsy.

"So, is the redhead, Kingsley, the carrot?"

She snorts so hard she actually spits and has to grab for the napkin to wipe her mouth before answering. "No, we never thought of that. I have to tell Bean, she'll get a kick out of it."

We each take a minute to compose ourselves, but I'm itching to know more. I have a million questions, but I patiently hold my tongue and wait for her to go on. Hoping she will give me the answers I seek.

It is an agonizing few minutes, of chewing my steak, while I watch her push her empty container to the other side of the island, then reach for two more bottles of brew. She opens them, placing one in front of me, before taking a drink of her own. I'm damn near bursting when she finally breaks the silence with a giggle.

"What?" I ask with curiosity.

"You look impatient, it's adorable. I'm glad you find my life so fascinating, but as I told you, it's rather dull."

She says this with another one of her eye rolls that I can only shake my head at. "There is nothing dull about you, and as I said, I want to know everything."

"Okay, but I can't promise I'll be as excited when the tables are turned." She offers a wink with her tease, but her words dig deeper than she'll ever know.

"Don't be so sure about that," I mumble and turn back to the last of my meal, which I no longer wish to finish.

Having lost my appetite, I push my container towards the other side of the island and lean in to slowly sip my beer. The silence would be deafening if it weren't for the gentle tickling of piano keys filling the air around us. I get why she listens to the music, it is soothing and probably helps wash away her daily challenges. It isn't strong enough for my life issues, though.

"I'm not opposed to shoving a lantern up your ass so you'll lighten the fuck up."

I turn in my chair to flash a glaring stare at her. I'm met with a mischievous grin, and eyes so bright with concern, they are trying to tell me everything will be okay. I wish I could be like her, in a place where being at peace is the priority and negatives no longer exist. Her tease does what she set out for it to do, though, making me laugh and feel certain that with her, my world isn't as bad I think it is.

With a warm smile of thanks, I answer her tease with one of my own, "Something tells me you want that more than you're willing to let on."

"Mmm, you have no idea," she purrs.

"Then finish your story so you can show me."

"Ooo, I'm always in the mood for some ass fucking, especially with a willing partner." She lets out an evil sounding giggle.

I tap her nose with my finger. "Why does that laugh make me think you mean mine and not yours?"

She shrugs. "Maybe I'm testing the waters. Or maybe, I'm just trying to get you out of your head for a minute. I'm sensing you carry around some heavy shit, and if I can get you to relax for even a second, it might help you come to terms with some of it."

She catches me off guard with this. "Have I been that transparent?"

She crinkles her nose while patting my hand. "A tiny bit, but I'm also a good judge of character. I have had years of practice reading people in my line of work. It's how I know you are different, caring of your people, protecting them, even if it is at your own expense."

She takes my hand in hers, pulling it to her breast as she

gets serious. "I notice you never butt in on an argument until you learn all the facts first, and even then, you wait to be asked for your opinion to be heard. And they all listen because they know you think things through from start to finish with extra options. You showed me that on the hill. The pack charged blindly and got caught up in the crossfire, shooting at each other. Magic or not, they didn't think it through, but you did, and that's not typical for a wolf."

She links our fingers, playing with a few of my rings. "So, tell me, who is Zander Paine? And before you change the subject back to me, I know that you know the ending of my story."

"Tell me anyway, I would rather hear it from your lips," I whisper with a swallow, knowing I'm not ready yet. Hoping she won't notice, I offer a smile and add some manners, "Please."

She chews her lip in the most sensual way as she decides, and just when I think she's seen through my guise and won't finish her tale, she takes a big breath and begins to unleash.

"I struggled too, for a really long time. Then one day I realized I'm stronger and smarter than I thought. Eventually, as I'm sure you heard, I built, what I hope, will one day be my legacy. Bear has been anything but supportive, always trying to sell me off to the highest bidder so he can get his greedy paws on everything you've seen today. When rightfully, it should all be mine. My land, my money, my everything. Yet, he has me funding the pack, the MC, and even doing some of their dirty work. This is why I make a point of standing as his second, that and I know it pisses him off. He said earlier I need him, when really, he's the one who needs me and he knows it, but the pack rules are in his favor."

She's smirking with a bit of attitude as she says the next part. "I look forward to the day females are accepted as Alphas. Just as the Queen has been accepted as our ruler, and her hybrid mate has been accepted as her King. I needed to be reminded of how proud I am of my heritage, my human Native mother and werewolf father. It's these differences that have not been easy for our kind and me. The Queen showed me though, that our diversity is what will make our future better. And thanks to you, for bringing me along today, I see that now, and I believe in her vision, too. Especially if it means I get to follow in my dad's footsteps and become an Alpha one day."

She stops to catch her breath and allow me to let this sink in. She's right, she is much stronger than anyone has ever given her credit for. I bet one day, she'll be a damn good Alpha.

I would follow her in a heartbeat.

"So, now you're the stranger with all my secrets. I believe it's your turn to spill." She leans back to allow me to take the proverbial stage as she sips away at her beer.

"Fair enough," I manage to say with some hesitation as my mind goes blank.

Where do I even start?

The temperature in the room seems to go up, I begin to sweat while trying to find words. I open my mouth then snap it closed and repeat until I resemble a fish out of water gasping to fill my gills with a liquid breath.

I stand, then think sitting might be better. I squeeze her hand and take her other one to do the same, so she can't use them on me or run away when she hears who I am. The thought makes me laugh for no reason and it sounds manic, which doesn't surprise me since I'm feeling somewhat deranged.

"Hey, relax." Her smoothing rasp tickles my ears and wiggles its way down my spine. "Our biggest battles sometimes can be the ones we fight inside the prisons of our own mind."

And in those few words of understanding, she silences my storm. Somehow, she's captured my chaos from raging and takes it away for safe keeping. I no longer feel mentally out of control. Instead, I'm lost in her blazing gaze. The kind of lost that's exactly like being found. After all these years of roaming, I feel as though I have finally found someone who gets me.

She feels like home.

"Okay, you're officially killing me, just tell me already." Her voice breaks through the last of my worry and I chuckle at her impatience as she goes on, "No matter how bad you think it is, I'll help you work it out. I've heard relationships are built on communication. To me, I think that means, if you can stick your face between my legs, you sure as shit better be able to talk to me about anything."

A laugh bursts out of me for her interesting comment. Then I break it down and realize what she's hinting at, a relationship.

Is she as serious about me as I am about her?

My laugh eases into a grin, fades into a frown at this revelation, and my heart starts to pound for a whole other reason.

Am I really thinking about commitment?

"For crying out loud, don't make me tie you up and whip it out of you," she warns with a look so stern, it makes me want to kneel.

Oh fuck, I might be falling in love with her.

"I would so let you," I whisper back.

She grins at me and it's so unbelievably sexy, I forget what we were even talking about. I gather her into my arms and pull her against me. She climbs across my lap into my embrace as I lean in for a kiss. Moving in slow to capture just her bottom lip between both of mine, sucking it into my mouth to run my tongue against the thickest part. I feel her body shiver as a shuddered moan expels from her breath and I know, without any doubt, she wants me as much as I want her. And as the kiss deepens with passion, I ache with need to have her.

"Stop." She brings her hands to my chest to nudge me back. "I've changed my mind."

Five boner killing words no man ever wants to hear.

What the fuck!

I inch away with a scowl creasing up my face. She clucks her tongue while grabbing the back of my head, staring me down as she boldly explains, "I'm going with my gut on this, and you better not make me regret it. But if I'm right, we'll have all the time in the world for you to tell me who you are. Meaning, I've decided, I don't care because a man with a tongue as useful as yours can't be all that bad. And I would rather you use it to slow dance with my clit than talk my ear off."

"So, in other words, you're telling me to put my mouth to work and suck your lady dick."

Her mouth opens as a gasp escapes, "If you do, I'll be a slut, just for you."

CHAPTER 9

Flames of desire flicker bright in Paige's eyes, a sign I can't ignore. I know Paige is a controlling female, dominant in everything she does, and I assume, that extends to sex. For her to tell me she'll be slutty, my slut, is a big deal, and I don't take it lightly.

"Understand, I will never try to tame you, *leannàn*. I only want this to be about you and me, and all the pleasure we can give to each other. No matter how wild you need to be, know I am here, willing to go along for the ride in whatever capacity you see me in."

She answers by grabbing the back of my head to crush her wet mouth to mine, taking control of my lips for a kiss that blows my mind.

Goddamn, she's fun to kiss.

I'm so wrapped up in her tongue fucking my mouth that I barely notice her working the belt and buttons on my pants. Not until the heat of her palm cups the tip of my dick, and she begins to swirl her hand around the head. My cock jumps in recognition, bounding forward to greet her like an old friend.

I try to catch my breath, but I'm overcome by a nose full of her scent and it makes me dizzy, drunk with lust. All my senses spark at this exact moment, screaming out with an urgent craving like nothing I have ever experienced before. I want to taste her, touch her flesh, feel her heat from the inside as I take her, claim her, mark her as mine.

All mine!

Some auto response takes over as I wrap one arm under her legs and the other around her waist, hoisting her up while I stand. I remember the rolling doors and go in search of the bedroom; never leaving her lips as I walk. It poses a challenge as I enter the closest door first, not being able to see the door frame as I bump into it. Then as the hardwood gives way to marble under my feet, my footing slips. I regain my balance, causing my pants to fall on my hips but not all the way down. I have to depart her hungry lips to get my bearings as we enter what turns out to be the bathroom.

I scan the small area and notice the shower is the go-between, a walk-through from the washroom area to a large walk-in closet, where the second rolling door exits. Unless I'm missing something, there doesn't appear to be a bed anywhere in the apartment. For a split second, I wonder if perhaps Paige is so busy, the poor girl doesn't sleep. It is but a brief and yet, amusing thought that crosses my mind, as I envision some sort of blanket fort in the living room in which we finally consummate our union.

The thought is gone before I can even acknowledge it with a laugh as Paige wiggles from my arms. I must let her go, with reluctance, or I will drop her.

"Shower," her purr is so low, it's difficult to determine if she's asking if I want to shower or demanding me to have one.

She hops down on the tile floor, her heels tapping with purpose as she struts across the shower stall. As she passes through, she turns the spray nozzle on, separating us by the jet of water. Her luscious figure blurs behind the rising steam. Thankfully, not enough to block the amazing view.

I'm hypnotized by her hourglass hips swishing with attitude as she makes her way to a stool in front of a vanity. She stops with her back to me to place her foot on a small stool. Making a slight bend at the waist, she glides her fingers down the inside of her thigh to the zipper at the side of her knee-length boot. With a steady hand, she starts the unveiling. Inching it down to unwrap the leather from her leg, she pulls it free from her foot and discards the shoe to the floor. Her hips deliciously shift as she reverses the position to the other foot and repeats the process.

It appears dreamy, watching the show through the veil

of thick steam. When this boot lands with a thud on the floor, she straightens to glance back at me from over her shoulder. When our eyes meet in the fog, I'm blown away. It's as though a completely different woman is standing before me.

The orange hue of her eyes blazes behind hooded lashes and a sharply raised brow. Her mouth is set into the ferocious smirk of a woman who means business. This is the confident attitude of a woman that knows exactly what she wants, and how she's about to get it. Paige, the dominatrix, has entered the building, and she's telling me with her come-fuck-me eyes, just how she's about to make my darkest fantasies come true.

Be still my throbbing cock!

"Why are you not naked and in that shower? Do not make me wait or you will be punished." Her deep rasp purrs out and sends such a jolt of heat into me. When I try to swallow, it's as though my mouth is full of sand.

She's ten feet away, not even touching me, and that damn voice of hers is an aphrodisiac, arousing me to the point of combustion. I have no intention of ignoring her demands. Yet, I also secretly want to push the envelope to see how far she'll go.

If the tables were turned, I would tease her with sexual torture. Working her up until she dripped with lust, painfully at the edge of release, which I would deny her. She would be begging, pleading with me to let her come, and when I finally allowed her my cock, I wouldn't stop fucking her until she couldn't walk.

The visual is so vibrant in my head it sends my cock into spasm. It jerks forward in painful throbs, pressing hard against the last button on my jeans trying to burst free from the bind. It has a mind of its own and right now, it desperately wants her.

I shrug out of my jacket, pulling my arms out of the sleeves with such force it turns them inside out. It hits the floor with a thunk from the weight of the leather. I unclip my shoulder harness, swinging it up and over my head. Dropping this down with the attached gun on top of the jacket with a little more care. The ammo holster is next, followed by the belt and knife sheath. As I remove them, I also toe off my riding boots and kick them back to my growing pile.

When I kneel to remove the smaller nine-millimeter from around my ankle, Paige whistles. "Jesus, you're a walking armory."

As I place this gun on the pile with the rest, I see her point, but when you ride alone for so long, the only one watching your back is you. "Preparedness is key for a nomad."

"I see that," she states, then adds with force, "But if you don't hurry up, I'll count this as making me wait."

I stand to face her, pulling the shirt over my head before releasing the last button on my pants and letting them fall. My cock springs forward and points straight at her, seeking her out.

She moans with approval. "That right there... well worth the wait."

I feel the heat of her stare as she eyes me from head to toe then gasps, "Dear God, what happened to you?"

I look down at where I know her eyes have landed. The jagged scar branding my chest, between my fourth and fifth rib, with a multitude of shorter grooves across my belly and hip.

"Shark attack," I offer a joke.

She plants her hands on her hips with a stern glare. "I'm being serious."

"And I don't want to be. Not right now, anyway."

I end the conversation by stepping into the shower, allowing the water to cascade down my body. I wash the day's grime from my skin and a lifetime of memories from my head. Now is not the time.

Once I have soaked my soul, I open my eyes to find her

watching me. I can tell she's curious, intrigued even. The questions are heavy on her lips as she nibbles away at the bottom one, debating whether to ask me or let it go.

I give her time to work it out in her head by reaching for a bottle marked as shower gel and squirt a thick glob into my hand. It doesn't have a scent but it does lather well, too well. Before long I'm coated with an overwhelming amount of bubbling foam. I hear her giggle as I attempt several ways to flick some of it off me.

"You only need a small dab of that," she states the obvious while she works the zipper of her suit, pulling it down the length of her body.

Her questions have been put on a shelf, for now, and she seems back in the game as she starts to undress. My soap issue is forgotten as I watch her in a frozen state. She unclasps the collar piece from her long neck and it breaks in two, dropping on either side. Then she does this shimmy of her shoulders, making her breasts dance for my entertainment, as she tries to get the material far enough down for her to pull out one arm.

Once her arm is free, I'm again greeted by the colorful images painted on her. They are a storybook written in a language of pictures that only she understands. Some seem obvious, the heart line, drawn as fast beats above her left breast, ending with the image of a wolf running. Others seem to just be filling in space, but I'm sure each one holds great meaning to her.

It appears we both still have much to share. I look forward to learning what these images represent, and hearing the stories behind them. My full attention, for now, is on the unveiling of her amazing breasts.

Two pillowy soft cushions, free of ink, jiggle out of the latex cat suit as she peels it down her torso, stopping just shy of her hips. The heavy ink everywhere but her breasts, is an optical illusion, making her tits appear gigantic. Add the sparkling gemstone on her left nipple and she has the perfect rack.

The dirty vixen knows it too, as she stops undressing to grab her own tits and put on a show. There's far more than a handful as she squeezes the heavy mounds. Lifting them both up to press together while she bends forward to give me the cleavage shot. I palm my cock to give it a good hard stroke with one hand and cup my painfully full balls in the other to give them a squeeze.

"If you clean that any harder you're going to set it off," she coos while pinching her nipples until they pearl.

I stroke my bone down to the root, gripping my shaft to make it bulge out, showing her my enthusiasm. "I can't help it; your tits are exceptional."

She lifts one breast with both hands, stretching the flesh as she bows her head so her mouth can meet the pierced nipple. She sucks in the metal between her thick lips. Flashing me a grin to show the ring clenched between her teeth, she rolls the pebbled bud with her lips. Soft moans follow her actions and her eyelashes flutter. I stroke myself harder from the sound alone, until pre-cum is dripping from my vessel.

She opens her mouth to cluck her tongue at me. "Don't you dare cum without me."

"Then get over here and jack me with those tits. If you do it just right, I'll reward your effort by coming in your mouth," I demand with a deep tone.

Her jaw clenches ever so slightly, with a growl sounding low in her throat, and a flash of annoyance crossing her face. She tries to blink it away while avoiding eye contact, ending with a laugh. "I'm not used to being told what to do, as I usually fuck submissive humans. I have a strong urge to punch you right now, just don't take it personally."

From what Paige has told me, I understand more than she knows. In order to keep everything she has built, she has to remain in control of every aspect of her life. She's distanced herself from relationships with her own kind, so she doesn't get hurt or so Bear doesn't use it against her. By doing so, she has never given herself permission to be free to explore her own sexuality.

"As you know, I take a punch like a champ. One from you, will be quite the turn on." I offer her a wink. "We will go at whatever pace you are comfortable with, and if you do let go, trust that I will never hurt you."

She shakes her head. "I know you wouldn't, I have trusted you from the moment we met. So much so, I want to give you a part of me I have never shown to anyone. Just know, allowing you to control this is new for me and I can't promise to be good at it. I'm warning you, I'll probably be quite defiant."

She ends with a wide grin that sparks fire into her eyes, telling me she's already thinking up ways to defy me. A challenge I am more than turned on by.

This is going to be one hell of a night.

"Challenge accepted." My cock springs forth with need as the switch flips in my head and my drake nature takes over. "Now, wipe that fucking smile off your face, *leannàn*. We both know the proper response is for you to drop to your knees."

Paige's body shudders at my command, making her skin pucker with thousands of tiny bumps as a gasp of excitement recoils from her lips. This time, there's no resistance as her eyes move to my cock and she licks her hungry lips while dropping down to her knees. She doesn't stop there, though. Bending forward, she places her hands on the floor before her and gets into her wolf position.

I watch her covered hips sway in a hypnotizing way as she begins a seductive crawl towards me. Her eyes locked onto her intended target, my cock, as she goes. Her shapely mounds squished together between her arms, heaving and jiggling on each forward movement, make my mouth water. The alluring way in which she moves is that of a woman on a mission.

Determination sits heavy on her brow when she comes to the edge of the shower stall, stopping just shy of the streaming spray and right before me. Sinking back to sit upon her heels, she assumes a waiting position. Her knees spread apart with her hands resting, palm side up, on her thighs. I'm not surprised she knows the position. I'm just shocked she's so willing to put herself eagerly into it. Once her eyes meet mine though, I can see it isn't without some fight.

"Good girl," I praise, trying to avoid a snicker as I take in her rebellious stare. "Now, tell me you are my slut. Mine to control as I see fit."

Her lips twitch into a smirk. She's quick to catch herself though, pulling just the corner of the bottom lip between her teeth and biting down. Her chest expands as she takes a breath, then as she blows it out, in a slow even exhale, she speaks with a calm voice.

"I'll do you one better. How about I empty your balls into my mouth." She licks her lips and adds a curt, "Sir," before opening her mouth wide to present me with her tongue.

I groan, "Close enough." Too anxious to really give a shit whether she obeys or not.

I lean back into the spray to rinse the remainder of the soap from my body. With eager speed, I turn off the water to step in front of her, with cock in hand. As I stroke it, a mew bubbles out her throat. Her rebellious stare instantly switches to deep lust as she watches me jack my shaft.

"Does it turn you on when I masturbate for you?" I ask and she nods her head. "Say it out loud."

She growls a little but eventually replies with, "Yes, Sir."

The words are punctuated hard and I like the struggle she's having with this, so I play on. "Do you want to please me?"

This time she's quick to answer as she watches my hand

move down my shaft. "Very much, Sir."

"I am going to use your mouth as my personal fuck-toy and you will let me."

Her eyes dart up for a second, I see some anger but mostly desire, and when she answers, her rasping purr is velvety smooth. "Please do."

A shiver rolls down my spine and starts a burn deep inside of me. I take the top of her head with my hand, gripping a handful of her hair at the crown to hold her in place.

"Then start sucking it like the whore you want to be."

She smiles up at me and it weakens my knees. Then she sighs with content and opens her mouth, to invite me in. I step an inch from her face and slap the length of my cock across her cheek. She squeals out a giggle so I do it again. This time, turning my hips to slap the flat of her tongue. Her head swings with my movement so she can suck the tip of my cock into her hot hole. Slurping at the head with her lips, and sucking hard to keep it in her mouth.

I loosen the hold on her hair and she takes over. Penetrating herself with my dick she eats me whole, right down her throat. Heat surrounds my cock as her throat tightens from a gag. She works through it and somehow keeps going. Not stopping until her nose is pressed firmly against my belly, and her tongue is tickling my balls.

Never in all my years, has anyone been able to achieve such an enormous feat. Then again, Paige is no ordinary woman. She is extraordinary in everything she does, right down to her cock-sucking skills. I would applaud her effort if I wasn't so engrossed in how fucking good it feels.

I cup the crown of her head, helping to guide her while she inches back from me. When she reaches just the head, she bobs a little while swirling her tongue around the area, flicking the underside before going back down. After a few back and forth passes, she brings herself to her knees, keeping them slightly spread for balance, as she lifts her breasts with her hands. Again, she puts on a show. Playing with her plush pillows to bring them forward to present her ample cleavage. My own tongue tickles for a taste of her nipples.

The show is more than I can handle. A moan escapes me with the visual of her pulling her head back, and the strings of our mutual admiration connect us like silken webs of sexual lust. It turns the slight burn inside of me into a raging inferno as my internal temperature spikes. She leans in at the same moment to combine her heat with mine, wrapping her beautiful tits around my cock to jack me between her cleavage.

It's a soft but firm double breasted hug. Which is only made better once her head bows forward, and she French kisses the head of my cock. The mixing sensations of wet and dry heat are the spark that sets me on fire. Deep in my mind, I hear the echo of a whoosh as my own pilot light is lit. I radiate from within, with an internal heat I thought was gone forever. It isn't lost on me that it has everything to do with Paige.

The way she's devouring my dick for the sole purpose of pleasing me shows me how much she cares. It both scares the crap out of me and calms my soul completely, and maybe, this is what it's supposed to be; a contradiction that balances out to love.

As the word sinks in my mind, Paige sinks her head right down my cock. With my hand pressing down on her head, I eagerly pump myself in her throat. The need to mark her is overwhelming and I can't hold off any longer. The eruption explodes from me, and I do my best to warn her before it happens.

"Swallow it, *leannàn*, it's all for you."

She doesn't miss a beat, taking each throb and spasm of my release in stride. She swallows every last drop and continues to suck me until dry. My blood is boiling, my heart racing. I'm weak in the knees, but she makes me want more.

So much more.

I retract my hips and drop to my knees in front of her. "I need to taste you."

Cupping her face with my hands, I plunge my tongue into her mouth. Our kiss is passionate and deep as I allow my lips to speak freely with everything I cannot say. She moans and I swallow her puffs of air, biting at her lip as I untangle my hand from her tresses to pull her into me.

She squeals as I stand us both up and pin her to the shower wall. Pressing my body hard against her, I go into her neck for a nibble. It reminds me of our first meeting when she told me not to bite her.

I test the waters again, raking my teeth across her jugular. This time, she doesn't tense. Instead, she arches her back and bends her head back, opening herself to me for the bite.

God, I'm so tempted to make her mine.

My whole mouth cups the sensitive spot between her neck and shoulder. My tongue swirls over her flesh as I debate branding her with my bite mark. Her flesh is warm against my teeth and tongue, making me salivate as I imagine the taste of her blood. I even press my incisors into her skin but don't break the flesh.

Somehow, in my lusting madness, I manage to stop myself. It isn't easy. When I do finally back away, Paige whimpers as though she too, wishes for marking. Looking at her face, I see that exact thought burning so bright in her eyes, my heart skips several beats. I don't give it time to sink in. I can't, not right now. I push myself to carry on and hope this isn't a missed opportunity.

I go for somewhat of a warning instead. "Your pants look uncomfortable, we need to get them off of you."

I strike with movements so fast, I don't give my brain time to be logical. I grip the rubbery material of her suit in my hands and pull it over her hips. It's shocking it comes off with ease, helped by her dancing in place to get it down her body to her ankles. Dropping to my knees in front of her, I lift each foot to free her from the outfit until she is finally unclothed. I feel this is more than me undressing her. I'm exposing her soul and maybe, exposing my own, too.

I sit back, throwing the latex over my shoulder to gaze upon her for the first time. My eyes dart wildly over every inch, flashing colorful images to my brain as it tries to decipher where one ends and another starts. A dreamcatcher drawn under and between her breasts with feathers that appear to float down her toned stomach. It mixes with others that join the word 'immortal' in fancy lettering crossing her right hip and under it, a six-shooter sits, forever ready to be drawn. Each secretly expressing who she is, but those parts I already know.

One painting, though, stops my scan and knocks me on the floor with the air in my lungs exploding out of me. It's a vibrant red image swirling up her left leg, twisting over her hip, and up her ribcage to disappear behind her back. It flows over her curves so well that when she moves, it appears to be animated in flight. I don't need to see the whole tattoo to know what it is. For the artist had talent, and added so much detail I swear I'm looking at a mirror image of myself, long ago in another time, when I could shift into my true form.

Before I can go down the road less traveled, Paige clears her throat with impatience. "If you take any longer, my virginity is going to grow back."

I snort at her comment but smile with thanks for getting me out of my thoughts. When I look up to give her the grin, she's staring down at me with such feral lust it damn near makes me ejaculate on the spot.

"If you think the unwrapped package looks good, then you should kiss me because I'm also quite delicious."

She sweeps her hand down her body, presenting herself as a prize. With the reveal of this tattoo, I wonder if perhaps she is indeed a gift from the sisters above.

The suggestion causes my mouth to salivate as my sight

drops down to where her hand has stopped. She's pointing me right to her pussy, lips glistening with a sheen of her dew. I sit up on my heels, front and center, to the intended target as she opens her legs. Any thoughts of whether we are fated or not are lost as I focus on what's right in front of me.

Earlier, I had a thirst my beer couldn't quench because it wasn't what I craved. Here, between her thighs, is the drink I've been yearning for my whole life. I dive into her spring knowing this will not extinguish that hunger, it will only make it stronger. I don't care, I welcome this consuming passion.

My mouth clamps over her, and I slip my tongue between the folds, tasting her flavor with greed. As I lick up her slit, the tip of my tongue comes in contact with something metal. It surprises me, and I jerk back to spread her lips with my fingers. Hidden between her folds, peeking out to greet me, is another ring looping through the hood of her clit.

The discovery, though a delightful one, has me questioning my memory. "Was this here before?"

"Mmm, no, I take it out when I ride my horse, which I had been doing before we met." A dirty smile spreads across her lips. "But from that moment on, I felt drawn to you. You entered my mind and became part of it until all I could think about was you. When I came back here to change, my urges got the best of me as I was putting the ring back in, and I masturbated to the image of you in my head. It wasn't nearly enough, so I inserted a butt plug too, with hopes we would be in this position later."

News of more hidden treasure sends my cock into spasm. "So, my sticky finger princess, you thought you could indulge without me, did you?"

I spread her pussy lips wide open until the little ring is dangling mid-air. Then I do what any dominant male would when giving out punishment. I lift my hand, flicking my wrist quick to give her clit a hard slap. When she squeals out a scream from the sharp sting, I rub my thumb over the nub to sooth the pain and a drop of dew trickles out her opening.

"I'm just a girl with naughty thoughts and sticky fingers, who obviously needs to be taught a lesson." She pouts while fondling her breast, teasing me to punish her further.

"Show me how you pinched those nipples when you masturbated to me," I command with a harder slap to her clit.

"Oh." Her mouth drops open with a long breath. "Ah," she hiccups as she twists the nipple ring to pinch the bud.

I give her one more stinging slap that has her hissing before I push my face between her thighs to plunge my tongue deep into her well. I hear her moan and her fingers are suddenly tangled in my hair, holding me in place as she rocks her pussy into my face.

I don't let her take her own pleasure, there's no fun in that. I want to be the one to give her what she needs. I pull away to slap her again, and this time, I use my other hand to seek out the hidden butt plug. I feel the heat coming off of her as I find the round end of the toy. It's saturated with her excitement and too slick to grip, so I push it up, deeper inside of her.

Adorable incoherent mews form on her lips. It prompts me on, wanting to hear her scream my name. I move in to devour her cunt, licking, slurping and sucking every inch until I feel her pearled clit throbbing against my tongue, beckoning for more.

"Are you a greedy whore?" I mumble against her with excitement.

"Oh, God, yes," she moans.

Moving my hand from her pussy lips to dip my fingers between her legs, coating my digits with her lust. Before I put them in, already knowing her answer, I ask, "Tell me what you want, *leannàn?*"

Her body sinks lower on the wall as she spreads her legs and rolls her hips forward. "I want your big cock thrusting deep in my cunt."

As she explains her request, I insert two fingers inside her, curling them in and up until her muscles clench tightly from the invasion. Her moans of pleasure echo back and forth between the tiled walls.

She's slick, dripping with lust, enough that I can slide in a third finger with ease. A quick flick of my tongue, back and forth, against her clit, and she becomes so aroused I can stretch my fingers apart and plunge them deep inside of her. As I work out a rhythm, she matches the beat from the inside as her cunt milks me back.

Her moans are endless, some are muffled and caught in her throat, while others are so loud they pierce my ears. When I hit just the right spot with the right combination of hard thrusts in her cunt with my fingers, and back and forth action of the plug in her ass, she shrieks then shudders. It isn't until I clamp her clit between my teeth and give it a good hard suck that I feel her completely tighten up. Her breath hitches and both of her hands grip hard on the side of my head.

"Yes, Zander, just like that, don't stop," she screams out just as her cunt lets go.

"Give me your cum, *leannàn*." My words vibrate against her pussy. "Show me how much you want me."

A flood of ejaculate squirts into my mouth, a water fountain of lust. It tastes of sunshine kisses. Sweet, much sweeter than even the honey from a bumblebee. I lap it up like a man who hasn't had a drink in decades.

I'm shocked, but it is outweighed by how aroused I am, to discover Paige is a squirter. It doesn't surprise me that the tiny bit of pain I provided on her clit was the part that brought her over. Considering she paints her flesh with art from a thousand needles. I'll wager a bet, Paige gets off on pain. A secret I am both fascinated and completely turned on by.

I continue to manipulate her with my mouth until her entire body trembles. When the last of her release is but a trickle down my chin, her legs give out and she falls forward over my shoulder.

"Uh-ugh," she pants as I catch her legs in my arms to prevent her from hitting the floor. "That has never happened to me before."

I hug her hips and kiss the side of her thigh, running a hand up and down my favorite image on her leg, hoping to soothe her. "That's the sincerest form of flattery I have ever been gifted. Thank you, *mo áilleacht*."

She snorts, "No, your boner is flattering. What just happened was just horribly embarrassing."

Her hands grip my hips and she wiggles her body up my shoulders. She tries to stand, walking her hands up my back for balance. I steady her on my shoulder as I straighten up, swinging us towards the door. I am not even close to done with this discovery, and in need of a flatter surface, in which to spread her out and fuck her senseless.

She gasps, just as the heat of her palms make contact with the flesh of my shoulder blades. Coupled with her words, it stops me mid-stride. "Oh, my, God, you're one of them."

Her light touch to this spot is an electric shock to my soul. It's so overwhelming that I stumble to maintain my own balance.

She slides down the front of my chest until we are face to face, and I can see her wide-eyed stare. "This is what you didn't want to tell me, that you are just like them?"

I blink as I try to understand how she could see the scars. I have been with many women, from all the different races, and none of them have ever been able to see these mangled forms of scar tissue that once housed the wings of my inner beast. For her to not only see them but for her touch to register deep inside of me, is perplexing.

"I'm nothing like them. I was never and will never be like them. I am just a nomad and that's all I can ever be," I snap with more than a hint of venom on my lips.

Her brow creases up into a frown, and she clucks her tongue at me. "Don't give me the bullshit you've been hiding behind. I'm not that gullible. I saw what you did to that warlock. I can see your aura isn't like any other, including the royals. I know you are different, and I told you I didn't care. You could be the Loch Ness Monster for all I know, and it will make no difference to me. At some point though, if you want this to continue to work, you need to be honest with me, and more importantly, with yourself."

I step back to glare at her, surprised by her candor and her ability to truly see me. "What if I am a monster, Paige? Will it scare you away? Will you want to have me destroyed just as my Father did?"

The frown deepens on her face and she reaches up to place her hand upon the scar on my chest. Again, a spark ignites and shoots right through me. The churning fire seems to be getting hotter with every minute I'm with her.

"Is that what happened? He must be a wretched man, full of hate and jealousy because nothing about you scares me. A monster stops being a monster when you love it."

The glare on my face falls as my mouth drops open. I'm beyond knowing what to say so I just stand there, blinking away the tears starting to prick the corners of my eyes.

She seems to not notice as she continues to speak, "Your Father better pray he never crosses paths with me. I'll make it known what I think of him, right before I stake the bastard in the heart for what he's done to you."

I laugh, "That's sweet of you, but he's already dead."

"Good, less work for me," she states with finality, then her face softens and she offers me a kiss on the cheek. "You don't have to tell me anything right now, Lockie." She grins with a wink. "But I'll be here when you're ready."

I laugh at her latest nickname, a reference to the Loch Ness Monster, but it doesn't last. I'm keenly aware of what she's saying and it makes my heart grow. I bend forward to pull her into my arms and stare into her eyes. "Thank you, that means more than you'll ever know."

Moving my head forward to capture her lips, sweet and tender at first. Slowly working up to something needier as I realize she is making me whole again. I let this kiss speak for me, softly conveying for her to be patient with me as I build my nerve to finally pour my heart out.

Her arms tangle with mine while her hands seek out the scars on my back. When her fingertips glide down the deformed tissue, the sparks she sets off from her touch cause a reaction. It's like being woken from a deep slumber by someone dumping a bucket of ice on you. I have the same jolt of adrenaline coursing through me, but mine is boiling my blood and changing me.

"I need to be inside of you," I mumble into her mouth, pressing myself against her body in an attempt to get closer.

She pushes back, hard enough to push me away as she pants, "I need to say something, first. Whatever you are, whether it is like them or not, don't expect me to share you."

This stops me dead in my tracks. "Are you staking a claim, *leannàn?*"

Her face crinkles up in an adorable frown. "No," she snaps, then adds in a whisper, "Maybe."

It's my turn to cluck my tongue at her. "I dare say someone is being possessive."

I chuckle as her frown deepens and I try to soothe her with fact. "If you are referring to the Queen and my sister having more than one mate, remember they are the only females in their relationships. Perhaps, I should be the one worried."

Her brows pop up in question and she tilts her head to the side, waiting for me to explain. I run my hands over her shoulders and down her back, tracing the outline of her one tattoo with my fingers, feeling some kinship to the painted beast. My feather touch makes her shiver out tiny goosebumps across her flesh that excite me.

I drop my hand between her legs and palm her cunt.

"You see, where I'm from, females often take multiple mates for many reasons. The Queen uses the bonds with her men to strengthen her powers. Whereas, my sister had so much love for her men that she couldn't choose. However, some take extra mates for purely selfish reasons. The more cocks in the relationship, the more satisfied the female, and ultimately, that's all that matters."

The heel of my hand presses her clit and I push my fingers into her wetness as I explain. Paige's legs automatically spread in response, and I begin to build her up again while I go on. "We have barely touched the surface of what I know you will need to be satisfied. While I look forward to indulging in this beautiful cunt of yours, a part of me wonders if I can keep you satisfied. What if I'm not enough for your hungry pussy? What then, *leannàn*? Will you wish for another bigger cock?"

As my fingers plunge inside of her she moans out the answer I seek, "No, I don't want anyone else."

"Are you sure, *mo áilleacht*? You see, I too, do not wish to share you."

I fuck her cunt harder with my fingers, feeling her body respond to each plunge as she screams out her answer, "Yes, oh, God, yes."

"Then say it, Paige. Tell me that this is mine. That from this moment on, you will be mine in every way, and only I will be the one to satisfy you."

Her hips push forward into my hand as she rakes her nails against my back, down the sensitive scars until my own body is erect with need. She seeks out my lips and crushes her mouth into mine, giving me her tongue as she gives me her body.

"I am yours, truly," she pants. "All of me, wherever, whenever."

My smile spreads across her mouth as it joins our kiss, knowing she just submitted. Her words are spoken with greed, as I knew they would be. While I will allow her the release she so desperately seeks, I shall do it on my terms, after I've worked her up past the point of painful need.

A woman like Paige is not easily sated with a simple orgasm, and I welcome the challenges that lay ahead. I also know she will not always be submissive to me, and when the time comes, I have no issue with giving her full control. She is mine, as I am hers, in every way, always.

CHAPTER 10

The light coming in the bathroom door has changed to a blue-gray shade, signaling the dawning of another day. There is still much to do to wrap up our official business here in Nevada, and for me to come clean with the court. The possibilities are endless when I think of the outcome. I may get punished by the Queen or be exiled once again. The mere thought has my heart racing, but I push it down before it festers. I will not go down this path, not when I wish to finish the one I'm on first.

This may be my last day on this realm as a free man, and I wish to make it count. I want to spend the next few hours blissful in Paige's arms, and between her legs. I pull myself from her grasp and take my hand away from her, leaving her cunt dripping with lust and just short of the orgasm she's on the verge of releasing.

She's crude as she screams in frustration, "What the fucking fuck?"

"Easy, *leannàn*," I chuckle and take her hands in mine, kissing her fingers while I lead her towards the closet door. "Let's get you comfortable so I can give you what you really desire."

She digs in her heels and stops me with an attitude laced reply, "No, what I need is for you to finish me off."

"Patience, *leannàn*, I'll take care of you." I tug at her arm again, but she still won't move.

Her head jerks up to meet my eyes and I see they are burning with need. While hidden in the shadows there's also some mischief dancing about.

Her lips twitch into that dominant smirk I'm becoming quite fond of. "Oh, I know you will, but it doesn't negate the fact you are leaving me hanging. I've never been a fan of being teased to the edge and left wanting. Normally, I punish my male subs for not being able to finish me off."

"Mmm, are you saying you'd like to give me a lesson?" I enjoy this sudden flip in roles, my cock jumps forward anticipating the shift I knew would come eventually.

She wiggles her hands from my grasp to grip my shaft. Moving her body to press into mine, she begins to stroke me off against her belly, while her other hand seeks out the scar on my chest. Her touch has me holding my breath while my heart picks up speed.

"I don't know if this is wrong or not, but these scars turn me on. They tell me you have endured great pain, and I think you know by now, I like pain." Her purr sends a shiver up my spine as she continues, "I like giving pain to others for the sole purpose of it becoming pleasure. Almost as much as I like receiving it. You're done with being in control, for now anyway. Your cock is just as much mine as my cunt is yours, and when you failed to own my pussy, you gave me the right to stake that claim first."

Her hand moves from my chest with a light touch, circling my shoulder to my back. She scrapes her talons down the length of my spine, hitting my left shoulder blade as she goes. I hiss and bow backward as the sensation of a million tiny pinpricks sting along the gnarled scar. She then strokes me hard and fast, making me weep as she turns the torture into wonderful pleasure.

"My way isn't going to be as gentle, but I guarantee it will be rewarding." She offers a wink of promise with fast jerks to my cock.

My initial hiss turns into moans of ecstasy over the fisting. It fades into curiosity for what she has in store next, when she starts to turn us around, backing up through the door. I'm digging the dog on the leash thing, her hand wrapped tight around my cock and balls as she guides me into the main room.

She stops beside the fireplace, a few feet from the side wall. The area is open, free from furniture and decoration, with only a couple of end-tables up against the wall about ten feet apart.

As her eyes settle on mine, the dominant part of her peeks out with an eager zeal. Her face is set in determination as she watches me with caution when she speaks, "I assume you know I'm more perverse than most, since I am the proprietor of a whorehouse I use to my advantage. What I don't know, is if you also have a depraved side too. Before I continue and make a real ass out of myself, I need to know what your sexual preferences are."

I'm touched she's asking me if I'm okay with rough sex, it shows what a compassionate and caring person she is. A good dominatrix. But, I knew from the moment I pinned her hard against the barn, and she got wet, she enjoyed her sex with a side of whips and chains.

"I'm open for whatever kink you have in mind, *leannàn*. As long as you know, whatever you dish out, you also better be willing to take. Whether it is red marks on your ass, bite marks on my thighs or the smell of our lust all over us, it will be our reminder of us belonging to each other. However you want that to go, I told you already, I'm in."

I'm not sure how she manages it, but the smile on her lips reaches equal parts sweet and innocent, mixed with shameless seductress. It leaves me not knowing whether to wrap her in my arms or drill her with my dick-- Which she has let go of to step in front of the wall. I straighten to pay attention, sensing her next move might be important.

"Okay, just remember you said that." She doesn't take her eyes from mine, while reaching halfway up the wall for a piece of leather sticking out. "And try not to judge me, too much."

The leather is a strap and as she wrenches on it, she walks back towards me, pulling a piece of the wall down on her. There is a mechanical sound, metal wheels rolling on metal tracks. Then a click, right before four thick square posts pop out of each corner of the wall face-- Which appears to be the bottom to this hidden secret. When the hole is opened all the way, a steel cage unfolds around a king-sized bed.

At first glance, it reminds me of a medieval torture contraption. The caged box seems to be holding the whole thing together, acting as bedposts between the black steel canopy top and the deep wooden base supporting the mattress. Once the bedroom is revealed and locked into place, Paige reaches up once again. This time, she tugs on a thick braided rope, releasing a leather mesh swing from inside the canopy top.

Holy shit! Paige is my kind of dirty.

"This is the most ingenious invention I have ever seen," I tell her after noticing a small blush on her cheeks as she unveils this latest secret.

First the squirting then this bed... Yup, she's my dream girl.

And as I think the thought, the inner fire bubbling deep in my belly bursts to life in response. The inferno seems to be moving outward towards my veins, igniting my blood in a backdraft of fire as it builds. A wave of heat flushes my skin and I break out in a sweat.

My desires take over, an ache so deep, I crave Paige more than any need for my next breath. I move, desperate in my search for the match to my flame, the calm to my inferno, the beat to my heart.

I'm not gentle when I hoist her on my hips, pulling at her hair to tilt her head so I can possess her lips. It's rough, even animalistic, as we crush our mouths together and give it everything we got. We don't just kiss, we strike a battle for ownership of each other, and allow our tongues to do the negotiations for surrender.

I manage to walk us to the edge of the swing, stopping when the thickness of the leather bangs against my thighs. The heavy craftsmanship shows this is no average sex swing. This jungle gym appears to be built for our kind, from the rugged woven mesh of the seat to the strong iron shackles dangling from the steel canopy. This playset is ready for whatever wild tussle our natural instinct dictates, and I'm more than willing to test out its superb quality.

I lean over to place Paige in the basket-style chair and wait for her to settle, holding the iron bilbo at the top of the mesh for balance. When she starts to grope me, seeming comfortable enough in the chair to take what she wants, I pull myself from her clutches. She whines as our lips part, then makes an adorable pouting face.

"You make me smile." I grin at her while positioning her feet into the stirrups hanging down from heavy chains. When her legs are secured and spread wide, I notice how wet she is and groan, "And also, super horny."

She giggles until I bend forward to lap at her dew, swirling my tongue tip around her opening and up her slit, preparing her for what's to come. She cries out, instinctively reaching forward, trying to hold me in place by my hair to direct my tongue. I'm quick to her actions, though, making an easy getaway as I swing her towards the wall.

"Wait a minute," she yelps, becoming aware of her surroundings. "How did I get in the chair? This isn't what I planned."

Her complaint barely registers in my head. I'm focused on the driving need to bury myself deep in her cunt. The chair swings gently back to me with a light bounce against my thighs. The height is perfectly set, placing her beautiful pussy open and ready in front of me.

I moan at the visual of her widespread invitation. My own cock throbbing forward to greet her. I palm my shaft and stroke it with vigor until drops of pre-cum are dripping from the tip. Using our natural lube, I position my hips in front of her and thumb myself against her opening.

"Your plan works, too," she moans out, tilting her pelvis up, eager for the first inch.

Her shift allows my tip to dip into her hole, and I have

to fight the urge to plunge myself in. There will be plenty of time for a hard thrust later. Right now, I want to savor this moment. I want to feel every inch of her, from the outside, and commit it to memory before I take her on the inside. If I do get exiled, I want this moment to be what keeps me going. I want this moment to be why I fight my way back, to be with her.

I slick up her slit with our mutual lust, feeling the metal ring glide up and down my bone as I masturbate her clit with my cock. Her nub hardens to a pearl, pulsing as a tiny beating heart against me. I pull back just to watch it throb. It excites me to see her so aroused, and I reward her by spanking her clit with the head of my cock.

"Ooh..." The low groan rumbles deep in her throat and her eyes roll back behind fluttering lashes.

I award her response this time, by tickling her opening with the tip of my dick. Slowly, pressing down into her hole until my crown disappears.

"Oh, God, you're hot," she screams out.

I chuckle, "Why, thank you."

Her head flips back and forth, and her eyes open wide. "No, I mean you feel really hot, you're on fire. Oh, fuck, it hurts."

My hips jerk back on instinct, realizing my inner heat is starting to project outward. I step away, not wanting to burn her. Panic starts to take over.

She whimpers, "No, more, I want it."

"Paige, I...uh," I struggle to find the right words to explain.

Her arm lifts as she gestures for me to come closer. "You don't have to tell me, I get it. This has something to do with who you are, the monster you believe yourself to be. But, I'm still here. I'm not going anywhere, honest. I'm not scared. Quite the opposite, in fact. It's fire-play on an extreme level, and in case you got sidetracked, that shit turns me on."

She spreads her thighs as far as they can go to show me the proof, and sure enough, the evidence is dripping from her. "Christ, you're sopping wet."

A knowing grin stretches wide across her face as she nods vigorously. "Uh-huh, and if you continue, I'm sure whatever fire burns inside of you will be extinguished, once I cum my brains out."

I snort from the comment, it's so Paige, and yet, without me saying a word, she's picked up enough of the gist to know exactly what to say. Her humorous insight might just be bang on, and the reason we seem to be so drawn to each other. This is the revelation I need, the slap in the head to bring me back to what matters, pleasing my dirty girl.

I move back between her thighs to manipulate her opening once more, slicking her up to play. My hand seeks out the butt plug, pulling it from her ass as I push myself into her pussy. I get in an inch and feel her tighten around my cock head. I pull back and push the plug in. I work this combination, back and forth, until her cunt starts to pulse and her hips are rolling up against mine.

When I remove the plug altogether, she shrieks her disappointment, until I fill her cunt.

"Oh, my, God."

Her voice is rough and pained as she takes on the mass of my member. I stop just shy of giving her the whole length. Rolling my hips and grinding myself against the tight muscles before pulling out of her in a super slow motion.

"So big," she mumbles. "So hot," she states while palming her breasts.

The touch of her warmth mixing with my own, and the sensation of her cunt milking me back, is almost too much to handle. I grit my teeth, feeling consumed by my lust. I watch her reach for her cunt, masturbating herself while I fuck her. This visual porn is pure, natural, and so erotic it makes me want to crawl inside of her and become a part of her.

"You are so beautiful, *leannàn*."

"No more pretty words, just shut up and fuck me." Her growl is demanding, prompting my hips to match hers of their own volition.

I increase my pace, force feeding her hungry pussy with my full length until I'm balls deep and she's coating me with her essence. Sweat drips from my brow as my internal temperature rises from our feral lovemaking. Except, the more she takes, the more tranquil I begin to feel on the inside. Until the raging fire is a swirl of controlled calm inside of me, and I'm able to manipulate it to where I wish.

I realize, in this moment, Paige is my sanctuary, and through her I have finally found peace. I assumed Livia had meant once peace was found for our kind, only then would I return to my true self. Then Paige said she could extinguish whatever fire burns in me when I make her orgasm, and the switch has been turned on-- I finally get it.

This is it, this is the draw. She is of magic, probably from the water sign and the opposite of my fire. She is the yin to my yang.

Namaste, motherfuckers!

I pound into her, palming her breast, and flicking my finger over the jeweled ring. She cries out and her cunt tightens. Her fingers continue to work away, rubbing her clit, twisting the metal to harden the nub until her pussy flutters against my cock. I grab a handful of her ass cheek to pump her as hard and fast as I can. Thrusting against the pulsing spot inside of her, over and over again, until her body tenses.

"Oh, yes," her breath hitches. "God Zander, yes."

A smile touches my lips as she calls me her deity, right as she releases a flood down the length of my cock. It seeps out and drips down my balls. I continue to fuck her, riding out every throbbing wave until her whole body is shaking in convulsions.

Her arm flings out of the swing and she flaps it down and around; she's trying to reach for something of importance. I slow my hips to a stop, allowing her time to recover, and wonder what she's reaching for.

I pull myself from her and she bows forward, expelling a shaky sigh.

While she regains her breath, my curiosity gets the best of me and I bend to examine the wooden base under the bed. It isn't obvious, but the frame has a small groove, about an inch from the top, big enough for my fingers to insert. It's a handle that allows me to hook the wood and pull out a drawer the length of the whole base.

The drawer rolls out with ease and is lined with a black velvet cloth. Once completely open, I see it has been sectioned off with compartments of various sizes, to accommodate the treasure trove inside the drawer.

"Whoa," I gasp.

I'm more than shocked as I take in the whips, canes, paddles, vibrators, dildos, and plugs. And those are just the items I can name; the rest leave me simply gob smacked. It's the same as finding a lotto ticket and discovering it's the million-dollar winner.

An interesting object in the third section over, between a neat pile of restraints and the various assortment of gags, catches my eye. I'm fascinated, even compelled to pick it up and see what it is.

In the drawer, it reminds me of a jockstrap with extra parts. After a closer inspection, I realize it's a strap-on, on steroids. The whole thing secures around the waist with a thick rubber dong attached. But there is an extra detachable strap, dangling down with two other detachable toys. This triple threat looks loaded for fun, I'm just not sure for whom.

I hold it up while shooting Paige a questionable glance. She answers slyly with, "I told you I'm more perverse than most."

"True, you were forthcoming about your kink." I chuckle then add, "So, who wears it and who gets the receiving end?"

Her shoulders shrug while a sexy smirk crosses her lips. "Depends on how adventurous you feel?"

Pulling herself up by the hanging rope above, she's a pro at lifting herself out of the chair, to perch on the edge. I can tell she's done the dismount more than a few times. I get caught up, distracted by the graceful way in which she slides from all the rope, steel, and leather. It isn't until she's tugging the banana-hammock-with-bite out of my fingers and stepping into it, that I tune into what she's up to.

I'm on the bandwagon now, shifting into high gear as I kneel in front of her. I take the straps from her long fingers, sorting them out to hang the right way and help her step into the sexiest pair of underwear, ever.

Remembering her question, I give an encouraging answer, "I've always thought myself a bit of a madcap, a daredevil even. You have to be somewhat of an adventurer to be a nomad."

I kiss her thigh while I dress her. I take the opportunity to run my tongue up the red tattoo, where I playfully bite at her hip. Her fingers slide through my hair, gripping a handful to jerk my head back. I'm happy to see her holding my gaze with a darker one of her own. It fills me with a giddy anticipation.

"Good answer." She grins down at me. "This will hurt less if you're more willing."

My cock flexes forward in answer to my willingness. My response has her grin spreading wider as she releases her hold on my hair, cupping my chin this time, as she directs my next move. "Put them on me and I'll make it worth your while."

"Yes, M'Lady, right away," I say this with a hint of English accent to make her laugh. "I'll do anything for the Mistress."

I'm placing the straps on her hips when she groans with annoyance. "Stop goofing around or I'll have to cane you first."

"Please do, Mistress, and start with my balls." I look up with a wink and watch her eyes widen with glee.

I don't give her time to respond further as I lick her slit to lube her up. I get distracted easily, and dive my tongue into her hole, slurping her nectar. I twirl her quick, pulling apart her cheeks to spit on her asshole. Her moans escalate when I add my fingers to the mix, rubbing the spit over her puckered hole and getting it slippery. It responds well, fluttering open as I bring the attached plug and dildo combination up, and slowly insert them for her pleasure.

While I'm pushing them in, first with the dildo, I notice a switch on the underside of the rubber. I flick it with my thumb and it buzzes to life.

"Hmm, slutty, I like it."

"Ah," she gasps. "Warn me before you turn those on."

Her skin reacts, goosing with excitement from the sensation.

"Mmm, not a chance," I tell her, wondering if I should add a few more buzzing toys to make her really hum.

I decide I have more than enough to please her with and get back on task, manipulating the dildo in and out. When she starts to hiccup with her panting, I insert the plug. Dipping in the tip to tease, then pulling it out to circle her rim with my tongue. She spreads her thighs to allow me to play. It's short-lived. Once I have them both buried deep inside of her and buzzing away, she's eager in her mission.

"Good job, but it's my turn to play." She grips more of my hair to pull me up until I'm standing. "You need to sit, now."

Her hand nudges my chest to move me towards the swing. Even though I'm a willing participant, and somewhat sure what's about to happen, I hesitate ever so slightly. Stopping at the edge of the swing, letting the leather rub the backs of my thighs as I play out what's going to happen.

I don't fear the pain of having my asshole penetrated. As Paige had said, I've endured great pain and this will be a walk in the park in comparison. It's more about trust and allowing her to control this that has me clenching my ass cheeks. I've never given myself to a woman this way. In all honesty, if I cross this line, I'll be giving her the most sacred part of me. A thought that paralyzes me with what ifs.

What if this is all there is between us?

I wet my lips and look at her with what, I'm sure, is this very fear in my eyes. "Don't hurt me, Paige."

She studies me for a minute, her eyes intently reading my face while she thinks over her words. She bridges the gap between us to place her hand over the scar on my chest and present me with a warm smile.

"I sometimes forget my badass exterior makes me appear heartless. I promise I have no intention of causing you anymore anguish. I believe you've had more than enough for one lifetime." Her honest comment relaxes me, something, I'm sure, she did on purpose.

The softer side of her doesn't last long. Within seconds she's back to being forceful, nudging me into the seat. Quick-handed too, when she locks me in the stirrups. She's not giving me time to change my mind with over processed thoughts. And once she's secured me in place, she's standing between my legs with a satisfied grin and taking my cock in her hand for a stroke.

"The invitation to my darker side isn't about me hurting you emotionally. While physically it can be painful, especially if you struggle," She grins at this, hoping I'll be disobedient. "It's more about you letting go of your inhibitions, and allowing me to give you pleasure. And maybe, through the experience, you have a cathartic moment that allows you to heal."

Most of what she says gets lost as my mind focuses on her hand stroking my shaft. I do understand the sentiment, though, because it's what I told her earlier. She was reluctant at first, but she gave herself to me. From that, she was able to achieve new heights in her sexuality. She trusted me without hesitation, the least I can do is to give her the same consideration.

I lean back, curling my arm under my head to rest and let myself relax with a sigh. "Take me to your world, *leannàn*."

The most beautiful curve on her body stretches wide and lights up her face from my acceptance. She licks at the smile, to moisten those thick tempting lips; lips that make a strong male like me feel weak in the knees and dissolving my most intelligent thoughts. She is so beautiful, and that isn't even a strong enough word to describe her. It's not just her exterior, it's in everything she says and all that she is.

I lay in the swing, spread-eagle, aroused and ready for her to take me on this journey. Her long, delicate fingers wrap my cock and stroke me with a gentle touch. Her thumb massages my head until it is swollen and dripping with drops of lust for her. When the first drop rolls out, she bends at the waist to mouth my crown. She's sucking in the juice, adding it to her saliva to spit back into her hand. She then swirls her fist, coating my length, and works in the fluid to a faster pump.

I'm moaning as I grow harder in her palm. My blood rushes into my appendage, bulging the veins, and lighting the fires that only seem to burn for her.

"You're getting hot again," she mumbles around a mouthful. The vibration wiggles down my shaft, and up my spine, causing another internal eruption.

My cock starts to throb with force in her hand. She switches her rhythm to longer strokes, right down to my balls, where she plants her face to suck on my heavy sacs. The heat of her mouth mixed with the tickle of her tongue, as she fills her mouth with my nuts, has me transfixed. This is so erotic to watch, but feeling it, is beyond stimulating. I'm aroused, my blood is pumping the heat through my veins so hard, I fear I will spontaneously combust.

I'm about to shout for her to stop, I don't want to burn

her. When she pops my balls from her mouth, to tongue my asshole. My words get lost as she lubes my hole, and I find the swirling tongue action soothing. When she inserts a finger, though, I tense from the sudden shock. I pucker up, but it's my cock that turns the traitor, jutting forwards and escaping her grip to bounce against my belly and drizzle me with pre-cum.

She comes back up to deep throat me, dropping all the way down my length. After a few pumps to coat my shaft again, she goes back to seducing my hole. This time, it isn't as shocking. Instead, the sensation is warm and enticing. It doesn't take her long to make the heavy manipulation of my cock, coupled with her tongue action, to have my ass fluttering open for her to insert two fingers.

I feel the pressure first, followed by a slight sting as she swirls those fingers inside of me. She seems to know exactly how to work the barrier, over and over, until I'm moaning for more.

"Oh, fuck, yes," I cry as the orgasm begins to push forward.

My hips flex and roll up, my cock pressing hard against her hand as I prepare to release. She reads this well, too well, switching her hard hand strokes to light swirls with a fist around my cock head, denying me the release. I punch my own fists down into the mesh seat, frustrated swears rumble off my lips.

"Damn, that was easy and made me so wet." She stands with a giggle. "But, don't think I'm letting you get off that quick, just yet."

She is eager, moving between my thighs, nudging them further apart with her hips while spitting in the palm of her hand. A thoughtful move, as she takes her cupped hand to slick up the dong attached to her pelvis. Once she has it coated, she begins to thumb the rubber tip against my ass. She plays, teasing my opening until I'm ready. The dong slides in with less restraint, and in an instant Paige pops my cherry.

I have never been penetrated before. Even during times of torture, I somehow got lucky. I have often wondered what the physical act would feel like, though. To know how the first push inside, past the resistant barrier, would feel. As Paige stretches me wide and takes me in this most intimate manner, I have an understanding of what being full means. This one act of penetration has made us one. There is no separation between us now, no more reason for secrets. She's right, letting go of one's inhibitions can be cathartic and from it, I found where I belong.

"Mother of God," I begin to beg. "Don't stop, please."

She's patient and persistently slow in her movements as she pegs me to a hip-rolling pump. The little vibrators buzzing away inside of her, tickle my balls. This is much more stimulating than I could ever have imagined it to be.

Her hand never stops jerking me. First, with long strokes, then building into faster fist pumps. I can tell she's done this a time or two, she seems to know the right buttons to push. Working my orgasm to a simmering pressure, on the verge of boiling over. And just as quick, she teases me back from the edge of deep craving, until I believe I'm going to go mad if I don't explode.

Her hips thrust forward, harder as her own need starts to come into play. She's rolling them in with a circular motion, hitting the right places deep inside her honey hole with her toys, masturbating herself as she fucks me.

"I'm going to ride you so hard, cowboy, it's going to make us both cum."

The feral look of determination on her face and domination set in her eyes put me right where I need to be, teetering on the cusp of the pleasure she promised. Feminine sexual power is not about physically overpowering a man. It's more about the strength of her attitude and the clarity of her desire. In this moment, Paige is the most powerful being I know. As she penetrates me, I believe in my heart, she isn't just taking me on her sexual journey, she's owning my body, mind, and soul completely.

I scream. "Take me, Paige."

My release hits hard, but not all at once. Small eruptions of lust shoot up from my crown in messy jerks. She strokes my bone to the root and squeezes my shaft hard, holding off the rest as she thrusts herself forward.

Her O-face starts to form but seems to get lost in frustration on her brow, when she can't quite get herself over the edge. My balls are heavy, full from the denied release, and at the point are starting to turn blue.

"Please, Paige, finish me off," I beg, reaching for her, but she seems lost in her inability to get herself off.

I squeeze my thighs against her and push myself away from her. The dong slithers from my ass as I swing, and I jerk everywhere from the odd sensation. It's an effort to roll myself, but I grab the rope hanging from the canopy to pull my body up. Wiggling my feet free from the stirrups, I'm able to unlatch myself from the binds. My dismount isn't nearly as graceful as Paige's had been. I'm not trying to be graceful, though, I'm trying to get to my woman and give us both a happy ending.

With clumsy awkwardness, I manage to escape the swing and land on my feet in front of a confused Paige. Her O-face has turned into more of an oh-shit-face when I come at her as the beast in hot pursuit of its prey. She squeals as I grip her arms in my hands. Her body tenses when I lift her and walk us towards an S-shaped chair in front of the fireplace. The backing of the leather lounger follows the same S-shape curve of the seat, sturdy enough for how I'm about to use it for.

I'm a man possessed with purpose, obsessed with need and consumed by desire. I'm not gentle or even kind as I manhandle her. Setting her on her feet, flipping her around to face the fireplace, I pop the snaps of the strap-on open and fling the dong on the floor. When I bend her over the back of the chair, pushing her head down against the smooth seat cushion, I notice the two toys still tucked deep inside of her. A wave of jealousy hits me as I see them, then I remember the toys couldn't satisfy her, and a laugh of madness escapes my lips.

I'm only slightly aware of how insane I feel, but not totally gone that I don't know what I'm doing. I do have focus and a steady hand as I remove the dildo from her cunt and watch a bead of juice trickle out. I can't help but lean in and lap it up with my tongue, savoring her sweet nectar as I lick her hole.

"More," she moans. "Give me more."

Her pleas have me standing back up and moving in behind her. When I pinch the plug in my fingers and pop it out of her ass, I decide this is the perfect place to start. My cock agrees as it bows forward, eager to make contact. I drop the plug to grip my shaft, directing it in place as I gape her hole with just the crown.

"Oh, yes, take my ass." Her arm comes up, reaching for the back of the chair as she arches herself in an invitation to take her.

I tease her some more, giving her an inch then taking it away. Repeating the process, over and over, until she's cursing in frustration and biting into the leather cushion.

"You want it bad, don't you *leannàn?*"

"Yes, fill me and fuck me."

I roll my hips forward and fill her full, pushing myself deep just as she requested. I now know how it feels, and I want to give her the same utopia. I thrust into her with long hard pumps until her entire body is spasming in uncontrolled jerks. A hot liquid explosion hits my balls and drips down my thigh as she screams into the cushion.

It's the trigger my beast has been waiting for all night, for centuries. I feel it stir from the fire within, waking from its slumber to reconnect with me. It steps into me, similar to how a person would step into a pair of pants. Covering me from within as a second layer, attaching itself to every muscle, nerve, and fiber of my being.

I pull back from Paige to allow the transformation to take place. My flesh bubbles from the internal heat. I watch as it turns a bright shade of red, appearing scorched from the sun. It does not burn this time, for my beast has given me scales of armor just below the surface of the tissue to protect me.

The process is quick, lasting only a minute, but I sense it when the beast is locked back into place. Home once more and somewhat at peace. I realize just how much I have missed this part of me, like I have also been asleep for centuries. My mind is clear, my vision is crisp, my senses aware and my powers are strong, in full control. Well, almost in full control. There is one thing that is not even close to being in control, it rages with a passion the likes I have never felt before.

Mark her!

The shout is loud inside my head. It's unclear whether it comes from my own conscience or my beast. It matters not, for we are now the same, man and beast as one, and our only thought is of her.

Mine!

I'm growling like my beast as I quickly return to Paige, placing my hips back between her thighs. She whimpers when I gather her hair in my hand, but she comes willingly when I pull her up off the couch, balancing her hips on the backrest. She cries out as I plunge myself deep into her cunt, thrusting my cock inside her and picking up speed as a possessed man, an even more possessed beast, desperate to mate.

"You make me feel so dirty," she screams out. "I love it."

I control her with my cock until the scent of her arousal is thick in the air. I breathe deep to take it in, flicking my tongue at the air to taste the hint of her sin, my mouth salivating for a taste. The beast starts screaming in my head to make my mark, and when I exhale, a plume of smoke curls out of my mouth.

I trail my fingers down her back, tracing the curves of her body with a lover's caress. I don't just want to fuck her. I want to show her how beautiful she is, how I can't get enough of her and how I will always crave her in this manner. I want to worship every inch of her, as often as possible.

My eyes flicker down the image on her back to the perfect place-- the claw foot on her hip. A smile spreads across my lips as I set my hand over the drawing and find it to be of similar size. I clutch this curve and dig my nails in, my own talons extend and pierce her skin.

She hisses from the sting then let's out a giggle.

"My dirty little masochist whore," I chuckle. "Do you want more?"

She doesn't even hesitate. "God, yes."

I slow my hip thrusts and add circular motions, to grind my bone in just the right spot, working her over. When she grunts with approval, I send a wave of magical energy into my hand to warm her skin.

She squeals with laughter, "That's amazing, more."

I grind myself harder and work her up, feeling her pussy pulsing on the inside. She's close and I know just how to get her there. Adding a touch of heat to mix with my energy, pressing my palm hard against her skin. Her whole body jerks back, and I pull her into my chest where she tenses up. I ride her cunt hard, as she wraps her arms around my neck to hold herself up, while I burn my handprint into her flesh.

"God Zander," she cries out in my ear, "I fucking love you."

The way she says those six words, naming me as her God to worship, and telling me she loves me, whether she means them or not, it's enough to make me come undone. It happens so fast I don't even realize I'm doing it until my fangs are already deep in her neck.

Mine!

I'm growling deep in my throat as I bite her vein and drink in her tangy essence. She stills in my arms, tensing every muscle as I start the mating ritual without permission. I have no choice but to stop mid-drink and lick her wound closed.

"Don't stop, keep going," she whispers. "I want this, I want you, I am yours."

I snarl and nip at her neck again, testing the water to make sure she is serious. She gnashes her teeth and snaps back like an Alpha she-wolf.

"Do it," she roars.

A low rumble of approval rolls out my mouth. "I give thee my body."

She answers, "As do I."

"I give thee my heart."

Again she answers, "As do I."

"I give thee my soul."

"As do I," she says and then we join together in the ancient prayer, "We are as one from this day forth, to love for eternity as my own, forevermore."

A loud crackle rings in the room, a wave of energy shoots out and wraps us in an invisible thread of warm silk, bonding us as a couple. I drink from her neck and feel her blood connecting with mine, merging our energies into one form.

My hips move on their own, slow but forceful, as I work to bring us both over the edge, sealing our union as we release. I lick her wound closed and move my hand from the burn on her hip. I have marked her in every way I could and now, I will make it official.

Pulling her up to hold against my chest, I gain access to her whole body and I start rubbing her clit. I know pain is what will bring her over, and that is what I will give her. Moving the fire inside my body, I project it down my arm and into my fingers. Like I had done on the mountain when I killed Cale, I let the light flow from my fingers to shoot sparks of my God-like powers directly on her clit. A glowing fire show like none she's ever experienced, something I think I'll call, the dragon's kiss.

Her whole body starts to shake and her cunt squeezes my cock. It gives me the friction I need to start the flow of my own release. A blood-curdling scream rips from her throat as she soaks me in her sin. I can smell it heavy in the air, and it triggers the full force of my orgasm. I slam my hips to a pounding drive against her, violently emptying my seed deep into her cunt and marking her with every thrust.

"Mine," I scream.

"Yours," she whispers back.

With my balls empty, my legs become weak and shaking. I'm wavering on the verge of passing out. However, I did just make an oath, and I will care for my mate. My own needs be damned. She's a limp body, easy to maneuver when I turn her in my arms to lift and cradle her into my chest. I'm slow and unsteady, walking us over to the bed.

I'm thankful for the mattress to sit upon as I hold her to search the bedside table. My fingers latch onto a cloth and when I pluck it from the drawer, I'm happy it's exactly what I need. Taking the soft hand towel, I clean her off as best as I can, then pile the pillows behind me. I swivel and shuffle myself against the puffy cloud at the headboard, sighing with exhaustion.

Once I settle, she stretches out lengthwise on top of me, curling her leg under mine and an arm across my chest, where she places her palm over my scar. We lay for a time, our panting the only sound in the room as we catch our breath. My whole body seems to tingle from the workout we just had. It twitches and jerks, but lulls me into a sleep.

CHAPTER 11

I'm somewhere in between the veil of deep sleep and waking dream. I have no idea how much time has passed, minutes, hours, maybe even days. My mind is replaying the night, over and over. I see the erotic images, the beautiful acts that led to what happened. My eyes pop open.

Holy shit, I have a wife!

I blink to focus and find Paige staring up at me, her eyes give nothing away as she watches my reaction. I'm not sure how long I drifted or how long she's been watching, but I want her to know, with all my heart, this has not been a mistake.

I'm about to tell her when she speaks in a calm voice, "That wasn't just sex, that was like naked poetry, in bumper cars, on acid."

I burst out laughing. "What?" I choke out.

She lifts up to fold her arm across my chest, propping her chin on a forearm to look at me. Her face is relaxed and her eyes are, different. I can't place my finger on this expression, but I feel warm from it.

After a minute, she begins to speak and it all becomes clear, "You are the love that came without warning; you had my heart before I could even say no. My grandmother once told me, my soulmate would be the stranger I recognize. You are my stranger, and so much more."

I tilt my head to kiss her nose. "Then tell all the wolves to back off because I'm home, and I'm here forever."

She smiles. "I never thought I'd say this, but I like the sound of that."

"Good, because I mean it and I want you to know, Bear will never be a problem for you anymore."

Her brows pop up. "Oh, you plan on taking him and the whole MC on, do you?"

"If I have too, yes. I just mated with you, which means, you are mine to protect."

She laughs. "One amazing roll in the hay and you became my savior. I know you have a stunning set of big balls, but don't get crazy. We can work this out, we just have to be smart about it, give him what he wants."

I grunt with annoyance. "You will give him nothing."

She jerks up as her eyes light with anger. "Why, so you can keep it for yourself?"

She begins to struggle to get up and I wrap my arms around her. "No," I try to tell her.

"You're just like all the rest, only looking to get into my pockets. Let me go," she shouts. "What have I done?"

I hold her to my body and sit us up, bending her in an awkward position so she'll quit moving for me to explain. "I don't want your money, I have enough of my own. I can prove it if you grab my phone from my jacket. I'll pull up my accounts and show you. I only meant you can't give Bear money to get rid of him. He'll only be back when it runs out, and you know it."

She stops trying to get away and sits on my legs, her head tilts sideways. "What do you mean you have money? I thought you were just a nomad."

I laugh, "Sure, sometimes I am. Other times, I put on a suit and go to my skyscraper office in Toronto to meet with the people that run my companies. We are not different, you and I. Cut from a similar cloth of entrepreneurs, and while you are just starting out, I've had a lot longer to build my own real estate empire. One you can even look up on the internet. I own a successful chain of hotels all over the world, as well as many other businesses in Canada. I have human employees running my companies to keep me out of the spotlight, and free up my time to do whatever I want. I usually ride a lot, moving shit for some of the MC, and recently I joined the court, which brought me here."

Her mouth drops open. "You're shitting me, right?"

I shake my head. "I'll get my phone and you can check it out for yourself."

She says nothing, she only sits and stares. It's only when I go to move her to get out of bed, and get the damn phone that she stops me with, "So, you're a billionaire shifter."

I turn back to sit heavily on the edge of the bed. "What did you say?"

A side smirk lifts from the corner of her lips. "You aren't the only one who holds their cards close, mister money-bags shifter from the heavens."

I run my hand through my hair, a nervous tick, as I try to work out my reply. Then I realize it doesn't matter anymore, I love this woman and I'll do whatever it takes to make her happy, including spilling all my dark secrets. I'm ready to finish our talk, except Paige seems to have already figured me out.

"So you know. How?"

She shrugs, then moves over on the bed to let me get comfortable. I sit back amongst the piles of pillows, pulling the duvet over my lap and pat it for her to join me.

Once she is stretched out on top of me again she asks me an odd question, "Can I tell you a story?"

This is not what I expect her to say and laugh out my response. "Sure, why not?"

Her long fingers trace the ridges of my scar as she begins to speak, as though it brings her comfort to do so. I find the sensation soothing and before long, it brings me warmth too as she tells me her tale.

"As a child, the elders in my tribe told me stories about where we came from, our history, and beliefs. It's how I found out the wolves were believed to be great spirits and why the tribe protected my father, then me, after he was gone.

My people have a lot of beliefs and many spirits; not all

of them make complete sense to me, but I'm also not a full native. I have this other side, a supernatural secret side, with its own beliefs and histories. It gets confusing trying to take it all in, and worse when beliefs start to cross into each other."

She shuffles to put her hand, palm side down, on my chest where she props her chin. She looks at me directly, her eyes connecting with mine as she continues, "Like yesterday, I heard Brigid call you *Ruadan*. I know in your language it means red-haired boy. This didn't make sense because your hair is more chestnut, and even with your manscaping, I still couldn't find evidence for the name reference.

Then you called her mother. Which I found puzzling since you told me you were older than dirt and I know she isn't even in her four hundredth year. The confusion went on, as I know she is a witch and so too is your sister, Lilith. But you are supposed to be a werewolf. However, Lilith is also a goddess like the Queen so then I thought maybe, it could be possible that you are like them somehow. I'm not sure how that could work, and the whole lineage thing left me confused as shit."

She winks at me with a laugh. "I imagine that's the point though, to keep the common folk guessing about the court."

I shake my head. "Not really, no. Some, like my sister and the Queen, didn't know what they were until their powers came to them. Others, like myself, had a more complicated transformation."

She chews her lips for a minute then starts again, "Yes, well, whatever the case, I don't think you realize that I love to read. You can learn some fascinating things in books, about mythology, religion, and beliefs in other cultures. While you were remaining silent about who you were, I was putting my knowledge to work as I watched you. Do you know what I discovered?"

I chuckle knowing exactly what my smart beauty

discovered. "You know who I am."

"That's right, I do, and it turns out you are just like them. You just don't see it as such, but you will, when I tell you why you're better in every way to me." She smirks at me with the attitude I love and it makes me laugh.

It turns her smirk into a full-blown grin. "I'm glad you're more confident with this conversation. It isn't all bad being a god and the first of the shifters."

I frown. "And how did you figure that out, exactly?"

She laughs. "From my books. You see, as we talked and I got to know you better; I remembered reading about Ruadan, son of Brigid and Bres, who were Celtic gods. I'm not sure how Brigid is now a witch, but I do know Bres had his son killed, which matches your story. And I remembered it wasn't because of the color of his hair, but the color of the beast he shifted into, that he got the name. It's why your skin turned red and why you shoot light, and heat, and fire. You have a beast in you and not like us, the wolves, but as the *ollphéist comhlàn*-- or as you think of yourself, the gross monster."

She looks smug for knowing the Celtic word for my beast, the only word they have for what I am. She also seems energized as she rolls out quickly, "What you don't know is, when I was a child, I dreamt of a great beast. My grandmother told me that only those who have been blessed by the Earth Mother could see him in his truest form. She believed I had to be blessed to see him in the dreamland. As a shaman, she too had gifts, and hers were visions of the future. On her deathbed, she told me the beast would come for me one day and he would be the stranger I recognize.

I know the story sounds crazy, but every night I would dream of him. I wanted to believe what my grandmother said was true. I wanted him to come to help get me away from Bear, but it never happened. Instead, my belief in the beast became my strength to overcome Bear's cruelty and build my own way out. In time, the beast became my symbol of hope, and I thought maybe that's what my grandmother really meant. It is why I tattooed his image on my body to remind me."

She shakes her head in disbelief. "You recognized the ink when you saw it, and that's when I knew you were my beast. Now you are here in person as my mate, and I find out we have similar business interests. We are some match made out of the heavens."

My suspicions had been correct, our paths crossed because the gods willed it. I'm not sure why, and I'm not sure what to say, as we lay wrapped in each other's arms, and in our own thoughts.

It doesn't take long before I have to ask the burning question, "So you dreamt of me?"

She snorts with an eye roll. "After all I said, the only thing you pick out is that I dreamt of you?"

"Well, yeah."

I caress the side of her cheek, tugging at her chin to make her look up at me so she can see the honesty on my face. "There is no man alive who wouldn't want to know that the only female he's ever cared this deeply for, has thought only of him since she was a child. It not only swells my ego, it fills my heart. To me, right now, nothing else matters. You make me feel wanted, loved, accepted for being different and it brings me peace, something I never thought I would ever have. I want to enjoy this blissful moment, with you in my arms, and the rest can wait."

Her sigh is pleasing to my ears. "I don't think I will ever tire of your words, I love them."

"And I love you." The words roll off my tongue with an incredible ease because they are the most honest words I have ever spoken.

Her lips crack into a smile but I notice a slight tremor in the bottom one as her eyes begin to shine with unshed tears. "Damn you. Not only do you make my downstairs parts tingle, you make my heart quiver, too."

I pull her up my body to capture her trembling lips, stilling them with reassurance from my own as we allow ourselves to get lost in our emotions. No matter where we go from here, I know in my heart we can get through anything as long as we are together. She's the one who will heal me with these kisses because she is everything I long for.

Our kiss builds from gentle and intimate into rough and animalistic, as the craving to take her again drives me. My hands begin to scan her body, caressing her shoulder, down her spine and ending with a firm handful grasp of her ass, as I grind my growing hard-on into her belly. I could have every single part of her body touching me, I could devour every inch of her, take her in every way imaginable, and still I would feel as though I can't get enough of her. She is my all-consuming madness while she holds the key to the door of my absolute sanity.

She pulls away to lean back with a giggle. "Someone's on the slutty side of the bed this morning."

I growl and try to pull her back, to continue what we started. I lick her chin and nibble on her throat while my hands caress her ass and my fingers play a game of hide-and-seek, in and out, of her pussy.

"Mmm," she coos. "You're incorrigible. Not that I'm complaining, but I do have to work and the Queen wants us at her meeting."

I lick a trail to her ear and bite her lobe, ignoring her request to return to reality. She lets out a hiss. I soothe it away by sucking it into my mouth. I'm not above playing dirty to keep her in this bed. I rub her clit, dipping my fingers into her cunt, trying my best to make her putty in my hands.

Paige proves she is not as easily distracted as I hoped, and again she leans back. "I would love to go another round with you, but I'm starving. Aren't you hungry?"

"Mmm, very," I moan and lick my lips for the tasty treat before me, even though it's not what she has in mind.

"I can whip something up." She sounds all business.

"How about some French toast?"

"How about a French kiss?"

I pull her up my body, her legs falling on either side of my waist, her breasts press into my chest, and her face is right before me. She snorts a laugh just as I crush my mouth over hers. She doesn't resist, instead, she melts into me and gives me her tongue, swirling it around my mouth to tango with mine. My hands, working with a mind of their own, grasp for her ass cheeks as my hips roll up to grind my length between them.

Paige gets roaming paws too, running her fingers through my hair, down my neck and arms. When she reaches my nipples, she's merciless, pinching and pulling at them with her fingers. The assault stimulates my nerve endings, shooting shockwaves of pleasure right to my dick until it's weeping in agony.

She nibbles on my bottom lip, I react with a bite to her top lip. We both moan and gasp, loving every minute of the teasing we both give and receive. She lifts her torso to tilt her hips and positions her slit on my stomach, scratching her perfectly filed nails down my abdomen.

"These are begging for attention. They make me want to be naughty," she whispers then licks her lips while looking at my belly. "The 'make me want to masturbate my clit all over the amazing ripples', kind of naughty."

My cock spasms and slaps against her ass over the suggestion and I eagerly reply, "Then use me as your plaything, my dirty girl."

Her lips curl up. "You have such great answers," she purrs out.

The musical sound makes me moan in response, but when her hips begin to roll and she starts to take her own pleasure from the ridges on my stomach, it's all I can do not to cum on her ass.

"Fuck, that's hot," I groan through gritted teeth, willing myself not to release.

The little noises escaping her throat only add to the pressure building in my balls. I reach for her breasts and help her along, twisting her ring hard until she's screaming, then rubbing my thumb over her nipple to soothe the pain. Her hips pick up speed and rock in a circular motion. The line on her forehead begins to crease as her own determination sets in.

"Flex for me," she demands and I comply, lifting myself in a partial sit-up. "Oh, fuck yes, like that. So hard. I'm going to cum."

I push some of my heated light into my fingertips and project tiny sparks out onto her nipple. "Then cum, my greedy beauty."

She screams then moans, "God, that's amazing. Give me more."

The show is just too much. I start humping her ass cheeks, pressing my cock up against her to get as much friction as possible. The need to grasp her hips and sink myself deep inside of her is overwhelming, but I remain patient, allowing her to have this moment of self-manipulation. All the while, I know once she screams from her release, I am going to flip her over and fuck her hard.

I build a little more heat in my fingertips and this time, I zap her with the full force of the magical fire. Her legs start to shake and she's panting in hiccups. I look between her legs just in time to watch her expel her sin on my stomach, the sight makes me damn near burst myself.

Her scream is loud but the words are perfect, "Oh, *Ruadan, mo ollphéist olc.*"

I almost laugh at her calling me her bad monster, but an abrupt pounding at the door stops me mid-chuckle. I hear the click of the knob before the door swings open and a panicked female voice calls out, "Pea, what the fuck is going on in here?"

There's a moment of shuffling as Paige reaches behind me, between the headboard and the mattress, for a weapon.

I swear inside my head, every cuss word I know, in several languages as I prepare for some sort of fight.

Paige's body turns then sags, her head rolls forward and her hair cascades over her face hiding her reaction, but I hear her annoyance loud and clear in her hissed cuss, "Shit."

I move with speed, pulling up the duvet to wrap it around Paige just as our visitor gasps, "Oh, Pea, no, what have you done?"

Paige lets out a sigh. She sounds exhausted, but musters her energy to straightens, swinging herself off my lap and off the bed. She takes the covers with her and leaves me exposed. My solider is still eager as it stands at attention. I doubt my team leader will go down, not without a good hard spank first.

I'm trying to save my dignity as I tug at the sheet, finding it tucked in well, with the only form of cover being the pillows. I shift to pull one from behind my head to place in front of my throbbing cock. I'm still painfully hard, and the heavily starched fabric touching my sensitive organ, is of little help.

While I fight the urge to allow my active volcano to erupt, Paige is speaking to the visitor with an angered tone, "What is so Goddamn important, Bean, that you felt it necessary to barge into my home?"

I turn my head to the door where the blond bartender from last night is standing, staring right at me with her mouth hanging open. I climb off the bed and offer a nod of acknowledgment before I slink off into the closet behind Paige.

Bean clears her throat a couple of times then finally answers, "We have a situation at Wasted."

As I walk into the closet, Paige is already wearing a pair of denim shorts and is putting on a black stretchy top that hugs her breasts. I whimper from the visual and press the pillow against my cock.

She hands me a towel with a sympathetic expression and

mouths, "Sorry."

I whisper back, "Blowjobs are better than apologizes."

She grins with one of her classic eye rolls then leaves me to clean myself. I listen as she questions her friend, "Why aren't you calling Ducky? He's the day manager, and he's perfectly capable of dealing with bar issues."

I make my way to my clothing clump on the bathroom floor to put on my pants as Bean answers, "We tried calling him, but he's not answering, and he isn't at the clubhouse either. Then we called you, and when you didn't answer we got worried, so I came here."

"Shit, I left my phone in the office. Whatever, you're here now. What's going on?" Paige sounds annoyed, and I feel a twinge of guilt for distracting her enough that she forgot her lifeline to her business.

"There was a drive-by. The front of the bar looks like Swiss cheese." Bean says this matter of fact, but it stops me in the middle of securing my pants.

I walk out of the closet holding my drawers and firing questions at the poor girl. "A drive-by? Is anyone hurt? Do you know if the royals are okay?"

Bean looks over at me with a frown. "I'm sure the royals are fine, just the bar got hit. Fortunately, most of the customers were gone and none of us got hurt." She turns her attention to Paige and lowers her voice, but it still sounds full of the attitude she just gave me. "Why is he here? You know it changes everything?"

Paige holds up her hand. "Zee is my guest, and it changes nothing."

Bean pushes the topic, "He's a nomad, Pea. The fuck it doesn't. When Papa finds out, you know what he'll do."

Paige turns back to me, her lips pursed as a deep crease worries her brow. "Then we wouldn't tell him."

The blond snorts, "A little hard to do, you reek of him and I can see his bite mark on your neck."

Paige swings back to Bean. "That's none of your

concern, or Papa's for that matter."

"It damn well is." Bean gets right in Paige's face. "You just broke the unwritten rule that gives Papa the right to everything. You'll become a fucking baby machine to his friend that he makes our Alpha, while Papa lives it up on the money he makes from selling you. The rest of us will become slaves to the new Alpha, and in case you forgot, the guy is a scumbag who only wants this for his own enjoyment."

I race across the room to get between the two females, seeing this escalating in a bad way. "None of that will happen, I'll make sure of it."

Bean turns on me, her steel grey eyes piercing me with her glare. "Oh, really, and you think you're the man for the job? I heard the True Alpha beat you senseless. What makes you think you can hold off Papa, nomad? Aside from an impressive cock, I don't see you being much of anything, but the problem."

"Jill," Paige snaps in warning. "That's enough, Zee is only trying to help."

I hold up my hand. "No, she has a right to her opinion."

Bean laughs. "See, he can't even stand up to me, Pea. How the hell will he stop Papa? I might as well pack my fucking bags now and move into the Pearl. I know that's where Papa's buddy wants me, flat on my back and a dick between my legs."

"I see this is more about you than it is about what I want. So, while you wallow in self-pity, I apparently have a bar to rescue, and until I determine otherwise, a business to run, too," Paige snaps back at her friend, twirling on her feet to head back to the closet.

"That's not what I meant, Pea," Bean calls after Paige then glares at me. "This is all your fault."

I snort at the girl but don't answer. I'm not pleading my case to someone only looking out for themselves. I turn my back on her instead and head to the bathroom for the rest of my belongings. Knowing I'll need to be well geared up for this day.

I enter the bathroom and find Paige waiting, her hostility-laced mask of attitude is back in place, on her face, as she holds out my gun belts, jacket, and shirt. I start to dress as she starts to give me an out.

"Look, what Bean said is true. Us, being together, is going to open up a huge shit-storm when Bear finds out. I won't blame you if you want to walk away."

I click my harness with more force than normal and shoot her a glare. "I'm going to file what you said under the 'fuck that' column. It isn't going to happen."

She places her hand on my chest and sets her shining eyes on mine. "You don't understand, Bean is right, Bear owns me. I might have been tough about it before, but the fact is, I have two options. One, I walk away and he gets everything, period, end of story. As much as Bean was being a whiny bitch, she's right. When I'm gone, there won't be anyone here to help her or the pack. And option two is exactly what she said. Bear hands me over to his rich buddy, who's had a hard-on for me for years. He'll get everything, which still doesn't help the pack. Either way, I just fucked this up. Unless you just walk away so I can do some damage control."

My beast stirs within, wanting to unleash a violent rage all over Bear as I listen to her. I start to tremble the more I hear until there is only a roar in my ears as my blood boils. The fire in my soul churns with force and I can taste the burn in my throat. The need to protect my mate is strong, the need to pulverize Bear seems to be stronger, and I break out in a sweat trying to stop myself. It's only when Paige steps into my body for a hug that I feel my common sense come back to me.

"I see we need an option three," she whispers in my ear.

"Damn right," I snap back, then pull her against me to speak in a lighter tone. "I'm not sure why, maybe it was fate, but my life changed the minute I met you. It changed again the minute I said those bonding words, and I take that vow seriously. You are mine to protect, period. I'm not walking away from this, and I will do whatever it takes to keep you from that cocksucker."

I have to squeeze her harder to stop the rage from starting again, and she melts into me with a sob, "Thank you."

The weight of those two words sits heavy as I realize what this means to her. She has waited her whole life for me to get her out of this hell. Maybe this is part of my destiny, part of the reason Livia brought me back, a test to prove myself as the god I once was.

This time, I will not fail.

I place a kiss on the top of her head with my silent promise. "I love you," I mumble into her hair. "Just don't thank me yet, we still need a solution. There's also a good chance a few of my skeletons might make an appearance today, too."

"Oh, for Christ sake." She pulls back with a laugh, and I see her eyes are moist from tears. "We are both disasters."

I wipe my thumb under her eye with a smile. "Yes, but together we make a beautiful blessing."

She sobs a laugh and shakes her head before straightening her shoulder and dropping the confident veil over her face. "Then let's go kick this motherfucking curse to the curb, so we can get back to making our own dirty secrets together."

I take her face in my hands and stare deep into her eyes. *"Cibè is mian le do chroi, mo áilleacht."* I place a sweet kiss upon her lips and feel her breath come out in a sigh.

"Never stop the pretty words, even if I don't know what they mean."

"I simply said, whatever my beauty desires."

She crinkles her nose. "I prefer the Celtic version. Hearing those words make me feel as though I'm a part of your secret world, as your special goddess. It's the fairytale I used to dream about."

"Well, I do seem to be only rolling with the goddesses, these days." I laugh at the truth of my statement. "So, mo bandia, how about you put on that attitude I adore, and we go tackle what awaits."

She nods her head. "Deal, but first I need shoes."

I love how even in the face of uncertainty, she still wants to dress-up her confidence. She wiggles from my arms and walks across the shower stall to the closet, where she bends over to pick up a pair of shoes. It isn't a sexual move, but seeing her ass cheeks peek out of the bottom of the shorts sends a shockwave to my erection. I hiss as my cock tries to escape out the top of my pants, it still hungers for her and is not at all happy with this change of plan.

My only diversion is to put on my jacket, but it does nothing to stifle my urges. My eyes aren't helping matters, as they remain fixed on her as she thumbs the shoe straps over her heels. Stilettos are meant for fucking and worship, two things I desperately wish to be doing. However, when I notice her sliding small silver knives into notches on the heel, and pushing them in to glide along the leather instep, I have a whole new appreciation for the female wardrobe.

"You are just full of surprises," I praise her with a laugh.

She lifts her shirt to show me a flashbang bra holster. "Yup, and these babies help hide my Glock 43, too."

"I'm not sure if I'm turned on or frightened by this." I wink at her then offer her my hand.

She walks over the shower stall to meet me, a playful grin on her lips as we link fingers. "I never promised you mental stability, but I can promise you, whatever doesn't kill us better fucking run. I'm one hell of a shot with the gun and even better with the knives."

I chuckle, "I don't doubt that. I'm just glad we're on the same side."

We walk out into the main room and find it empty. I

glance at Paige with a questioning frown. "Where's Bean?"

Paige shrugs. "If she's smart, she'll be at the bar cleaning up and keeping her mouth shut."

I'm surprised by her quick dismissal of Bean as we hit the staircase and head down to the stable. I am not as easily swayed into thinking the girl won't try to cover her own ass. There is also a chance Bean is acting on Bear's behalf, and the story about the drive-by is just the bait to get us into whatever trap awaits.

As my head spins with uncertainty, a cheery-sounding female chirps out a greeting as we hit the bottom steps, "Good morning, Aunty Pea."

As we move into the foyer area of the stable with the standing desk, a beautiful human girl, in her mid-twenties, is standing behind the neat paper stacks waiting for us with a smile. I understand the family greeting as soon as I see the girl, she could be the younger version of my beauty, before the tattoos graced her flesh.

"Good morning," Paige answers as she goes to the girl with open arms.

The human comes out from behind the desk to embrace her aunt. "Do you want me to get Nitro ready to ride?"

"Not today, Denver. There's an issue at the bar I have to deal with. Let him out with the others for now, but ask Clay to work him later. We don't want Nitro to think he's on vacation."

The girl giggles. "He still might if I put him in the pen next to all the fillies."

Paige laughs back, "You are cruel."

Denver steps out of the hug and starts back to the desk when she spots me. She jumps with a start but offers me a shy smile before ducking back behind the safety of her paper stacks.

In a lower voice, she asks, "Should I get Mama to clean the apartment?"

Paige turns to me with a grin. "Yes, and tell her the

sheets need changing."

Denver averts her eyes, and a red blush colors her whole face. "Yes, Aunty. Do you want me to do anything else?"

Paige's grin drops and she turns to address her niece, "Yes, I want you to be extra careful on the trails today. Bring a rifle with you, and if anyone you don't know comes at you, shoot at them like Clay taught you, then get your ass back here. Do you understand?"

Denver's head pops up. "I know the drill, Aunty Pea."

"That's my girl." Paige gives Denver a loving smile then starts for the door with me behind, but stops before opening it to add, "And Denver, don't shoot this guy, okay? He's pretty important to me."

"Uh, sure." The girl frowns. "Who is he, Aunty?"

Paige opens the door and waves me through with a laugh, "He's your Uncle Zander."

I freeze halfway out the door and turn back to look at the girl with wide eyes. She has a big grin on her face. "Nice to meet you, Uncle Zander."

I'm speechless. I just stand there gawking at the girl, my niece. The magnitude of my mating with Paige hits me, and it is something I hadn't even considered. Paige has a human family, I now have a human family. My mouth starts to form words, but they come out as blurts of noise.

Paige, thankfully, takes pity on me and guides me backward through the door into the Nevada heat. Under my breath, I mumble, "You could have warned me."

She breaks into a laugh. "I could have, but it was more fun to watch you almost shit your pants."

We walk up to my bike and I fish the key out of my pants pocket. "You're evil."

Unfastening the helmet from the saddlebags before putting it on her head, she turns while threading the strap under her chin. "Maybe a little evil, but I had a means to my madness."

I swing my leg over the bike seat and take my beanie

from the handlebar. "Oh, and what exactly would that be?" I ask with curiosity.

She steps on the footrest and swings her other legs around to mount the seat, sliding down to press her body up against mine for a perfect fit.

As we adjust, she answers, "I wanted you to see that you aren't a nomad anymore. You have a family now, my family. They will welcome you, just as they welcomed my father, and they will treat you better than your father treated you."

I turn in my seat to look at her, the love in my heart bursting for her. I lean in to kiss her forehead and say the only thing I can, "Thank you."

I don't wait for a reply as I know it's implied in her smile. I turn back and kick the bike to life, revving the motor to warm up the cold engine. Paige snuggles against my back, crossing her arms over my lap and resting her head between my shoulders. The comfort of her position makes me realize what she said. I'm not alone anymore and she will forever have my back.

I push us off and make a wide turn in the yard to head west, up the wagon trail to the main road. We pass the foundation remains of Paige's family home just before the turn and my mind starts to play out the events of the last twenty-four hours.

So much has happened since I stepped off the plane, about this time yesterday, with Sunshine. I had just been trying to make my way back into the court by coming here. Making up for my past mistakes by showing my loyalties to September. I had no idea what awaited me. The return of my mother, gaining a sister, finding a mate and inheriting a whole new life as my old one came back to me.

I used to wish for my old world, to be back in the heavens in my true form. The more I think about it though, the more I realize how empty it had been. These last few hours have shown me that. I only wished for what I had because it was all I knew. It was what I thought were my glory days, but now that I have found Paige, I'm seeing I haven't even begun to explore my best moments yet.

I want to have a million moments with Paige. I want to be a part of her family and have them all meet my family. I want to experience her love, her sexuality, her life, and watch it grow to new heights. I want it all and so much more, and it makes me want to fight for this day and a lifetime of more to come. Whatever waits for us at the bar, with Bear, or even with the court, whatever happens from this moment on, I will fight to stay here. Even if I have to give up my beast as punishment. I will endure that pain again for her.

As I pull us into the parking lot, I vow to make this work, no matter what.

CHAPTER 12

There are perks to living out in the middle of nowhere so close to your work. With no traffic, the ride is stress-free and we arrive at the hotel in minutes. A far cry from the usual downtown Toronto traffic I deal with to my office.

Paige directs me to park at the back of the building by a side door. I roll the bike to a stop, then drop my legs to balance us as I walk the bike backward onto a sidewalk. I kill the motor and we dismount. A process that only takes a few minutes, but it's enough time to realize how quiet it is. Considering the building had been shot up, I imagined there would be more of a buzz of activity. My beast shifts inside of me as an uneasy feeling settles in.

"Is it just me or does it seem calmer than as it should out here?" Paige mumbles low under her breath.

"I'm right there with you."

I head for the steel door marked as an emergency exit. Paige stops me by gripping my arm. "Wait, something seems off. There's no cop cars, no noisy neighbors, nothing…" She trails off as she walks off down the side of the building.

I have to stop her, tugging her shoulder to swing her around. "Let me have a look."

She steps aside, but not without some grumbling, "I'm a grown ass woman."

I love her independence and strength, but she's going to have to get used to the fact she isn't on her own anymore, and I'm not taking any chances with her sticking her neck out there. I go on ahead to the corner of the building, peeking out from the wall to get a look at the front of the bar. I immediately notice the line of bikes parked in a line down the sidewalk. I also notice obvious bullet holes pocking up the face of the building.

"It was hit alright, and it looks like the whole MC is inside surveying the damage." I turn back to tell her.

Her face crinkles up in anger. "For fuck sakes."

Taking her clenched fist for a comforting squeeze, I ask, "What do you want to do?"

She huffs out a breath and starts moving forward. "I'll go deal with this."

"And I'll come with you." I remind her I'm a part of her world, too, with a gentle tug on her arm.

Her head makes a slow turn towards me until she meets my stare, her anger fades into realization. "I do want you to."

I snort. "I hear the *but* in there, loud and clear."

"Yup." She bobs her head then gives me a wink. "But, I think you should go check on the Queen while I go see why the MC is on this, and not the cops. Besides, if we walk in there together we might as well be announcing ourselves to Bear. I know we talked about it, and I'm all for working something out, but I want to tackle one problem at a time."

I think this over, she makes a good point, but I'm still not convinced. "I'm not sending you in there alone. As Bean said, my scent is all over you. It won't take Bear long to figure it out, and I am not letting you be the sacrificial lamb."

"I can handle Bear," she snaps out.

I snap right back, "I'm sure you can, *leannàn*, but I am not giving you that option. Not now and not ever."

Her arms cross in front of her breasts for a defiant stance. "Well, aren't we bossy."

I mimic the pose and add a dominant glare at her. "When it comes to you, damn straight I am. You're mine, remember."

"It would seem you two are at an impasse," a deep voice announces behind us.

Paige jumps from the intrusion while I look up calmly, knowing by the signature of magic who is standing behind us.

"Laz," I greet the angel and see the rest of the court

walking up behind him.

"*Dearthàir*." His greeting me as his brother stops me.
Does he know who I am?

I have a second to think this through and realize, he's with my sister and it makes him my brother now. This is not about past history. Although, with Lazarus anything is possible.

Paige curtsies beside me, it startles me from my thought, as she gives her own greeting, "Good morning, my Queen."

Both September and Lilith push past Lazarus to attack Paige in a hug, taking her by surprise. Lilith's perky voice chiming, "Welcome to the family."

While September announces, "You're family now, Paige, you can just call me by my name."

I'm not sure who is more in shock, me or Paige. Although, between Lazarus and Lilith's gift of visions, I'm sure they have already seen our life map. Not that either one of them would be willing to share that information.

I bet they know my secret. They must know.

"How…" Paige stutters while inching her way over to me. Her eyes are wide and I detect a light scent of her fear.

Lilith giggles in a carefree manner, totally unaware of how overwhelming this can be to someone like Paige. "I saw a vision of you two, yesterday in the barn. I didn't know when you would actually unite, until now, seeing the magical bond around you. I'm so happy for you both."

There is a round of congratulations, handshakes, and pats on the back from everyone. Paige thanks the well-wishers with a masked face and pasted on smile. We haven't been together long for me to know all her tics and tricks. However, it is clear that underneath the rough edges of her exterior, Paige has no idea what just hit her.

I sympathize with my beauty, it can be a bit overwhelming to know others see your path before you live it. I wrap my arm around her and squeeze her in a side hug, happy to be the shield she seeks for comfort.

While I feel honored to be a guardian of sorts for Paige, my own mind races with a heavy dose of guilt. I'm being welcomed with open arms, yet, I haven't told them my secret. I'm deceiving them when they only wish to give me nothing but love. I can no longer hold my tongue. I care too much about every one of them. I have to come clean.

My legs just give and I drop to my knees in front of September, bowing at the waist until I'm almost touching her shoes with my nose. "My Queen, I can no longer lie to you."

"You are doing this now?" Paige squeaks out just before she kneels beside me.

She takes my hand in hers, holding it in a death grip while pressing her body into mine. I'm honored she would support me. Having her here is of great comfort and makes me want to do this even more. I must make it clear, she is not to be reprimanded for my indiscretions.

"What are you talking about, Zander? You haven't lied to me." September's kind voice almost breaks me.

"But I have, my Queen, and not just to you, but all the supernatural."

"What the hell are you talking about, Zee?" Gage growls out. I don't blame him for being angered by my confession, he has known me the longest and this will break our trusting bond.

"Please stand, Zander, you don't need to kneel." September is gentle with her instructions.

Sabre is a bit more practical when he whispers, "Darling, perhaps we should take this elsewhere." His firm grip takes my arm as he pulls me to my feet while speaking more to me, "This is not exactly a great place for a private conversation."

"I know," I tell them and meet every single one of them with my eyes. "I've just been holding this in for almost nine thousand years, and I'm tired of doing so. It's time for me to repent my sins."

Gage blows out a long whistle then crosses his arms over his wide chest. His pose is authoritative and demanding of answers. It is not unlike Sabre's, on the other side of his mate. If the men didn't look so different, one could mistake them for twin warriors protecting their beloved Queen.

Paige, on the other hand, gasps from hearing my age. Another wave of guilt hits for not telling her more when I had the chance. Somehow I know, though, that she will understand. So accepting, my beauty, and why I will forever love her.

Lilith, however, is on the same page as I am. "Let my brother speak, he's earned the right to do so. I'll take care of the privacy part."

She steps a few feet away from us, Lazarus joins her by moving a few feet in front of us, and together they get to work. I watch them look at each other, their eyes dancing glances back and forth. Lilith's head shakes then a blush crosses her cheeks, while Lazarus gives her a dirty grin. Something I'm not accustomed to seeing on the angel.

It's obvious they are having a conversation telepathically, and I don't need to hear it to know what it's about. I drop my eyes, feeling uncomfortable with my friend's affection for his mate, my sister. This new emotion is a brotherly instinct, I'm creeped out to know my sister does the nasty with my friend.

I clear my throat to clear this from my head, just as I sense Lilith tapping a line of energy. It's a strong pull from the Earth as she welds it around us, then shoots it at Lazarus. He weaves the energy up and over, connecting the circle to lock us inside it. When the energy is placed, Lilith adds some reinforcements to build an invisible soundproof wall around us. My beast stirs, recognizing her magic, for we are from a similar cord. Something I had not noticed, until now.

I'm pondering this when September comes to me with a smile. "Zander, if this is about you're past as a god, we already know. Brigid told me yesterday who you both are, were, I mean."

I nod my head, more to clear it than to agree, as I get back to our conversation. "Good, then I don't have to tell you that part. That's not the lie, Ruadan is who I once was. It's after my father had me killed and sent my soul to the Underworld that my mother knows nothing about. It is also where the lying began."

September frowns, her amber eyes glowing with concern. "Brigid said my mom brought you here and blessed you with a second life."

Again I nod, this time, to agree with her. "Yes, Livia got me out of the Underworld and gave me a new life with her creatures. Except, I have never been one of them. I am not from a supernatural species you know. I assume it is what you believe me to be and, until last night, it is what I believed myself to be."

"For Christ sakes, this shit is getting annoying. If you aren't like us, then what are you?" Gage demands, pulling September back from me.

I understand his concern and I get to the point. "In my god form, I am the *ollphèist comhlàn*."

September seeks out Sabre for clarification, "What is that?"

For her to ask the questions and not seem embarrassed for not knowing, shows a side to her I never saw with Livia. September's crown is a heavy burden for her to carry, and yet, she wears it as though it weighs nothing more than a feather. There is such strength in her, but she stays humble. She has the determination of a fighter, and the soul of a warrior. She is every bit her mother's daughter, but in my eyes, she is the better Queen.

Sabre opens his mouth to answer, except Paige sounds proud as she jumps in to do it for him, "He's a dragon shifter, my Queen."

"September, please." The Queen reminds my mate then turns to me and cocks her head. "I can't say I'm surprised.

You are the god of mystery, and it explains the fire you killed Cale with. I still don't see how this is a lie, though. We are all something different, some of what we are is thanks to my mom. Yours is just who you have always been."

"Yes, it is who I am, but you all believed in stories about your mother because of me." I wince even saying this for the first time.

Aside from Lilith and Lazarus, everyone wears a similar expression of confusion. I carry on to explain while my momentum is strong. "When I came out of the Underworld, Livia took me to her island, cared for me physically until I was healed. Mentally, however, I was fucked up. At the time, my head wasn't straight from what had happened to me, and Livia's kindness clouded my judgment. I thought we were in love, and I promised her I would do whatever I could to help her in the war. Later, I realized I mistook her affections and created something that wasn't real from it. It didn't matter, I remained by her side, as it was all I knew."

Paige shifts beside me and I can't look at her. I do take her hand for comfort. I'm just not sure if it is for her or me, at this point. In my head, I promise to apologize to her later for not telling her about my relationship with Livia. Knowing Paige, she'll want to punish me, and if I get through this, I'll gladly allow her to give me whatever form of pain she wishes to dish out.

September's eyes widen and her hand clamps over her mouth when she figures it out. Then she blurts the question I knew, from the moment I met her, she would. "You were her mate?"

I think on how to answer her without it being any more of a shock, but the truth is what I seek, for it will set me free. "Yes, I was the last mate she took. Which, in essence, makes me your step-father."

There's a commotion amongst the group, comments and curse words are thrown about. Most coming from one pissed off Alpha wolf. I take it in with wide open ears. I have been waiting my whole life to come clean, and the more I hear from them, the more I want to tell them.

I can't seem to stop myself. I don't wait for clear responses, I just keep bounding forward. "After Lazarus had disappeared and was presumed dead, and the fallen had been lost, Livia knew she would not win the war with the gods. We were out of time when she gathered David, myself, and Andras, the last of her mates still alive. Andras's ties to the Underworld prevented him from being a part of her final plan to use the magic from the elves, and transport herself into a future time. Once there, she stripped herself of her powers, cursing herself to live as a human. Until, of course, she could have a child and pass on her legacy."

"Why did she choose David over you?" Gage asks, holding September between him and Sabre for support.

I can tell by the firm grip she's holding them both with, this news is shocking to her. It's bad timing on my part, to tell her when she is with young, but she needs to know. They all need to know.

"David was her true mate, he'd been at her side long before they came to this realm. I also knew there was a chance the elven magic wouldn't be strong enough to transport the three of us. Had I gone, Livia wouldn't have made it. It was during the teleportation, when the whole elven race died, siphoned dry of their magic, like what happened to Sunshine yesterday. After that, I stuck with the plan Livia gave me, for the first few centuries anyway. I did stop believing, after a time, when she never came back. Then I met September in Toronto. I wanted to say something then, but there was a lot going on…" I trail off, exhausted by the heavy burden of the story, but finally relieved to get it out.

There is a long quiet pause as they digest. I watch September, her eyes mostly, for signs of anger and possibly her demon. Neither one seems to come forward. Her usual warm-colored skin, however, does appear a shade paler, and she doesn't seem to have anything to say as she studies my face with curiosity.

Sabre turns his head to Gage and they pass a glance. Some sort of direction or question is decided before Sabre takes over. "While this is new information, but we still don't see how any of it is deceitful. What aren't you saying?"

I take a breath and roll my shoulders. Holding September's eyes with my own, I tell her how I lied to her people. "Livia thought by spreading fear it would put the races into hiding. I volunteered to stay, to be the one to plant the seeds of fear. I came up with the story of an Overlord who wanted to destroy the races. I used Lazarus, not only because I assumed he was dead, but because he was known as the Punisher. Many elders of the races had known him and it made it easier to believe he was the one to deceive Livia. It worked. The supernatural went underground soon after, where they stayed, for the most part, until the curse was lifted."

Gage sneers at me, "You started all this?"

I bow my head with a simple, "Yes."

"What of the prophecies, did you make those up, too?" Sabre asks with disbelief.

"No, but I did help spread them. I wanted there to be hope for the future. A world without war, as Livia saw it. When I'd hear that one of the seers had predicted September's birth, I made sure the word got around during my travels. I embellished a few of the stories to make them sound more convincing, and it did the trick. The races believed, with great hope, there would one day be another Queen."

"And you kept this secret, this whole time? Why?" Sabre's astonishment is clear and written on his and Gage's face.

When I open my mouth to answer, September holds her hand up to stop me. "It's quite obvious, to me."

"It is?" Gage turns to flash September a glare of disbelief.

She smiles at Gage, cradling her baby bump with her hands, to rub her growing belly. "While Zander did lie to the people, he did it to protect us, and he did it on Livia's orders. Even when he thought the elven magic didn't work, he still followed those orders through. If any of Livia's plan got out, there's a good chance none of us would even be here. I might not be here, and my baby wouldn't be growing inside me now."

I frown with confusion. "But, my Queen, what I did…"

She cuts me off, "Zander, what you did saved our kind. I can't even imagine how difficult it must have been for you. To hold such a powerful secret. To live amongst us and never be able to tell anyone who or even what you really are. This is a brave sacrifice, and you are an honorable man."

She walks to me and wraps her arms around my neck for a warm hug. This isn't how I envisioned this going, and I have to make sure she understands.

"My Queen." I step back, bowing my head with respect. "I'm confused. Are you not mad that I didn't tell you? Even angered that I used Lazarus in my deceit?"

I hear Lazarus snort, but I pay him no attention. The bastard could have given me a heads up about this, I'm sure he knew. Instead, he made me sweat it out for the last few months, hell, the last few centuries.

The fucker.

September chuckles too, and I focus back on her. "Don't be ridiculous, I could never be mad at you for this."

Gage asks the same thing I'm wondering, "You're sure you aren't even a little miffed he didn't tell us, like maybe a few hundred years ago when I first met him?"

September clucks her tongue at her mate. "Don't you dare get pissy at him. I know you feel slighted by this since you have been friends for so long, but think of it another way. Zander keeping his promise to my mom shows us just how far he would go for her, that's commitment. His lies kept the races safe for centuries until I could be passed the legacy, which shows his allegiance to our Kingdom. By telling me today, I suspect he's expecting some form of penance, but I only see his loyalty to me. I have four men I trust with my life. Today, Zander proved to me I now have five."

"I'm not as convinced," Gage grumbles.

Sabre has been quiet this whole time, taking in the words of his mate and Gage. He's not easy to read as he watches and listens to what we say. I don't know what his reaction will be before he verbalizes his decision. I fear it, though. My short time with the court has shown me Sabre has September's ear. She will seek his counsel over the others, and she has been known to change her mind based on his advice.

He takes September's hand and kisses the back of it, then offers me his other for a shake. "I think you just cemented your position in the court, and I'm honored to have you aboard. A note of caution though, don't expect me to call you Dad."

Gage seconds this with his two cents, "Hell, fucking no, we are not calling him that."

While there are a few chuckles, it's Paige's snort that reminds me why we are out in the parking lot. Since I have the court's favor, maybe I can use it to our advantage while they are here.

"My Queen," I start, but September clucks her tongue.

"I told you, it's September. We are family now, a really mixed up family, but one none-the-less. Only speak of my title if we are in front of the people. It makes me uncomfortable when I know I'm so young compared to all of you. Even Chris is older, not by much, but still."

Gage clears his throat. "Baby, you're babbling."

September's hands go straight to her belly. "Gah, damn pregnancy brain. My apologies, Zander, what were you going to say?"

"No apologies necessary, my..." I stumble and start

again, "September, I should warn you, saying your name might take me a bit to get used to. Your mother was not as tolerant, even if we were alone."

She frowns and her eyes flash a little on the yellow side, it's her warning of caution. As she speaks, it becomes clear that the warning is more of a mood shift. "The more I learn about who she was, the more thankful I am for who she became as a human. It is why I will always hang on to my humanity, it helps me stay grounded. Some think it makes me weak because I allow the human emotions to come out. But, if I stifle that side of me, I fear my beasts would make me more of a tyrant than my mom ever was. If you think of it that way, it might ease your own fears about using my given name."

I understand her completely, having my own beast to contend with. "For a long time, I hated Livia for this second chance. I thought I was stripped of my beast forever. It forced me to be more human, to live with those emotions. Now that my beast has returned, I realize, like you, the humanity is what has kept me grounded enough to deal with the secret I vowed to keep. It has also made me think out my problems, rather than react to them. This is why I wish to ask you for a favor, rather than taking action on my own."

"Whoa, hold up," Gage breaks into the conversation and nudges September aside to get in my face. "You can't just start asking favors right after you offload this shit."

"I agree, my timing is bad," I tell him as humbly as possible. "I wouldn't be asking if this wasn't important."

"Gage," September cautions her mate with her tone. "Let Zander speak."

Gage's jaw clamps closed, and works back and forth as he grinds his teeth, hissing out defiantly, "Yes, my Queen." He steps back to stand at September's side, pinning me down with a dominant Alpha stare.

"Thank you." I bow my head again with respect, then stand to take Paige's hand. "My favor is requested as a friend, not as a member of the court. Although, it is pack related. It has to do with Bear's claim of ownership on Paige and her business."

Paige tugs her hand from mine to stand her ground, her hands on hips pose I know well. "No, we are not getting them involved."

"Paige." I try to reach for her, but she quickly avoids my advance. "I'm only asking them to help back us up."

"No," she verbally puts her foot down. "This is an arrangement between me and Bear, enforced by pack law. Even they can't change Bear's right of privilege as an Alpha."

"Wait," September butts in. "Am I hearing this right? The Alpha somehow owns you?"

"Yes," Paige and I both answer in an abrupt snap.

September ignores our bark to investigate. "How can he own you? This sounds so medieval like you are some type of slave. Which is just ridiculous considering Brigid told me you, Paige, are the proprietor of all this."

Paige shoots me her sink eye then turns to September with a sigh to explain. "My name might be on the deed, but Bear is the Alpha, and I am the oldest of his daughters. With no sons to pass on the pack, the law states that everything I own is his until he can secure a suitable successor. Once a deal is struck, the successor becomes Alpha, and in this case, the new Alpha will own all that I do, including me."

September turns her curious gaze towards Gage. "Don't you have to kill an Alpha to take over a pack, like you did with Leland?"

The harsh stare Gage has been nailing me with fades as he takes in his lover's question. When he answers her, his voice becomes understanding of her innocence to our world. "There are a few different ways for an Alpha to get his position. A challenge, like what I had with Leland, is just one way. An Alpha can also retire his position, by handing it over to his heir."

Paige blurts, "As long as that heir is male."

Gage twists his head like he's cracking his neck, a tic signifying annoyance over Paige's comment, which he ignores. "The reason the Alpha passes his pack to the first of his sons is to keep the bloodline pure, and our species strong."

September is listening intently to the information and asks the most obvious question for someone who doesn't know the laws. "And what if the Alpha doesn't have a son?"

"The Alpha has the right to claim his first daughter as the next in line. It gives him the right to secure a deal for the next pack leader by offering the daughter as a suitable mate. This is done so that the Alpha can avoid a challenge."

"So, you're telling me, Gage, as the True Alpha, if we have a daughter, you will sell her to ensure a strong bloodline? Even though our daughter will probably be stronger than any male out there, including you?" September growls the questions and adds, "Think really hard before you dare answer."

Gage purses his lips and glares at me again. His nostrils flare as he takes a calm breath to answer. "Of course not, I would never sell our daughter."

"How the hell can you allow Bear to sell Paige? This is the stupidest, barbaric bullshit I've ever heard. We don't sell our people."

Sabre moves beside the Queen, his hand going to her back where he rubs up and down her spine, he too speaks in an unexcitable tone. "Easy darling, these are not Gage's rules, and he can't change them."

"Then I will because I refuse to have my people bought and sold like livestock." The growl September lets loose has me stepping back and pulling Paige with me.

To Paige's credit, she stands her ground to touch the Queen's arm, saying words I know can't be easy for her. "You have no idea how much it means to me that you would try to update the laws. For years, I have hoped for that, but it isn't something you or the True Alpha can do. After our last Queen and True Alpha were thought to be dead, the wolves made it so our laws can only be amended if all the current Alphas agree to the changes."

September twirls back to face Paige, who jumps into me and I have to catch her before she falls. As I stand her up, she turns into my chest where I can see over her head, September's eyes have dipped into shades of red. I've seen this before, and I remember the outcome so vividly that I am backing away from the building, out towards the parking lot, to protect Paige.

Gage and Sabre cross in front of the Queen, blocking her from our path as they try their best to calm her with soft coos. After a lengthy whispered conversation, there's a few minutes of silence. Though the body language of the three tells me they are having an internal conversation. Looking over at Lazarus and Lilith holding the magic around us, I see they are having an equally intense conversation through their telepathic link, if their eye movements and facial expressions are any indication.

Then, out of nowhere, the Queen snarls out, "That's just fucked up."

Paige moves her head up so her lips are to my ear, to whisper, "I might have an attitude, but at least it doesn't come with a split personality."

I snort just as September blurts, "But, she's Zander's mate, won't that make him the successor?"

Paige seems to take pity on the inexperienced Queen, turning in my arms to face her, but not moving from my protection.

"That's not the plan Bear has for me. When my parents died, Bear started a pack so he could use the law for his own personal gain. When I became of age, he had the right to find me a mate. Except by then, I had built a profit machine for him to live off of. So, we came to an understanding. I make him money and he leaves me alone, as long as I don't show interest in any pack member. Having sex with Zander has voided the arrangement, and now he has the right to sell me to his friend, whether I have a mating mark or not."

September's eyes are more amber than red, and she seems to be more in control of her beast as she listens to Paige. Both Sabre and Gage have their beloved in a hug between them. I wonder if like me, the Queen finds her peace in them as I find mine in Paige. I seem to have more in common with our ruler than I thought. Maybe, one day, she and I can find some time to discuss our similarities. Right now, I just want to figure a way out of this current situation.

September comes to my aid, "To hell with protocol, this just became official court business. I might not be able to change the law myself, but I will stand with you both and do whatever I can to help you find a way around this. Chauvinistic, jack-ass Alpha, be damned."

Just hearing her support is a relief, like a heavy burden has been lifted off of me. I seek out a hug from Paige, who happens to be laughing at the Queen's comment. "She's got sulfuric acid in her attitude, I love it."

I roll my eyes. "I don't think you both together is such a good idea."

September laughs. "I don't know, Paige and I would make a great team."

I turn to look at September and see Gage rolling his eyes before he comments, "God help us all."

We take a minute to share in the tease, passing a few more comments back and forth that show just what normal folk the royals are. The energy wall around us shifts, then falls while we kibitz, bringing the sounds of the world back into focus. There's a car getting closer, the whirl of wind whipping past us. All signs of the reality we must face.

Lilith steps back to our grouping next to me, placing her hand on my arm to get my attention. "I have faith we will figure this out together. No matter what, I am here to help."

"I too, have your back, *dearthàir*." Lazarus claps me on

the back then adds, "What would you like us to do?"

Their kindness touches me. "Thank you," I choke out, for it is all I can say.

CHAPTER 13

It takes me a minute to clear my head, holding Paige in my arms for comfort, for strength. She seems to understand I need this connection because she wraps one arm around my waist, while her other hand slides under my jacket, and right over my shirt, to the scar on my chest. I've never felt more accepted and loved than I do in this moment.

Looking out at the people around me, I realize, we've been through a great deal together in a short time. I couldn't be prouder or more humbled to be a part of this court. To know they trust me and have my back, something I never thought I would ever have. And to include my mate as one of their own is not lost on me.

My emotions are heavy and all over the map. I chalk it up to sheer exhaustion from the events of the last day, but mentally kick myself to get back on track. I can sort my thoughts out later, Paige is what matters most right now.

I finally answer Lazarus with an explanation, "Paige wants to deal with the drive-by incident first. The pack is inside already. With the absence of human police, I'm guessing the MC has decided to deal with this themselves. Either way, Bear calls the shots and as soon as we step in there, he'll know we've been together."

"That makes this a bit of a sticky wicket," Lilith comments.

Paige stands tall, escaping my arms to face the group. "I'll go in first, to get a feel for the situation, before we make any announcements or decisions."

"We can't let you do that," Lazarus booms out.

Paige turns to the giant and looks him square in the face with zero fear in her beautiful eyes. Her hands find their way to that position on her hips as the confident attitude comes forth. "You damn well can, and you damn well better."

To the angel's credit, he doesn't even bat an eye, but his lip does twitch as he tries his best not to smirk at her ballsy comment. He does add his own statement to fuel her fire, "Still not happening."

Paige huffs at Lazarus then tells it like it is, "Look, as much as I appreciate the help, it's still my business. You all marching in there will be a huge red flag for Bear, and he'll react. I'll go in first and try to work it out. You can stay in the foyer and wait. If I need help, I'll call." She extends her hand to Lazarus and adds, "Deal?"

This time, Lazarus just snorts but shakes Paige's hand to seal her deal. "You, little miss attitude, are trouble and a perfect match for Zander."

He is so bang on, she is my everything, and she damn well knows it. She turns to me with her classic eye roll then gives me a grin. "Are we ready?"

Glances are exchanged amongst the royals with some internal conversation before Gage turns an assertive expression towards Paige. "I'm not comfortable with this flimsy plan. It's too risky to go in blind, and alone. However, Zee trusts you and I trust him, so I am willing to take a supportive role as your back up with one stipulation. If Bear makes even one derogatory comment or tries to attack you in any way, this becomes my show, and that is not negotiable. Are we clear?"

Paige blows out a frustrated breath. "Fine." She throws her hands in the air like she's surrendering to the heavens, her patience wearing thin. "Can we just get this over with?"

September links her arm with Paige's and starts to walk towards the side of the building. "I know this must be frustrating to accept help. I sense you are quite independent, but we're on your side. We only wish to keep you safe, please let us help you."

Paige gives in with a sigh. "I know you are, September, it just might take me some time to trust that you are here to help."

I join the ladies to take the lead in escorting them to the front of the bar. They continue to chat in low whispers as I round the corner, where a taxi is pulling away. The front door, missing of its glass window, is swinging closed. It's the only sign that there are others around us.

The rest of the landscape gives off a ghost town feel. Deserted, but for a few cars and the line of bikes. War-torn in appearance, with bullet holes marking up the building and glass shards sprinkled on the walkway.

My anxious energy awakens my beast and it stretches to life inside of me, making my skin prickle. Below the surface of the tissue, there is a ripple as the scales of armor lock into place. The churn of heat inside me billows up and radiates outward through my veins causing my brow to perspire. I seek out the weapon under my left arm. The cold steel in my hand feels like an old friend, my security blanket. I'm not expecting a fight, but I'm more than ready for one.

Coming up to the front door, I take the handle and then wait for the rest to come in behind me. Lazarus moves to my side, guarding my six as I swing the door wide and duck my head around the frame. The foyer is empty, but the act has my blood pumping. An adrenaline rush of excitement fills me as everyone steps over the glass to enter, moving as quiet as church mice to fill the circular room.

Paige steps away from our group to take the lead, moving towards the outer curve of the wall that will guide her inside the club. She stops just shy of the broken glass water fountain, cocking her head as though she is listening to something beyond the foyer. She turns to face us then motions with her hand for me to come forward.

When I approach her, she leans into my ear to speak so low that her voice is barely a puff of air. "Bear's in the bar with one of his girlfriends. I hear about five or six others."

Bobbing my head to let her know I heard, she starts to move away. I grab her arm to pull her back and she startles, turning a questioning eye to me. I press myself against her, brushing my lips at the soft flesh of her ear, causing her to shiver.

"Don't be a hero in there, we'll work this out. I just found you, and I'm not giving up without a fight."

Her lips spread wide and she bows her head to let me know she heard me. I say one last thing to sweeten the deal, *"Tá mé i ngrá leat."*

Her head jerks up at my statement of love and her grin is breathtaking. She adds a wink in return before shaking her head back. Her hair falls behind her shoulders, which she straightens as she takes a big breath. I watch her mask slip into place, and like a commanding warrior, she heads for the door.

Lazarus grips my shoulder with his massive mitt, holding me back as my body automatically tries to follow her.

"She'll be okay, she's tough," his voice rumbles inside my head

Some form of grunt escapes my mouth to agree, as I listen to her high heels tap with forced purpose across the tile, and then the wood floor of the bar. The sound becomes faint as chairs scrape on the hardwood, then Bear's voice cuts into the commotion.

"Well, look who rolled herself out of bed and decided to grace us with her presence."

"Papa," Paige greets her father-figure with an uninterested tone. "What is the MC doing here?"

I hear heavier footfall like Bear might be walking towards her. I brace myself, ready to bolt at a moment's notice. I'm struggling to hear through the blood pounding in my ears. Waiting with my breath held for any move from Bear that will jolt me forward to protect my girl.

"We are being responsible and taking care of what's ours, unlike you," Bear snarks out a reply that has me clenching my fists.

Paige spews back with enough venom to make me

proud. "Responsible my ass. It looks more like you're drinking the profits by helping yourselves to my liquor."

"We had to do something while we waited for you. Besides, what's mine is yours." He pauses then slyly adds, "Unless, the situation has changed. If that's the case, then none of this would matter because it would become all mine."

My heart leaps in my chest with fear. The bastard knows, and he's playing with her. Paige doesn't take the bait. "The least you could have done is patch the holes in the front of the building and fix the door. Has anyone even called the cops yet?"

Bear barks out a laugh. "Call the humans; that's funny, Pea. This isn't a human matter, this is a club matter. Roller saw the Warlocks pulling away after they sprayed the place with bullets. This is retaliation for their fucking warlock getting offed by the nomad. I knew this would happen. I warned the royals, but our Alpha seems to bow to his bitch like some pussy-whipped puppet. If brains were lard, he wouldn't have enough to grease a skillet."

Gage rumbles a low but deadly growl, and he moves towards the door. Sabre shoves me against Lazarus to get at the wolf, manhandling him with force to pin him against the side wall. September takes the opportunity to blow past the commotion with Sunshine hot on her heels.

They are both so fast I don't see them blur by. It's not until we hear September's voice that we know she's gone in without us.

"Do you have a problem with my rule, Bear?"

September's question has the rest of us shitting ourselves. There's a mad dash to the door as we crowd through to get in behind the unguarded Queen. The shuffle doesn't end until our group has a lined position with Gage and Sabre standing on either side of the Queen, Lazarus, and Lilith on Sabre's left, and me on Gage's right. The MC members lounging at the tables jump up in response and reach for their weapons. They make a line to mirror ours, standing with Bear. Paige is the odd one out, caught in the middle.

This showdown at the Elegantly Wasted Bar is like a scene out of the Wild West. Except on the one side, the pistols at high noon are Glocks at ten in the morning, with hands of magic at ten and two on the other. I reach for my Sig, lifting it from the holster to release the safety, but don't pull it all the way out. I wait at the ready, willing to pounce for my girl and get in whatever shot I can in the process. Whether it be a bullet or my power, it won't matter, either one will create damage.

"Well, now we have a party," Bear states. "I was wondering if you'd all show up so we could get down to business."

Gage marches forward, taking the ballsy approach to stand right in front of Bear. "The Queen is in your presence, show some fucking respect."

Bear eye fucks Gage in a battle of stares that is lost in seconds when Bear snarls in submission and drops down on a knee. The rest of the pack follow and collectively they hail, "My Queen."

Paige falls back, stepping to my side to mumble, "He knows, it's why he insulted Gage."

"I gathered," I agree, but hold my position, waiting to see how it will end.

"We already established that Zander killing Cale had nothing to do with you, your pack, or this gang." September walks over to the wolf, her voice is colder than ice and I'm willing to bet her eyes are slipping towards red. "Brigid already spoke with the coven about what took place, and vengeance was never brought up. Whatever happened here has nothing to do with Zander, Paige, or even my court, and I find your accusations disrespectful. I don't like to be called a liar, Bear."

Gage rips out a growl and Bear sags lower while

backpedaling, "I never called you a liar, my Queen. Roller, one of my pack members, saw the Warlocks pulling out of the parking lot after the attack."

"Who was here when this happened?" Sabre asks the group.

The wolves take turns looking at each other with questioning glances, as though they are hoping the others have answers. It makes me think that none of them had been here during the shooting.

"My daughter, Bean." Bear names his flesh and blood so fast it's like he's throwing her under the bus to save his own skin.

"Where is she?" Gage demands.

"I sent her up to the office to keep her safe." Bear's caring words don't match the harsh tone of his voice.

My suspicions of his lack of concern for his daughter are validated and my head jerks up to the dark window up above, where Paige's office overlooks the bar. I curse myself for not remembering it. It is the perfect position for an ambush.

"I'll go get her," Lazarus announces while walking off. Lilith falls right behind him, she's guarding her mate and protecting the Queen from whatever threat might come from that office.

The two go to the staircase, but only Lazarus heads up. The office door opens before he reaches the top and Bean comes rushing out. Lazarus waves her forward and lets her pass him on the narrow staircase, then watches her descend. Only once she is with Lilith does Lazarus continues to climb alone to the door, then disappears behind it.

Less than a minute later, he reappears with Mac Tire. The wolf walks out in front, he's slow and cautious as they make their way down to join Bean and my sister. Neither wolf tries to make eye contact in our direction, they are showing submissive postures as they take up positions beside Bear, kneeling to pay respect to September.

"My Queen," they both mumble.

September turns to the blond. "Are you Bean?"

The girl glances up briefly, to answer with a shaky voice, "Yes, my Queen."

"You were here when the bar got hit?" Sabre starts a line of questioning.

"Yes, me and another girl, who I sent home."

"Was there anyone else?"

"Not staff, but Reg and his buddy were at the bar drinking." She points out the two wolves in the back I had shared a drink with last night.

Sabre motions them forward. "Any of you see what happened?" He presses, as these two wolves slowly come over, standing with hesitation by a table.

It's clear they are nervous and uncertain of whether to remain standing or not. They also can't seem to find words as they both shake their heads, leaving Bean to explain, "We didn't see anything we just heard the gunfire. I ducked behind the bar and they jumped over to join me until it was stopped."

"Where was this other girl?"

"In the kitchen," Bean answers. "She was doing dishes and didn't hear the gunshots over the dishwasher."

Sabre nods in understanding, there are no windows in here and her explanations seem sound, but he continues, "Did you hear anything before it happened?"

The three witnesses shake their head, Sabre keeps going, "What about after?"

"I heard a car door slamming, then the spinning of gravel under tires, before a vehicle drove off?"

"Wait," Gage stops Sabre with his own question, "A vehicle, not a bike?"

"Uh-huh." Bean nods abruptly.

"Did you hear any bikes at all?"

The girl frowns in thought, her eyes flicker to her father then she bows her head to quietly answer, "No."

Gage turns to the rest of the MC. "Who's Roller?"

A gruff looking male, covered in dirty denim, stands at attention by the bar. "I...I am," he stutters.

"Did you see any bikes?" Gage pegs the guy with his bright blue eyes.

"No, sir. I saw a van." Roller meets Gage's eye with what I can see is the truth.

Gage grunts, "A van? Then how exactly did you know it was the Warlocks?"

"Uh, sometimes we move..." He trails off with a guilty expression to quickly think of better words. "When we trade goods with the Warlocks, they use a white van to do the pick-up. It looked like the one they use."

Gage rolls his eyes. "So, when you sell them illegal shit they show up in a van. Is it marked? Did you see faces? How do you know it was them and not someone else?"

The wolf looks perplexed. "I...I just assumed."

"You assumed," Gage snaps then huffs out a grunt in frustration.

He turns to Bear with a deadly glare. "And you called me the stupid one. At least I'm not willing to start a war over an assumption."

Bear sneers at Gage, "No, I suspect your balls are being held too tight to start anything."

"What the fuck did you just say?" Gage growls out.

Sabre grabs Gage's shoulder, holding him back from what we can feel is about to explode. The tension in the room spikes to an extreme level, the smell of male dominance is thick in the air. When I lick my lips, I can almost taste the fight that's brewing. My beast rolls inside of me, itching to be released and I inch forward to stand with Gage, prepared for the battle.

There's a silence that falls over us, the only noise is a buzz of electricity coming from the fluorescents overhead. No one moves and no one speaks as Bear gets to his feet, standing toe to toe with Gage. The two men shoot deadly glares at each other. Low, threatening snarls rumble deep in their throats as each male adjusts his posture into a fighting stance. Bear has not verbalized his challenge, but they are both acting as though it is implied.

Somewhere, in the far back of the bar, there's a creaking of metal like a door with rusting hinges being opened. The sound fills the silence and I tense. It's followed by footsteps, sharp and tapping on the wood floors. I recognize the clicking as high heels. There had been a female in the bathroom.

I mentally curse myself, yet again, for not thinking to clear the room, but who could predict there to be so many hiding spots in a bar. It's not like I can do anything about it now, except for maybe bracing for the worst.

Lazarus is still by the staircase and from the corner of my eye, I see his frame move off towards the incoming female. I don't dare take my eyes off the Alphas or the pack. If Bear chooses to challenge Gage, this is the best opportunity, and it could go south fast. Gage will need me to protect September from any advancing pack members.

My posture is rigid, but I'm ready to pounce like a cat to a mouse when I hear my sister gasp. Then she sharply breaks the mood of the room with an angered tone. "And what the devil do you think you're doing here? Haven't you caused enough trouble?"

My eyes are glued to Gage and I don't see anyone's reaction. A few feet shuffle like some might be turning to see what has Lilith so riled. There is no sound of attack and no scent of danger. I'm guessing whoever came out of the bathroom isn't a threat.

I'm about to relax when September growls with venom, "I knew I should have killed that bitch when I had the chance."

In response to September's reaction, Bear, not Gage, breaks the stare down by turning first towards the Queen, then to the back of the bar. His brow pops from shock so quick it gets my curiosity up and I move my head to see what's going on.

Down at the end of the bar, where the stage ends and the hall to the bathroom starts, my tiny and sweet little sister, has another female pinned to the ground. Lilith is on the girl's back with her arms secured around her neck in a headlock. I can't see the face of the girl, but her hair is a shade of red I would know anywhere. If this wasn't such a tense and fucked up situation, I'd laugh. My sister has some serious fighting skills and she's using them to kick the crap out of Gage's ex-wife, Cassandra Kline.

"Oh, shit," I curse just as a body knocks me sideways.

I catch myself and twist to react, just in time to see Gage and Sabre, tackling September in a collective bear hug to pull her towards the front entry. The Queen does not sound happy, she's snarling like a rabid dog. Just seeing them care for her has me swinging back in search of Paige.

My eyes seek her out, on her butt, and on the floor. Gage had knocked me in his attempt to get to his mate, Paige also got knocked down when Sabre ran to September. This is something my vixen doesn't take kindly to. If looks could kill, Paige's would be murdering our King from her dagger-filled glare.

"Get the fuck off of me." I hear Cassandra scream in the back corner.

Followed by my sister's response, "I'm saving your prissy ass, you idiot."

"Let me at her," September roars from inside the foyer. "I told her I would kill her if I ever saw her again."

"Jesus," I swear, moving to Paige to help her up.

"What the hell just happened?" Paige asks, taking my outstretched hand.

"History," I tell her while pulling her up. I don't know the whole story, but I do know Cassandra tried to blackmail Gage and end his relationship with September. Apparently, September has not let that go and is willing to wage war over it.

"That must be some history to inspire the Queen's inner serial killer, and your sister's martial arts moves."

I snort at Paige's comment but don't get to answer as Bear is suddenly at our side. "That didn't go how I planned, but it's a good enough distraction."

I turn to face the man with a glare. "Distraction from what?" I blurt.

His face curls into a malice-filled grin. "From me, thanking you for dumping a load in my daughter, and breaking the deal she and I have. I've waited a long time for her to give in, even paraded a harem of wolves in front of her as bait, and she ends up caving to a twinkle-dick nomad. I guess there's no accounting for bad taste."

I growl at his crudeness but he cuts me off, "Don't bother getting defensive and planning some takeover, you know the laws are in my favor. She's mine to do with as I wish, and you, nomad, can't even challenge me as Alpha because you aren't even a part of a pack."

"I'm part of the court," I blurt, thinking up a plan of attack in my head. As a member of the court, I am under the True Alpha's pack, and as such, I'm no longer a nomad. I could challenge him and end this here.

"Really? Show me his mark or the Queen's mark on your flesh and I'll reconsider the case," he says this with a smug tone.

My beast rolls with anger, knowing he has me there. I have no mark from any pack, from this Queen or the first. This is why I have kept my distance from the wolves. I have no ties to them because I am not one of them. The fact that he's mentioning this means he knows more than I suspect, and I wonder how he even got the information.

Bear lets out a satisfied laugh. "I thought not."

My body starts to shake and I coil my fists to prevent myself from hitting the smug bastard; he is still Paige's father. "What do you want, Bear?"

He straightens his shoulders and cocks his head. "From you, nothing. You are worthless to me. But Pea, now she has worth. From her, I will soon have an empire. Maybe, if I play my cards right, even a Kingdom."

Paige huffs and rolls her eyes.

"One of these days, Pea, you are going to roll those eyes of yours so far in the back of your head, they'll get stuck. You better cool that attitude of yours because I promise you, it will not go over well with your new mate. And I'm not talking about this mutt," he snaps at her.

"Fuck you, Bear," Paige coldly throws back, and the bastard whips a hard slap across her face.

My hand flies forward to grab the guy by the throat. I start choking him, cocking my other hand back to beat him senseless, when I'm hit by something solid from behind. There might be a lot going on in the bar, but Bear's goons haven't left his side. Two loyal wolves pull me off their Alpha and throw me to the floor with force. The bigger of the two lands on my chest, pushing the air from my lungs as he elbows me in the jaw.

Paige screams and tries to come to my rescue, but Mac Tìre is there to hold her back. She's kicking at him, using the spike of her heel to stab into his shins. The Viking rattles off a few colorful words in a combination of languages as he wrestles her into submission. Not an easy task.

Watching the distraction gets me a punch in the face. When I slug the ugly fucker on top of me back, his partner gives me a boot to the side. I roll, not from the pain, but to catch the first guy off guard by bucking him off me. A wolf on the other side kicks at my back.

This goes on for a few more blows until Bear calls out, "That's enough."

The wolves back off and Bear steps over my torso on his way to Paige. I roll to grab at him, only to get one last kick to the kidney.

"Give it up, nomad, you know you can't win this," Bear

says this like he's doing me a solid.

I roll back with a grunt from the kick, taking in what breath I can to spew my threat, "I swear I'll fucking end you."

"Ha!" The bastard laughs, stepping up to Paige to add, "Your toy has spunk, Pea, I'll give him that. But, I saw the Alpha kick the shit out of him, and his threat is as weak as he is. I do feel sorry for the mutt, though. I'm sure this wasn't what he thought would happen when he pumped his dick in you."

Paige spits in her dad's face, "Go to hell."

"I won't be the one going to hell, my dear daughter," he coldly replies while wiping her saliva from his face. "And to show you I'm not the heartless one, I'm giving you a day to say some touching goodbyes before the new Alpha arrives. Cassie has set it all up so I suggest you spend the time wisely. Get your affairs in order, Pea, and prepare to be the pack's new pull train mama."

I spring to an attack position, but the wolves anticipate my move and haul me back to start hitting me with brute punches. They might be holding me down, but they also fuel the fire burning within. I vow, whatever it takes, I will get Paige out of this and away from her father.

Paige screams, "Over my dead body." She wiggles against Mac Tìre, trying to break loose.

Bear cackles, "My dear sweet Pea, either way, you've lost."

He slowly turns to check the rest of the room before he slinks off, leaving his goons to beat my face in. I might not have attacked Bear, out of respect to Paige, but I'll be damned if I let these two pricks finish me off.

Their punches are hard, but not nearly as damaging as Gage's had been. I take the hits until Bear's steps fade, then I make my move. Bringing my knee up, I kick the wolf on top of me hard in the ass. It jerks him forward and I use the momentum to flip him over my head to land on his face behind me. The other wolf steps back with surprise, his hesitation gives me enough time to jump to my feet in front of him.

His head whips up, his eyes widen as I cock my fist and let him have it. I use some of my extra drake strength to land the strike square between his eyes. It makes a slight popping sound and a snap against my knuckles, telling me I broke the guy's nose. He howls and falls against a table, landing on the wood top with a thump. The table can't take his heavier weight and one of the legs snaps, causing the table and wolf to go skidding in two different directions when they hit the floor.

With this wolf down, I twist back to the first one. He's already on his feet and running for the door, the last of Bear's goons hot on his trail. A quick scan of the room shows the royals have disappeared, taking Cassandra with them and leaving just Paige and Mac Tìre with me.

I turn on my friend with a low warning growl, pulling on my powers to light flame to my hands as I curl them into fists and ready myself to take the Viking on. To my surprise, he lets go of Paige, taking a step back with his hands in the air.

"*Cairde èasca, ciallaíonn mé tú aon dochar.*"

"If you meant no harm and truly were my friend, why did you just side with Bear?" I snarl at him, pulling Paige to me and away from him.

"I had no choice, my brother, you know I can't go against me own Alpha," he says in a pleading tone. "We go way back, yeah. You know I be only protecting Pea."

Paige huffs then snaps back, "I don't need your protection, I never did."

I pull her closer to try to soothe her, but she turns on me too, pushing at my chest with her hands. "Don't," she warns.

I blink at her, trying to understand the cold shoulder. "*Leannàn,*" I begin to say, but she cuts me off.

"No more pretty words and no more bullshit. That's

what got me in this spot in the first place. I was so stupid, thinking we could be something, thinking you could really help me," she spits out then screams, throwing her hands in the air as if she's giving up.

"Paige, we can work this out," I try to tell her.

She comes at me with her talon extended, poking it right in my face. "No, you obviously can't because Bear just walked out that fucking door, and you did nothing to stop him or fix this situation," her angry tantrum rolls off her tongue. "I just lost everything because of you, and the Goddamn royals. Who, I might add, are nowhere to be found. They sure had our back on this one, the fucking liars."

"Aw, Pea, don't be blaming them now. Tis not their fault," Mac Tìre tries to calm her down. "And Zee took the blows for ye."

Paige whips her head to glare at the Viking, her eyes have darkened from her mood and stare right through Mac Tìre. Her voice drops a few degrees as she coldly purrs, "You're right, the fault is all mine. I let myself believe. I allowed myself to hope I could finally be free of this."

She turns back to me, there's a hate in her eyes I don't understand. "I thought my dreams came true and you would finally save me, but I've been a fool. You didn't even stand up to Bear, you just laid there like a wet noodle."

I growl with frustration and snap at her with disgust, "Would you have had me kill your father? Is that why you decided to mate with me? Could you have lived with that? I know I couldn't."

"No, it's as Bear said, you're worthless. Just go tuck your tail and run, it's what you do, right?"

Mac Tìre grabs Paige's arm with a jerk to make her face him. "Now, Pea, don't be saying things ye be regretting 'morrow."

"The only thing I'll ever regret was fucking him," she says this with so much loathing it gives me whiplash. I feel the proverbial backhand to the face, and the shockwave sting it leaves is a spike straight through my heart.

She wrenches her arm from Mac Tire's grip and backs away, heading toward the emergency side door. "Do what you want with the bar, fix it, burn it to the ground, I don't care. I'm done with trying to keep it all together for everyone."

When she reaches the door, she pushes the latch-bar with her backside. I watch her take one last sad glance at the room before she turns and walks out of the building into the bright morning light. There's no goodbye, no parting words, not even a final look back. She's just gone.

"Son of a bitch," I scream into the emptiness she left, smashing my fist into the closet table top. "Paige, get back here, Goddammit."

"Easy brother, don't be going off half-cocked and trashing th'ee place. Pea be a stubborn lass, yeah. A real hothead when shit don't go her way. Give her time to cool off and see the truth."

The whole scene is replaying in my head, over and over. My anger gets the best of me again, when thoughts of her using me cross my mind. The chair closest to me takes a flight across the room when I kick it.

"And what exactly is the truth?" I turn on the Viking.

He startles with a jolt of fear and backs up.

"You and I are about to go find out," Gage announces from the doorway.

I twist around, at the ready, to charge at my so-called friend. Mac Tire jumps in front of me to block my advance. "Calm down, ye feisty bugger. It not be his fault either, Bear's trying to feck ye, turn ye on each other to drop ye guard, and tis be working."

"Mac Tire is right, Zee. Bear's playing us, digging where he knows we're weak to get what he wants," Gage explains fast.

"I don't give a rat's ass what that fucking piss stain

wants," I growl with impatience.

"You should, it includes your mate."

Reality sets in and I freeze, thinking Bear might have grabbed her as she walked out the door. "Where is she?" I bark with panic.

"She's fine. She's with the others outside, Sabre will keep an eye on her," Gage says.

Mac Tire snorts, "He be needing more than the luck of the Irish for th'at, eh."

He is so right. Paige is wild and she won't be easy to contain, but Sabre has more patience than anyone I know. If anyone can calm her down, it would be him.

I sigh with relief, knowing she is with the court. No matter what just happened, I trust them to keep her safe until she comes to her senses.

"Thank you," I say with a respectful bow.

"No thanks necessary, I owe you this for not having your back earlier. I can see how you feel about the she-wolf and I want to help you fix this, but we have to figure out Bear's endgame to do it."

I nod in agreement with Gage while Mac Tire answers the Alpha, "Tis be simple. Bear wants what many of the Alpha do, your crown, and they all be chomping at the bit for it. He's not the only one moving an heir into power to prepare for the challenge, but not all the Alpha's want the position. Those that don't are taking advantage of the shuffle to build bigger territory."

Gage snorts with disgust. "And we just helped to put Bear at the top of the list, as the next successor, by being here."

"Aye," Mac Tire agrees.

"That sneaky son of a bitch," I hiss.

Again Mac Tire agrees with a nod. "This isn't on you, Zee. Ye just be in the wrong place at the wrong time, my man."

"Bear said we have a day before the new Alpha arrives,

and he prepares for what I assume will be him challenging you," I explain to Gage.

Gage scratches at the whiskers on his chin while he thinks this over, his eyes flicker from me to the Viking. "Can he be trusted?" He motions to Mac Tire with a head bob.

Mac Tire snarls at the accusation, "I just be telling ye the damn plan, how much loyalty do ye fecking want?"

"You said you couldn't help me earlier because you belong to Bear's pack. How do we know you won't switch sides again?" I demand of the man.

A sly grin spreads across his lips and it puts an odd spark in his eye. "No, mate, I said I couldn't go against me Alpha's wishes. My loyalties be with your lass and why I protected her. I don't wear Bear's mark and I'm not the only one."

"Ducky," I whisper, still unsure as to how they can be in this pack without pledging allegiance to Bear.

"Aye," Mac Tire agrees with a smugness.

"Bean said she couldn't find him, where is he?"

"Bear sent him to the city to collect the Alpha when he arrives."

Gage jumps in with a question, "You said we have today before Bear makes his move, and there's a handful on our side when he does, right?"

The Viking and I both nod, prompting Gage on. "Okay, then we go to the Warlock leader and get his help. If he's willing to join us in a fight with the pack and I take out Bear, the pack becomes a part of my territory and dissolves the claim on Paige."

Mac Tire glances at me with worry. I'm not sure what he's thinking, but I know what I am, and voice my concerns. "I can't let you do that, G. This isn't your fight and if you lose, I can't be responsible for your young growing up without a father, and potentially a mother. If Bear wins, I can't even imagine what he'd do to the Queen. I won't let you do this."

A laugh bursts out the Alpha's mouth. "Thanks for the

vote of confidence, Zee."

I wince and try to do some damage control, "I didn't mean you couldn't handle yourself…"

He raises his hand to stop me. "I know you didn't. You are looking out for my family and I appreciate it."

Shaking my head, I interrupt him, "This isn't your fight, though."

He smirks, "The hell it isn't. You do know what my position is, right?"

He waits for me to offer a shrug of acknowledgment before going on, "This isn't my first challenge, nor do I expect it to be my last. I have been underestimated my whole life, and as such, I have every arrogant asshole, like Bear, coming at me until I prove I'm worthy of the damn position. But none of them seem to remember, I used to hunt the rogue. In hindsight, I guess it was my training, and lucky for me, I don't have to track down the idiots anymore. They now come to me willingly."

Grunting, I get his points. Thanks to his father, Gage was never liked or respected in the wolf race, and becoming the True Alpha put a big shiny target on his head from those who don't believe he's deserving of his title. His history isn't unlike my own. This is why I always felt a kinship with the male, we had an unwritten understanding of each other.

"I want to go on record as not liking this plan," I begin to explain. "However, it's the only one we got, so let's go talk to Shax."

Gage's eyebrows pop up, adding to the quizzical expression on his face as he asks, "Shax? Isn't that a demon name?"

"Aye, tis his road name," Mac Tire answers with a laugh. "Though, he ain't nothing but a pussycat."

"I prefer to think of him as fair. I've never had a problem dealing with the guy," I agree.

"Sounds like he might just be the one we want on our side then. Let's go make this happen before the other Alpha gets here," Gage concludes as we start for the door.

As we walk, he changes the subject. "So, Mac Tire, who's this Alpha anyway? I should probably at least thank him, for being one of the only fuckers who doesn't want to kill me."

I chuckle along with Gage as we file out of the building into the bright sun and hot desert heat. Mac Tire doesn't join in our amusement, stopping just outside the door with a wince. Once he sees his hesitation, Gage turns to the wolf with a curious expression on his face.

"What?" He asks, cocking his head to the side.

The Viking clears his throat and shifts uncomfortably on his feet. "I thought ye knew," he says, sounding nervous.

I look at Gage, wondering where this could be going. He's got a frown, indicating he's wondering the same question. "If you mean I know which Alpha is coming in, the answer is no. I didn't even know the packs were shuffling members until you told me. Most of the Alpha's won't talk with me; I've been getting my brother to communicate with them."

Mac Tire winces again, bracing for the bad news he's about to give. "Aye, and tis perhaps why ye do not know. Just because they be blood doesn't mean they can be trusted, eh."

"What are you saying, wolf?" Gage demands in an authoritative tone.

"Ah, bollocks," Mac Tire curses. "Don't be shooting me for telling ye now, I be only th'ee messenger. Bear made this deal years ago, tis only been within the last few months he be looking to move the Alpha in."

Gage steps in front of Mac Tire, putting his face right in the Viking's to make his demand clear. "Who are you talking about? Which Goddamn Alpha is it?"

I watch Mac Tire swallow hard, then try to wet his obviously dry lips to say the name. After a short pause, he finally blurts, "Tis be Garo, your kin."

CHAPTER 14

"Are you shitting me?" I can't even believe what I hear.

I'm rooted to my spot on the dirt road in front of the bar, staring at Mac Tìre in shock. Garo, Gage's brother, is my competition. *Un-fucking-believable.*

Gage isn't as frozen in disbelief, he's more reactive as he goes to the wolf and pushes him up against the outside stucco bar wall.

"You're lying," he screams.

"Am naught, I swear it," Mac Tìre says calmly, but his face is twisted in anger. I know the wolf well enough to know he does not like to be called a liar, nor does he like to be pushed around. He's showing tolerance to Gage, proving his loyalty to us.

"G, Mac Tìre might be a lot of things, but he isn't a liar." My words are low but bold, warning him to back off.

He turns to me with rage on his face, this news is not sitting well with him. Then again, hearing your own brother is a sneaky fucker, taking advantage of your position for his own gain, never sits well with anyone. I feel bad for the guy, no one should be betrayed by their own family. But from where we're both from, that's par for the course.

Gage vibrates from his anger, his fists clench and his body tenses. I motion for Mac Tìre to walk away, to get out of range in case Gage decides to unleash. To the Viking's credit, he doesn't move. Instead, he claps a hand on Gage's shoulder and gives it a squeeze.

"I meant no disrespect, me brother," he says this with sincerity.

"Cock-fucking sucker," Gage screams up to the sky, I'm not sure if it is to the Gods or to just let off steam. "I'm sick of this shit."

"I'm starting to remember why I became a nomad," I

mumble.

Gage barks out a laugh. "Don't think you're getting away from the politics, just yet. Hell, you've only been in the court for a few days. Wait until it really gets interesting then come whining to me."

"If I was in the court officially, this whole situation would be playing out a whole lot different," I snap back.

He jerks his head up to offer his curious gaze. "What do you mean? You're a court member."

My patience is thin and I let Gage have it. "I've never been given the Queen's mark, G. In fact, I've never had a mark of any kind. If I did, I'd be the one challenging Bear, not you. And now, with Garo in the picture, I'm out of options."

He huffs then rubs his chin to scratch his five o'clock shadow with annoyance. After a minute, he comes to some decision. His hand goes into his pocket, where he digs out a key.

"I still owe you, Zee, that isn't changing. I'm a man of my word and the plan remains the same. We go to Shax for help, then wait for Bear to make his move," he reaffirms.

"What about Garo?" I ask, knowing he won't want to fight his brother.

He snorts, "I'll deal with him later, but it won't be an issue. Mac Tíre said he's just one of the Alpha's looking to profit from whatever coup the wolves are planning. He won't fight me, it's not his style."

He starts to walk off into the parking lot, to what I assume is the car that goes with the key in his hand. I grab his arm to stop him, and he turns with surprise as I stare him down.

"I won't let him take her, G. I won't let either of them take her- whether he's your brother or not, whether I have a damn mark or not. I'll break pack law, I don't care. Paige is mine, and I'm at my limit on patience trying to work this out the right way," I warn in a dead calm tone.

Gage's eyes flicker over to Mac Tìre, who's been standing off to the side listening quietly. He grins at the wolf and starts to chuckle. "I believe our boy here is in love, and by the inflection in his tone, I'd say it's pretty damn deep."

"Aye, the bugger's balls be already snipped." Mac Tìre claps me on the back as he laughs in my face, "Ye poor bastard."

"I'm not fucking joking here, I'm serious," I throw back a last ditch effort to make them understand.

Gage nudges me toward the lot where a few cars are parked. As we walk, he continues to razz me to change the serious mood. "We know, but we're going to have fun at your expense, anyway. You, Zander Paine, getting mated... It isn't something any of us saw coming. Especially to a she-wolf like your Paige. That girl has a hair trigger temper and one hell of an attitude. I wish you luck with that."

"Aye, you'd be best to start wearing the dress in yer relationship, mate. That one can't be tamed, and she's got bigger balls than the lot of us," Mac Tìre adds his own take just as we come up to a car I know well.

The sight of it has all other thoughts evaporating instantly. I walk over to the black Cobra, with two gold leaf stripes painted up the hood and down the trunk, and let out a whistle. "Is this the same '65 Shelby that was the only 427 to capture championship titles in both countries?"

"Nice change of subject, my man, but yeah, the one and the same," Gage answers with pride.

"Tis a two-seater, mate," Mac Tìre voices the obvious.

"Yup, it is, and one of you is going to have to two-wheel it to Shax." Gage laughs as he opens the door to climb behind the wheel.

I'm closer to the passenger side and rush to join him in the car. Hoping over the door frame into the seat, I leave the Viking standing at the trunk in dismay.

"Sorry, buddy, but I can't pass on this ride."

Mac Tìre grumbles a few hard, choice words under his

breath that I ignore. In a pout, he heads to the bar, where his bike is parked on the walkway out front. I want to feel bad for him for missing this prime opportunity to cruise in a classic, but then Gage brings the car to life, and I forget Mac Tire even exists.

"Oh, man, she's got a sweet purr to her," I praise, then add, "A V8, right?"

"Of course, and she hauls some serious ass with it, too. Hold on, we're about to take this bitch for a ride," he warns with good humor, putting the car into gear and letting her take off.

He punches the gas hard enough to spin the tires. The car twists into a fishtail, spreading gravel out behind us. It's part of the show, the rush Gage loves. This is the guy I know. The guy that used to get off on fast cars, parties till dawn, and equally fast women. He had a real zest back in the day, and I remind him of it. "Hey, you remember the first time you and I came to Vegas together?"

Gage carefully steers the car out of the parking lot, swerving around the craters and heaves of the road to avoid damage to the undercarriage of the Cobra. Once we are clear of the obstacles and on the less bumpy road leading us to the highway, he turns to me with a cocked brow to ask, "Wasn't that like sixty years ago?"

Nodding my head, I answer, "Has to be about that, yeah."

"Oh, man, that was back in the glory days of Vegas. We sure did have some fun," he says with a jovial chuckle then adds, "Hey, wasn't that the time you spent the weekend with the pinup model?"

I frown at the question, trying to remember. "Pinup model? No, buddy, I think you're thinking of yourself on that one."

He downshifts the car and rolls us to a halt at the intersection. We wait for a few cars to pass before he makes the left and guns it down the highway. This road is much smoother and he's able to open the engine right up, showing what this beauty can do. The landscape flashes by as grins of excitement spread across both of our faces.

"She's a beast," I call out to him over the wind.

"Yeah, and so was the pinup model," he chuckles out. "Come to think of it, her name was Page, too. You seem to have a theme, but it is Vegas."

The comment jars my memory until I remember flashes of the weekend he's referring to, with the famous brunette. "I forgot about her," I say with a grin.

"Well, you are old as fuck, maybe the dementia is starting to kick in," he ribs me then changes his direction of topic. "I didn't realize you had a taste for the fetish lifestyle."

I frown at the thought, at his reference to both women, having an interest for bondage and kink. "Huh, I guess I never realized it myself."

He nods. "I'd say it was a wolf thing, but as I understand it, you were never a wolf."

I turn to him with a smirk. "I see where this is going. You're still pissed I never told you."

He shrugs, gripping the wheel to take the curve on the road. "I wouldn't say I'm pissed, more like confused as to why you didn't feel you could trust me. Especially after you helped me cover up my father's death."

I shift uncomfortably in my seat. I knew sooner or later Gage would corner me with this, I didn't expect it to be today. "I do trust you, G, more than you know. You're family to me, I love you like a brother. You don't know how hard it was not telling you."

"If you had, it might have been different for me and September. We could have been more prepared for what she had to go through," he snaps out then sighs.

I get where he's coming from, September's transition into our world had not been easy, and because of it, she ended up bonding to four males to feed her powers. I suspect Gage wishes he was the only one she needed, but that's not how it works and I explain it to him.

"It wouldn't have mattered if I told you or not. September's path was already mapped out. She had to experience what she did to become who she is. It's the only way she can be the right heir to the throne. Besides, if I had told you, Livia's curse would have been broken, and September would not have even been born."

His face pales when he realizes what I'm telling him. He swallows hard and grits his teeth as emotion overcomes him. It renders him silent for a while. I give him the space he needs, turning in my seat to watch the brown desert landscape rush by. I'm not really taking in the sights, I'm lost in my own thoughts about life.

Had I told Gage my secret all those years ago, September wouldn't be the only one not here. Even though I volunteered to stay behind and protect the races, my own life was hanging in the balance of the same curse. It was Livia's fail-safe. If I said even one word, I would have gone back to the Underworld where she found me, as punishment for ruining her plans. The bitch had me by the balls, in so many ways.

It brings me to Gage's comment about my like of the fetish lifestyle. He's right, I have always had a taste for that world. It used to be so I could inflict pain on a sub, as a way to stay in control of my own chaos. Since I met Paige though, it's all changed. We laughed earlier about her being untamable, but that's exactly what I crave. She's my driven equal in every way. She's someone that needs the pain to control the chaos, almost as much as I do. I just didn't realize how much until now.

I got frustrated and angry with her outburst back in the bar. Thinking she had used me or even played me somehow, to get her out of this deal with Bear. What I didn't clue into is, she feels caged, at the end of her rope. She masks herself so damn well with attitude, I didn't see her fear. I didn't recognize the pandemonium the stress was causing inside of her. My poor beauty wasn't trying to push me away or hurt me. In her own complicated way, she was pleading for my help and I let her go, alone.

I'm about to curse myself out when I hear, "Thank you."

Turning to Gage, I'm surprised to see we are on the interchange from the one-sixty to the fifteen, heading north towards Las Vegas. It's a short jaunt to bring me back to reality before I point him east on the two-fifteen to take us into Henderson.

We're quiet as he navigates the traffic, waiting until we've made all the right turns before explaining his compliment. "As my much smarter mate pointed out earlier, which I was too pigheaded to realize until you just mentioned it just now, I thank you for keeping your vow. It couldn't have been easy for you, holding the secret in. Knowing our entire world's existence rested on your shoulders, and if you said one word, you could potentially destroy us. Even if you had no idea what the outcome would be or when. If it wasn't for you, September wouldn't be here. I'll never be able to thank you enough for keeping your mouth shut. It's because of you she's in my life, and there's nothing I wouldn't do, to keep her there. I suspect, though, you can relate."

I sigh out, "More than you know."

He chuckles loudly. "Oh, I think I know exactly where you're coming from. When you find the right one, you'll do whatever it takes to keep her. Hell, since I met September, I've done things I swore I never would. I'm the True Alpha, for fucks sakes. That's something, the guy from sixty years ago, would never have contemplated, and yet, here I am. Not to mention, I'm about to be a father. Me? So, yeah, I get it, and it's why I'm helping you."

After a speech like that, I say the only thing I can, "I appreciate it, but promise me you won't lose."

He snorts with confidence, "Please, have some faith." He's gearing down to make another turn just outside of

Henderson onto the five-fifteen towards Boulder City.

At mid-day, the traffic on this highway is thick. Most of the plates are from out-of-state, tourists heading off to Hoover Dam for an afternoon adventure. Gage weaves and bobs around the motorhomes and campers like a pro, while we hold a casual conversation. If he didn't have this new responsibility, I'd recommend he start a career as a race car driver. Although these days, I doubt he would be interested. He's finally content with his life. He's happy, and as he said, it's something the man I knew sixty years ago would never have thought possible.

About ten minutes outside of Boulder we turn north on an unmarked secondary road, running parallel to Lake Mead. We follow it a few miles to where it jaunts a bit west, into another quarry situated at the basin of the surrounding hills. It's a perfect location, providing significant protection for both the illegal aspect, and the supernatural element of the Warlock club.

Gage rolls the car to a stop in front of two hanger-style buildings, making way for a big rock truck barreling by. The driver swerves the truck to the right, just missing the front end of Gage's car. Gage leans on the horn and flips the driver off. I doubt the driver even notices us through the cloud of dust the big wheels kick up.

"Jesus," Gage coughs out, batting his hand at the air in front of his face to clear the dust.

"Maybe bringing the Shelby to a rock pit wasn't the best idea," I say, and regret the decision to speak immediately. Fine sand particles fly into my mouth, I wad it with some saliva and spit out over the door.

"You better not have hit the car," he grumbles while cranking the wheel to the right.

He's aiming us between the two hangars, away from the large machinery and the quarry part of the property. At the end of the buildings, where the dust is settled, the area opens up to a parking lot of mostly bikes in front of the clubhouse.

The saloon style building is straight out of the old western movies, complete with the veranda catwalk and dancing girls.

"Did we just go back in time through that dust storm?" Gage muses.

"Nah, it's just how Shax rolls. He's not your typical MC president, or coven leader for that matter," I fill him in.

Gage groans, but doesn't respond while pulling the car into a parking spot close to the saloon door. When he shuts the car down we hear loud voices, laughter, and music coming from inside the saloon.

"Looks like we made it just in time for happy hour," I muse then add, "Shax hasn't changed one bit."

We get out of the car and meet at the hood. Gage is in full guardian mode as he checks out our surroundings-- eyes shifting, nose twitching, ready to pounce at a moment's notice. Being that I've been here on several occasions, I'm well aware of the lookouts and verbally point out their stations. "They have one guard in the tower of the saloon, one on the roof of each building, and there are three bunkers up in the hills. Each bunker is armed with enough firepower to stop an army from getting in. Shax makes sure he's guarded better than the United States President."

"And yet, I detect no wards or magic of any kind," Gage throws out the statement as a curious question.

I lean against the car to sit on the hood while we have a casual conversation and wait for Mac Tire. "I told you, he's different."

He rotates to face me but doesn't look at me. He's still surveying the landscape to get a feel for what he's going into. "What's Shax into that he needs the kind of protection magic won't help him with?"

"Drugs, and some guns too, but Bear has most of that avenue covered. They both have substantial territories. Bear has most of the West, up to the Canadian border. Shax has the South down along the Gulf. Of course, the lines get blurred and deals get changed almost daily, so they fight over it, and not just with each other. It's why they use the firepower and not the magic."

He snorts with disgust, "Not real smart if you ask me."

I shrug. "It's their way of blending into this world, and to be honest, I fit in better here than with our own kind."

Gage pops his brows with surprise. "Why would you say that? We've always got along alright."

I give him a half smile. "Sure, but think about it for a minute, was I ever around on a full moon? I've never shifted. Hell, up until yesterday, I didn't even think I had powers. The guns are my protection, my powers when I need them. And this world is a lot easier to hide a secret in."

He rotates to take a seat next to me on the hood, clasping my shoulder as he sits. "I'm sorry, brother, for what you went through."

"Well, at least it's out and we can move on, if Mac Tìre ever gets here. Geez, did the guy switch his Harley for a Vespa?"

My dig at the wolf gets Gage laughing. It moves us away from my past and into the present. He's back on his feet and walking around the car, making it look like he's checking the paint for rock chips as he kneels down beside the passenger door. With the hangars in front of us and the hills behind, there are many places for someone to come running at us for an ambush, Gage is just keeping an eye out for one.

After a long look at his car door, or rather over the door to the hills, he stands to make his way back to me. "So, does this quarry act as a front?"

His jitters are making me just as agitated, but I don't move. I don't want to spook the Warlock guards watching and have them get on the defensive. I sit instead, keeping it calm and casual, like two old friends having a conversation while they wait for a third. It's not a lie, it is what we are doing and I keep to my end of the chinwag.

"Nah, it's just a convenient place for him to hide the

Warlock clubhouse because he owns the land and business. He also owns the quarry next to Paige's place too, it's how he keeps an eye on the pack."

"How do they filter all the cash? I can't imagine the quarry being able to launder it."

"Paige runs Bear's cash through her bar and brothel. It's how she was able to hold off this arrangement for so long. Bear needed her brains for business. Shax, on the other hand, is connected. When hotels and casinos started popping up on the Vegas Boulevard, he made friends and partnered with them. All his drug money goes through the casinos, and he keeps the hold by doing loan-shark work and providing a high-end escort service to the hotels. Prostitution isn't legal in Las Vegas, but escort services are because they don't promise sex."

With a snort, Gage adds, "That's a thin red line to travel."

I shrug. "Yeah, but it's worked for him for a long time."

"How do you fit into all of this?" He asks with interest, just as I hear the telling sound of a bike motor approaching.

Getting off the hood to turn in the direction we came and wait on the Viking, I begin to explain. "I met Shax just after I bought the old Thunderbird Hotel. At the time, he was moving guns for the mafia crime families and needed a way to get them in the country. He heard I had the hotel in Vancouver, and came up with the idea to move his shit from the port there, using my hotel connection and trucks. Back then, the border was easier to cross if you were transporting food or linens from one hotel to the other, and we took advantage of it. We made a shit load of green until the late seventies. Shax was so well connected by then he predicted the fall of the mafia and the overhaul of Sin City. He reinvented himself to fit with the new landscape. I took my money and ran back to Canada, building legitimately in Toronto, then branching out overseas."

While I tell my tale, Mac Tire comes into view between

the two buildings. I notice a white piece of cloth wrapped around his front handlebar, and he's driving the bike so slow, he's practically using his feet to push himself.

"What the hell is he doing?" Gage asks with impatience.

"Easy," I tell him, crossing my arms over my chest to inconspicuously reach for my gun. "His cut announces he's with the Wicked Ones on the Warlock territory. The white rag is his way of saying he's coming as a friend, not a rival, but it doesn't mean these guys won't try to take a shot at him."

I check the skyline, to the saloon watchtower, the buildings, and the hills. There's no movement as the Viking crawls his bike towards us.

"Why didn't you warn me I might need my own gun?" Gage grumbles as he too scans the horizon.

"You aren't wearing colors and I'm neutral, didn't think we'd need to worry about it," I say, then add, "Mac Tire's the one taking the risk here. He's showing loyalty to you, which is a big deal for him. Don't take that lightly."

Gage grunts, but he waits in silence until Mac Tire finally pulls up next to the car. He cuts the idling motor and kicks the stand down to dismount the bike with a comment, "That be an intense ride in, eh."

I greet the wolf with an arm handshake to show our allegiance to those watching. Gage steps up to do the same, adding, "I appreciate the effort, and trust you have our backs on this."

Mac Tire bows his head with a grin. "Aye, I do that."

"Okay, let's go meet this Shax." Gage starts for the swinging doors.

Mac Tire stops him with a question, "Ye know what ye be giving him as leverage to help, then?"

Gage stops, turning to frown at the wolf then looks to me for help. I nod my head in understanding, he has no idea how this works. "I told you who Shax is, his history here. He isn't just going to jump at a chance to help you out, he needs incentive."

"What kind of incentive?" Gage asks with hesitation.

"If Bear does challenge you and you win, his territory becomes your territory. Shax is going to want a piece of it as payment for helping you," I outline the bigger picture.

Gage snorts in understanding. "This got a lot more complicated."

"Exactly," I agree.

He makes some more grunting sounds as he thinks over what has to happen. "I know nothing about Bear's deals."

I grin and cock a thumb to Mac Tire. "You don't, but he does."

"Aye," Mac Tire says then adds a deal of his own, "And for a price, I can negotiate for ye."

The Alpha rolls his eyes and shakes his head. "I see your loyalty to me only extends as far as you getting something in return."

The Viking grins like a madman. "Bloody right."

Seeing that he's cornered, Gage sighs. "Fine, what do you want?"

Mac Tire takes up a thinking pose, stroking his reddish beard while staring Gage down. It's not a challenging exchange. It's more like he's weighing his options and determining what Gage is willing to give up to help the cause. He rolls his tongue over his lips to wet them before he grins.

"If ye take over the pack, ye take the club too. Except, as the True Alpha, ye can't be taken on the club's business. Ye also have more than yer fair share of territory to control, tis a lot more to handle. Ye'll be needing a good second, as well, someone to deal with the club, yeah."

"You want to be my second, here?" Gage asks with a smirk, seeing where Mac Tire is going with this.

The Viking shakes his head. "Nah, I ain't greedy. I'll watch over th'ee club, but only under Pea. Make her yer second and I'll go in there to make whatever deal ye need, to save Pea."

My mouth drops in surprise from his request of not asking for anything for himself. Instead, he selflessly asked to make history by giving Paige a spot as Gage's second of the Vegas pack, provided he wins the challenge from Bear. This would be a monumental change for the wolves, one that has been a long time coming. I'm just not sure Gage wants to be the one to start this movement, as it will probably bring more threats for him and the Queen. I can see an uprising coming from this, a civil war between the packs and the True Alpha.

Stepping back from the wolf to cross his arms over his massive chest, Gage gives him a long hard stare. I can see the flicker of thought behind his eyes as they move back and forth, up and down, thinking in every direction. His one eyebrow is cocked from this dare, his mouth is frozen in a smirk of defiance of the test. After a few minutes, he comes to some decision with a loud huff.

"Fine, consider it a done deal," he starts, and Mac Tire is right there with his hand extended forward to shake on the terms.

"Not so fast," Gage adds, "I will only give this position to Paige, with you taking control of the club, if, as King to the court, I have my own second-in-command. This decision will cause a revolt, and it's apparent I can no longer trust my blood to help me fight it. I need the right male for the job."

Mac Tire looks confused and I'm right there with him. "Ye want me to be yer second in the court?" There is disbelief in the Viking's question.

"Oh, hell, no, not you. The court has to maintain a clean reputation. I need someone with ties to the corporate world, not the crime world."

Mac Tire and I turn to present each other with the same befuddled expression. We're wondering where Gage is going with this, and who we have to find to fit the profile of this second he's wanting.

The Alpha laughs at us and shakes his head. "I can't believe I have to spell it out."

I pull a Paige, and it feels cathartic to put my hands on my hips to blast him with attitude, I'm starting to see why she does it. "Either spit out whatever the fuck you want to say, so we can figure out how to get you the perfect second or step aside, so we can go talk with Shax. My mate's future is hanging in the wind, and time is slightly critical."

"It's that spirit that is going to take you far." He stops to chuckle when my eyes practically bulge from my head with impatience. After a minute, he finally gives us his punchline, "I want you to sit on the court as my second, Zee."

"Me?" I spout in a surprised shout, from being hit out of left field with this.

Gage smiles at me and offers a shoulder clap. "Yes, why not? You have more connections than Garo ever did. Couple it with your usual calm nature, level head, and firm stance on important matters, I think you'll make a fine officer of the court. You've already proven to me you'd do anything for the Queen, and I want you to have the title for your efforts. And I can't think of a more trustworthy person to have at my back when the shit-storm hits. So, what do you say, want to shake up the Underground and make some history?"

Before I shake the guy's hand, I clarify my only purpose for being here as part of the deal. "This all hinges on Paige getting out of this deal clean, am I clear on that?"

"Crystal," he agrees.

I'm not satisfied with his answer and make one last attempt to warn him. "Once she's free, then the rest of the pieces will need to be put into place. Only then, will I take the seat. Until that point, we have a lot of obstacles to jump."

"Aye, we get it, ye love-struck bastard. Now can we get on with it then, time be ticking, yeah."

Gage chuckles at the Viking but it's me he extends his hand to. "Do we have a deal, Commander Zander?"

"Bollocks, makes ye sound like a big wanker that," Mac Tire says with a burst of laughter.

"That's your majesty, wanker, get it right," I tease the guy while stepping forward to clasp Gage's hand. "Let's go start a revolution, together."

CHAPTER 15

Stepping through the swinging wooden-slat gate, we seem to go back to the time when the saloon still sat in Rioville, before the town became submerged deep at the bottom of Lake Mead.

The old brick floors and large wooden beams survived the move from the old mining town, the few cracks adding to the charm of the place.

The antique player piano is new since the last time I visited. It sits alone in the corner but is full of musical life as it belts out an old rag-time tune for the Warlock members, sitting around the parlor drinking and gambling the day away. They are being entertained by period-clad scarlet ladies dancing about while seeing to the needs of the notorious biker gang.

It's more surreal every time I come. I'm not the only one watching this real-time flashback with bewilderment. Gage has one of those discombobulated expressions on his face, and it's so comical, I burst out laughing.

He swings his head at me to offer a frown of disappointment. Which I respond to with a sarcastic rib, "Festive, isn't it?"

He rolls his eyes, then leans in to whisper, "It's not quite the place I thought we'd find a revolutionary army in."

I shrug with a laugh. "I don't know, judging by the burlesque dresses alone, I'd say we're at least in the Civil War period."

Before Gage can get in his reply, the music stops and every head seems to oscillate in our direction. From a table in the far corner, cloaked in shadows, a strong male voice declares our arrival.

"An Alpha, a Viking, and a nomad enter the tavern." The male speaking takes a dramatic pause as though he's building to some sort of tension, you can feel it growing in the room.

He breaks the silence with an amused tone, "I feel like I should have a punchline for this odd combination of visitors, and yet, I am at a loss. Perhaps I should be asking why the True Alpha has decided to grace us with his presence? And why he thought he should bring the likes of a criminal and a scoundrel with him?"

The male takes this moment to leave the table in the shadows, walking out to officially greet us. He swaggers to the door with an air of confidence, as though he's daring us to make a wrong move. He shakes his long, dark, curly locks from his darker shaded face with a neck twist, stopping just a few feet in front of us. He plants his steel grey eyes on Gage, then down at me, studying our stance and postures, before finally extending his hand to me with a grin.

"Zander Paine, my old friend, it has been a long time. How the hell are you?" He asks with disbelief.

I clap the males rough hand for a shake. "Arro Gunn, it's been far too long, my brother."

"Indeed," he agrees and pulls me in for a hard hug. After a firm pat on the back we part, then he's back to business with a serious glance up at Gage. "I take it this isn't a social call?"

"Arro Gunn, this is the True Alpha and our King, Gage Blackwood," I begin the introduction. "Gage, this is the leader of the Las Vegas coven and Warlock MC, Shax."

Arro bows his head with respect. "Blessed be, my King. I am both humbled by your visit and curious. To what do I owe the pleasure of your company, today?"

With a smirk, Gage asks, "Do you have somewhere we could talk, privately?"

Arro frowns, but I can see he's indeed curious about our visit. "Yes, of course," he says to us, then he turns to the room to add, with a hand gesture towards the piano, "As you all were."

Someone gets the piano fired up again, filling the room with another zippy tune. A few of the scarlet ladies grab some of the bikers and begin to do an old cakewalk-style dance. Before our eyes, the bar is back in the swing of the nineteenth century.

"Delightful," Arro chimes at the floor show then gestures for us to follow him.

He takes us to the table in the shadows, but doesn't sit. Instead, he turns left to a red stained door and opens it, waving us through before closing it behind him. The music and party voices are still apparent, but muffled enough for him to give instruction. "Down at the end of this hall is the club's meeting room, we can talk there."

At the head of the line, Gage leads us to the room. As we file into the large space, I notice nothing special. The absence of windows and wood walls weathered to a dull gray make the room especially dark. Arro flicks on an overhead florescent with one dead bulb. It doesn't help matters any as what little light it does have flickers and spurts down on us.

He motions for us to take a seat at the large rectangular table in the middle of the room. Gage sits first, picking a leather office chair at the head of the black-stained flat top. I sit to his right, Mac Tíre to his left, leaving Shax standing at the door with hesitation. It would seem Gage has taken his seat, and he's unsure as to where he should plant his ass.

Arro shakes his head with a flicker of annoyance, his tight curls bouncing around his strong masculine face. He moves around the table to the far end of the room, stopping in front of a counter cluttered with cups and kitchen items. After a flurry of shifting shit on the counter, he bends to open a cupboard door to produce a kettle. Turning to a sink, he fills the electric appliance with water before plugging it in.

Once he's pulled four mugs out and is satisfied with his set up, he finally turns to us to ask, "Would you like some tea?"

Gage has been watching the male with amused interest

and cocks an eyebrow at the question. "Uh, sure," he answers with wonder in his tone.

Mac Tìre isn't as agreeable, "I'd rather a whiskey, mate."

Arro nods at the Viking. "I'm sure you would, Mac Tìre, but you know I don't discuss business with drink. It clouds judgment, and I have a feeling I'm going to need all my sensibilities for this conversation."

"Ye th'ee only bloody Scot I know who doesn't," the Viking grumbles about Arro's decision to have a dry conversation.

The warlock laughs off the dig. "You might be right, wolf, but from the darker shade of my skin, you have to know I'm not completely Scottish."

"Aye, pity that," Mac Tìre agrees with defeat. "Tea it is, then."

The kettle whistles and Arro quickly turns his attention on fixing our drinks, with the fussing movements of a domestic housewife. With his back turned, Gage shoots me a questioning, *what-the-fuck*, glance. I assume he's wondering if Arro is of sound mind, which I can't honestly answer. So, I offer him a shrug and a wink to really confuse him.

Arro deposits hot mugs of herbal tea in front of each of us. He plops down a tray of sweeteners and cream in the middle of the table before settling in a chair beside me. Picking up a cream packet, he squeezes the plastic to squirt the shot in his mug.

He doesn't stir it, he just picks it up and slurps a gulp with a lip-smacking, "Ah."

Once the first sip is tasted, Arro relaxes in his chair to finally address us. "If I may, my King, I'm curious as to this visit. I already spoke with Half-Pint early this morning about what happened yesterday. Cale's opinions and actions were his own, and I do not share a similar view. I have no quarrel with our Queen or with her court, and on this matter, I have no reason for a dispute with the Wicked Ones or Bear's pack."

"Half-Pint?" Gage questions.

Mac Tìre answers, "Aye, tis Brigid's road name, that."

"Ah," Gage says with a nod of understanding. "Yes, Brigid explained this to us. However, Bear seems to think you shot up his daughter's bar this morning, in retaliation for Zander's actions against Cale."

"Does he, now," Arro muses with a snicker. "I assure you, I would never attack Pea. She has had to overcome some shit odds to be where she is. I have nothing but the utmost respect for the she-wolf."

Gage grunts an acknowledgment, adding a pertinent question of Arro's slip of words. "So, you're saying you didn't attack the bar for this matter, or at all?"

Arro sits forward to place his arms on the table, leaning forward to meet Gage's hard gaze. "I'm saying, I didn't hit the bar this morning or ever, for any reason. I wouldn't. If I had an issue with Bear, either through the club or his pack, I wouldn't be taking it out on his daughter. If you want to hit Bear, you go after his cash flow. But, I'm not interested in gun running anymore, so I have no interest in him."

Gage isn't convinced of Arro's honesty and he keeps up the twenty questions game. "If you have no interest in him, why is he accusing you of the attack?"

Arro blurts his response with confidence, "I own Vegas and he doesn't."

Gage frowns as he tries to understand. I decide to help him get there. "The gun and drug business isn't as profitable as it once was. Not when every human MC has their fingers in the game, too. Arro's deals with the casinos and hotels make a huge profit, something Bear has had his eye on for a long time. By us showing up to deal with Cale, it created yet another opportunity for Bear to hopefully take a slice of the profit pie."

Gage makes a disgusted snort. "It's never enough for

him, is it? He wants his cake and the whole fucking bakery."

"Aye, Bear's a greedy bastard and he won't think twice about taking out whoever stands in his way, to get what he wants," Mac Tire announces while slapping the table top with his hand to make his point.

Arro, having heard enough to piece the puzzle together, starts to laugh. "I get what this is, Bear set me up. He threw me under the bus in an attempt to take me out so he can take over. Damn, I honestly never gave the guy that much credit, he's smarter than I thought."

"And quick on his feet," Gage interjects, then turns to me. "You've only been here a day. How did he not only come up with this plan, but execute it in such a short time?"

Leaning back into my chair, pausing to think, I realize Gage is right. In less than a day, Bear somehow used the court's presence as a way to hatch his scheme.

"How did he know the court would even be here?" I ask to no one in particular.

Gage and Mac Tire both answer in unison, "Garo."

I gasp when I get what they are both hinting at. "Do you think Garo and Cale worked with Bear to get us here?"

Gage clamps his jaw and grinds his teeth together as he growls low in his throat. Mac Tire inches his chair away from the Alpha, staying clear of whatever explosion might hit.

Arro has been watching us with his keen gray eyes, listening to the unveiling plot and finally asks, "So, why did you come to me? Where do I fit into this, aside from Bear trying to eliminate me? And for that heads up, I thank you."

Gage rolls his shoulders like he's working the stress of this situation out of his muscles. It can't be easy for the guy to hear his brother is a rat-faced-prick. If the hints of deceit are true, this just got a lot more complicated.

After gathering his thoughts and a few deep breaths, Gage directs response to the Warlock, getting down to the business at hand. "Initially, we came to ask for your assistance with a somewhat personal matter. After hearing more of the story, I now suspect Bear has bigger plans that directly involve you as well. I believe this just became an all hands on deck type of situation, and I'm no longer asking for your help, I'm demanding it."

The warlock chews on this for a minute. There is uncertainty in his eyes, questions seem to flicker in his facial twitches as he tries to understand. Arro doesn't know the whole story and in order for him to trust us and join our fight, he needs to hear the whole truth.

I blow out a breath and sit forward, feeling the weight of my past once again, as I start to unravel my tale to another friend. I trust Arro, always have, and he deserves to hear the words from me. It's time-consuming, recapping who I was, how I fell, and the secret I kept. I often wondered, when the truth finally came out, how I would have to deal with it. I never imagined it would be for love. I thought love would never happen for me. I am, after all, used goods. A damaged soul.

If it wasn't for Paige, I doubt I would be telling Arro my story now. But fate has a strange way of showing up when you least expect it, and if truth be told, if I had to do it over, I wouldn't hesitate. I know in my heart I would do anything for my Queen, for the court, my friends, but most importantly, for Paige. I have already lived through a personal hell, this is but one more obstacle I must jump to finally be free. Knowing she is my reward, my salvation, and my home, I'd die a thousand more deaths, and live through another lifetime of demon torture, for her.

I hold nothing back as I tell my tale. I share every secret from my past, my reason for loving Paige, our suspicions about Bear's challenge to Gage for the throne, and how Gage's brother Garo might have worked with Cale to put Bear in position to gain wealth from Gage's death. When I'm done, we sit for a long while in silence. They seem to be digesting what they have heard, while I feel relief from getting it out.

After what feels like hours, I start to fidget. My leg shakes with a stress spasm under the table. I itch and twitch as I wait. Fearing Arro will either not believe me or worse, reject me with disgust, has me on edge.

The warlock stretches back in his chair, placing his hands behind his head like he's about to take a bloody nap. A bubble of laughter starts to rumble up his throat before it comes bursting from his lips.

"Jesus Christ," he exclaims, shaking his head in disbelief. "After a hundred years of knowing you, thinking you were just an odd duck, I find out you're a god. And not just any god, shit no. You're the shape-shifting, all-powerful, god of mystery-- said to be able to turn invisible as well as into dragon form. I even heard you could perform miracles, like bringing people back from the dead."

He stops with a gasp, running his fingers through his long length of curls to pull his hair back from his face. "Seriously, this is fucked up," he blurts with astonishment. "I'm trying to wrap my head around it, but I keep coming up with why the hell didn't you tell me?"

"Join the club," Gage chimes in.

Arro grunts, adding, "Yes, I suppose you would feel the same, Alpha."

"I do," Gage answers with a nod before continuing, "And no matter the outcome, the Kingdom is still under threat. Bear is trying to claim the throne, and he won't be the last. As King, I must build an army to protect the Queen from these continued threats. I need to know you will support us and that we can count on you to join the fight when the time comes."

"Gee, no pressure," Arro sarcastically comments.

"Look, I know this is a lot to take in and a big ask on our part. But you know me, Arro, and you know I wouldn't be asking you to help us if this wasn't important," I beg my friend, hoping he will overlook the fact I kept this monumental secret from him, and still trust me.

He picks up his cup to take a big gulp of his tea, swishing it around in his mouth before swallowing the liquid. When he's done, he slaps the mug on the table with a hard thud, like he's using it as a gavel in a court, to announce he's made his decision.

"I'll be honest here, when you three showed up, this isn't what I thought we'd be talking about. I actually had no idea what you wanted from me, but asking me to be a part of this..." He trails off at a loss for words, shaking his head.

Mac Tìre jumps in with an angle of his own, "Tis be good business, Shax. Tis not all about the royals, it's about alliances over a commonality. Ye respect Pea, yeah?"

When the warlock nods at the wolf, Mac Tìre continues, "Ye know I vow my life for th'ee girl. I love her as me own sister. But it breaks me heart th'at Bear has this hold on her. The plan Zee and the Alpha have tis her only way out. If ye side with us, mate, I be making it well-worth the ride, for ye."

Arro's dark brows pop with interest. "I'm listening, what do you have in mind?"

Mac Tìre settles forward at the table with a smug look set on his face. "As I said, tis be good business. The Alpha assures me, he wants me to oversee the Wicked Ones when he wins th'ee challenge. As the President, I vow, we'll combine our business interests. Ye need Pea's brothel and I need the Vegas escort talent, together we create a legal empire."

"I'm intrigued, but will Pea go for it?" Arro sits forward on the edge of his seat, he's obviously enticed with this deal.

"Aye, tis an idea we've been kicking about. She already built additions to the brothel, to keep it separate. We'd be planning to do it ourselves but, if ye be willing to help the Alpha with the rest, I'd partner with ye myself."

"What are we talking? Movies, webcam, virtual, what?" Arro has excitement in his voice. Mac Tìre nailed this offer, but good.

"All of it, mate. I said it be an empire, and Pea don't half-ass shit."

Arro's steel gray eyes light up and a smile stretches across his lips. He's happy about this deal and I thank the heavens we decided to bring the Viking with us. "Alright, that's solid, but what part do I have to play to receive this generous cake?"

Gage takes the conversation from here, explaining to Arro our plan to wait for Bear to announce Garo as the new Alpha, and the challenge he will most certainly give to Gage. "When he throws it out, I want you and your people to be ready to defend the Queen and court, while I take Bear down."

"The plan is sound and you seem convinced Bear will challenge. I'm convinced he will, too. Bear won't pass on this, not when he sees the bright pot of gold as his endgame." Arro pauses, perusing the picture we painted. His cheek twitches as a satisfied smirk breaks his lips, an evil glint of excited anticipation sparkles in his eyes. "Count me in. I haven't been to a good dust-up in a long while, it could be fun."

I have been holding my breath during the negotiations, knowing we need Arro and his coven to make this work. As he accepts the deal, my whole body sags with relief as I extend my hand to the warlock.

"Thank you," I almost weep with joy.

His smirk spreads wider as he laughs, "Damn, Zee, that girl is deep in your veins. You got it bad."

I shift uncomfortably in my seat as Mac Tire adds, "Aye, she's got him by the short and curlies, but they'd be good together, yeah."

Arro stands to clap me on the back. "Agreed. A strong woman can stand up for herself and doesn't need anyone. A stronger woman, like Pea, stands up for everyone else and deserves an equal to stand with her. You, my friend, are the perfect male for that partnering. You're willing to go this far for her, and I have no doubt you'll obsess over her for the rest of your lives. I'm envious, to a point. When it comes to her temper, though, all I can say is, good luck."

The boys take another minute to share in the ribbing, throwing comments around about my manhood. I don't mind the jokes, they are true. Paige has me in every way imaginable. I know I'll never stop falling in love with her and I'll never stop trying to protect her. Which brings me to my next topic of conversation.

"All jokes aside, I have one more ask," I say with a serious tone.

The three offer up confused glances while Arro falls back into his chair, giving me his full attention.

"And that is?" He asks with speculation.

I meet Arro's eye to show my sincerity as I get right to it. "If this happens the way we plan, there's a good chance this will cause an uprising from some of the other Alphas. As Gage's commander, I am going to have my hands full trying to stay one step ahead of new attacks and threats to him and the Queen. It will leave Paige somewhat alone, and vulnerable to threats to her. Many Alpha's will consider her an easy Alpha to challenge. I know I can count on Mac Tire and Ducky to help her, but I need more of a guarantee that when I'm away…"

Arro cuts me off with a wave of his hand. "Say no more, my love-struck friend, I get what you're throwing around. Considering I too will need Pea for Mac Tire and my deal to work, she has just moved up to be my number one priority. I will personally make sure your mate doesn't even get a split end on that pretty brunette head of hers."

"Lord help us if she does. The bugger be a fecking dragon, mate. I'm not sure about you, but I don't want to be 'is supper."

Arro snorts at Mac Tire's honesty, "Perhaps I bit off more than I can chew on this deal of yours, wolf. You better get used to my gorgeous face because you will most certainly be seeing it around a lot. And on that note, unless you have anything else to add to this laundry list of expectations awaiting me, I suggest you allow me my leave to get my crew prepared for the upcoming showdown."

As Arro gets out of his chair, the rest of us follow his lead. Gage is the first to shake the warlock's hand and thank him for his cooperation, before heading out the door.

Mac Tire turns to follow the Alpha, but Arro calls after him in a serious and somewhat warning tone, "I'll be seeing you soon, wolf. We have much to discuss."

The Viking pops back in the door with a grin on his face. "Aye, but cheer up, fuckface, tis going to be good for us both, yeah."

Mac Tire roars with laughter as he walks down the hall, leaving me and Arro for a private moment. Once the wolf is gone, Arro groans, "He is going to make me regret this, I just know it."

"Mac Tire is just busting your balls, he really is a good guy," I reassure him. "And for what it's worth, I appreciate what you are doing for us, for me."

"Damn right, you appreciate me," he says with a laugh before getting more serious. "But straight up, Zee, I would have done it without the deal. I owe you that much. All the races owe you for the sacrifice you made for our kind. If it wasn't for what you did, none of us would be where we are today, and I am truly grateful."

He comes at me with an extended hand and when we grip elbows, he pulls me into a one arm hug. "And all kidding aside, I'm happy you and Pea found each other. I agree with Mac Tire, you two are made for one another, and I wish you all the best."

I slap the guy on the back before pulling away. "Just keep an eye on her for me, okay?"

He grins. "It will be an honor to watch over your girl for you. Even though she isn't going to like it, and I'll probably get a ton of flack."

I snort, then frown, feeling it deepen across my brow as I think about how my last conversation had gone with Paige. I don't even know if she's still interested in us. This whole plan, and the deal Arro and Mac Tire made, might have just turned into time wasted.

And as my mind shifts into what my life would be like without Paige in it, my heart starts to race and I know I have to get back to her ranch. I have to see her, to work this out, beg, and plead. Hopefully, after a bout of punishment, she'll forgive me for not doing more earlier. And I hope she can see this new plan as a solution for our future.

Arro, having seen the change of expression on my face, begins to question me, "Everything okay? You aren't thinking of backing out, are you?"

I shake my head. "No, not at all. I'm ready to do this. I have to square up with Paige first is all. I tried to protect her earlier, but I went about it all wrong, and things got left a little rough."

"Ah, I see," Arro comments with a grin. "A word to the wise, when it comes to that she-wolf, learn how to beg for forgiveness, and allow her to take it out on your hide."

He says this like he knows more than he's saying and I'm suddenly wrapped with jealousy. "Is this experience talking?" I ask with a low growl.

The fucker laughs. "Down boy, it was a long time ago. We only played to scratch each other's fancy, we knew it would never amount to anything."

I throw him the old stink eye of doubt, with a smirk of insecurity, too. There is no doubt Shax is a catch, with good-looks, charm, and ambition, it's easy to see how Paige could be attracted to him. Except when I really think on it, knowing them both, Shax more than Paige, he's right, they are just way too different to be together. *Thank the Goddess.*

It does strike me as interesting that my little she-wolf and I have run in similar circles all these years, and yet have never met before now. It would seem fate made sure to guide those I trust the most, to protect her, until our paths were destined to cross and we could finally be together.

As I contemplate my thoughts, Arro comes at me with another clap on the shoulder and a warm smile of reassurance, pushing me towards the door. "No worries, my friend, Sweet Pea is all yours. Now go be with her, and work out whatever differences you have. Tomorrow is a big day, alliances will be built, enemies will be gained, and I must find my duster jacket and six-shooter to join the fight. I can't attend a showdown this big without the proper attire."

Picturing Shax in an old style duster, boots, and hat, with a stalk of wheat between his teeth, brings back memories of our adventures from the old frontier days. It's enough to change my sullen mood and has me laughing in no time.

"And you said you thought I was the odd duck," I remind him.

"It takes one to know one…" He trails off to curl his arms up and starts to flap them up and down like a bird in flight. "Quack, quack."

We both bust out a laugh, tensions break and our friendship rekindles as we head towards the bar. Whatever happens tomorrow, I know Arro will have my back and I his, just like old times. If we can survive the birth of our individual nations, we can certainly survive whatever awaits us with Bear.

CHAPTER 16

"Zander, over here," a sing-song greeting from my sister knocks me out of my preoccupied fog as I enter Elegantly Wasted.

The bar is hopping tonight, packed with a mix of patrons of every race, from biker to tourist, and everything in between. Including the royals, set up in the center of the room at a large round table overflowing with food plates and drinks. They seem misplaced, like they took a wrong turn and got lost on their way to the supermodel convention. I notice many at the surrounding tables even appear star-struck, enamored by the beauty of the Queen and High Priestess as well as their combination of mates. It does wonders for my ego as I'm called over to join them.

"Dearest brother, where have you been?" Lilith asks as she jumps from her stool to embrace me in a loving hug.

Since returning from our meeting with Shax and dropping Gage off, I have been searching for Paige. Either she does not want to be found or I have lost my abilities to track, because I came up empty-handed. As a last ditch effort, I'm trying the bar one last time, in hopes she just gave me the slip. A quick scan of the room tells me she is not here either, and this does not make me happy.

Lilith ends our embrace and I take an offered stool between her and my mother, making pleasant greetings as I get comfortable.

"So, what have you been doing?" Lilith asks once again, this time I detect an urgency in her tone. One full of hope, and I suspect she knows of my search, but I fill her in any way.

"Looking for Paige, have any of you seen her?"

Several heads shake with a few verbal no's, then Sabre's final answer, "Not since this afternoon, after you and Gage left."

My forehead works itself into a worry of creases and I fidget with anxiety in my chair. My mother pats my hand while Sunshine offers support, "Don't worry, she just needs some time to process. I have no doubt you will be seeing her soon."

Lazarus picks up an empty glass from the table, along with a bottle of bourbon, to pour a few fingers of the drink before sliding it my way.

"Here, this will help," he says with a knowing grin.

I nod my thanks and pick up the drink, sucking it back and draining the glass dry, like it's nothing more than water. I cough on the burn, which does take my mind off of Paige's absence. It's only for a second, of course, because I can't seem to get her out of my head. There isn't enough booze in this world to make me forget about the women I love.

I clear my throat and decide to make an attempt at being social. "What have you all been doing?"

"Why, isn't it obvious?" September asks with a laugh. "We are taking advantage of this time away from our responsibilities, and your mate's wonderful hospitality. I for one am enjoying a night out like a regular person and to tell you the truth, I could get accustomed to being an average Joe."

"Isn't that the truth," Sunshine chimes in. "Although, I'm having a hard time with everyone staring. I mean, it's like they've never seen a couple of goddesses before. Sheesh."

There is a chorus of laughs shared around the table as they make fun of what I noticed earlier, only from their perspective. The grass isn't green on either side, no matter what the circumstances.

Samuel suddenly clears his throat to excuse himself. It's the first time I've seen him since the barn chaos. I notice he still has dark bruises on his face and bright red marks on his neck, from Cale slashing him open and Paige biting him. The healing process will be human slow for him until he has his first change into wolf, but for someone that just came back from the dead he seems full of energy when he stands from his seat, then leaning down to give Lilith a kiss. It's not a quick peck on the cheek, but a full-on mouth fuck that only two lovers, quite intimate with each other, can give. I find myself staring with envy and wishing for my own lover, wondering where the hell she could be. The clock is ticking and I want to spend the rest of the night making up from our fight, but for some reason, Paige is being stubborn and staying away.

All afternoon my mind has been going to that dark place, reliving her telling me I was a mistake. My heart lurches, even now, thinking about it. I feel a hollow hole deep within my chest, and it aches with each minute she is absent from my life. As the thoughts swirl, my anxiety peaks. Questions begin to form, like what if Bear has already taken her to Garo tonight, sealing the deal before we even have a chance to put our plan in place.

Before I let the panic from that idea sink in, I work it over. This can't be the case since Ducky has yet to return from Vegas with the traitor brother. It does little to calm me, as there is always the thought of Paige at her brothel with some random stranger, working through her own chaos at the business end of a whip.

Fuck, she's making me an emotional mess.

Picking up the bottle half filled with bourbon, I debate between refilling my glass or taking the drink straight from the source. It isn't even a fair fight, the bottle wins hands down. I wrap my lips around the opening and guzzle until I can no longer feel my throat from the burn. Only once I have drained the bottle dry, and I'm coughing up a lung, do I notice the stares of sympathy and understanding.

Samuel finishes hugging my sister and begins to leave the table. He stops behind me, placing a hand on my shoulder to lean in. "I've been in your shoes, my man, and all I can say is, hang in there. She'll come around, I have faith, and it's so worth it in the end," he whispers this bit of encouragement in my ear.

I place the empty bottle on the table and offer the newly turning wolf a nod of thanks. He would understand, after what he went through to be with my sister. It gives me hope, although that could just be the booze talking.

Sam walks off, heading for the backstage and the band setting up to play. I follow his exit, and notice Mac Tire on the stage, shamelessly chatting up two stunning women. They both have guitars slung over their shoulders, an indication they are the band, but that ends the similarity between the two.

One appears to fit in with the rugged biker crowd, draped in leather and tattoos, reminding me of Paige. The other female, however, has this freakish doll look to her. It must be a rock and roll thing.

Her bright pink hair, done up in curls, matches the color of the tattered tutu and ripped corset she has on, and her makeup is done so well, she actually resembles a doll. Mac Tire must be into that kind of thing because he's all smiles, something the Viking only does when he's chopping up body parts or being a smartass.

Whatever floats his perverted boat.

Sam hops on his riser and parks his ass behind his drum kit. He gives the kick drum labeled with the words *Avenging Angels* a test beat before picking up a set of sticks and running through a pattern of notes for the sound check. The crowd instantly applauds and delivers loud screams of excitement as the band prepares to start their set.

"Chris said these girls are incredible live," September speaks out over the cheers.

"Oh, they are. We heard them at setup earlier, so good!" Lilith yells back with a big grin.

"Not that you're biased or anything," Sabre teases her with a wink.

Lilith laughs and keeps the tease going, "Well, maybe a tiny bit, but only because the drummer is fantastic."

"Did Sam know the girls were of magic, before?" Gage asks of the two females Mac Tìre had been chatting up, and whether Sam was aware of their race before his introduction to our wild kingdom.

I turn back to the stage to appreciate the view of hot females again. There isn't an obvious magical signature around them, but I do detect something familiar. It's hard to say what it is exactly, and I study them while listening to Lilith's answer.

"No, he only just sensed it. I think he was surprised he didn't know they were one of us since he's been friends with them a long time."

"To be fair, they do mask themselves well," Brigid adds. "I didn't detect their gift the first time I met them, and that says a lot."

It's true, being an ex-goddess herself, my mother would have known of the girls' magical gift. I'm intrigued to know how they manage to hide it and why. Not nearly as much as I'm interested to know how the great Goddess Brigid became a simple witch in this realm, present day. There are still many questions on the table, and no answers, at least not to me. Although, I have been somewhat preoccupied.

"This might be promising for him. I mean if they can keep themselves shielded enough to not be found out, then maybe Sam, and even Chris, can too." September's comment has me swinging back to the table and the conversation.

"Is Sam thinking of quitting the music scene?" I ask with curiosity, sensing where this is going.

Lilith shrugs then frowns with worry. "We all know he can't remain in the public eye forever. In ten or fifteen years, his fans will start to notice he's not aging."

I nod with understanding. "I thought Defeat the Darkness had a new album coming out, though. Are they putting a stop to that?"

"No, not stopping it," September begins in a lower sad voice, "But, they are wondering if it should be the last one they make. It's not an easy decision, it is what they love to do."

Sabre takes September's hand and kisses the back of it. "It isn't something we need to decide right away, they still have time."

I sense this is a hard topic of conversation for the group. Chris and Sam's fame can't remain public for long, and not just because they won't age. The Queen's wedding to her four mates isn't something easily explained in the human world and will be difficult to keep a secret from the paparazzi that seem to follow Defeat the Darkness everywhere they go. I'm surprised the gossip hounds haven't shown up here in Nevada with Sam, but the night is still young.

I feel for September and try to offer her hope. "Living amongst the humans can present challenges, but it isn't impossible. Hell, I've managed to reinvent myself more times than I can count. Sometimes I had to go underground to disappear for a while or overseas to start fresh. The possibilities for our kind, however, are endless. It's not like they can't form another band in a hundred years or reinvent the way they do their music."

"Dear Goddess," Lilith gasps, leaning to speak in a lower tone. "I never even considered how often you would have done that or how many times you would've had to fake your death, even. Not to mention the people you would have watched die as you went on. It's heartbreaking, to know you did this alone. It won't be the same for Sam and Chris because they have us, but you had no one..."

She trails off and puts her hand to her trembling lips while unshed tears form in her emerald eyes. I can't help smiling with affection. My sister is so empathetic, so loving, and I'm so grateful to have her in my life, now.

Cutting into this touching moment, Lazarus groans and

rolls his eyes at me. "He wasn't as alone as you think, I know because I was here with him."

"Sure, a few thousand years after you left your precious island," I reply with sarcasm.

"True, but it wasn't as though you suffered in isolation, unlike some of us. You were down here finding adventures of your own making, like that time in Spain. I distinctly remember you getting caught with a priest's daughter. Then that time in Africa, when you were on the run after an indiscretion with a tribesman's wife. Both times, I had to bail your ass out." He stops to laugh, then quickly adds, "Don't worry, my little dove, your brother never had to worry much about being alone."

Gage barks out a laugh with the angel, then adds his own commentary, "Apparently, you haven't changed over the centuries. What Laz is describing, is exactly how I remember our misadventures together. And here we are today, planning yet another."

"It might be true of Ruadan in the past, but you have to admit this person before us, the Zander of today, is quite different. There is a sense of purpose, a glow of renewed light I've never seen in him before. I believe this will be the last of the adventures, for love has seized its hold on him." A mother always knows best and Brigid just summed it up in a nutshell.

Judging by Gage's snort and Lazarus's chuckle, though, I sense they still have doubts about my feelings for Paige. After all, I have been with more women than I could even count, never mind remember.

"Brigid is right, I am different. Only because Paige is different," I tell them, then try to explain. "You know the feeling you get when you meet someone for the first time and your heart just stops for a beat?" I ask as a way to make my point.

Gage barks out another laugh with his comment, "Yeah, humans call that arrhythmia, and apparently, they die from it."

The males crack up, the females aren't as amused. Especially September, who elbows Gage in the ribs.

"I'd say go to hell, but I wouldn't want to end up with you there, you fucker." I take his joke in stride, with my own human dig of sarcasm in return.

"Gage," September snaps in warning. "You of all people should understand what Zander is going through. Allow him to explain."

Gage frowns in thought for a second then picks up his mate's hand to link his fingers with hers. "As always, Baby, you are right, and I apologize. Zee, you have just as much right to happiness as any of us. Please, continue with what you were saying."

I could make a comment about which one of us is the most pussy whipped, but I refrain. I'll save the jab for another time. Instead, I clear my throat to start again.

"I was trying to put into words how Paige is nothing like the other females I've been with. If you ask me how many times she entered my mind today, I'll tell you once because she has never left my thoughts. Not from the moment I met her. I'm consumed with my obsession for her. We have this unbelievable connection that is beyond anything I've ever felt before, and from our union, she has made me whole again. So, go ahead, tease me about my past, it means nothing. In my mind, Paige is the only adventure now and forever."

Lilith sighs a sob while fanning her face as women do, in an attempt to hold back tears. Brigid places her hand on my forearm to give it a comforting squeeze while September is more forward, speaking from the heart like only she can.

"I understand exactly what you mean, Zander," she starts. "People come and go from our lives all the time. Some are habitual, boring, and even bad for us like a cigarette break. While others are wild, spontaneous, and make us feel alive like a raging forest fire. From what I see, you and Paige love hard because you know what it's like to be loved so little. It's part of what shaped you into the wildest of these fires, as two lost souls burning out of control as single beings, waiting for that transcendent moment for the merge with your other half into a perfect unit. No matter what bullshit happened to get to this point, it doesn't matter because together you are an equal force of light and dark, intertwined in a multitude of colored flames. You are meant to be as one, and if that isn't worth fighting for, I don't know what else is."

I'm speechless, staring at the Queen with my mouth gaping open. I can't believe how observant she's been of my life, especially with so many other important matters on her own plate. Yet, her words, which I can only assume are coming from her own experience, are the truest words ever spoken.

"Thank you, for your profound insight," I mumble with a bow of my head.

September laughs in a carefree manner. "It isn't profound insight, as much as it is learning from my own mistakes. And there isn't a single one of us at this table, who hasn't tripped a time or two when it comes to a relationship."

Sabre lifts his mate's hand to kiss the back of it as they share a knowing glance. "You are so right, darling."

"And think of the make-up sex you'll end up having," Gage adds, which gets him another rib jab from September's elbow.

I smile at the playful couple, seeing Paige and myself in their actions. "Sex is a great motivator, but I have to find my partner first, and she doesn't seem to want to be found at the moment."

Sabre shoots a grin in my direction but his eyes are fixed somewhere over my head at the crowd behind me. "I wouldn't be so sure about that."

September's face lights up as she follows Sabre's glance. "And I'd say she's dressed for the challenge."

"It doesn't appear as though your she-wolf is looking to play fair, either," Lazarus barks out.

"Oh my goodness. Is that a panier she's wearing, without the overskirt? Ballsy!" Lilith screeches.

September frowns. "What's a panier?"

Lilith explains, "It's the French word for basket. In my day, you wore the steel cage like basket under your petticoat to extend the width of your skirt, to make it spread out more to see all the embroidery and lace detail. I hated them, especially being at a vertically challenged size. Under most fabrics, I resembled a marshmallow, and I was forever tipping over. The damn things were such a pain in the butt when you wanted to sit, too, and I mean that literally."

I remember the seventeenth century fashion trend Sunshine is referring to. It wasn't my favorite style either, but for a whole other reason. The accessory was better than a chastity belt in the heat of the moment. Unwrapping a female in those days meant you couldn't just throw up the skirt material and get down to business-- not without impaling yourself on the metal frame wrapping her waist. Instead, you had to spend boner killing time, trying to free the girl from the frills and lace of corsets, skirts, and hooped cages. By the time you got her naked, you almost lost interest in the prize.

To hear Paige is wearing something so old-fashioned has my curiosity piqued. It doesn't suit her usually revealing style and I can't even imagine her in something as full-length as Marie Antoinette's court dresses. The mere thought makes me laugh, and I have to turn in my chair to see for myself. Except, once my eyes land on her, I'm stunned to silence and paralyzed by the pain of a rapidly growing erection in my own constricting garment.

Lord have mercy.

Paige's outfit is nothing like the dresses I remember, from that century or any other. In fact, this one has barely enough material to even be considered an article of clothing, never mind a dress. The short version of this black panier, wrapping just the curve of her hips, isn't made of the usual steel. This has a thicker and wider leather frame, similar to her sex-swing, and it hugs her form like a second skin.

Under this crisscross binding is a simple pair of panties-sheer, black, lace. They leave nothing to the imagination, especially in the right light. The top, if it can even be called one, also in the black sheer material, has perfectly placed embroidered flowers artfully sewn around her breasts to hide her areoles, but nothing else. She is literally on display.

"Fuck me..." I groan in appreciation of the view, and also, from the deep ache of need growing inside of me.

My beast wakes with a roar as it recognizes this desire for our mate. Every one of my senses is triggered. I crave to hear her sultry voice screaming my name, to smell her desire, taste her sin, and feel her quiver beneath me as I bury my cock deep inside of her.

I'm not a jealous man, but seeing her like this, showing off to the world, makes every fiber of my being wish to publicly and savagely mark her as mine. Even the mere thought has my beast purring with excitement to make it so.

"Wow, people with tattoos are way more fun to look at naked," Lilith giggles behind me.

She has no idea.

Damn, am I ever horny.

There is some sort of conversation from the rest at the table, even the sound of chairs moving, but none of it registers. I'm locked into my target, hypnotized by her beauty and the *in-your-face* outfit that I know she wore to provoke me. It has me zeroing in on the sway of her hips as she struts around the room, checking in with patrons on her way to the stage.

What a fucking cock tease!

She hasn't glanced my way, but she knows I'm here and I'm watching her. She's being obvious about it, putting on a show, flipping her hair while laughing with the girls in the band. She's torturing me like only she can, playing the tease while leaning over to say something to Sam so her magnificent ass is front and center. Her hips shifting from side to side is a temptation that is hard to resist. Somehow, I manage to stay in my seat, even though, every part of me is drawn to her.

Goddamn vixen is playing dirty.

This is her way of punishing me for our fight. By turning me on in public, she knows it will make me hard for her, painfully erect. She wants to torture me, to know I am in agony over her, it gives her the sick satisfaction she craves.

Ah, but two can play this game.

The more Paige taunts me with her nudity, teasing me with her beautiful booty while flirting with others in an attempt to drive me wild, the more turned on I know she's getting from my suffering. She might have said I was the mistake and implied we were through, but her actions now are saying otherwise.

I have to will myself to turn away and put my back to her, to avoid doing something I know she wants me to. I won't be the one making a scene, not here. Mentally, though, I promise to make her beg forgiveness later for this little stunt, and I happen to have just the plan.

A grin spreads wide on my lips when I see Mac Tire has joined our table, taking Sunshine's seat beside me as she takes Sam's vacant one. The conversation is about his chat with the rocker chicks. Of course, Gage is the one leading the charge.

"Is it a gimmick or does she have daddy issues? I mean, I'm all for roleplaying, but I draw the line at changing a chick's diaper."

September makes a disgusted groan. "Gage, really, it isn't for you to judge," she snaps at him.

He shrugs his shoulders. "What? I'm just asking, inquiring minds want to know."

A few of us laugh, a few of us do not. Gage doesn't seem

to care, and Mac Tìre is enjoying the conversation like the sick bastard that he is.

"There be nothing wrong with a little piss exchange between th'ee sheets, mate."

"Okay, all this talk about body fluids makes the pregnant girl have to use the facilities. And hopefully, by the time I return, you've got this topic out of your system," September warns with good humor.

"I second that," Brigid adds while also leaving her seat.

"Me too." Lilith twists in her chair and follows the others towards the hall, at the back of the bar, to the washrooms.

"Was it something I said, then," Mac Tìre roars with laughter, the rest of us join him.

Sabre's the first to recover from his chuckle to add, "I somehow doubt that really offended them." He's talking about the conversations his mate and my sister probably have had.

"You aren't kidding, some of the things they say have made me blush," Gage says this so seriously, I believe him.

As the topic changes to one of a domestic nature, I turn to Mac Tìre and whisper a requested favor in his ear. The wolf snickers with a grin.

"Here ye be blasting me about me fancies when you'd be asking for something on the sadistic level. Now, who's the dirty dog, mate?"

Everyone turns to me, having heard the bastard's outburst. I don't elaborate, I just get to the point, "Can you get it for me or not?"

"Aye," he answers and picks up the pint of beer in front of him.

Right before it gets to his lips I interrupt, "I meant now."

His eyes, full of love for his beer, flicker to me with a sudden change of disdain. "Serious?"

I nod. "Yeah, now would be good."

He snarls, "Bloody hell."

Placing his drink back on the table coaster, he frowns at me as he gets off the stool. "Tis damn good I be in a giving mood, ye fecker."

I try not to laugh as I thank him, "Appreciate it."

"Don't touch me beer, I be right back," he snaps at the table, but under his breath, he's cursing me right out the door. "Proper jizzmonger, fuckwit."

"The wolf has a temper," Lazarus states the obvious.

"To be fair, I did get between him and his drink. Not something you want to do to an Irishman." I chuckle then realize Laz is being serious. "Don't worry, he's not as mad as he seems. He's a good shit."

"I hope you're right. We don't need any hot heads tomorrow."

I frown at the angel. "Like we don't have a few at this table," I point out.

"Zander's right, Lazarus," Sabre agrees. "We've all lost our heads at one time or another, sometimes it even works to our advantage. I'm not worried about a few tempers flying, I'm more concerned with trust in this case. There are a lot of people we don't know, with pieces in this plan we can't control."

Of all the males at this table, Sabre is the only one who doesn't know me. It plays a big part with how he sees our plan. For him, September is the only one that matters, and he knows it will destroy her if something happens to Gage. He's being protective of her, and of our Alpha, by being cautious of me.

Gage interjects, "You make a good point, Sab, but I trust Zee, and he knows these people and the circles they run in. The deals made today were better than anything we could have offered, thanks to his connections with Mac Tire. They both stepped up, showed loyalty to the crown. I'd say they earned their worth, and in my book that equals trust."

Sabre frowns, I can see he's not as convinced. "Are you sure there is no other way we can approach this?"

Gage blows out a tired sounding breath. "I wish there was, we got lucky on this one as it is. If it wasn't for Zee and his friends, we might not have seen this coming."

"Luck has a funny way of running out, and we might be on our last save," Lazarus reminds us, referring to events of the last few days. "We can't rely on blind faith anymore, something needs to change soon."

"Is that coming out as the obvious warning for things we already know or is this one of your angelic predictions?" Gage inquires.

"Does it matter?" I ask. "We don't need a prediction of the future to see the crown is vulnerable. Just look at how many times there's been a threat in the last four months."

Sabre glances nervously towards the back of the bar. "He isn't wrong."

"Relax, Lilith and Brigid are with her, she's fine," Lazarus reassures the King of the Queen's safety, then adds a warning, "For today."

"Okay, we get it. We need a serious overhaul of the court, but this is not the place to be debating it," Gage snaps at the angel while pushing his drink away. "I would love just one fucking day, where we don't have someone slinging shit at us."

Lazarus smirks, "You picked the wrong mate for that, my friend."

Gage rolls his eyes. "Jesus, do you have to be such a buzz kill all the time?"

"He can't help it, G, his kind are just assholes," I joke.

"Says the fire-breathing serpent," Lazarus shoots back.

Gage snorts, "He has you there."

"By the sound of the insults being flung, I'd say we didn't miss much, ladies," September says, announcing they have returned.

"At least they moved to immature name calling. I'd rather this subject to the last one, any day." Lilith says with a giggle.

We adjust our postures upright, having been leaning into the table for our private conversation. There is a shuffling as Sabre turns to Brigid, Gage to September, and Lazarus to Lilith, to help them back into the high seats. Being the odd man out, I turn to search for my mate, only to come face to face with the redhead bartender, Kingsley.

She gives me a flirtatious wink then speaks to the table, "Y'all doing okay here?"

My gaze follows Kingsley's scantily clad body around the table, while she clears plates and empty bottles. I'm not sure what Paige and her friends have against cloth with their clothing, but I for one think the whole female population should follow suit. The female form, in every capacity it is presented, should be worshipped, especially one so banging. But, as I listen to September place another food order, Paige makes her approach to our table with a breathtaking smile spread across her lips. As soon as I see it upon her face, I realize her smile alone excites me more than the nudity of any other. I forget every woman I've ever known before this moment, none of them compare in any way with my Paige.

I could literally start fires with what I feel for her.

"Is Kingsley taking good care of you all?" Paige asks, in that velvet tone, when she reaches the table. The vibration tickles my eardrums, and I feel the sensation all the way down my body to my balls, as they start to throb.

She slides between Lilith and Gage, placing a hand on each of their shoulders like she's giving a group hug. She seems relaxed in posture, but her eyes don't miss a beat, darting around the table to take in the scene before landing on our Queen, and offering a slight bow of her head in respect.

"Yes, she has been quite attentive," September comments with a genuine smile in return. "If she ever wants to relocate, we'd welcome her at the Silverclaw in a heartbeat."

"She would give the twins a run for their money, that's

for sure," Lilith adds with a laugh, and I'm sure this is some inside joke about her Canadian co-workers.

Kingsley waves her hand like she's presenting the room. "Give up this glitz and glamor for cold and snow? Never going to happen."

"It's only cold for like eight months out of the year," Lazarus says dryly.

"Really?" Kingsley asks while twisting her face into a horrified expression. "And you like that?"

"It's not that long," Lilith scoffs at Lazarus. "And if you dress for the elements, it isn't that bad."

Paige bursts out laughing. "What's the point of having sexy underwear if you have to hide it under layers of wool? I much prefer showing them off."

I prefer seeing them bunched in my hand when I rip them off of her, but each to their own.

"We were just admiring the way you chose to show them off, too. Wasn't that right, Lil?" September grins at her friend.

"Oh, yes," Sunshine brims with excitement. "I love the modern day spin you put on the panier. It's sexy. I could never pull it off."

Lazarus growls then mumbles under his breath, "Nor would I allow you to."

Sunshine giggles at the comment and snuggles up to her mate. "Yes, well, it wouldn't suit me anyway, but on Paige, it's a statement. Wouldn't you agree, Zander?"

There's an uncomfortable silence at our table as some turn to me for an answer, and others turn to Paige for a reaction. I don't even have to look at her to know she's adjusted her posture to scream defiance, and slapped a smirk of attitude on her face. It's just what she does, and I wouldn't expect anything different. It's part of my feisty vixen's charm that makes me hard and wanting her.

I meet her eye with a determined stare of my own. "It's a statement alright. I'm just wondering if it's a perverse lesson or a blatant fuck you."

She doesn't answer, not like she needs to say anything when her body language screams out the vexation I know she carries. It can't be easy sustaining the heaviness of that weight. I want to take it from her. It is partly my responsibility to lessen her load, but she is too proud to allow anyone to help her. Not here, anyway, in front of the royal's, her staff, and the members of her pack. So, instead, she hides it behind the confident guise, masking her worry, frustrations, and anger as best she can until she is able to channel the energy through a riding crop to a submissive.

She is as broken as I am.

Christ, I love her even more.

Someone clears their throat. Someone else coughs. There are even some words spoken. It's just more noise to blend with the rest of the sounds swirling around us. Neither of us seem to notice as our eyes remain heatedly locked across the table, connected by the magnetic sexual tension burning between us. A fire so hot it puts my beast to shame.

"So, uh, Paige," I hear Gage try to interrupt. "Any word on your guy coming back from Vegas?"

Paige shifts ever so slightly as a wave of fresh annoyance ripples across her face and up into her eyes. The burning gaze of sexual heat, in which we shared, fades in an instant. It is replaced by hostility she shoots toward the Alpha.

"I have not heard from Ducky and I don't suspect I will. My future is apparently no longer in my control," Paige snaps with a volatile eruption.

Gage seems unfazed by her outburst. "I wouldn't say that," he says off cuff.

Kingsley slowly backs away from the table to get out of the line of fire. I don't blame her, Paige appears as snarly as a mama bear protecting her clubs.

"Really?" She asks, her eyebrow spiking with intent. "So, you asked me for my opinion today, while you were making deals?"

Gage's face darkens as he sees what she's hinting at. "I have a responsibility as the True Alpha, to protect you by whatever means necessary, and I did just that."

Paige's jaw clenches tight and her nostrils flare from her anger. "I never asked any of you to protect me. You were the ones who voluntarily promised to help, to save me from this situation, but when I needed you earlier, you failed to be there. And now, you're making plans on my behalf, giving away a part of my business as though you have some right to do so. Not informing me, of course, until after the ink is dry. You're no better than Bear, except now, I have a lot more of you to deal with."

Her body is vibrating with her anger as she speaks. I'm out of my chair in a heartbeat, heading around the table to wrap her in my arms. When she sees me coming she starts shaking her head, while her eyes shoot hateful daggers in my direction.

"No, don't," she snarls and begins to turn away.

"Paige, wait," September reaches forward in her seat to grab Paige by the arm and keep her at our table. "You have every right to be angry. We did fail you today, and it was all my fault. My duty is to protect our kind, and I got too caught up with my own emotions that I didn't come through on my promise to you. And then, I tried to make amends with this plan, but I didn't bother to include you, even though it does directly affect you. My intentions were coming from a good place. However, the way I went about it was not fair to you, and for that, I am sorry."

As September takes responsibility by humbly apologizing, Paige seems to relax enough to hear the Queen out. When it looks like Paige isn't going to bolt, September releases Paige's arm and sits back in her chair with a loud sigh, before starting again in a more lecturing tone. "If you must place blame, put it on me and me alone. Just know that anger is not going to get you out of this situation. You might not have been involved in the plan, but you have to admit, it's the only option we have. Tomorrow, Bear will make his play and we are ready to deal with him. You have to decide if you can put your differences aside, and trust us enough, to work together to get you free. That's our endgame, nothing else, and I will do whatever it takes to make it happen."

"I appreciate your apology, my Queen," Paige says with a bow of her head in acknowledgment. "Accepting help is not easy for me, I told you that, then you kind of blew it today. Restoring trust is going to take time, but if this plan works tomorrow, it will go a long way in getting me to forgive you."

"Noted," September says with a grin then taps the table with her hand. "Come sit, we can start rebuilding our friendship with a drink."

September barely finishes before Paige starts doing some sort of one-foot dance. She's fumbling one hand in the leather of her boot, near the inside of her thigh, while her other hand is making a one finger gesture, asking the Queen for a minute. It doesn't take her long to produce a phone, which she promptly puts to her ear. We don't hear her answer because it is in that moment when the band suddenly comes alive.

The room fills with a classic orchestra sound, but with a loud electric twist. It's so unexpected, I'm turning on the spot to understand what I am hearing. Earlier, I thought the girls had guitars strapped to them. Seeing them now, I realize it was an easy mistake to make. The instrument the brunette has standing upright between her legs does resemble a modern guitar or even a bass, except this is played with a bow.

"Is that an electric cello?" I ask loudly for anyone to answer.

"It is," shouts Lilith over the melody. "Don't you just love it?"

Hell yeah!

I am digging the brunette's vibe, and the crowd is right there with me, as screams and heavy applause erupts around us. I give the girl credit, she is putting her heart and soul into rocking that cello, complete with head-banging hair flips, adding a crazy flair to this classic sound. And just when I think it's over the top, the chick with the pink hair jumps down from one of the speakers into a knee slide to the front of the stage while walking her fingers down the neck of her guitar to a heavy rock riff. Sam comes in with a booming beat, turning the classic into a rock masterpiece.

As I watch and listen, I keep thinking I've heard this before. Something about this music, not necessarily the modern sound as much as the actual written work, and the two females, is registering as familiar. It could be possible I have heard them play before, perhaps in a different century. I believe these girls are a classic example of how the supernatural reinvent themselves.

With the thought swimming in my head, I turn to the table to ask if anyone knows more. Once I'm facing the court, I see Paige is no longer with us, and the band's identity no longer matters.

"Where did Paige go?" I shout the question in a panic.

Lazarus cocks his thumb to the front door. "It got too loud so she went outside to take her call."

My eyes flicker to the entryway. "Did she say if she was coming back?"

"Don't know," Lazarus answers with a shrug.

I stand, watching the door, staring it down as I will her to come back in. In what feels like an hour, which is probably only a minute, Lilith touches my bicep. I respond with a jerking twist of surprise as I meet her concerned eyes.

"You need to go chase her, Zander. You need to run out the door, find her, and tell her how you feel. Do whatever it takes, whatever needs to be done to get her to see what's in your heart. Only then can you be whole."

I blink a couple of times trying to understand. Sunshine

is telling me something that isn't unlike Livia's words from so long ago. I'm not a stupid man, but I am a man. We don't think in over-processed thoughts about every deep feeling, and I don't have another nine thousand years to figure this out. It would be easier if those with higher powers would stop speaking in riddles and just lay it out in black and white.

Lazarus leans against my side to speak directly in my ear. "Just go find her and do what you do naturally. In other words, let your dick do the talking for you."

I swing my head towards the angel and see the widespread grin on his face. He offers a wink before he roars with laughter. "You wanted simple truth, there you go."

"Christ," I snap at him. "Would you stop going in my head."

He sobers quickly with a serious expression. "I promise you, if you make this work between you and the she-wolf, I'll never be in your head again unless you will it."

I roll my eyes, knowing it's another of his cryptic lessons. I don't have the time nor the patience to debate the coded message. Instead, I walk away from the table without so much as a goodbye and head out the front door in search of my female. It doesn't take a genius to understand what they are trying to tell me.

I love Paige, and tonight, I am going to do whatever it takes for her to finally accept she loves me, too.

CHAPTER 17

"You're back again, Uncle Zander," chirps Paige's niece, Denver, from the mouth of the stable as I enter the foyer.

She walks towards me in greeting, a blanket folded up in her arms. Her eyes are bright, full of innocence, as she grins at me. I genuinely return the smile, liking the idea of being included as family more and more.

"I am, but this time, I'm certain I have followed your Aunt here. Is that her truck outside?" I ask with hope.

She places the blanket on one of the saddles in the showroom as she answers, "Yeah, that's her truck. She just got here a minute ago to take care of a rattler out back."

Right on cue, two shotgun blasts echo down the chamber of the stable from somewhere outside. I don't even think when I reach for my gun, pulling it from the holster to aim towards the rolled-up door at the end of the hall. My thoughts are to protect Denver as I step in front of her, guarding her with my back until I clear the stable. I heard what she said about the snake, but I'm not taking any chances.

Making my way cautiously down the long wide hall, I feel Denver's presence following me. From worry, I turn to face her with a stop gesture from my hand. I'm warning her to stay, but she's watching me with curiosity in her eyes.

"Ah, whatcha doing?" There's an inflection in her tone, it suggests I'm overreacting or I've gone crazy.

"I'm making sure Paige is at the firing end of that rifle, and not someone looking for trouble," I explain in defense of my actions.

"Oh," she says while cocking her head at me, in a way that says the idea never dawned on her.

Oh, to be a sweet and innocent lamb amongst the big

bad wolves.

"All clear, Denver, I got both of them," Paige's voice announces from the opening of the garage style door. "You can go get the horses from the other pasture and bring them in now."

I turn to face the door just in time to see Paige stroll in, gun slung over her right shoulder. *It's so badass.*

She stops upon seeing me, surprise registers in her eyes as she takes in the gun in my hands pointed in her direction. I watch her blink a couple of times, then her left hand slowly lifts to the barrel, readying herself against me.

"What are you doing here?" Her words are thick with venom as they lick at my ears.

I lower my hand with the gun and surrender with the other to show her I mean no harm. I acknowledge her, "Easy. I heard the gunshots, and was coming out to investigate."

"It's true, Aunty Pea. He told me he thought someone might be outside with you," Denver confirms from behind me.

Paige huffs, "Now you decide to be a knight in shining armor."

I catch her eyes rolling as she wanders over to a cupboard just inside the door. Opening it, she clears the Winchester then stores the weapon in a secured cradle. I take the opportunity to holster my own gun. When she's done locking the rifle away, she swings around to face me, but her eyes are directed towards the desk.

"Denver, go tend to your chores so we can lock up the stable. It's getting late."

The girl walks past me, stopping in front of Paige with a familiar hand on hip stance. "I won't let you yell at him. He was worried about you all day, and he tried to keep me safe just now. He's the nicest one you've ever brought around. Don't get all bitchy and scare him away."

Paige glares at her niece. "Girl, this is none of your damn business, and do not make me tell you again about your chores. You might be a human adult, but you are still young enough to go over my knee."

"Whatever, Aunt Pea," Denver huffs while throwing her hands in the air, marching herself out the door to disappear around the corner and out into the well-lit yard.

"The apple doesn't fall far from the tree," I mumble then chuckle at the similarity of the two women.

"What do you want, cowboy?" Paige snaps.

Her tone is hostile-heavy, reminding me of our first meeting at the barn when the cure for her sass was a good fingering. I debate this as an option but stick to my guns on my initial plan. "I came to talk, *leannàn*."

"Ah, more of the pretty words that got me into this mess in the first place. Well, there is nothing I have to say and nothing I want to hear from you."

In a move much like Denver's, Paige pushes past me and heads for the front entry. I don't let her get far, curling my hand around her arm and pulling her to me until we are standing face to face, locked in another heated glare.

The tension is extreme as I address her, "Ah, but there is, *mo àilleacht*, and I'm not leaving until we work this out. I see the anger in you, let it out. Scream at me, tell me how you feel. Give me the side you keep masked from the world, let me carry some of the burden for you."

"Phew," she spews. "Why would I do that again? Fool me once, shame on you, fool me twice... Not going to happen, pretty boy."

She pushes at my chest to move me away; I don't budge. A wave of annoyance flickers through me, though, and I snap back. "What would you have had me do this morning, Paige, kill your father? Right there, in front of your pack, your family, and your sister? What do you think it would have done to Bean? Watching me tear apart her father, knowing I was doing it for you. She would have hated you for it. *You* would have hated me for it and it wouldn't have solved anything."

She pales as I speak and I know I'm getting to her, but she is so stubborn she won't back down. "You didn't even try to fight. You just let his flunkies beat on you, and then he literally walked over you. It makes me wonder if you are even who you say, your actions seem to suggest otherwise."

"For fuck's sakes," I swear through gritted teeth, pulling my fingers through my hair in frustration. "You know damn well I can't challenge Bear as my true self or as an unknown, and I couldn't take over his pack, even if I did. Me killing Bear would mean Garo would still own you, and we'd be right where we are now, but with zero options."

Her eyes squint as the frown deepens across her brow. "Yeah, well, maybe your precious royals should have stepped in like they said they would. Instead, they went behind my back to make deals with my life and my property, like I'm a fucking commodity. They don't care what happens to me, they're only in it to make themselves look good."

"That's not true and you know it," I snap.

A smirk recoils across her lips. "You always defend them, but you're no better. What did you get out of the deal today, by the way? Oh, that's right, Mac Tire told me you are going to be the new commander, the Alpha's high and mighty second. Well, la-tee-da!"

She barks this in my face, she's goading me and it's working. I'm so irritated, I have to force myself to stand still or I'm going to slap her hard across the face.

"You're acting like a spoiled cunt."

"Fuck you," she snarls like a rabid dog, snapping her teeth an inch from my face.

My irritation might be beyond belief, but there's also a part of me that loves this ballsy sass she's throwing around. It's the same tough girl stance that turned me on at the barn and started my fall into this land of foreign feelings.

I knew coming here, we weren't going to have a civil conversation. This isn't going to be simple. Paige isn't wired like most. She communicates on a level all her own and sticks to what she believes, even if she's wrong.

She's tightly wound in her blanket of anger, feeling deceived, betrayed, unsupported and even unloved. Though I doubt she would ever admit to it. And telling her otherwise will do little to change her mind. No, it will be up to me to break through her hard shell in the only way I know how.

I came here to work this out, by whatever means necessary, to get my mate back, and I am going to do just that. A grin crests my lips. It's the only warning I give her before I bow forward to scoop her up and over my shoulder. Holding her legs tight against my chest with one arm as I stand, and head for the winding staircase behind the desk.

"What the fuck do you think you're doing? Put me down, you jerk," she curses me and starts to buck against my body, making the climb up the stairs more difficult.

With my free hand, in an attempt to settle her down, I slap her ass cheek as hard as I can. "We are going to talk this out the only way I know both of us will understand."

"You can't make me do anything I don't want to."

Her scream of protest turns into a muffled moan as my hand meets her ass on the second spanking. The sound of the moan, so deep and sensual in her throat, is the aphrodisiac my libido has been craving.

"Is that so?" I comment, racing up the last of the steps and rushing to the door of her apartment, managing to awkwardly open it with a bang.

"Jesus, put me down before you break something."

She's insistent, thrashing against me in an attempt to get away. I'm not letting go. If anything, I'm holding her with a firmer two arm grip while entering the kitchen area.

I pause, allowing the sensors to pick up our movement and turn on the overhead lights. I'm not expecting the blasting blare of music flooding the space, making me wince from the heavy metal sound piercing my eardrums. The screaming is full of rage, reflective of how her mood seems to be at the moment.

I swing left, then right, searching for the stereo to turn off this demon dribble. There is no obvious box, console or even a cabinet housing the sound system. Turning to the kitchen cupboards, I shift Paige higher on my shoulder and begin a one hand hunt, opening and closing each door for the elusive equipment.

"Stereo off," Paige shouts the command and like a witch performing magic, the music vanishes.

"Well, that was easy," I chuckle at myself for overlooking the obvious solution.

"It's the only damn thing in this house that is," she snaps then adds, "In case, you were thinking otherwise."

"Never said you were, *leannàn*, but you are stubborn as hell." My hand finds her ass one more time, making an audible fleshy slapping sound as it stings my palm in satisfaction. Her groan makes me smile and warms me internally.

She hiccups out, "This, changes nothing."

I don't bother with a response. I'm on a mission to allow sex to do our talking for us. My eyes flicker to the countertop, a solid surface at waist height, it has possibilities. Until Paige tries to wiggle down my back, and I realize the counter will be too easy to escape from.

I hoist her back up while scanning the room, glancing towards the fireplace and the empty space for the bed. It has been tucked into the wall, but beside it, where the closet door has been rolled closed is something that makes my cock instantly hard.

Bingo! We have a winner!

My feet start moving before my brain can comprehend the action.

I'm across the room in an instant, and when we near this latest discovery, my heart starts pounding with excitement inside my chest as I take in the equipment.

Smooth, black painted boards have been placed at a crossed angle with horizontal straight pieces bolted a few feet above the top and below the bottom, to create this simple apparatus. About a dozen carabiner clips are secured in strategic locations, along with two sets of wide steal cuffs. One set of cuffs on the cross pieces is a foot from the bottom, to lock-in ankles, and the other, on the top horizontal board, locks the wrists. The whole rig is roughly of a similar dimension to the barn door, so when it rolls closed, the cross is hidden completely from view.

"A St. Andrew's cross, eh?" I mumble with a chuckle. "You never cease to amaze me, *leannàn.*"

Paige spits out a laugh. "Tying me up isn't going to make me your bitch. I won't submit to you, not again."

Kneeling down, I place her feet on the floor before the X-frame. As I stand, I press myself against her body, groping her soft curves as I show her I think otherwise.

"Really?" I mock, but I don't give her a chance to speak.

My hands are steady and strong as I manhandle her, gripping her hips while forcibly pushing her against the boards. I kick at the heels on her boots with my own and use my knee to nudge apart her thighs. She opens them willingly to me. While holding her in place with the weight of my hip, I grip her wrists tight to stretch her arms over her head, only to have her press her giant pillows into my chest.

I'm showing her, with my body, she can be controlled. To my surprise, she's not resisting and seems to be taking pleasure from it. Even giving me a slight head nod of consent, so I'll continue to do more.

I lean into her personal space, working the cuffs around her wrist. Her breath waivers slightly on the exhale against my neck. Once her wrists are secured to the board, I trail a line with my fingers down her arms to the edge of her breasts, tracing her outer shape with my fingertips. Again, there's a slight shake in her breath. Glancing at her face, I watch her suck her bottom lip into her mouth as though she is craving to taste something delicious. She has been verbally resistant, snapping and snarling at everything I say. Yet, her body is a contradiction of actions.

It is as I suspect, Paige is desperate to be set free from her internal chaos. But due to her strength and pride, she is unable to bring herself to ask for this surrender of control. There is a disconnect between her body and brain. One screams her defiance loudly while the other craves to succumb. Staring deep into the cognac coloring of her eyes, the glimpse into her soul, shows the battle taking place. Words will not win this war.

Swiftly I move, keeping our eyes locked. I capture her mouth and devour her thick lips with my own. I'm rough, possessive as I bite the fleshy part of her bottom lip, tasting a hint of blood as I break the skin. She gasps, then moans, and finally allows her mouth to open, inviting me to consume her.

I'm gentle at first, sucking her bottom lip into my mouth to kiss away the sting. Once my tongue slips past her opening, she tastes like the sweetest honey ever made. I am suddenly the candyman in search of a sugary fix. I lose restraint, dominating her with my tongue for a rough and savage mouth fuck.

My beast recognizes the flavor of our mate and wakes with a roar that barrels up my throat and into Paige's mouth. She whimpers as her eyes widen, right before I pull away.

"Ahh," she gasps, whether in fear or to catch her breath, I don't know.

I'm hoping for the latter, as my fingers squeeze into the soft mounds on her chest, lifting and pushing her breasts together to create a big plump mountain. My only warning is a seductive wink of desire before I attach my mouth to the perky nipple with the ring. I'm all teeth, biting her through the sheer fabric top and suckling at her tit, pulling the ring and nipple into my mouth for a hard draw.

"This isn't going to change anything," she screams over my head, while she pushes her breast against my face.

More contradiction that I address, "Why not?" I ask,

lifting my head to meet her wide open eyes. "You can't lie and say you don't want this. Your body is telling me otherwise. Let me help you, Paige. Let me take away some of your fears, your stresses, your problems. Let me in, for Christ sake. Accept me as your mate and give me this, so I can take care of you."

Her eyes shine with the glossy glow of welling tears. She is frantically blinking them away while her head is slowly moving side to side. "I can't," she whimpers out.

I move my thumb up the side of her breast to circle her areola around the ring. "Tell me why," I whisper.

When she doesn't answer, I sink my teeth around her nipple and give it another long hard pull, flicking it with my tongue.

"No, I can't." Her snarl is followed by a deep moan and rhythmic hip thrusts.

Letting go of her left breast to reach down, I cup her pussy in my palm and she immediately grinds herself into it. Her lace panties are so thin I can feel the spot of wet heat soaking through the fabric. It is right where the heel of my palm rests against her clit. I use the natural lube, pushing in with a circling rub to apply enough pressure to stimulate. Her hips jerk, back and forth, as she humps my hand. As a reward, I flicker my tongue over her nipple to the same movement, nipping periodically to encourage stimulation.

The light scent of her arousal tickles my nose. She's close to a climax, and my cock is throbbing in anticipation. Judging by the pleading whimpers though, she can't seem to get enough traction to complete the task. This is exactly where I want her, teetering on the edge of pleasure. It will make her emotionally vulnerable, and if I do my part right, she will release more than just a few orgasms.

I grin against her breast with eagerness for the challenge ahead. I step away, briefly handling my manhood with a squeeze, to relieve my own building pressure.

"No, wait," she orders. "I'm not done," she demands in

frustration.

I'm snickering at her directness while kicking off my boots. "No, you aren't even close to being done, *leannàn*. Be patient, I will get you there."

Her eyes automatically roll and a huff of disgust bursts from her mouth. "I don't have time for whatever game you think you're playing. In case you forgot, tomorrow is a big day for me. What with my new mate coming to claim me and all. So, either get me off or let me go because I have shit to do."

A growl of jealousy rips from my mouth, but I suppose she wanted the reaction. "Why must you be so stubborn?"

Her eyes darken as she fixes them on me. "I'm not stubborn. This is me being realistic. I made the stupid decision to believe in the bullshit fairy tales. I actually trusted you'd be the one to get me free, but it was a ruse so you could get what you wanted. You didn't choose me for love, you chose me for personal gain. Now I get to suffer the consequences. Not you, not the royals, but me."

She spits the words with hatred as she says them, but that's not what stops me from removing my jacket. It's the sound of anguish in her voice that does.

I step forward to bridge the gap between us, needing to see the truth to my question. "You're convinced I've betrayed you, aren't you?"

Once the words register, the pain is written all over her face. "Trust is a fragile thing, you know. Easily broken and lost, not so easy to get back."

"Oh, *leannàn*," I sigh, placing my hand at her neck to pull her close enough for our foreheads to touch. "I'm not sure how to defend myself against your claim, when I know you won't hear me out."

"Then don't bother," she starts in a quiet voice. "Sometimes betrayal can be a blessing. I've been holding this deal together with paperclips and duct tape forever. I'm tired."

The sound of defeat in her voice rattles me to the core. "Screw that," I tell her, stepping back to really take her in with my eyes.

Her head pops up, along with her brow as she stares at me. "Excuse me," she snaps.

"Don't you dare put me in the same category as the others before me. I'm not them, Paige. Do you know, since I came to Nevada and met you, I haven't thought once about my own shit? I haven't checked in with my companies. Hell, I only looked at my phone today to make sure I didn't miss your call."

As I begin my lecture, my temper gets the best of me and I let it out with both barrels. "Dammit woman, you have consumed me from the first smart-ass comment at the barn. I didn't fight Bear because I didn't want to hurt you or your family. And the deal we struck is to get you out of this. I don't care if I become the commander. I only said yes so Gage would keep to his end, making you his second once he kills Bear. All I've done today is think about how to change this fucked up situation so you wouldn't have to worry about it anymore. I want to help you, to protect you, to take away the pressures and stress because that's what a mate does."

The fire inside me is churning and from it an energy builds, my beast is wound up. I begin to pace in front of her to burn it off, nattering as I stroll back and forth in front of her.

"Yesterday, the only thing that mattered to me was protecting the crown and avenging my sister. That was all I knew, what I thought Livia left me here to do. If I could help the Queen gain peace for our kind, then maybe I could finally be whole."

Stopping a few feet away, in the empty space where the bed should be, I notice the leather handle sticking out of the wall. I swear the damn thing is taunting me, telling me what we both need is but a tug away. I reach up to firmly grasp the strap in my hand to give it a good yank. It doesn't take much effort. Like a drawbridge, the wall begins to fall, dropping the bed frame so fast I have to get out of the way.

Once the bed has landed, I turn back to finish my rant. "Then I met you, and my whole fucking world changed. Now my only thought is of you. My only cares are for your well-being. My only hopes are for your happiness. I chose you to love, and I will never stop choosing to love you, now or ever. Maybe you don't believe it because you are so damn pig-headed, but I promise you…" I trail off as I remove my jacket and place it on the bed.

I notice her attention is on me, and like any guy, I'm loving it. Even giving her the show as I run my hands down my torso to the gun holster, which comes off with care. The shirt is next, and I feel her eyes all over me as I toss the garment on the bed. I remember the plastic baggie from Mac Tire, who I saw when I left the bar.

This puts me back on track as I pull it from my coat pocket. It doesn't stop my floor show as I bend, ass front and center for her entertainment, while I open the long drawer hidden in the bed frame. There are many appealing options to choose from, but from my memory of the contents, I already know what I want, and make the selection.

"Oh good, more empty promises to be disappointed by, can't wait." Paige suddenly bursts, and I realize her attention hasn't been on me, but for me to finish the rest of my sentence.

Or is it?

Setting the objects on the side table between the bed and cross, I walk over to stand against my woman. Getting right in her personal space, chest to chest, face to face.

"Your sarcasm isn't just an attitude, it's a goddamn art," I tell her while pushing two fingers in her mouth. "Perhaps you just need to put your mouth to better use."

Her eyes widen with revolt and when she starts to mumble out a reply, I add another digit. "Shut up and suck or I'll make you."

She growls and tries to bite. I push in another finger and scissor them open until she has no other option. I place my other hand on the front of her neck, using my thumb and forefinger to apply pressure on either side of her throat.

"I'm trying to tell you, Paige, I don't want to tame you. I don't need someone to submit to me. I need someone who I trust, who will challenge me, and who will be at my side as an equal. Last night, you stood unafraid in my darkness and helped me to become whole again. Let me do the same for you tonight. Forget everything, turn it all off and let me take control. No words need to be said, our bodies will communicate for us."

I watch her face as she works my offer through her head. her eyes dancing about with uncertainty. I'm pushing my fingers in and out of her mouth, preventing her from speaking, but she doesn't need to be verbal to answer. The moment she decides to let me in is perfectly clear. Using her tongue, she swirls it around my fingers, coating them with her spit. She presses her lips against my flesh and begins to suck, bobbing her head ever so slightly.

Her reaction is the only answer I need. I pull my fingers from her mouth as I whisper, "Good girl."

She smiles wide and it reaches all the way up to her eyes. It's such a beautiful smile that I capture it in a kiss. Her lips are wet and warm against mine, like a slip and slide for our tongues to play on, and she's willingly participating in the fun.

Fuck yeah!

The kiss turns electric, stealing our breaths until there is a buzz of dizziness in my head, and Paige starts to sway like she's drunk. It's powerful enough to make my skin tingle, my blood boil, and my whole body heat from the fires within. A few minutes longer, and I hear her whimpering like a hurt animal.

I've been so into the lip lust, I didn't notice I'm projecting my heat externally. If she hadn't cried, I could have consumed her with it. In a panic, I pull away and we both gasp for air.

"Where are you going?" She whines so sweetly.

Around her lips is what appears to be a red sunburn. As soon as I see I've hurt her, I snort with disgust. A plume of smoke puffs from my lips, and we both watch it drift up between us. There is a moment of silence in which I berate myself for not being in control of my beast.

"I've burnt you," I groan, running my thumb down the side of her jaw and around her chin, trailing the outer line of the burn.

She licks her lips with a slight wince before she laughs. "I know, but if I couldn't take the heat, I wouldn't have provoked the dragon."

This takes me by surprise. I stumble back a step while shaking my head as I try to understand. She holds my eyes with a look more heated than the kiss. This time, I snort in confusion.

"Do you have a death wish or are you just that sexually depraved?"

Her smirk says it all, but she follows it up with a great comeback, "My naughty is naughtier than your naughty, and I'll happily demonstrate it for you."

"Ah, *leannàn*," I groan, grabbing my package for a squeeze as it throbs with an ache in my pants. "My dirty girl, I fucking love you."

"Then prove it like you promised," she growls low in that tone I love. "I want to be used tonight. I want you to take it all away. Do whatever you want to make me forget."

"Are you sure? It might be too much, *I might be too much.*"

She laughs. "You could never be too much for someone like me. It's why we are fated to be. I know it in my heart, because before you, I could never get enough, but together we have both met our match."

This isn't forgiveness, it's a step. This isn't quite

resolved, but we are on the way. The grin on my face probably says enough, but I want to never keep anything from her. I broke her trust once, I will never do it again.

I palm her cheek and softly kiss her forehead. I'm conveying my respect, my honor and loyalty to her as my unequivocal equal, partner, and mate. Carrying on to whisper kisses on her temple, her cheek, her nose and at the corner of her lip. This isn't about sexual appetite, it's me telling her without words I love her, and I'll do anything for her.

With each brush of my lips, her breath catches. When my teeth graze her chin, she gasps. She practically hyperventilates when I work the mating mark on her neck over with swirls of my tongue and deep sucks from my lips.

My cock grows hard inside my denim. I try to rub it off on her hip and she's right there with me, thrusting herself against me. The damn cage wrapping her waist keeps getting in the way, though, just like its seventeenth-century cousin.

On each roll that Paige makes forward with her hips, the hard leather straps ripple up my erection in all the wrong ways. I'm thankful for the protection of the jean material until the basket slips behind the waistband. When we both rotate our hips back, the leather strap pinches the tip of my cock head and I almost lose my mind from the pain.

"Fuck," I curse and slam my hand against the wall behind her head.

Like the sadist that she is, she giggles, knowing exactly what went down. I growl at her with an angry stare, she snorts in my face. She's daring me to take out my aggressions on her.

"You think that's funny?" I demand.

"Yup," she says with sauciness, then unleashes the most mischievous grin. "And thank the heavens for the entertainment because this sensual foreplay is starting to bore me."

Never underestimate the power of a mischievous

woman with a sharp tongue. The mere hint that I am not enough, that I can't take care of her needs, is more than a challenge. It's about to become a fucking conquest.

I reach for the sheath at my hip to unclip my blade and step in front of her, clutching her throat to push her hard into the cross. Her eyes widen then fill with fear when I place the knife tip against her chin. She whimpers slightly when I drag the cold steel, oh, so, slowly down her throat. She gasps from the nick I make, a tiny cut in her skin above her left breast. The whole time, though, excitement dances in her stare and her scent grows stronger, punctuating her arousal. I know she's getting wet from this.

Curling the flat part of the knife around her breast, I stop at the center of her chest, pressing the blade lengthwise, against her shirt, between her ample cleavage. I'm barely touching her, but I can feel her heart pounding. The look on her face is anticipatory. The scent of her arousal is overwhelmingly intoxicating.

It appears as though Paige has a secret craving for something more sinister. As the god of mystery and a male of my word, it is my duty to bring her wicked fantasies to life, with pleasure.

"Game on, mo chailín salach," I tell my naughty girl, flashing my beast forward and presenting her with a what I imagine is his yellow-eyed greeting. She squeaks out a tiny scream of fright that tickles my beast with joy. "And welcome to the dark side."

CHAPTER 18

"I'm not scared of you." Her voice says otherwise as it cracks.

My grin stretches wide across my face. "Good to hear."

I lift the handle of the knife so the tip of the blade is pressing against the fabric of her shirt, making it pull snug across her tits. "If you aren't frightened, does this mean you trust me?"

I watch her close while I move the knife. It's a fraction from her skin, just enough to remind her which of us is in control.

"In theory..." She trails off, ending with a scream as I slash down her cleavage.

The blade's sharp edge makes a shredding mess of her shirt as it rips open, exposing her big beautiful breasts. The thrill registers quickly, pearling her nipples to hardened buds and puckering her skin. I hear her heart boom to life in her chest as a shaking breath exhales from her mouth.

"I'll ask you again, do you trust me?"

She starts to nod her head then stops when I frown at the action. Her tongue juts from her lips a few times as she tries to wet them.

She swallows hard to answer, "Mostly."

Before I can say anything, she clears her throat to correct herself with a more curt response. "I mean, yes. I trust you, Sir."

This warms me and makes me smile. I drop my head to kiss her breasts. I lick away the small drop of blood from my earlier nick with a swirl of my tongue.

"Good, now we can sink into deeper places and expose our darker thoughts, playing with them together, "I mumble into her cleavage.

It's a cozy and inviting area, her pillowy mound. I sink

my face between the folds and worship her with my mouth. Nipping at her skin, sucking my way to her nipples, but never forgetting the knife. I keep the edge of the blade pressed against, and slightly under, the side of her left breast. Showing her how the fear can turn into something more pleasurable if she's open to it.

By the sound of the heavy pant coming from her mouth, I'm guessing she's more than open to it. Testing the waters, I draw a line with the tip of the blade, scraping with a light touch down her torso. It leaves a trail marker, even through the tattoos, as the first layer of tissue is scratched off.

I follow the etched-out blade path with my mouth, kissing it and the sting away, to make my way down to the top of the fashion basket ringing her waist. My first instinct is to slice the fucking thing up, but why waste good effort on something so trivial. Especially when the snaps at the front are easily pulled apart.

"Remind me to burn this later," I tell her as I toss the bouncy, spring-like-cage across the room. "So you'll never wear the medieval torture device again."

"But I like it," she pouts, blinking with a put-on innocence.

I bite the spot on her hip where I burned my claw mark on her last night, making my point clearer.

"I do like you biting me more, so consider it a pile of ash," she moans.

"Good girl," I mouth the words against her hip, tucking the knife blade beneath the edge of lace above her pubic line.

"Do you like these too?" I ask of her sheer underwear.

She gasps, "You won't!"

I smirk, "Oh, but I would."

With a quick flick of my wrist, in a down and outward motion, I slice one side open. The fabric comes away to reveal just the top of her pubic area, freshly shaven and smooth. It's a calling card of sorts, beckoning me to eat her pussy with zeal. As tempting as it is, and to my taste buds dismay, I move on, kneeling before her to continue securing her for play.

Nudging her knee with my shoulder, I guide her leather covered foot to the cuff on the left of the cross and fasten her ankle in the shackle. She doesn't fight, she just watches my hands with an eagerness in her eye. I notice her cheeks are flush, and when I curl my fingers around the back of her thigh, to slide her right leg to the other cuff, there's a damp heat rising from her like she might have a fever.

I grin up at her as I finish locking the cuff. "How turned on are you, right now?"

"Mildly," she sarcastically drawls.

It makes me chuckle as I mumble to myself. "Obstinate right to the bitter end."

"You could beat that out of me, you know. It would probably turn me on more." This time the sarcasm isn't as obvious, but I imagine it's because she actually wants me to hurt her.

"I have other ways of inflicting pain, *leannàn*. And they don't involve me actually punching you." I kiss the inside of her thigh just above the cuff of her tall boot, demonstrating a gentler approach.

"Well, that's a shame," she pouts again.

It doesn't last long on her face. Not when I kiss another spot by the side of her left butt cheek, where the tail of the tattooed dragon starts to curve up her back. Her moans continue to grow as I do some worshipping. With swirls and licks, kisses and sucks, I show my gratitude for the drawing and our connection; honoring and praising her hip and my mark. My other hand is just as busy, drawing another scratching line up her other leather-clad leg. Hopping over the boot cuff to her hip, I tuck the knife under the remainder of the underwear material.

I wiggle the blade to pull at the lace. "Are you wet for me?" I ask this time.

"No," she snaps the answer too fast, a tell to her lie.

I flick my wrist up and out, cutting the material in two. The torn bits fall away, exposing her cunt right before me. Her clit has pearled and the flesh around it is a bright pink. The excitement has her pulse racing enough to flush her everywhere. My mouth salivates as I crave a taste from her well. I know she's wet, I can see it glistening on her pussy lips. But she lied, and that deserves a punishment.

I press the tip of the knife to her clit, right in the center of the bud. It is only a light touch, like being pricked with the head of a pin.

"Jesus fuck!" Paige yells with a start.

With a jerk, she tries to retract her hips, but she can't get far, and struggling too much will prick her harder. She settles quickly, using her sharp tongue instead, to snap back. "What the hell do you think you're doing?"

I ignore her to carry on. "I'll try my question again."

This time, I'm more insistent with my demands, putting some pressure on the blade to prick her harder. "Tell me, *leannàn*, and it's best that you don't lie, are you wet for me?"

"I am, now." She swallows a moan to add, with a forced snarl, "And the fuck you is implied."

I chuckle while pulling the knife away, placing it on the floor to slide out of the way.

"Good girl," I praise before I bury my face between her legs.

With the flat of my tongue, I lick her from asshole to clit and taste the cream coating her cunt. It's the sweetest of prizes, and I make sure to reward her for the gift by lapping at her hole before plunging my tongue deep inside her. She's more than just wet, she's also ready for action as her cunt flutters against my tongue. I work her over, stimulating her clit with quick swirling circles between long plunging strikes.

"Keep suck… No, go back to the, oh… Yeah, just like… Fuck."

She rocks against my face, cursing out unfinished

instruction in frustration. I'm hitting all the right parts, sucking her clit until it throbs then hardens. Moving back to her hole to fuck her with my tongue, over and over, until it's pulsing at the edge of a release. That I refuse to give to her.

We have embarked on a journey, her and I. One of great pleasures, with the highs of extreme thrills that lead to absolute satisfaction. And the only way to make it to the end of this sinister voyage is for her to give, as well as take. I am going to make her tell me her deepest and darkest secrets simply by reducing her to a drooling, eye smudged, lipstick smeared, mess. When Paige is done she will be the epitome of rode hard and put to bed wet.

"Would you just…" She starts, then screams out a long grunt followed by a deep moan. "Yes, that spot, suck it… Hey, did you bite… Oh, fuck yeah, bite me, harder."

The mellifluous tone of her voice has me shivering with sexual need. Her deep rasp is so sexy, I swear she could make me blow my load just by reading to me from the dictionary. The more aggressive I am with eating her cunt, the lower her tone goes until my jeans are soaked from my own lusting desires. The need to fuck her is overwhelming. I want so badly to be deep inside of her that I ache all the way to the depths of my soul. It's this intense connection with her that gives me the ultimate heart erection.

But it's not about you, you greedy bastard.

I growl at myself for being selfish, it vibrates against her clit and she gasps a telling breath. The change of stimulation is enough to tip her over the edge. She pushes her cunt into my face and starts to grind, jacking herself off to complete the orgasm. I change directions again, not wanting her to release, yet. Shaking my head vigorously against her pussy while drawing a hard suck at her nub, stops the release at the gate, and has her howling from the agony of disappointment.

"No," she cries.

"Please," she begs.

"Let me cum," she demands.

I drag myself away with reluctance to crawl up her body. Sliding myself against her, scratching her flesh with my nails up her body, then tangling my fingers in her hair to hold her head, and stare deep into her eyes. I'm making it roughly apparent which one of us is running this show. The rush of exhilaration is glowing in her eyes, but the pout of disappointment is quite obvious on her lips.

"Let this be a lesson for the next time I ask you a question," I lecture. "Answer quickly, without the mockery, and I will consider a more suitable ending. Understand?"

She pegs me with a sly glare. "You know I barely take suggestions, never mind an order. A leopard can't just change its spots to appease the hunter."

"Then you'll have to face the consequences." I grin at her. "And to tell you the truth, this form of resistance is inspiring my filthy mind."

"I'm up for the challenge." She winks then lowers her voice an octave to a purr, "Show me what you got."

"Mmm," I moan at her willingness to play. "Good answers."

Dropping my hand between her legs I finger her opening, circling the entrance to wet my fingers before plunging them in. She tries to roll her head while her mouth opens. There is no sound at first, but the silent moan becomes deafeningly loud with each stroke I give her cunt, in and out at a slow pace.

"Do I make you feel good, *leannàn?*" I ask.

"God, yes," she purrs.

I add a finger and continue my assault. "Do you want me to make you cum, *mo àilleacht?*"

"More than you know," she gasps as her hips roll forward to meet my thrusting movements.

"*Is é mo chroí mianach?*" I ask.

She hesitates, rolling her eyes forward to meet mine. I wonder if she doesn't understand and ask her again. "Are you mine, *leannàn.* Does your heart belong only to me?"

She squints her eyes and bites her lip, prolonging her answer. I move to pull out my fingers and she gets the point as she whines and thrashes against the boards. "No, don't stop."

"Tell me," I insist.

"It's not an easy question," she blurts then screams as I step away.

"It's yes or no, pretty straightforward."

"It's not, and you know it," she barks back.

Going to the small table by the bed, I pick up the bag and a toy. A battery operated vibrating wand with a solid round head for stimulation, to be exact. The wand handle is attached to a belt, which I return to Paige with, wrapping it around her waist and securing it. There's a swivel for the wand, which I put above her pubic bone then move it around to adjust. It takes not even a minute, where she hasn't said a word. I'm not here to play fair, so I flick the switch to test its power. It comes to life with a vibrant hum and she tries to bow forward to get away from the toy.

"Ahh," she puffs. "You're playing dirty."

The wand is tucked in the valley between her cunt and thigh, not even touching her most sensitive parts, yet, and already she's fighting it. Her body stiffens and she struggles against the cuffs. It makes me chuckle, knowing once we get to the painful foreplay, she's going to be singing like a cat in heat.

"Explain your comments, Paige, it's that easy," I smirk as I twist the wand a fraction of an inch to sit against her pussy lip. She'll feel the tingling tease of the buzz, but won't be able to get off on it. "I can make you talk, but it's up to you."

Her words are shaky as she snaps, "I told you I'm nobody's bitch."

"And I told you I don't want a submissive, and it isn't what I'm asking you for now. Do you understand the differences of what I'm asking?"

"Of course, I do," she snarls.

It's a right answer, and still, a wrong response. I chew on my next chess move of how to capture my naughty princess.

I drag the wand to rub her clit, circling my wrist around to perk up her nub. It will expose nerve endings, making her clit extra sensitive and her cunt extra wet, ready for penetration. I can hear the exact moment when this happens; her breathy pants become mumbled cries. I can hold her here, teetering painfully on the edge of the release for as long as I want, and she knows it.

"Just tell me, Paige," I whisper in her ear while I circle one fingertip around her wet pussy hole. "Give me the truth and I'll give you some relief, that's how this works."

"Fuuuck," she drawls out. "You are such an asshole."

"And you are so Goddamn stubborn."

Leaving the wand pointing straight down with the round buzzer resting a hair above her clit, I turn my back on her and walk away. I have to before I explode. The whole sight of her is stimulus overload. I can smell and feel the wetness of her arousal, see every emotion playing out in her face, even when she resists it. The scent of her dampened skin is tantalizing, but when it puckers from the slightest touch, reacting to me more than she's willing to admit, I just can't take it. I have never wanted to fuck anyone so bad in my life, and not just for the sake of getting off.

I do own her; body, heart, and soul. Her mind, on the other hand, that is a tricky bugger. Until I can break through the titanium wall she's built in her head to prevent anyone from truly getting in, getting close enough to love her, I must resist her. I walk away, but the sound of frustration and agony in her pleading cries stops me a mere foot away.

Well, doesn't that sound just make my cock harder.

I hiss as I squeeze the front of my pants, painfully gripping my erection to hold off my urges.

And she thinks she's in agony.

I turn back to face her as I unbutton my pants. She is grinding her hips while her whole body appears to shake, but she can't get the traction she needs to get off. The irritation is heavy on her curled lips. It's a sight to behold, and as soon as the last button on my pants is released, my cock springs towards her dripping its own tears of frustration.

A sob gets lost in her throat as she gulps in air. Her throat bounces as she swallows then she tries to speak. "Need... please... you."

My pants drop and I kick them off on my way back to her. "Are you ready to answer me?" I ask with hope.

She throws her head back and bangs it on the board while growling, "Not this shit again. Just fuck me."

I bite the inside of my lip, until I taste blood before I lose control of my tongue, and say something I'll regret. Breaking someone is never easy, breaking Paige is going to kill me. I cup my balls to give them a squeeze. Pulling at them to also grip the root of my dick, where I hold it firmly. She licks her lips as she watches me, so I stroke myself to show her what she's missing.

"You could stroke that inside me." She's not at all shy with the hint. "I'll even deep throat you with my cunt to help you empty your balls.

Damn, that's tempting!

She's tormenting me with her seduction, making my next words sound rudely curt. "Not until you tell me what I want to know."

Trying to make up for my sharpness by rolling up on my toes, I slap her sex hard with my swollen cock. "Come on, Paige, let me in. It will be so worth it."

After a couple more taps, I have to pull back before the combination of buzzing and beating my meat sets me off. I'm just as much on the edge as she is and it's driving my beast crazy. Internally, I'm a volcano ready to erupt. The fire within has drops of sweat beading on my brow. My beast is even starting to show on my skin. I'm glowing in shades of red while my flesh tingles from rippling, a warning of the shift. At this point, if I let loose a burp, I'll probably shoot out a fireball.

It's been a long while since I felt the shift. I'm close to having it happen, though. I don't blame the beast, wanting to claim our mate, but she's not ready for that. *I'm not ready for that.*

I manage to control it from happening. Although, there's no guess as to how I find the restraint. It's because of Paige, she keeps me on my toes and wanting to be a better man. Without her, I'd either be a shell of myself, as I have been for centuries, or an out-of-control monster, as I once was in the heavens. Neither is my preferred choice now.

"This, with you, is the only choice I will ever make for the rest of my life, *leannàn.* You already own me. You have my heart completely, and I will fight to my last breath to prove my love to you," I whisper in her ear while caressing her cheek, her breast, her arm, anywhere and everywhere.

"I know this isn't easy for you to believe, my sweet little sadist with trust issues, but it's true. All day, I lived and breathed for you. I even brought you a gift to prove it."

She grins at this news. Moans when I bite her areola to pucker the nipple, heightening sensitivity to make the bud a hard point. I then twist my head with the ring between my teeth to cause a sting. Once I hear her gasps become deep hiccups, I swirl my tongue aggressively, around the whole area, to soothe her from the pain.

She responses with a deep moan that registers in my cock, and it bounces up with zeal to greet her cunt. Rolling my hips back and forth, I masturbate myself against her clit, feeling the strong buzz on my bone.

Paige gulps in a shaking breath and holds it while mouthing words I can't hear. Her brow is pinched when she meets my eyes, and I can see the tears rimming her lashes, yet they refuse to fall. Whatever she can't say out loud will be wept soon enough.

I dip my head down to capture her lips, kissing her like it's our first, making it last as though we will never have another. She starts to gulp in air and when I pull away, a single tear rolls down her cheek. It warms me to the pit of my soul and makes what I'm about to do next, worth it.

Licking her breast again, this time it's to wet the area around her nipple. I finally open the crumpled baggie in my hand. I never stop rubbing myself on her as I work, pulling out a small dab of moist white cotton from inside the plastic wrap before discarding the bag to the floor. I have to manipulate the cotton, tugging it apart, then rolling it into a long line like a piece of twine. Once it is of a perfect shape, I place it around her areola and tap it down. I also step away to rotate the wand on the swivel so it points to her hip.

With the stimulus out of the way, Paige physically sags from the wall. The cuffs are the only thing holding her upright. I can see her heart pounding in her chest as she tries to catch her breath. Her whole body is shaking from her fight. She must be exhausted, but the burning determination is still in her stare as she watches me.

"What is this?" She asks, barely above a whisper.

"Nitrocellulose," I tell her.

Her brow pops up with surprise. "Gun cotton?" She squeaks out.

I smile at her brilliance. "I'm happy to hear you know your flammable compounds."

A worried frown creases her brow and she stands herself back up to pay attention. "Uh, yeah, I do have a gun collection. I'm just curious as to what you're planning to do with it?"

My smile turns into a grin as I tweak her nipple to make it pearl. "To give you what I call my dragon's kiss."

"A what now?" She shrieks the question while bracing her back against the cross.

I trace my fingertip, back and forth, over her hardened nipple to make her whimper. I continue to flick it, to make it retract even more, until she's squirming.

"This is where I need to be sure you trust me, Paige, completely."

I channel my powers to heat up my hand. I use it to cup then lift her whole breast, warming her skin until it is on the cusp of a burning sting. With my other hand, I cup her cunt and finger her hole, pushing the same amount of heat out, to warm her pussy. I know she's getting off on it when a drop of her lust hits my fingers and hisses from my heat mixing with her liquid.

"Ah," she moans and bucks her hips. "So good."

"I'll make it feel even better, *leannàn*, just say the right words."

I plunge my fingers deeper inside of her, working them in and out until her cunt is dripping. I inch my other hand away from her breast, keeping it far enough back from the flammable cotton, to safely snap a magical flame of fire to my fingertips.

Her eyes widen and a sob escapes her mouth as she prepares for what's about to happen. I smell her fear, yet her cunt tightens and she begins to ride my fingers with anticipation.

I know she wants this when she finally speaks out. But Paige wouldn't be Paige without a warning. "Damn-it, I trust you. I have always trusted you, but may the gods strike you dead if you ever hurt me again, Zander."

The tears roll a little more from her eyes with her confession, and I want to kiss them from her face. The need to reward her for this honesty is much greater, though.

"That's my good girl," I praise.

It's my signal before I flick my fingers, throwing the magical flame at the heart-shaped cotton swirl around her nipple. The nitric acid soaking the cellulose is so flammable, it catches in an instant, and sparks a flash of fire around her areola.

"My God," she screams into the space between us. Her

whole body bows and tenses, from the singe that the quick match-like flare creates.

I'm right there to kiss away the pain with my lips to her breast, continuing to fuck her fiercely with my fingers. Her cunt is so stimulated, it's squeezing my digits as she greedily humps my hand. I speed up the thrusts and add a third finger to fill her full. I combine the use of my thumb to manipulate her clit, pushing my powered heat into her hole. Her whole body spasms with a jerk as the floodgate opens. Her sweet lust soaks my hand, causing an audible sizzling sound. She's literally extinguishing my flame, controlling my beast.

I listen to her mews as I milk the last of the release from her. Her body is sagging forward with all her weight on me. I prop her up with my hands to keep her standing up. Heavy pants mix with the sobs, and when I brush the tangled hair back from her face, her mascara has gone rogue. Black smears smudge her eyes and run a trail of ink down her cheek to mix with remaining hints of red lipstick. She is wearing this wildness as though it's her crown, owning it in the most unapologetic way.

"You are so fucking beautiful right now," I'm heartfelt in my praise.

She groans, then tries to laugh. "Anyone else saying that I'd swear they were being a smart ass. You saying it, with that damn look you always give me… I know you really mean it."

This makes me frown. "Of course, I mean everything I say to you, *leannàn*."

Her face pinches in a way that suggests she might cry, and more tears start to well in her eyes. "I know," she hiccups. "And I know you didn't really lie or try to betray me today."

I wipe her face with my thumb. "Then what was with all the hostility?"

She shakes her head and blinks away the rest of the tears. "It doesn't matter, it's just stupid."

I growl at the audacity of her statement. "If it matters to you, it's not stupid."

She snorts so hard a clear snotty bubble burst from her nose. A sadist no more. No, she's my masochist and she's more than a mess, she's a beautiful disaster. I turn to the night table drawer to get a towel, then use it to dry her face and wipe her nose.

"Why me?" She asks as I care for her.

"Why not you?" I counter.

A deep frown forms on her brow as she works this over. She seems to come to some resolve when she blinks but shakes her head like she's shaking the thought away, and changes the subject. "Would it be wrong of me to say, I need you? I need you in ways even I find disturbing. I need you to be something for me no one else can."

Looking right at her, I see the secret anguish she's been hiding. A secret she's kept hidden for years. She's not asking me to tell her she's the reason I live or that I need her too. This is her complicated way of asking to be punished again. The pain, for her, is freedom.

My smirk is dirty, my wink suggestive, but my words are honest. "No more wrong than me telling you I still have some flash cotton in the bag and the mere thought of using it on you has the veins on my cock standing at attention."

She rolls her eyes then giggles and the sound is enchanting, bewitching me to her will. I kneel for the bag and decide to unclip the cuffs from around her ankles. When I stand she wraps one leg around my waist to pull me in.

Her smirk is deadly. "Great idea," she purrs.

I twist the wand down over her clit and crank up the volume. "Even better idea," I laugh.

A spasm rips over her, making her leg instantly drop and she cusses me out, "Motherfucking bastard."

"Bastard is not a safeword, *leannàn*." I chuckle while clicking the volume down a few notches, and roll the rubber head along her slit.

It has her moaning in seconds and spreading her legs open. "That's my girl," I praise. "You like being dirty for me, don't you?"

"Yes," she slurs out.

"And you trust me, right?"

"Yes," she moans as I ride her hole with the wand.

These answers are quick and true so I test the waters. "Do you belong to me, Paige?"

Her head rolls up so she can look at me, she's undecided. I can see she's still too afraid of something to give me the answer. She nibbles on her lip, working the thickest part between her teeth like she's working on the problem that prevents her from giving a verbal reply.

Putting the wand directly on her clit, I stroke my cock against her opening to coax her along. "Stop hiding. It's just you and me here. You're safe, I got you. I will always have you."

"Ahh," she cries, and the tears start to form.

I shift to put my hand between her legs, plunging my fingers inside of her and thrusting them hard and fast. Her pussy reacts, fluttering in response to the invasion, then tightening as she speeds closer to the finish line. I let her cunt milk my fingers until I feel her juice coating my hand, then I pull out, and raise my hand to plunge the same fingers into her mouth. Pushing her head against the board as I fuck her mouth with my hand.

"You can't tell me I don't own you. Taste what I do to you. Everything I do is for you, for this. Taste it, then tell me what you know is true in your heart."

The tears are falling now, she's close to breaking and I'm not prepared for the reward. I fumble with the bag, flicking it open with one hand then shaking out the remainder of the cotton. I'm not as graceful as the first time, but the clump comes out and lands in her cleavage. Using her ample mound, I finger stretch the blob against it, to a bigger size. Once I have a circle about an inch in diameter with a hole in the center, I take the material and place it over her clit.

"Mu-huh," she protests, but her mouth is too full for me to understand.

I pat the cotton around her clit between her pussy lips and twist the wand away. Her eyes are wide as I pull back my hand, leaving just my fingertips resting on her bottom lip. "Talk, and I will reward you. Don't talk, and the foreplay continues all night. The choice is yours, Paige. What will it be?"

Taking my hand from her mouth, I slowly stroke my cock head at her opening, warming her with the heat of my powers. Hinting the idea of how this is going to go down. The crack of the breakthrough is almost audible as some form of relief flashes across her face, and words just start flooding from her lips.

"I've spent most of my life being told I've never been enough. Good enough, strong enough, smart enough, just enough. Not one person I know has ever believed in me, completely. Until you came here and made me feel invincible. It made me happy, you made me happy." The tears are streaming down her face, now. I'm losing focus, wanting to wrap her in my arms to protect her.

"I'm petrified to be happy, Zander. It never lasts. It's why I got mad at you and the royals. I felt caged, lied to, and used, just like everyone has used me in my past. I promised myself I would never allow anyone to walk over me again, but here you were trampling me and staking a claim. It hurt."

"Jesus," I mumble, not knowing whether to hug her tight or spark the flame.

She leans in as far as the cuffs allow her, getting right in my face. "Don't think it through, please. You know what I need, only you. It's how I know I'm yours. You have me. I belong only to you. As long as there are stars in the sky and air in my lungs, you have me."

I take her lips with my own and violently devour her

with aggression. In this moment we both need the emotion, it's what speaks to us best. There will be time for sweet love and devotion later, but for now we need this. She kisses me back with the same intensity, scraping teeth on tongue until one of us gets bitten. It's rough, emotional, fierce, even violent, but real. It's the best damn kiss we've ever shared.

My beast reacts, flashing heat until I burn and through me to Paige. "Fuck yeah," she screams into my mouth.

I pull back, not because I'm hurting her, but because I want to be the one to hurt her right. I place the wand right to her clit and kick it up to full speed until the hum is about as loud as her screams of pleasure. With her legs freed from the shackles, she can maneuver herself at will. Buck her hips in just the right position to feel the intensity.

With my powers, I light a flame to the tips of my left fingers and begin to play with it. I tickle her left nipple, then the right. Her breasts dance and jiggle as she jumps from the quick singe.

"More, please," she begs in the purr that compels me to comply.

I spark her nipple again. This time her breath catches and she's on her way to tripping over the gate. I'm more than ready to give her what she needs to get her there. My hands move fast as I unclip the belt from her waist and the wand hits the floor with a thud. Once it's out of the way, I step between her spread legs and trail my flaming finger across her hip, from my claw mark straight to her pussy. As I near the spot just above her clit, I grip my cock with a steady hand, waiting for that perfect moment to invade her.

The flame from my fingers licks the cotton, and a burst of fire consumes her cunt. I dare say, I've never been more jealous.

"Motherfucking-shit," she screams as her whole body goes rigid.

This is my cue, and I'm not at all gentle. I extinguish the flame in my hand to grab her hip, and as I pull her forward,

I roll up on my toes and plunge my cock in deep.

"Holy God," she coughs out what little air she has left as I possess her completely, this time with my manhood.

I'm so eager I lose control, and begin to pound her hard and fast. She starts sliding as her legs become too weak to hold her up. I cup her ass with my hands and hoist her up so she can wrap her long legs around my hips. This position allows me to drill her deep, over and over, feeling her cunt tighten around me as it milks my erection. It's too much, seeing and feeling how lost in the pleasure she is.

"Christ, I'm going to blow," I warn her.

Fortunately, she's already there.

I feel myself release just as her tidal wave flows. In an explosion of molten heat, Paige's cunt erupts like a fountain, spraying out her erotic lust and covering me with her sweet sin. It's so fucking arousing. My beast roars as we both get off. Together, we are one, whole and so sexually stimulated, I climax a second time as I ride her with a greedy need until she completely extinguishes my sexual heat.

My knees grow weak and I bow forward, resting my head on her breast to catch my breath. I hear Paige panting heavily above me, between soft murmurs that sound like words. I lift my head to look at her and there is this big goofy grin plastered on her lips.

In a soft voice, she whispers, "And sometimes, a girl just needs someone to light her pussy on fire to make the world seem right again."

I bark a laugh and my cock jerks inside of her. She groans as if she's in pain, wincing as she rolls her head against the board.

"Okay, maybe I'm being too enthusiastic." She tenses up and I get the message. In a quick motion, I pull myself out of her.

"Ow, Christ, I'm going to feel that tomorrow," she hisses while I drop her legs gently for her to stand.

"Mmm, I like the sound of that." I chuckle louder when

she gives me her classic eye roll.

We do a bit of a dance, her leaning on me as I free her wrists from the cuffs. Once she's clear though, she just drops like a limp biscuit, sliding down the cross while whimpering.

As fast as a bullet, I'm there to capture her in my arms and help her in the descent until her butt is planted on the floor. I hold her for some time, thinking about what we just accomplished. The breakthrough is a start down the road to what I hope is a long relationship. I pray for many more nights like this, where we both get to free ourselves.

"Put a fork in me, I think I'm done," she sighs and I hear the exhaustion in her voice.

It tickles my beast to see she's thoroughly sated and warms my heart to want to take care of her, even though I'm just as tired from our escapades. This still isn't about me, and if I'm honest, it never will be again. To me, there will never be anyone more important than her. There will never be one task or job more significant to take me away from her. In this moment I know the rest of my life, from here on out, will be devoted solely to her because without Paige, I am but a ghost. With her, I have purpose.

CHAPTER 19

A sharp, bitter, and yet, sweet smell fills my nose, nudging me from my deep sleep. The heavy slumbering fog inside my brain starts to lift as I blink my eyes open, and it takes me a minute for the beautiful vision before me to make sense. When it does, I have to remind myself I am still on this realm, and not back in the heavens where a seductress like Paige would thrive.

"Good morning," Paige whispers from her straddled position over my torso.

She's peering down at me with a magnificent killer grin, holding a mug of coffee in hand and waving it, back and forth, in front of my nose.

Damn, that smile. There is nothing better to wake up to.

My eyes scan her, taking in every sexy inch of her before me. Her hair is wet and wildly tossed around her head like she just washed and towel dried it but forgot to use a comb. A few strands have even tucked themselves beneath the collar of the t-shirt she is wearing. I can see from the wet spots on the shirt, they are laying on top of her breast.

And why wouldn't they... The lucky little bastards.

The shirt looks suspiciously like the one I had on yesterday. It fits her well, hugging her breasts and the curve of her hip in a possessive embrace. I'm slightly jealous that my shirt has the pleasure of feeling her up, and I'm not.

"Good morning to you, mo àilleacht," I say in a sleepy voice.

My voice and brain might not be fully awake, but my cock sure feels as though it drank the mug of coffee in Paige's hand and is ready to go for a twenty-mile jog down her dark tunnel.

Down boy!

"I brought you coffee, black. I hope that's okay. I didn't

know how you take it."

Paige's words halt the mental lecture going from my brain to my erection, and I have to think about what she just said before I answer. "Uh, a triple-triple usually, but black is fine."

Her head cocks as her brows pop up. "A what?" She asks with an abrupt bursting laugh.

Her body vibrates against me from her chuckle causing my dick to jump in a spastic jerking dance. Thank the heavens for the thin bedding sheet over me, or my morning wood would be beating itself raw against her ass. I muse at my inner monolog and realize she's staring at me, waiting for my reply.

"It's… ah… a Canadian thing," I tell her while getting myself back to the conversation. "When we place our orders at the local coffee shops there, most people ask for a double-double. It means two cream and two sugar in their coffee. I, however, like my coffee how I like my mate, extra sweet and creamy." I give her a wink with the punchline and her mouth drops open.

Not from shock, though, as she rolls her eyes and begins her rebuttal, "You almost had me there, but you can stop with the corny pickup lines, player. You already got the girl." She stops for a minute, thinking over some thought then adds with a warm smile, "Fully and completely."

I sit up and take the cup from her hand, twisting sideways to place it on the nightstand. She slides down my stomach into my lap, making my morning wood a happy camper as it settles against her ass crack. I ignore its urges while wrapping my arms around her waist to pull her close so our eyes can meet.

"I'm more than happy to hear it, but I wasn't trying to be a player. The coffee thing is true. I only brought it up, then added the joke, because I was just having dirty thoughts about you. I either have to sound like an idiot with random chatter or give into temptation and ravage you."

She gives me a serious look that has me worried my confession has offended her somehow. "So, what you're saying is, you want to take this hug and turn it into something with naked, heavy thrusting?" She is fucking with me and her grin is as playful as the comment.

God, she's the perfect mate. Perfectly perverted.

I roll my hips up, masturbating myself on her ass crack around the bed sheet. "Mmm, my cock would appreciate that kind of hug from your pussy."

She lets out a giggle that turns into a scream as I roll us both to put her on her back. There's a brief fight with the bed sheet that ends with it getting torn, as I untangle it from my torso to settle myself between her thighs. Her hands meet my dick in a double-fisted squeeze, stopping me an inch from her opening.

"Still sore?" I ask with concern, kissing her forehead to let her know I won't be disappointed if we go no further.

She strokes my bone with both hands. "A little, but we both know the masochist part of me just wants to fuck you hard to make it hurt even more," she finishes with a knowing grin.

"Jesus," I groan, "And the sadist part of me wants to give you your wish."

She laughs, "We are seriously messed up."

"Uh-huh," I agree, "But dirty minds work better together."

I lean in for a kiss; she stops me with a firm grip on my length. The move is confusing and I question the action, "Do you not want me to kiss you?"

"Not at all," she states while both of her hands slowly work over my cock. One strokes my length while the other fists my swollen head, coaxing out pre-cum to be used as jerking lube. "I'm just demonstrating how some of my best kissing, is done with two hands."

A deep groan rumbles up my throat. "Christ, you inspire me to be a better pervert.

She grins up at me in a way that screams of her own carnal desires. "Hmm, I like that. And now I want to see what else I can do to inspire you. Playing with it is good and all, but what if using my mouth is better. Like maybe you need to check my gag reflexes."

"Oh, *leannàn*," I moan uncontrollably, meeting her downward hand strokes by rolling my hips up.

I'm not sure if it's from her dirty suggestion, the deep rasp of her voice, the incredible hand-job or all of the above, but the need to mark her with my seed and scent is undeniable. She seems to read the signs of my impending orgasm and slows the jerking action to a long and steady fist pump between her legs, using the crown of my cock to masturbate her clit. I feel her wet heat and it tickles my beast awake, causing a fire to light within me.

Paige is trying to control me, keeping me on the edge like I did to her last night. The only difference is, when I'm around her, I can't be controlled. I crave to be in her, it's become my favorite feeling. Once I get to experience it, I want nothing more than to mark her, again and again, until her sheets are soaked in our sin and her scent is all over me. I can't get enough of her, and it's doubtful I ever will.

She slides my cock through her slit, up, down, and over her clit until we are both slick from our mutual pre-cum admiration.

"You're so hard," she moans.

I dip my head to her ear to whisper, "You make me so."

"Are you saying I own you?" There is a hint of challenge in her voice.

I trace the shell of her ear with my tongue, feeling her shiver before I answer with honesty, "Wholeheartedly, forever and ever."

I rock my hips forward to grace her opening with my crown, brushing against her to ask for permission to enter. She moans from the connection, opening her legs wide to me, then groans out her reply, "Now which one of us is the hopeless romantic?"

"A romantic with a twisted mind, but I think you like that." I push my pelvis forward as I speak, penetrating her with a quick thrust.

Her head rolls and her back arches as a gasp shoots from her lips, "More than you know."

My thrusting movements are slow, precise and practiced, as I work my length inside of her to hit all the right spots. I know I've achieved the next level when her coos turn to screams, which I egg on with words she seems to want to hear.

"Then you know my cock is yours, *leannàn*. It is here for your pleasure, and you may do with it as you wish."

"I wish for it to fuck me," she purrs, "Like it owns me, too."

When I entered her, she had to release my cock, freeing up her hands to explore her own body. I watch as her fingers play, tickling my length while she rubs her cunt. The sight of us connected and her stimulating us both is a piece of erotic art. With our bodies this intricately laced, there doesn't appear to be an end to where I start and Paige ends. We are of one interwoven link, completing the other. The mere idea of us each belonging to the other has my thrusts becoming more apparent. I sense an urgency within, as though nothing else matters except filling her with my sin. I speed the lovemaking to an unnatural pounding pace to get us both there.

"Yes, harder, make it hurt," she screams her demands at me, abandoning the finger playing to grab at my shoulders just to hang on.

As soon as her fingernails sink into my skin, piercing the scars on my back, my beast fights to take over. The first time she touched the mangled tissue it had only prickled. This time the scars seem to burn from the inside out, and as they do, so too does the beast within me.

My whole spine ripples from head to tailbone, and even

further as it seems to lengthen. My flesh not only heats from the internal fires burning deep in my soul, but also starts to smolder. My whole body turns a deep red while my skeleton covering stretches to allow for the scales to form.

"God, you're so hot," Paige shrieks with absolute delight, panting and moaning in ecstasy as she fucks me back.

Realizing what is happening, I panic. Using my arms, I try to push up and away from her. Her long legs are strong from hours of riding her horse and she wraps them securely around my waist to pull me back down, to ride a completely different beast.

"I have to stop," I'm pleading with her in an urgent tone.

"Don't you dare," she snarls the ferocious demand, sinking her talons deep into the scars to hold me tighter.

I use all of my strength to push myself up, fighting not only Paige but the beast who is slowly taking over. "I'm shifting, Paige. Let me go."

I'm frantic in my speech, fearing the worst and for her safety. I'm physically struggling against her while I mentally grapple with myself to stop what I feel is coming. If I shift at this moment, I will rip her apart. And if the shift doesn't kill her, my beast form will savagely assault her until there is nothing left.

I am a monster.

Paige's cool hands are suddenly on my sweat covered cheeks and she pulls me down so we are face to face. "You will not shift, my love. I got you."

I stare into the cognac color of her eyes and see her concern. It is only a small flicker before it is replaced by something new, something more powerful than any other emotion. It is what I concentrate on, even though I am panting out breaths of smoke at her. And true to her badass personality, she does not flinch.

"There is a reason I dreamt of you, Zander. There is a reason we are fated. I've just been stupidly fighting it like I do with everything," she speaks in a low and calming tone. It's soothing, pushing me forward and dragging my beast back into the hole deep inside me. "I'm stubborn, but you know that."

I don't laugh, I can't. I'm still trying to control myself, trying to keep my true form from getting out. She is helping me, soothing me with her enchanting voice, and grounding me to her with her incredible touch. I fall into her as she speaks, hypnotized by our connection and the way she caresses me. My pulse seems to slow from it to a normal rhythm. Not quite human or wolf slow, but not dragon fast either.

"You know my mother was Native and from a long line of female shaman. What you don't know is, her family came from the Aztec culture. Our legend says her ancestor had an affair with the moon god, Tecciztecatl. Important only because his parents were the god of fire and the goddess of water. The affair produced a child that started my family line. The union gave us strong powers, as well as strong ties to those elements.

I might have been born a supernatural werewolf, but I am still from my mother's family, and I too have powers. I just never bothered to recognize them, until I met you. There's a reason we have been drawn to one another and it isn't because of the phenomenal sex, though that has been a huge bonus." She stops to chuckle, and this time I join her.

She has been able to captivate me with talk about her lineage, allowing me to regain control of myself. As my beast slowly retreats and my mind settles, I'm able to place the last pieces of the puzzle together.

"You don't fear my fire because you are from it," I state as realization sets in.

She nods with certainty. "I am your beast whisperer," she says while wiggling her eyebrows at me.

I roll my eye. "Don't get cocky."

Her hips roll up as she grinds herself against my

erection. "I'm not being cocky, but I would like some more of your cock," she says in a low rasp.

"You are incorrigible, *leannàn*," I groan, growing harder by the second for her.

She reaches down between us to guide my cock to her opening again. "It's true, I am unashamed to take what I want," she boldly states, "And I want you, now."

She certainly is a beast whisperer, for as soon as she says this, I am drawn to comply with her demand. Lowering my body against hers, I penetrate her without thought, as though my body knows it is but a puppet, and she its master controlling the strings.

The thrust inside of her is hard because I know it is what she likes, and the deep moan on her lips lets me know I'm right. I dip my head down to taste that moan of desire off her lips. She opens her mouth to me and I invade her with my tongue. She is indeed the heavenly flavor of sin, and as I savor it, the urge to mark returns. Along with the threat of my beast taking over.

Her hands snake up my back to my shoulders and as soon as her nails pierce my skin I feel the spark. A spark that ignites the flame. A flame that has me burning hotter than the hellfire in the Underworld. I break our kiss as a feral scream rips from my throat just as the beast takes over.

I feel my arms move, my hands gripping her hips to hoist her up as my body rises so I'm on my knees, pounding my length into her at an unnaturally hard pace. I can no longer contain the beast. I have held it back for too long, and it finally wants to be free.

I want to be free.

No more hiding in the shadows. No more lies. No more pretending.

"I am Ruadan," I hear myself whisper.

"One and the same," Paige screams the reply and continues to repeat it, over and over, in whining pleas as though she's wanting to convey some sort of message.

At first, I don't realize it's her speaking. It's just a vibration of the air, kind of resembling words. But after she says the phrase a few more times, my head jerks down towards the sound, and that's when I see her.

She has stretched herself up the length of the bed, her back arched so her arms can reach the iron headboard, where her fingers are curled and white knuckling one of the rods. She's not hanging on for dear life, she's using it as leverage to fuck me back. Her eyes are fixed on me, the coloring has changed to a caramel shade, highlighting her emotions.

From my towering position above, savagely defiling her, I realize what she is saying. Me and the beast are one and the same. I don't smell any fear from her, just an overpowering scent of her arousal. One glance down, and I see it coating my cock.

She's taking this volatile assault as some perverse punishment, getting pleasure from the pain it is causing her. Seeing her in this state, the lusting desire burning as white-hot in her eyes as it is within me, I understand all she has said.

There is a metaphorical click in my head, and I suddenly see the light of Livia's blessing. This is my peace, here with Paige, and it has been because of her that I have been able to let go of the darkness that once consumed me. By letting my past no longer haunt me, I can finally be myself. Ruadan, the god of mystery and powerful dragon, as well as Zander, an average guy, living a normal life in a supernatural world. We are one and the same.

"Zander, baby," Paige pants out. "I can see you're having some monumental moment, and I'm sure it's profound, but I'm about to cum my fucking brains out, and I'd really like for you to be here in the moment with me, when I do."

Her voice is what makes me glance down, her flushed crazed look is what makes me tune back in and get down to business. I am a quick learner and she has taught me that even a beauty needs a beast, and she is built for a savage. As her barbarian, I can't deny my beauty of her deepest desires. I might be a combination of things, but she is my world, my everything, and I would give her the last beat of my heart just to make her happy.

"*Cibé is mian le do chroi, mo áilleacht,*" I tell her. "You are my reason for being. You make me keep wanting more. *Is leat mo chroí, leannàn,* forever."

"Goddamnit, your pretty words make me wet," she whimpers.

The truth of her declaration is all over my cock, but it isn't enough. It's never enough. I want her to cover me in her passionate lust, and the only way to do that is to speak the language she knows best.

Unfortunately, there isn't anything readily at hand to provide the painful pleasure I know she craves, but I have my hands and the element of danger.

She's already on her back, stretched out, her legs locked around my waist. Moving her isn't an option. However, leaning forward to pin her down against the mattress with the full force of my weight is. In this position, she is crumpled over like a pretzel, completely in my control and with no chance of escape.

I wrap my hand around the front of her neck, using a pinching pressure with my fingers to choke her. There is an immediate response of fright in her eyes. I play it up in a menacing manner by allowing my beast to flash forward. I feel it stir, igniting in flaming heat until a puff of smoke swirls from my lips.

"Zander," Paige cries with a gasp and her eyes go wide.

I hear her heart bolt to life, pounding at an abrupt pace. I smell the hint of her fear tickling my nose, and I breathe it in to alert my beast to be at the ready. She has registered the possibility I might be losing control of myself and that the beast is taking over, putting her in danger. It won't because I won't, we are the same being. She doesn't know of my breakthrough, though, and starts to struggle, pushing against me to get away. The bucking of her hips allows my cock to go deeper into her, and as it does, her cunt responds with a flutter and more wet heat.

I have achieved what I set out to do. Her brain and body have disconnected. One is screaming at her to run, while the other is getting off. I work on the latter, pumping my hips into her to fill her completely. She mews out like a scared rabbit.

A few deeper plunges and she starts moaning, but with a murmured uncertainty. Using the hand not choking her, I make my way back to her ass, giving it a hard full-on cheek spank. It stings my palm, but I feel her cunt tighten, and her moans rumble deep in her throat. It's music to my ears.

She's so close and I want her to have her reward. With the same hand, I dip two fingers down her crack. It is already well lubed with her excitement, and my fingers easily slip right inside her. This time, her breath hitches and her eyes roll until her lids close. She's almost at the finish line. *And man, does that ever turn me on.*

I'm all in now, down to business. My cock is throbbing inside of her. With each rough penetrating thrust, I'm about to burst. I combine my long cock pumps in her cunt with faster finger plunges inside her ass, until there is one continued scream shooting from her mouth. What little movement possible her pinned position beneath me, she uses to rock and meet each plunge, thrust for thrust, until the spasm hits and she howls like an animal in heat.

Her hips jut forward, and I literally impale her with the length of my cock, like ramming the door open to allow the orgasm to flow. Her floodgate unhinges, soaking me, the bed, and her in a spray of liquid lust. It is the most beautiful sight, and she is the most beautiful soul to gift me with her pleasure. I'm so enthralled by this experience with her that my own pleasure is of less importance, and before I realize it, I've lost the moment.

She goes limp beneath me, as soft as a pillow, breathless and panting. I descend with her, but hoover just above to cradle her between my forearms. Her eyes flutter open and she attempts a smile.

"I don't know what I did to inspire that, but you have to tell me so we can do it again." A small giggle ends the sentence followed by a sigh of contentment.

I've never wanted to be tender and caring with a woman before. I'm more than compelled to shower Paige with my affections now. Lavishing her with soft butterfly kisses to her cheek, her jaw, her neck.

"Mmm, I would love nothing better than to stay in this bed for the rest of the day, and continue to help you make similar sighs of satisfaction."

She moans, "Don't ruin my postcoital buzz with a big o' butt—kick of reality."

Her hands snake up my back and she scratches her nails over my scars, teasing me like the seductress she is, to turn my thoughts back to sex. "Just stay here," her low voice begs.

The building fire from her touch shoots down my spine and straight into my already engorged erection. Droplets from the orgasm I missed secrete from my crown as I hiss, "Christ, *leannàn*, you're playing dirty."

"I know," she purrs in that deep rasp while lifting her hips to press herself against my swollen manhood.

I damn near explode on her belly. It is only through deep panting breaths, and thoughts of anything other than her, I am able to hold myself back. The temptation is strong, though, and I reluctantly roll myself over.

She follows the turn I make to my back by laying across my chest, licking the scar across my rib and up to my nipple. It is beautiful torture and I want to give in, but we have much to do today.

"We can continue this later, *leannàn*," I moan out. "After we get you free from Bear."

Her head pops up and a deep frown creases her head. "There is no rule that says I have to be present for the fight," she snaps.

Her response surprises me. "That doesn't sound like the control freak I know and love," I muse at her.

She shrugs. "Maybe I finally realized last night, I don't always have to be in control. When you try to control everything, you enjoy nothing. Maybe I want to live in the moment, have some fun for once. My physical part in this is over, and like you all said, the True Alpha has got this covered."

I sit us both up and pull her into my lap, where she curls into me and nudges her head in the crook of my neck. "Where is this coming from?"

She leans back to look at me, and I see the exhaustion in her expression. "I think I'm just done with fighting this life."

I cup her chin with my index finger and rub my thumb against it. "Life is tough, but *leannàn*, so are you. I never thought you would surrender, not to this."

"Yeah, well, most have that image of me, but really, no one gets the true picture," she snaps and tries to climb out of my lap.

I wrap one arm around her to hold her in place, continuing to cup her chin and keep eye contact. "I'm not just anyone, Paige. I see the picture you're painting clearly. The woman I love and admire is strong, and you didn't get this way by letting shit work itself out. Strong people don't come from easy pasts and you are proof of that. When shit went wrong, you handled it. This time, you get some help, but it doesn't make you any less of a person."

She frowns at me and bites her lip as her eyes well with tears, but she says nothing. I try coaxing words from her with a more demanding tone, "Tell me what this is about, Paige."

She swallows and blinks a couple of times, but in the end, she gives in to the emotions. "I'm scared, Zander," she states through quivering lips. "I've been fighting this problem my whole life, and there's a good chance I'll be free from it today. Then what do I do? This fight has shaped who I am, what I stand for. Who will I be after? What will I have to fight for? What's my damn purpose?"

"*Mo àilleacht*, you will always be you. Being a stubborn, hardheaded woman is in your DNA, and it's never going away." I stop to chuckle, which brings a small smile to her lips.

It's enough to make me continue, "My point is, after today, you will still have your businesses to run, which come with plenty of issues, I'm sure. You'll also have a pack to lead in Gage's absence, as well as the MC because we both know Mac Tìre is going to need someone to keep him focused. And I hope, most importantly, you'll be my mate. An equal partner in all aspects of my life, and especially, my bed."

This makes her smile widen until it reaches her eyes. "The latter could be a full-time job in itself," she teases with a wink.

I wrap her in a hug. "Mmm, I love the sound of that."

"And I love you," she whispers back.

Although she hasn't been lacking with a show of her affection, this is the first time she's ever voiced the words, without being prompted during sex. It takes me by surprise, and I gasp from the unexpected way it makes me feel. Happiness, overjoyed and overcome with my own emotions that I'm hugging her tighter because I'm unsure how else to respond.

It might be the Universe's way of giving me a reprieve when bells and buzzing suddenly fill the quiet around us. We both sit up, with the same bewildered expression on our face.

Paige is the first to clue in, "Shit, it's our phones."

She hops from my lap and out of the bed, running for the kitchen island, where I assume she's left her device. I follow suit, rolling off the bed to search for my own phone, finding it handily on the nightstand beside me.

I hear her voice a greeting just as I swipe my finger across the screen to answer my own call, "Paine."

"Wake up ye wanker, there be a shit-storm brewing."

CHAPTER 20

Ending my call with Mac Tìre, I'm deep in thought when I turn to find the room empty. I need to speak with Paige, and I'm about to call out to her when I tune into the sound of water running in the next room. A recent image of her from the night before last, naked and wet in that very shower, fills my head. It is powerful enough to chase away the swirl of contemplation, from the conversation I just had.

Mac Tìre who?

In seconds, I'm across the room and rounding the corner of the closet to stand just at the edge of the shower stall. Paige is facing the other side of the shower, with the water rinsing suds from her backside. Her head is cocked down and to the side, so the spray can hit her neck, but avoid her hair. As the water washes away the soap, her dragon tattoo appears to glisten in the light like it is wrapped in a halo of coloring. If my erection wasn't guiding me to her, I would consider this a sign that I have indeed returned to my greater self as a being from the heavens. But, with an ass so perfectly defined in front of me, who the hell has time to debate such divine intervention?

"Need a hand washing the important parts?"

She twirls herself around and steps out of the spray, making room for me to get in with her. By the serious expression on her face, she's back into business mode. Sex is miles from her mind, at the moment.

What a shame…

She offers a reassuring smile and blurts a response, "As much as I love hand games, I'm afraid we'll have to wait to play again. Ducky called from the airport; the Alpha's brother arrived with an entourage. I'm not sure what's going on, but he had to wait for a tour bus to show up to move some guy in a coffin. He wants me at the bar to clear out the storage room, to stash whoever is in the coffin for the day, while keeping it on the down-low from the humans."

She leans against me to give me a quick peck on the cheek before stepping out of the stall, reaching for a towel from the shelf as she goes.

I'm disappointed, but I don't let it register in my voice as I explain a part of her story. "It sounds like the Queen's human, Chris, is here. He's in the same band as your pup. They must have asked Samuel to send his bus to the airport to transport Magennis, the Queen's vampire King. Looks like the gang's all here."

I step in the cascading water; the warm heat engulfs me and does little to take the edge off my boner. It's spring-loaded and trigger happy to the point of painful. Reaching for the lever on the wall, I crank it all the way to the right and wait for the blast of cold to hit while I soap up. It doesn't come. Instead, a lukewarm drizzle falls down on me like I've been caught in a summer's day sun-shower.

I'm scrubbing my body with vigor and mentally cussing out the ingenuity of an impressive hot water tank when she blurts out, "If all the Queen's men are here, then I wonder who the other two wolves are that also arrived."

"Must be Garo's men," I say without much thought. Rinsing the soap from my face, as I turn to face her.

"Huh," is all she says.

It takes a few seconds for the soap residue to clear away before I can open my eyes; and when I do, there's instant regret. My heart leaps to a double-time beat, which escalates the flow of blood through my veins and directly into my cock. My left-hand reaches out to the wall to keep me balanced. My right-hand grips my length with the tightest of squeezes to defuse the impending explosion.

Paige has toweled off and started to dress. I don't think she realizes how provocative she's being, bent at the waist with ass wiggling in the air, rolling a magnificent pair of mid-thigh boots up her long sexy legs. The mere sight triggers my hand to begin an urgent stroking of my bone. The snow-white of the leather footwear makes her skin appear darker, which intensifies the shades of color in her tattoos.

It'd be a shame not to spray them with a good cum-shot.

I view her in a full-length mirror as she stands and shrugs on some type of harness. Her movements seem to bring her flesh to life like dancing art. I watch the animated pictures in utter awe as she straps the stretchy elastic around her voluptuous mounds.

Am I drooling?

Then she's slithering into a piece of latex, laced together in the front with a crisscrossed string. She only pulls it down her torso halfway. When the action stops, I notice my jerking strokes do, too. Until she begins the elaborate adjusting process.

Have mercy!

The muscles in my forearm flex to the same rhythm her legs teeter back and forth on her stilts, while she works to hide a treasure trove of items in her footwear. Blades in the arches of the heels. A tactical combat knife tucked in a pocket of the boot, down the inside of her left thigh. A lacy garter strapped just above her right knee with a Glock 42 slipped in the attached holster. Once the leather has been dragged up her leg there is no visible evidence of any weaponry. The mere knowledge of what arsenal lies beneath has my cock dripping with excitement from the element of danger.

My warrior princess needs to come sit on her rock-hard cock throne.

Her breasts jiggle, flashing me back to the show. The shake is from the way she lifts then separates her tits, positioning another holster with a Smith & Wesson Shield through the strings that run the front length of the dress. She clips the gun to the strap across her ribs then slides the weapon under her left breast.

When she stands this time, she smooths the rest of the dress down and over her hips. You can't see the handgun, but you can see a whole lot of her. The string is straining across her chest, showcasing her impressive rack, and plays a sexy peek-a-boo show of her freshly shaven pubic area.

"Christ, you're wearing that?" I blurt.

Her eyes dart to the left as she views me through the reflection in the mirror. A smirk crests her lips as she raises a brow at me. Her question purrs seductively from her lips, "What's wrong with what I'm wearing?"

I plunge my hand down my cock and choke the life out of it, hissing from the pain as I speak. "Absolutely nothing, and without a doubt, everything."

She snickers at my response. "What does that mean?"

I glare at her reflection with a heat filled stare, holding myself back from stalking her like prey and taking her like the wild animal that I am. "For starters, that dress barely covers... Christ, Paige, when you bend over I can see your cunt. What if you need to defend yourself today? Perhaps a pair of pants would be a better option."

Her eyes roll with one of her classic glares. "Seriously, you're concerned about a clam flash? Think about that for a minute. If I do fight today, in all probability it will be with a male. A flash is my upper hand to throw them off their game, and I need all the advantages I can get. It seemed to work on you." She smirks knowingly, then grins with her next thought. "Is that maybe a hint of jealousy I'm detecting?"

I take a step forward, halfway between the safety of the shower and my greatest temptation. "I'm not going to lie and say I'm not, Paige. I am, however, a confident man, and perverse enough to admit I love watching you work a room. You ooze assertiveness, control, and sex. A tease to the poor douchebags who think they'll get in your pants. They don't have a chance or the proverbial balls to manhandle you, but I do, and I do it really well. But, if I have to watch you walk around in this..." I groan and wave my hand at her outfit.

It's too much, she's too much.

I stalk over, pushing her against one of the long doors of the built-in armoire. My chest at her back, heaving from panting anticipation, holds her in place. My hands grab onto her perfectly shaped fuck-handle hips so I can pin her there and grind my erection into the divot of the material stretched across her ass crack.

"I just spent the last fifteen fucking minutes watching you, beating my cock into submission because all I want to do is blow my load inside your spectacular ass. So, no, this isn't jealousy. This is me, concerned about my need to mark you, fuck you, and keep you sexually satisfied getting in my way of staying focused on important life matters today."

She turns her head to peer at me over her shoulder. "I have a solution. I can just put on some underwear."

I damn near choke on my laugh. "How is a pair of underwear going to help the raging erection I get every time I'm around you, *leannàn*?"

There's another wicked grin on her lips, indicating she has a plan. She reaches for a drawer on her right, opens it and fumbles around with her hand until she produces a silky black number.

"These will work," she muses.

She elbows me back. I move only enough for her to thread her legs through the openings of lace. Once they've reached her thigh, though, it's game fucking on. I'm shoving her right back into the cupboard door, showing which of us is in the driver's seat.

"What wickedness have you cooked up in that slutty little mind of yours, *leannàn*?"

As soon as her fingers begin to trail up her hips, rolling the latex up and over her curves to her belly, I know I don't have any of this under control.

"I'm finding it quite erotic to have the scent of the man I love, and sex on my skin. When you see me across a room today, receiving all the attention, I want you to think of my cunt and how it's covered with your cum. It is your scent I choose to mark me, and I no longer care who knows it."

While she paints me this graphic picture, she reaches back between her legs, curling her fingers around my cock to guide the firm length down her crack and through her slit. Rolling her hips forward, she strokes my length on her cunt, while fisting my crown with her lace filled hand.

I groan when understanding hits. "You're going to jerk me off into your panties?"

"Uh-huh," she purrs. "A million men could give me their attention, but it wouldn't matter because it couldn't compare to how you give me yours, like this."

She slides her hips forward and releases my cock, just enough for me to sink into her wet heat.

"I love how dirty you are," I moan.

After I give her a few hard pumps she shifts forward again, popping my cock from her cunt to continue fisting it with the silk. The material, slick from our mutual juices, slips with ease around my crown, intensifying each stroke.

"I'm only dirty for you, Zander. Your secret harlot. Your temptress. Your depraved slut." On each syllable, she uses her hand to enunciate the strokes faster, harder, until my urges grow deeper, more apparent.

"I love how you use me until I hurt," she continues to mind-fuck me verbally. "I love how you claim me as yours. Treat me as yours. I am yours, Zander, mark me. Spill your seed and I'll rub it into my cunt, wearing it like it's the most precious jewel."

"Oh, fuck," I drone out while my hips thrust forward, meeting her stroke for stroke.

Her free hand winds up to my head, where she grasps a fistful of my hair to guide my face to her neck. "I want you to bite me when you cum. Make a fresh mark to show the world who I belong to."

The request ignites my fire and before she even finishes her demands, I'm not only sinking my teeth into her neck,

I'm also burning my claw print back on her hip.

"Oh, God," she screams, "You're making *me* cum."

Her confession drives me. I feel the weight of my balls as they harden, ready for the release. My frantic hip pumps become increasingly erratic when her thighs cross, capturing my cock in a tight embrace between them. Her wetness warms my length as she lets her small eruption go, coating me.

"Cum for me, Zander, do it now," she demands in a low raspy tone.

Knowing she got off is my trigger. Hearing her deep voice command me is my breaking point. She cups her palm around my crown just as my seed starts to spurt. She captures some of it in the garment and clasps it into her pussy, rubbing my sin into her clit with the head of my cock. I have done a lot of explicit, erotic shit in my life, but this, hands down, is at the top of the list.

Dear heaven above, I love this female with all that I am.

I wrap myself around her body in an affectionate embrace while tenderly licking the bite closed on her neck. I place a soft kiss on the mark, causing her to shiver and another sigh to expel from her lips. When I'm done, she turns in my arms, kissing me in the most loving manner. Warm and sweet, like sunshine and honey.

"You complete me," she sighs into my mouth.

We stay in the embrace for a few minutes, allowing our lips to say what we both feel in our hearts. It's a beautiful moment. Something I long to experience more, but for now, I soak it in to savor.

"Your multi-tasking talents of making my heart sing and my panties literally wet are amazing," she laughs in the most carefree manner.

It is a winsome sound that warms me to the depths of my soul while nudging reality back into place.

"Promise me something?" I ask with a light kiss on her forehead.

Stepping back so our eyes can meet, there's no hesitation in her reply, "Anything."

This one gesture shows her faith, and that she no longer hides behind her walls from me. It makes me smile and take her hand, not caring when I bring it to my lips to kiss her sticky palm.

"Whatever happens with Bear's challenge and possible fight, promise me you'll stay safe and out of trouble. I know you're a badass, but you are my badass, and I want as many years as possible worshipping your greatness. Please, for me, don't do anything to jeopardize that."

The warmth of her affection glows brightly in her eyes, but her spunky response, is the reminder of why she captured my heart in the first place.

"You're asking *me* to stay out of trouble?" She asks with dismay, then carries on with an attitude-laced lecture complete with the hand on hip stance I've grown quite fond of. "I'm about to go stuff one of the undead somewhere between my turnips and canned soup for a secret supernatural Queen. I can only pray to the powers that be that the health inspector doesn't come for a surprise inspection, which will shut down my bar, and possibly toss my ass in jail because dead bodies in coffins are not easily explained and should never be stored with food. I'm sure you can see how there are many complications in your request, making it clearly impossible for me to commit to."

I can only chuckle at her rant and offer a simple, "Point taken."

"Good," she says, signaling the end of our conversation while walking off to the shower. When she reaches the edge, she half turns back, towards me, and softly adds, "Please don't die today either, because I need you too."

A wave of emotion damn near brings me to tears. I'm smiling like an idiot and staring at her like a love-struck fool. My only response is one that has her grinning back.

"Yes, Ma'am," I say and offer a submissive bow.

She snorts a laugh and turns away, attempting a wash-off in the stream of water without physically going into the spray. I reach for a towel to begin my own cleanup. There's a comfortable silence as we both work on getting ourselves ready, which for me involves a hunt for the clothing I had strewn across her apartment last night in the heat of the moment. I'm pleasantly surprised when I find my gear, including the saddlebags off my bike, neatly folded and arranged on the seat of the curved couch.

My badass domestic princess had been busy this morning.

The thought has me smiling.

I hear the water shut off and Paige's heels clicking across the tile. I pick up my pace, jumping into jeans, pulling on boots, clipping on holsters, and digging out a fresh shirt to put on under my jacket. The rushing actions help direct my thoughts to what awaits, and the important reasons I need to be performing at my peak today.

There is much on the line, and not just getting Paige free and clear from this deal with Bear. I have a responsibility to the Queen and her court, and I must be willing to protect them at all costs, defending our kingdom as its loyal soldier, a nomad no more.

No more shadows. No more games.

This is why Livia blessed me. This is my purpose.

My beast wakens with an anticipated enthusiasm, kicking on the heat by stirring the embers to stoke the fires within. This time I welcome his return, allowing the connection to bind us as one. One and the same. Ready for battle. Ready to protect my heart, home, and the crown.

The tapping of heels grows louder until Paige is standing at the closet door. Her expression is full of shock as she gives me a top to bottom once over.

"Oh, you're ready?" She states the question with surprise.

I give her a deadly glance of seriousness. "More than

you know, *leannàn*. And may the gods have mercy on anyone who dares cross me today."

CHAPTER 21

"Holy shit, the parking lot is jam-packed," Paige comments while speeding past the long line of vehicles bordering her bar, to weave her truck to the back of the building. "And it's not even noon."

She pulls up to an empty area between the hotel and bar, stopping just shy of a loading bay, and slams the truck into park. It jolts forward, then slowly rolls back to a stop when she cuts the motor.

She turns to me, a creased frown of worry denting her forehead. "What the hell is going on?"

Realizing I hadn't yet told her of my conversation with Mac Tire from earlier, I take a deep breath to explain the increase of customers. "Bear has been busy. Mac Tire said he called every supernatural leader within a few hours' drive. Promising them wealth and power, if they'd come join him in the fight. He doesn't just want to take out Gage. He's trying to take over. By the looks of the parking lot, I'd say there's more than a few who think he might succeed. We have a lot of work to do to convince them otherwise."

I reach for the handle to open the door and hop down from the truck to make my way in, knowing Mac Tire will need all the help he can get with those inside. When I don't hear Paige's door close, I turn to see what's taking her so long. I assume she's strapping on more weapons, it would be so her. However, what I do see confuses me, and fills me with panicked worry.

She's still in the driver's seat, frozen, with hands stuck at ten and two on the wheel, as she stares out the windshield. When I reach her door and open it, she's crying. I'm not sure why this would be her reaction, it isn't like her. It breaks a small part of me and I immediately wrap my arms around her.

"This is all my fault," she sobs, burying her face into my chest. "I'm so sorry I did this to your family."

An uncomfortable sensation grips my heart when it dawns on me what she's saying. I lift her chin to meet her eyes, wiping the wet trail of tears from her cheeks.

"*Mo àilleacht*, my sweetest love, this is not your fault. You had nothing to do with this."

Her eyes darken as she spews, "I have everything to do with this. If I just accepted the damn deal with Bear years ago, this wouldn't even be a thing now. But, like everything, I had to fight it. Drawing out my drama helped make the conditions perfect for Bear, and now look at the mess. Your whole family is in danger, you're in danger, and it's because of me."

It warms me to hear her worry and know it comes from her heart, but I hate the tone she uses to criticize herself. "Paige, stop beating yourself up. It wouldn't have mattered whether you took the deal or not. This attack on the royals is another test and would have happened with or without Bear's interference. He was just weak enough to take the proverbial carrot that was left dangling for him. He's not the first or the last, to fall victim to the gods' games."

She seems to understand what I'm saying and sags against me with relief. I take it as a sign and continue, "Whatever the case, it's how we deal with the test that matters, and ultimately it's the Queen's decision to make. She's the one they watch because they fear her strength. What they fail to realize, is the more of us that stand with her, the stronger she is becoming."

Her eyes burn bright with excitement as she adds, "And from the alliance, you and the court have become stronger too. It's why your sister grew wings and why your dragon returns to you now."

"Yes, but there's more to it," I tell her. "The Queen acted as the fates' messenger by sending me here, which got me to meet you, my destiny. But there is no guarantee, destiny can go either way. You could have as easily been destined to kill me, as to love me. The Queen played a role in this too. She believed in me, in us, and her faith is powerful. It helped encourage us enough, to find the peace within ourselves to give love a chance. It's from this bond my powers and beast have returned, and your love that keeps me grounded."

"Really?" She asks with a chuckle, and when I nod, her face breaks out into a huge grin. "So, in the future, if you do something to piss me off, I can kill you and claim it as my destiny?"

"You would go there, wouldn't you?" Shaking my head and stepping back to pull her from the truck. I get us back on track by walking towards the bar. "It doesn't work like that and you know it. Besides, a minute ago, you got emotional thinking I might be in danger."

She stops walking to face me and jabs her talon into my chest. "Hey, don't confuse my emotions for weakness. I promise you, I have zero issue slitting some fucker's throat while tears stream down my face. And when I'm done, I'll use their blood as lipstick just because I can."

Pulling her in for a tight embrace, I kiss her temple and whisper, "Spoken like a true beast."

She wraps her arms around my neck to hug me back. "Takes a beast to tame a beast."

I chuckle, "Ah, yes, my self-proclaimed beast tamer."

"No, beast whisperer," she corrects me with a serious tone, lifting her head to share a wink. "There's a big difference."

Going in for the kiss, I give one last comment before tasting her lips. "Leannàn, you can be whatever the hell you want, as long as it makes you happy."

The crisis seems to be averted since she's taking the conversation in stride with good humor. I want to make sure, though, before I send her off on her day. Curling my arms around her waist, I lean her back and off one foot as I deepen our kiss. Her arms tighten around my neck as she moans with delight over my swoon-worthy move.

That's right, I'm adding some points on my man card.

"Zee," a familiar male voice calls out.

Knowing this is a friend, I roll Paige back to her feet, finishing our kiss and adding a few sweet pecks to her nose, cheek, and forehead. I'm not in a rush to end this moment, and her sigh is the ultimate reward, but her smile gives me a complete heart erection.

I'm about to signal to the approaching male, to give us another minute, when Paige cups her palm to my cheek to keep my attention.

"Thank you, for making me the strongest beast of them all."

"Your smile is thanks enough, my beauty," I whisper back. "No more doubt, okay?"

She nods, but I'm already seeing a flash of something new in her eyes. A set-the-whole-fucking-world-on-fire look. My girl is back and she's sending out her badass vibe. "Oh, no more doubt here. I'm ready to get on with this. I want this over so I can start my life with you."

"I want that too," I agree. "But, you know when this goes down my responsibility is to the crown. Which is why I want you to stick to Mac Tire, Shax, or any of my family today. I trust them to help keep you safe, and you should, too."

She frowns for a quick second, as though she's thinking about arguing, then stops herself with a head shake. "Okay, but only because you asked."

I'm taken back, staring at her with dismay. "Wow, someone is going to get a huge reward later."

She laughs and starts to walk off. "Or maybe I just said that so I can disobey, and get an even bigger punishment."

"Paige," I warn.

"I'm kidding," she half laughs and I can tell she's only teasing. "I'll stick with the royals, they seem the least likely to get me in trouble. Now, leave me to my boring storage cleaning so you can go save me, my knight with scale armor."

She winks while she walks backward towards the receiving doors of the bar.

"And by the way," she calls out just as she places her hand on the handle. "This smile I'm wearing, the one you liked so much, it's the one you gave me this morning when you woke up, and every minute since."

She jerks hard on the metal handle to pry the door open. The smile she's talking about is radiating from her lips, as she slowly slips into the darkness of the bar. Before she vanishes, she blows me a kiss, and like a fool in love I reach out to catch it.

"I'm going to thoroughly enjoy throwing this disturbing display of affection back in your face for the rest of my life, Paine," Shax teases then roars with laughter.

I shrug, then reach out my hand to greet the warlock. "By all means, my friend, tell everyone. It will only help keep the male admirers away from my mate, especially when I'm away."

Shax clasps my forearm and pulls me in for a man-hug. "I don't think you'll have to worry about competition. I've never seen Pea act like that or look so happy. She's all yours, my brother, lock, stock, and barrel."

We break our hug and I nod in agreement. "She is, and it's why I need to ask a favor."

He raises his hand to stop me and gives me a knowing grin. "I'm well aware what you're about to ask, and while I already promised to do everything in my power to keep an eye on your girl, you do understand she is not going to like it."

I laugh, "Yeah, she is a challenge."

He snorts at the comment like he's experienced this difficult task once or twice before. "You're going to owe me big for it, and I look forward to cashing in," he says with a wink.

His expression then darkens and his tone changes to something more troublesome as he continues, "But first, we need to get through today, and it's going to be more than what we bargained for."

"How so?" I ask with dread, not wanting to know what surprises await.

"One of my girls called at midnight, said there were some new faces in town moving product on the strip, of the fentanyl variety. You know I don't play with that shit, and Mac Tire has also kept the Wicked Ones off the playground," he says in such an urgent tone, his concern is thick in his voice.

I nod my head to acknowledge what he's saying and he continues, "By two, I had reports of all kinds of deals going down, in and around Vegas. Everything from the drugs to a goddamn shipment of AK's coming off a truck by the airport. Mac Tire called a couple hours later to tell me about the increase of patrons in Pea's bar and I finally put two-and-two together. We have a lot of illegal trading going on and it's spreading like a wildfire."

"Bear?" I ask.

He gives me a hard glare. "You think?" he sarcastically comments. "This isn't something he started yesterday either."

I frown as I question him, "What do you mean?"

"The quantity of product coming in isn't something you can scrape up in a day. Not to mention, the Dead Stallions showed up just before sunrise." He turns towards the parking lot to point out a streamlined bus with blacked out windows.

"It's a two-day drive from New Orleans," I blurt when I realize what he's saying.

He rotates back to me with eyebrows lifted. "Exactly. And they haven't left Louisiana since they settled there in the seventeen-hundreds. Any time I've dealt with them in the past, I either go to them or they send out their human slaves.

Bear must have promised them something substantial to motivate this road trip," he says with a hint of curiosity.

A much bigger picture, of the plan Bear has drawn, forms in my head. "Shit," I swear and start for the hotel.

"Wait." Shax grips the collar of my jacket to jerk me back. "If you're looking for the royals, I saw them in the bar having breakfast earlier."

"Thanks," I growl with annoyance.

It isn't for Shax, as this isn't his fault. It is, however, for the whole situation, which seems to be bigger than what we anticipated.

Gage better take Bear out because if he doesn't, protocol be damned, I'll kill the fucker myself.

We reach the newly hung front door of the bar; Shax swings it open and waves me inside. From the first step into the entryway, I notice immediate differences. The large glass fountain is absent after getting shattered in the gunfire the night before. The empty base is the only reminder of the beautiful sculpture that once sat upon it. Aside from this missing piece, there is no other evidence of the shooting. The holes have been patched and painted, the cleaning crew has been through and meticulously cleared away the tiniest shards of plaster and glass from the chaos. It's a testament to how efficient Paige is with running her business.

A tattooed stunning beauty, a deliciously filthy mouth and the most brilliant mind, I couldn't have asked for a better mate. I truly am blessed.

Shaking my head, I notice the other obvious difference is the loud chatter, echoing into the small alcove from the bar. The volume inside the bar is almost deafening as it pierces my ears. It speaks for the mass that has crowded together inside. In my past, this would have triggered my urge to run. I hid from these kinds of confrontations as I had feared my secrets would be uncovered, and I never felt like I belonged.

Oh, how the times have changed, there isn't any other

place I would rather be.

Walking through the curved entrance into the overly packed room, a surge of adrenaline hits as I take in the many faces. A few I recognize as past business partners and acquaintances, others are complete strangers, but they all carry the similar vibe of danger. This is an intimidating crowd of thieves, hitmen, crime lords, and gang members. People who deal in drugs, guns, trafficking, everything and anything illegal. They reek of havoc, a stench of the terror they wish to inflict drips from their pores. A warning for the weak to not go into the dark underbelly of this realm, at night or alone. And yet, as I stroll through the throng, I'm aware of how at home I feel. I also chuckle to myself, for it is not lost on me that I'm more frightening than all of these people put together.

Shax taps my shoulder. "Down in the back corner by the stage, mate," he directs.

Scanning the crowd, draped in various MC patch colors, I spot the giant angel first. His sheer size makes him stand out, even in this crowd. But it is the ring of golden light wrapping his form, marking him as a member of the deadliest gang of all, that catches me off guard. To the rest of the world, this mark isn't visible. From the moment I reconnected with Lazarus, after Livia cursed herself and he returned from his island, I had not been able to see this mark. To see it now, as bright as sunshine glowing from his pores, is the sign of confirmation.

"Ruadan," Lazarus calls out my given name as though he is acknowledging the thoughts in my head.

I bow my head to him and Lilith as I approach the table. "Laz, Sunshine," I greet them casually.

Lilith jumps from her seat to attack me in one of her child-like hugs, wrapping her whole body around my torso. An adorable cheer erupts from her lips, "Welcome back, dear brother."

She isn't meaning my return to the bar, but my return to

myself. She too can see who I am, as easily as I can see the same brilliant light coming from her and Lazarus. We three are cut from the same heavenly cloth, and I suspect when I see the rest of the court, they will also be glowing with the same light. It is this banded circle of growing power that makes us the force the gods fear, and what will be the strength to get us through this day.

Bear is as good as dead.

An uncontrolled burst of laughter ripples up my throat. Lilith tilts back to look up at me, confusion settling on her face.

"Was it something I said?" Her eyes scan my face as she seeks out a justification for my outburst.

"I believe Zander just got a whole new perspective on things," Lazarus muses with a grin and a clap to my back with his giant mitt.

"Ah, am I missing something?" Shax sounds dumbfounded and when I rotate my head, his eyes are darting at the three of us like he's trying to understand some bad punchline to a joke.

I place Sunshine upon the barstool she had jumped from and turn to the warlock, making room for him to join us at the tall table.

"Sorry, my friend, we were having a family moment." I chuckle again, then quickly make introductions, "Shax, this is my sister, the High Priestess Lilith, and her mate, the angel Lazarus."

He offers his hand in greeting and I continue, "And this is my old friend, the warlock Arro Gunn, but around here they call him Shax."

Lazarus takes the warlock's outstretched hand in his own while Lilith chimes, "It's a pleasure to meet you, Arro."

"Any friend of Zander's is a friend to us," Lazarus says, then adds, "I also wish to thank you. I understand you have offered to stand with us today."

Shax blows out a breath. "Sure, except I bit off more

than I can chew with the deal."

Lazarus arches his brow and stares down at the warlock like he's about to interrogate the guy. "Having second thoughts, warlock?"

Shax shifts uncomfortably on his feet and his eyes widen as he realizes how his comment sounded. "No, not at all," he begins to backpedal.

I jump to his defense to explain, "Shax is just pointing out that we didn't expect a certain someone to call in reinforcements."

Lazarus peruses the crowd over our heads with a nod. "Yes, this is rather interesting."

"But, not surprising," Lilith chirps. "Goddess knows we've seen this before."

She's speaking about Toronto when Leland Kline had brought pack reinforcements to his Alpha challenge, but it didn't end well for him.

"Either way, this crowd is going to start attracting the attention of the human cops. It might have already. I don't want to deal with the blowback." Spoken like a true criminal, Shax is covering his ass.

Lilith frowns. "Nor would the Queen, but are there not wards up to prevent this?"

The warlock lifts his brow in curiosity. "This is a legal business open to everyone, there's no need for wards."

Lazarus drops his head to stare at the warlock with dismay. "Are you really that ignorant?"

I can see Laz hit a nerve with the warlock as Shax stands tall on the other side of the table, ready to defend his statement to the angel. "Not all subs take extreme precautions like the court does. Especially someone like Pea, who relies on the humans to frequent her establishments."

Sunshine's usual perky glow starts to cloud. "The Blackwoods also rely on human business, but they still have protection wards up, and have had them long before our Queen was even born. That's just good business. This is sheer stupidity," she lectures.

Putting my hand in the middle of the group to tap the table and stop the discussion, I lower my voice and rein us in. "You're arguing over semantics and it isn't going to get us anywhere."

"This is your show, Zander. Tell us what you want to do," Gage's voice booms behind me.

Turning to greet the Alpha, I notice the ring of light around his figure, just like I predicted. Although it is faint and wrapped in a shade of green, marking him as a male of importance to the crown, it is still there and equally as brilliant.

As I soak this in, Gage continues, "This is your coming out party, so to speak, you might as well take the lead. I already know you are worthy of the position as my second. Soon, everyone else will too, and this is the perfect situation for you to show off, to shine. So, lead away, Commander."

Bowing my head with respect to this honor, I swallow the emotions it brings with it. This is a moment I only ever dreamed would happen. To be living it now is simply a blessing. I will never take the second chance that Livia gifted me for granted again.

When I lift my head to meet his eye, I notice an excitement on his face. He's not only happy to see me succeed, he's thrilled for the coming day. Not surprising, Gage always did enjoy a good duel. I am going to do everything in my power to make sure he wins this challenge.

I blink away the heavy emotions of the moment and switch gears. Turning to my sister, who is grinning from ear to ear and bubbling over with positive energy for me, I smile back then begin to take charge.

"We need to put up wards around Paige's property."

Lilith nods in understanding. "I'll build a similar spell to the one I use at the hotel back home, but on a grander scale."

"This property stretches for miles, you'll need help," I

tell her.

Shax jumps in with his own suggestion, "You could ask Half-pint. She built some wards for my quarry when she lived with me, maybe she has some here too."

Sunshine glances at Shax, then at me, and we share the same expression of wonder. Whether our mother and my friend had been, or are still a couple, is something to ponder on another day. We both seem to shake our heads of the thought at the same time, and I continue with the subject at hand.

"You and Lazarus can get Brigid to help, and maybe your friend too," I recommend.

"Jamie? I don't know about that," she sounds discouraged. "She's not in my good graces after the part she played in Cale's plan to kill me."

"If she wants to build a trust with you and the Queen again, she should be leaping at a chance to help. And right now, we can use all the help we can get."

While Lilith curls her face into a frown, Lazarus wraps his arm around her for comfort. "Zander is right, my little dove, we need to take advantage of what we have. We need more numbers on our side. I know you are still troubled by Jamie's deceit, but if she is truly on our side, this will be her chance to show us her loyalty."

"Fine," she huffs, "But keep her away from me."

"I'll ask Brigid to work with Jamie. Since rescuing her from the barn your mother has been trying to help Jamie work on her issues and what led her to help Cale. If anyone can get through to Jamie and help reform her, it would be Brigid," he coos, soothing her further with whispers in her ear and gentle caresses down her back.

"Okay, we'll go take care of this," she says and they both head for the door.

Gage and I watch as they disappear through the curve in the entryway. Once they're out of earshot he quietly comments, "Is it just me or did the winged bastard just school us in relationship one-oh-one?"

I chuckle, "I'm considering taking a lesson from him. Paige would never bend as easily, not without a fight."

Gage snorts, "Yes, I've had the pleasure of your female's attitude, not five minutes ago. She's rubbing off on my soon-to-be wife because they kicked me out of the kitchen."

"You left them alone?" I question him.

His head jerks back and he glares at me like I've lost my mind. "No, I left Sabre with them, and he has more patience in his thumb than I have in my whole body. Trust me, he's the better man to be back there."

"Will they need a hand unpacking the bus when it gets here?" I ask, eluding to moving the vampire's coffin.

"No, Paige has Mac Tìre back there helping, Chris is on the bus with his two guys, that's plenty of hands. If they have a problem unloading one coffin, then we have bigger issues for today."

"Fair enough," I chuckle. "Did Mac Tìre say when or where Bear plans on starting this event?"

"He hasn't heard yet, but I suspect Bear will wait until tonight. He'll give those he invited plenty of time to show up so he has backup and witnesses. He'll also need to debrief Garo." He stops there and I get the sense this is a sore spot for him.

It's a sore spot for me. "Position or not, Gage, I won't let Garo have Paige. I know he's your brother, and you are my friend and King, but I will wage a war, I promise, none of you will win if he lays even one fucking finger on her."

Gage sighs and runs his hands through his long hair. "I know," he snaps through gritted teeth. "Christ, I know all too well."

He turns away like he might be going somewhere, but then he stops and just stands with his back to us. I can see the tension in his neck, the hesitation in his body, he's thinking hard about something. Shax looks at me with a questioning brow, I know he's wondering what this is about.

I had heard rumors about the night September and Gage had mated. The word was, Garo had been chosen by all the Alphas to become the King. It's common knowledge Garo is a pushover, and the wolves believed he would be easily manipulated. But, September surprised everyone when her magic called to Gage, and she crowned him. She picked the most worthy wolf, but the old guard will never accept her decision. This is why Gage is constantly being challenged, and until he kills every last one of those dicks, they will never let him rest.

It is also how Garo has slowly gathered more territory for himself. As the second, Garo takes over the territories when Gage kills off an Alpha. It's all ruled by the True Alpha, but run by the second-in-command. Whether Gage wins the challenge with Bear or not, Garo would still run this pack. As an Alpha, he can take any mate he wishes. The only way to stop Garo's accumulation of power, him claiming Paige, and the old guards' influence over the wolves, is to eliminate him permanently. A heavy decision for anyone to make, harder still when the person needing to die is your brother.

Thinking we should leave Gage to make the decision alone, I nod towards the door, to tell Shax we should go. He starts to head off just as Gage turns back to face us. Shax stops, looks at Gage then to me for direction. I can only shrug until Gage makes his motives clear.

Gage leans into the table and right in my face. "No one is sent by accident to anyone, we are meant to cross paths for a reason. We were meant to meet, on that ship to the Americas five-hundred years ago. I once thought it was so we could build our riches together. Then I thought it was so you could help me cover up my father's death. I now know we are supposed to be here for September, and not just you and me, all of us who have crossed paths."

He stops to wet his lips, maybe he thinks I need to let

this information sink it. I don't, I've known all along, but I give him this moment to collect his thoughts before he goes on.

"Bigger things are coming, it's why we are growing as a group, and why September is gaining power. My loyalty, life, and love, is and will always be to my wife, my Queen. It gives her strength. She needs Sabre, Mag, Chris and me, as much as Lilith needs Laz and Sam, and Paige needs you. You are an honorable man, Zander Paine, and you have every right to do what needs to be done to protect your mate. Even if it means killing my brother, I won't stand in your way."

CHAPTER 22

"Your cheeseburger with extra pickles, my Queen, and one super chocolaty milkshake," Red announces as she brings September her meal.

"Thank you, Kingsley," September says, eyeing her plate like she hasn't eaten in a month.

"It's my pleasure. Do you need anything else?" Red asks glancing over her shoulder. "I only ask because I'm not sure when I'll be back to check on you next." There's a hint in her eyes that suggests she'd rather be anywhere else than serving this crowd.

"God, I hope not. This is my fifth burger today. If I eat anymore, I'll be needing bigger pants," the Queen grumbles.

"I'd give my left tit right about now, to be wearing your maternity suit and sensible shoes, my Queen." Red turns back to September with a laugh.

September scans the girl's tight black corset and shorts combination, with stiletto leather boots, and offers a sympathetic sigh. "Yes, I suppose you have been running today. All the more reason I wish you would reconsider our offer to come work for us in Canada. We could really use someone like you at the Silverclaw, and you won't be run off your feet."

Kingsley grins. "If the customers there are half as nice and Canadian polite as you all, I might reconsider."

"Well, that's debatable," Magennis chimes in. "There be bad batches in every lot."

"True, some of our staff are quite rude," September agrees, then turns to Magennis with a grin. "We could sweeten the deal. Flynn does need to do a mass hiring soon. He could use someone with Kingsley's expertise to train the newbies. We could hold an open-ended position for her, as the manager of serving staff. She can help us out for a few months until everything is settled, then she can either stay, or come back here until we need her again."

Magennis shrugs. "Seems reasonable."

"Then it's done," September claps her hands as though the decision has been finalized. "Kingsley is coming back to Canada with us."

"Wait, what?" Kingsley looks confused, and she should be.

The Queen and Magennis have been trying to recruit the poor girl all day, sweeting the deal with every round to our table she made. It has been comical to watch as we wait to hear when Bear will make his move. There hasn't been much else for me to do.

"Just say yes, Red, it doesn't appear you have much choice," I chuckle out.

"Give me a minute and I'll come up with something," she says, blinking quickly as she thinks about it. "I'll be back."

She rushes to the bar to retrieve a drink order, giving us our privacy again.

Magennis grins at his bride-to-be. "You're so devious when you put your mind to something, my little minx. The poor dear doesn't stand a chance. She might as well pack her bags and get on the plane now."

They share a laugh and continue to chatter; I tune them out. I've been listening to them for hours and it's boring me to tears. We've been waiting to hear from Bear's camp. Mac Tíre and Ducky have been relaying messages to us ever since Ducky returned this morning. There hasn't been much news, only that Garo had been dropped at the clubhouse and has been in a meeting with Bear. Something I also don't want to dwell on, as it churns the fire in my belly and makes me want to lash out, knowing Paige is at the center of their talks.

My phone vibrates against the table and the screen lights up.

Thank God for small distractions.

Magennis and September both halt their conversation, having heard the phone, and like me, they turn their attention to the device. I flick the phone to activate the screen; a message appears from Ducky.

Guards heading out to the base of the hills behind the old barn. Good cover and away from human gawkers.

"We have a location," I say and twist the phone around for the Queen to see.

She reads the text and nods. She's silent for a minute then asks, "Gage wants to know when."

She's been communicating with her men through their mental connection. It has given Gage and Sabre the freedom to work the room and get a feel for how this crowd will turn. I glance across the room to find Gage at one of the tables. He appears relaxed as he chats up a couple of suits like they are in the middle of a business deal.

I've always admired Gage's professionalism. The guy is a chameleon of sorts, able to mask himself to become whatever he needs to be to get a job done. It's what he's doing now, becoming what the suits are, in order for him to entice them to his side. It's the same type of manipulation September has been using on Kingsley, and I see where she learned it from. The royals are a force of power, one this crowd should be leery of.

Picking up the phone I relay Gage's question back to Ducky and then wait for the reply. There's no immediate response.

September is studying my face, I see she's anxious. It's hard to tell if it stems from worry or if, like Gage, she's also eager to fight. I've seen her in action, she's an impressive warrior and enjoys the battle. Although in this situation, I suspect her worries over the fate of the father to her child will be what triggers her warrior tendencies. God help anyone on the receiving end of her wrath.

I punch in another message, this time to Shax, to tell him to move his people closer to the barn. "My Queen, can you reach out to Sunshine and give her an update?" I ask.

"Already done," she plainly replies then offers a smile. "Lilith and Lazarus are coordinating with Brigid. Her coven will be in place when the time comes. Whenever that is."

I blow out a breath. "If G is right, Bear's waiting until sundown. Which gives us a few more hours to kill."

"The bugger will wait, mark my word," Magennis announces. "He wants every race in attendance for this challenge, including the New Orleans vamps."

September curls her arms around her plate and leans into the center of the table. Magennis and I follow her lead, sensing she wants a bit more privacy. She emphasizes this by speaking so low, it's barely audible, making me strain to hear her over the loud ambient sound in the room.

"I don't understand how this guy can be so confident. He has Cassandra with him, she saw what Gage did to her father, and how our tiny group won that challenge. Why does he think he can win this?"

"I've been wondering much of the same, my love. With these many witnesses, the guy must think he's indestructible and will easily win this match. My question is, why so many witnesses? And knowing what some of them do, what is he cooking up with them?" Magennis adds his two cents and it gets me thinking.

"You're right, this does seem off," I say. I scan the different packs represented in this room, and pockets of people from the vampire, fae, and magical communities, until it dawns on me.

As soon as the thought clicks, I'm typing a new message to Ducky on my phone.

Who's in the meeting with Bear and Garo?

His response is immediate.

Not sure, I thought it was just them. Why?

I type back.

Where are all the Alphas, the leaders of the MC's sitting in the bar?

His answer is a simple question mark, then he follows it up.

I can't get inside the house to find out. Is something up? I quickly respond.

Not yet, just trying to figure something out. Keep me posted.

"You seem to be on a mission," September remarks. "Care to share?"

I nod at her. "I will, but not here. Tell Gage to meet us upstairs."

She turns in her chair to dismount her seat, stretching her long body like she's warming up for exercise. After a day of sitting, my ass is feeling a bit stiff too, but I ignore the kinks and head for the stairs. A quick jog up the steep incline and I get a good leg workout.

At the top platform, I open the door, waiting for September and Magennis to enter before I follow them inside. Gage is hard on our heels.

"What's up?" His ask sounds more like a demand.

"Aye, what brainstorm have you got brewing?" Magennis sounds quite curious.

I gesture for them to take the couch in front of Paige's desk. September settles in the middle with Magennis beside her, Gage stands like a sentinel at her back. Not wanting to worry them, I lean against the front of the big desk, even crossing one leg over the other to appear relaxed.

"We were talking about Bear's confidence. The way he's gathered these people, to have on hand as witnesses to his win. It's like he knows it's going to happen. The guy is a cocky bastard, but this is more than just bravado. That's when I realized, there isn't one single leader downstairs," I pause to meet Gage's eye and watch him work this over.

As soon as he understands, his face shifts to neutral stone. "No fucking way," he spews the obscenity.

"So, this is about more than just your lass, yeah?" Magennis asks, also aware of what I'm getting at.

September isn't as quick, having less experience with challenges and our world in general. She spins around on the couch to face Gage, confusion set in the frown on her brow.

"What's going on?"

The muscle in Gage's jaw flexes as he grinds his teeth. He slowly in-takes a breath to calm himself, before coming around the sofa to sit with September. He takes her hands in his. Magennis at her back, running his hand up and down the length of her spine. They work well together, calming their beloved, knowing she is not going to like the news that's coming.

"Baby, remember you are pregnant, and getting upset is not good for the young," Gage starts with a fair warning.

His bride grumbles out, "You don't have to sugar coat it, I know what lives inside me. It reminds me, at least once an hour, with either nausea, a craving or heartburn. Just spill it, for Christ sakes."

Gage takes a moment to gather his thoughts, even though there isn't much that will make this news sound better.

He wets his lips and begins, "Zee pointed to the lack of leaders amongst the gang member's downstairs. Bear isn't just planning this challenge for him and me. He's setting it up, so if he does lose, another Alpha is on hand, to bring forth the next challenge, until one of them kills me. He's also got leaders from the other communities to challenge Mag, Lilith, even Sabre. He knows we are outnumbered, but not who sides with us. He's prepared with additional people to take out whoever else is on our side. He's trying to break the court to get to you. No matter whether he lives or not, the leaders have formulated a plan to make sure their side wins. Being they're all criminals, it's possible they think they can rise up against the human world, too."

"That rat fucking bastard," September growls. "This had nothing to do with Paige and Zander, they were just pawns in the game."

"Yes and no, my Queen," I tell her. "Bear's still offering Paige to Garo, along with his territory and that of any of Alphas who don't make it out. It cements Garo's position as the second, no matter who wins. I believe it's his payment for the intel he's been feeding them since you were crowned."

A heavy knock sounds at the door before it opens. "Why are you knocking? It's my office, just go in," Paige harshly instructs.

"I'd rather take yer ball-busting over disrespecting the female in there," Mac Tìre snaps back.

"Get out of my way or I'll be the one busting balls," Sabre curtly announces right before he appears in the room.

He goes straight for September, crouching before her, to take inventory of her state with his eyes. "Are you alright, my darling?"

She doesn't get the opportunity to answer as the room starts to fill up. Mac Tìre and Paige finally enter, moving to the desk to stand behind me. Walking in behind them is Lazarus and Lilith, with Sam, Chris, the two humans from their band, and surprisingly, the two girls from the show last night. I can't get it out of my head, these girls seem familiar, but this isn't a time to dwell.

The newcomers shuffle inside the room to position themselves in their respective places. Mag, Gage, Sabre, and Chris are with the Queen. Lazarus and Lilith behind the couch, with the girls behind them. An odd stance considering they are not part of the court. However, the shocker is Samuel, who stands with Paige behind the desk. It's an affirmation he's chosen her pack, and not Gage's, to run with. This is a powerful statement he's making, and choosing her would be a testament to her strength as an Alpha. Sadly, because she's not male, in our world, it means nothing.

"I sense your distress, my Queen, what has happened?" Lazarus asks of his niece, touching her shoulder in a comforting way.

"Is it the baby?" Lilith inquires with panic. "Where is my mother? She can look you over."

"I am here," Brigid calls out as she and Arro rush through the door. Lazarus must have summoned the whole group to this meeting.

My mother goes to September to check her over while a few more fussing questions are flung at the young Queen. The rest say nothing but look on with boldly written concern on their faces. In a short amount of time, September has endeared these people to her. It is this formidable circle the gods fear, and one, I am proud to be included in.

"No, I'm fine. The baby is fine. Thank you, everyone, for your solicitude," September expresses in a kind voice. "It is not me you need to worry about, but all of us, I fear, are being threatened."

The concerned expressions fade into confusion, and a rumble of more questions begins to fill the space.

"Everyone, please," Sabre booms out as he stands, hands waving in the air to shut the group up. "Let's be quiet for a minute so someone can explain what's going on."

He turns to Gage as the someone with the answers. Gage inclines a nod to Sabre and begins a quick summary of the update of news. When he's done, a pin could drop and it would sound like a hammer hitting the floor. It's just that quiet.

"This man is like a bad rash that won't go away," Lilith snips then looks at Paige with apologetic eyes. "No offense, Paige."

My beauty snorts a laugh from behind me. "None taken. I've been dealing with that very prickle on my ass for years."

"Well, we can't just let this happen," the Queen interjects. "And, I'm afraid, our option pool is running empty."

"We also have the small issue of the sun, my Queen," Magennis reminds her.

"What difference does that make?" Mac Tire blurts.

"The Queen gains power from her mates, the bond they share makes them all stronger. Without Magennis present, it weakens the circle. It could be enough to give Bear an advantage," I tell the wolf. "I wouldn't want to test the theory."

"Zander is right, we need to stand together," Sabre says to September then he turns to look at Paige. "If we are going to win this, we all need to pull our weight."

His comment, coupled with his stare, makes me think he's sending Paige some type of message. A survey of the room tells me no one else is noticing this, except Lazarus and my sister. Lazarus is also sending Paige a similar expression, while Lilith is watching me with half a smirk on her face. A quick glance behind at my mate breaks the connection. Paige meets my eye with some renewed form of determination on her face.

What the hell are they up to?

My thought gets shelved rather fast when Chris, who has never spoken at a meeting with the court-- or much in general-- suddenly stands before us with his own idea. "Why not attack this guy now when he's not expecting it?"

September takes his hand in hers and smiles with pride at her human. "That would be a great idea."

"But, it will mean you fight without me," Magennis points out.

"Not necessarily, Mag." The grin on Gage's lips speaks volumes to how excited he is about this idea. "Our inside guy said the location is the barn, right?"

I nod while Mac Tire answers, "Aye, I trust Ducky's word it tis."

"Bear has no idea we already know this, so if we move in now, we can take him by surprise when he shows at sundown," Gage sounds giddy as he tells us his plan.

"Great idea, but the minute any of you walk out the bar, Bear will have a call from someone sitting downstairs, warning him of your movements," Paige points out.

"Not all of us," Chris speaks up again. "No one will think it odd if Defeat the Darkness and Avenging Angels go backstage. We can easily slip out the back, then load Magennis in the bus from the kitchen delivery exit, and take him to the location without anyone knowing."

"While I do not wish to be jostled about in that bloody coffin again, the lad does have a remarkable plan," Magennis muses while patting Chris on the arm for a job well done.

"It doesn't get us all out of the bar, though." September's frown of worry is heavily imprinted on her face as she looks to Sabre and Gage for answers.

"Lazarus, Lilith and you could leave from here. There's no other exit and no one knows of your gift of travel. They would just assume you are in this office," Sabre explains, but he doesn't appear happy about his mate going on without him.

"What about everyone else? What about Gage and you?" The hitch of stress in September's tone tells me she is equally uneasy with going out without her men.

Gage works his way around the sofa to stand beside Lazarus. "No, no, there's an easier way around this," he says, as he grins up at the angel with a wink. "Isn't that right, Lazarus?"

The angel chuckles deep in his throat and a devious smirk graces his lips. "I'm surprised you would even consider it. Since you protested quite loudly when it happened to you."

"I'll be the first to admit your magical tactics scare the shit out of me. But, I'd also be an idiot if I didn't think to use them for our benefit."

"Want to fill the rest of us in on this beneficial plan?" Shax speaks with some doubt from his position by the door.

"It's simple," Gage boasts with confidence. "Chris will take his group out as he said and head to the barn. Once there, the Queen and Priestess will have protection for when they magically teleport. Then, the angel here, will put a spell of paralysis on those in the bar, which will allow the rest of us to walk right out the front door. We'll be able to catch Bear off guard. He's such a hothead he'll attack first, long before his crew is able to get there to back him up. By the time they arrive, this will be over."

"Let's not get cocky about it, Bear's doing enough of that for all of us," September unleashes a warning.

Gage circles the couch, kneeling before his mate to take her hand in his. "We have been looking over our shoulders for months, wondering when the next threat will come, and I'm tired of it. The perfect scenario is before us, now. All these Alphas, in one place, chomping at the bit for their chance to take the crown. I say we let them give it their best shot because they won't win. And do you know how I know this?"

He waits for her to answer, but she only shrugs. He gives her a smirk and it's as optimistic as his speech. "We've been looking at this all wrong. We aren't the average supernatural anymore. Together, with the people in this room, there's more than a few secret talents, and powers so strong, the gods fear us. And if they are that uneasy about us, then this thing with Bear is going to be a cake-walk. I'm not cocky, baby, I'm confident we got this."

I have been watching September's face as Gage gives this enthusiastic pep talk. It goes through a transition of phases, worry and concern, to doubt and dismay, and finally a similar smug smirk of conviction on her lips. It is a pivotal moment for the Queen, realizing she doesn't have to be paralyzed by these simple threats because she doesn't bat in the same league anymore. And when it registers in her head, there's a new look in her eyes. The look of a woman about to win this battle and declare it her victory.

She uses Gage to stand herself up, positioning herself to be the focal point to address the room. "I believe Gage's prediction, we will win today. And when we do, the ones still standing who fought against us will be given an option. They either kneel and swear allegiance to me or be executed for this treason. I don't want to rule like my mother once did. Unlike her, I'm convinced we can build a world for our kind, amongst the humans, and live in peace. However, like her, I know an example must be made or this will never end."

Her pause has a purpose, to allow her words to sink in. She wants us to see this is more than just her pivotal moment, but ours, too.

Her eyes move to each of us as she reads it upon our faces, and only then does she continue. "I'm asking you all to join me in making these first steps with this plan, for our future. As the official court of this crown, my warriors, my guards, and my people, what say you?"

As her people, a collective group believing in this Queen and her faith for our future, we kneel at her feet.

"Long live the Queen," Lazarus calls forth.

"Long live the Queen," we chant in reply, and together we add, "Our life for thee."

"Now, let's do this," September cheers, clapping her hands to get us into action.

"Wait, my Queen, may I?" I ask to take the floor as I return to my feet.

September gives me an approving smile and gestures to the room. "It's all yours, Commander."

I nod humbly for the respect she has just given, then turn to address her people. "Since we made a mad rush up here, suspicions will be high downstairs. They will be expecting us to make a move and will be watching us closely. I think we should carry on where we left off, make it seem like nothing has changed. Give it about thirty minutes, then Chris can make it appear like they are setting up. We'll wait another thirty before Magennis ducks out, and so on."

"Good idea, keep suspicion low," Gage agrees. "Anything else?"

"Yes, I think Mac Tìre should go with the first wave," I

say to Gage's cocked brow of question.

I quickly explain, "He's believed to be with Bear's camp, so him leaving here or showing up at the barn, won't raise questions. He can also divert any trouble that might come up at the other end, and I trust him to guard the Queen and Priestess when they arrive at the barn."

Gage squints at the wolf while he chews on this.

Sabre isn't as confused with his decision. "I agree with Zander's additions. In order for this to be a surprise, it must go smoothly. Mac Tire can ensure it at the other end, and I'd feel more comfortable having as many as possible with the Queen, in that barn, in our absence."

I turn to Mac Tire. "You got this?"

"Aye," he agrees with a dubious grin. "Not one of them bastards will touch the Queen, ye have me word."

"I know I do." I reach for his hand to seal the deal. "Fill in Ducky and have him meet you there, too."

The wolf nods. "Aye, will do."

"Okay, let's move out," I instruct the troops.

The movement to the door is slow, September and her men being the first to leave. "At least I have time to finish eating," she comments to Sabre as they disappear out to the catwalk.

"See you in an hour and a half, Commander." Gage grins at me when he follows the Queen.

I chuckle, knowing as the clock ticks, those minutes are going to make him one antsy fucker. Gage is not a patient guy; the next ninety minutes might drive him to the edge of crazy town. But, I'm banking on his crazy, and the power of this court, to finally settle this score.

Chris and his gang are the last to go, and when the door clicks closed behind him, I exhale some of my anxiety. Long gentle arms wind around my torso as the weight of a magnificent set of breasts settle against my back from Paige's embrace. A gratuitous moan rumbles from my throat, and I tilt my head to her shoulder to breathe in her scent.

"I like these hugs from you," I tell her.

"Yeah?" She questions.

"Mmm, yes," I moan again. "It's your big boobs, they make everything better."

Her carefree laugh tickles my ear. "Sounds like someone is having a rough day at the office," she teases.

"You have no idea," I groan, remembering my hours of useless chatter with Magennis and September.

"Don't I?" Paige asks while running her nails down my abs to my belt-buckle, causing my dick to instantly react. "You weren't the one stuck in a kitchen, rearranging the shit out of it to hide a coffin that's about to be moved. Such a waste of my day, and talents, really."

The idea of Paige doing kitchen duty is both humorous, considering the outfit she has on, and quite provocative for the same reason. I have to stop my mind from going to the latter.

"Okay, so we both had mind-numbing days, but things are looking up."

"Mm-huh," she agrees while her hands unclip my buckle. "I was so bored, that all I could do to keep myself from going insane was to think about playing with your zipper."

Chuckling at her, I tease, "Too bad for you, I wear button-flies."

"Even better," she coos in my ear.

Her fingers curl into the waistband of my pants and she gives them a hard pull, popping the buttons and opening my pants. My cock springs free from the confines of the denim, and her palm is right there to capture it with a long stroke.

I hiss with delight, then moan with remorse of this needing to end. "What are you doing, *leannàn*?"

Her stroking hand continues to work my length with a slow steady motion until my cock is pulsating with need. "It isn't obvious that I'm distracting you?" She giggles, but it turns quickly into a purr. "I'll just have to try harder, then."

I can't seem to bring myself to stop her, it feels so good. My hips begin to rock, meeting her stroke for stroke. Then, when her other hand slips down the opening in my pants, and she palms my balls, I damn near blow my load.

I groan regretfully, "Leannàn, we don't have enough time for this."

She slows the strokes, and I think she's going to stop. Instead, the vixen walks around to face me with a smirk so profound on her lips, I'm panting in suspense of her next move. That's when she drops seductively to her knees.

"I better hurry this up, then." The rasp in voice sends chills of excitement up my spine.

Her tongue tip rolls against her upper lip, curls back against the bottom, as she wets them. Her eyes lock in with mine and don't leave, as she opens her mouth, taking me between her lips. The heat of her breath causes a quivering pulse, throbbing down my cock and into my balls, making them swell with an expectancy of the coming release.

If just her breath causes this reaction, it won't take her long to finish me off. I'm torn between my greed and generosity. I want her luscious mouth sucking me to completion, and yet, I desire to bring her pleasure. And the more of my length she takes down her throat, the harder it becomes to decide which to choose.

A groan in her throat vibrates deep in my bone and my mind goes blank. There's no more hesitation with my decision, I know exactly what I want.

Her, now, mine. All of her, mine.

My hips buck forward, pressing another thick inch down her throat. She gags, swallows, tilts her head higher and gulps in more of my length. With her head at this angle, each pumping thrust I make in her mouth bulges deep in her throat. Showing just how much of me she's swallowing. I'm not a small male in this department, many a female have refused to even attempt this act. Yet, Paige is eagerly sucking me like she wants more.

This eagerness to please is a talent of sorts, and it is blowing my mind. A few more strokes of her hot mouth, a swirl of her tongue on the underside of my crown, and I'm like an adolescent male getting my first blow-job. There isn't any control as I spurt a shot of lust down her throat. She recognizes the taste of me and begins to greedily suck and swallow it down.

"No," I grunt out, willing myself to stop the rest of the explosion. Taking away the temptation by gripping her hair to pull her off my dick. "It's your turn, *leannàn*."

She gasps as I manhandle her. Hauling her body up, and walking us into the wall, overlooking the club. Her back hits the two-way glass pane with a thud and she lets free a giggle of joy. She is enjoying being roughed up. I'm about to wonder why when I notice her rolling her tongue out to lick the mess of my lust dripping off her chin. I don't think she's trying to be seductive, but I'm a male who can't help but think otherwise. It's such a turn on watching her that I'm overcome with the urge to taste myself on her lips.

My mouth is on hers before the thought finishes in my head. I devour her, lapping my own sin from her lips, with as much enthusiasm as she just gave me. The flavor, though bitter, mixes with her sweetness nicely. I can't get enough. She can't seem to get enough. We lock into this aggressive tongue tangle as our mouths demonstrate our savage need for one another.

I've allowed myself the greed of her mouth giving me pleasure. It took the edge off but cutting it short only increased my lust for her. I want to indulge my hungry slut. I want to fulfill her deep needs of desire. I want to fuck her like this is our final hour together.

In a violent move, I spin her around, slamming her face into the glass, and pinning her body between the wall and me. Whipping up her dress, I expose as much of the dragon inked across her back to appreciate the art, as well as her amazing ass. She is my beauty, a stunning masterpiece.

There is a familiarity to this. I've been here before, at the barn only a few days ago. We were just strangers then, being pulled together by fate, and bewitched by magical lust. About to head into our first battle as allies, but fighting each other like enemies, fearing our secrets would destroy us.

In a few short days, we have come full circle. This time, we'll fight together, we'll fight for our freedom, and we'll fight for our love. But, unlike last time, our desire for sex isn't from a magical spell. It's from our bond as a couple and attraction to one another. We have come a long way in a brief blip of time. I can only imagine what a lifetime together will bring, and I can't wait to find out.

May the gods grant me this favor.

Paige clears her throat to break me from my thoughts. "The clock's ticking, my feral beast. My penance must be served or I'll voluntarily self-impose my own punishment."

"Someone's been awfully impatient, or were you getting off on sucking my cock?"

She snorts. "Your pelvic sorcery isn't that good that I'd succumb to you with ease."

She's taunting me, willing me with that saucy mouth of hers to prove her wrong. Of course I take the bait, there's no reason not to. I head straight to her panties, pulling them off to the side with a chuckle. To see she's still wearing them after this morning only makes me want to mark them, and her, again.

I'm already hard, painfully so, after holding back half of my release. Even touching myself to guide my length to her, triggers a weeping of pre-cum to seep from my crown. When I slide my cock across her ass, and into her sopping wet cunt, my cock spasms from the increase of blood rushing into my appendage.

"Your wet cunt says otherwise, *leannàn.*" I slam my hips forward, and vigorously beginning fucking her.

She moans out her next words in that deep rasp. "A

blowjob seemed better than an apology."

The low smooth tone of her voice loses me in the minute, and I just disappear in my obsession with her silky tone. It's one of my favorite things about her, next to her amazing hot pussy, of course. Riding it to a pounding beat is one of my favorite things to do. I'm in my happy place, on the verge of reaching utopia when her words finally click, and I get what this is.

"What aren't you telling me, *leannàn*?" I pant out, digging for the answers she's not so obviously hinting.

She whimpers, but says nothing, forcing me to punish it out of her. There's no way I can't handle a long session of sexual torture to get her to talk. I also can't deny her of what she needs. As one broken person to another, I know we must learn to fit together for this to work or we will destroy one another beyond any hope. That's not something I'm willing to risk.

Slowing my hips to fumble with the front of the dress, I try to release her breasts from the latex prison. It ends poorly for the garment, as I rip the string from the eyelets, and the seam splits wide open. It does expose one of her big beautiful breasts that I cup and fondle.

Mission accomplished.

Getting back to my hard cock thrusts I ask her another question. "Does this have to do with Sabre?"

She pants heavily, "Yes, he told me something earlier that will change everything."

Drawing on my magic to light a flame to my finger, I reward her with a sparking jolt of heat to her nipple.

"Oh, fuck." Her groan rings right down in her cunt as she squeezes my cock tight.

Inside my beast is wild with lust, burning outward to light up my skin. I roar a welcome and allow myself to take her harder still.

Incoherent babble spills from her lips and I try my hand again. Except my own words seem to come out in hiccup blurts.

"Is it… about… the fight?"

"Yes," she cries, though, it's unclear if this is the answer or just her pleasure talking.

I'm fighting myself to keep on fucking her at this point. I'm close to letting go, and a man can only hold off his release, with this kind of simulation, for so long.

"Can you tell me what it is?" I ask the question I already know the answer to, it's why she's being so resistant.

This time, she tries to shake her head, but the glass prevents her from doing so. I get the gist and reward her for it with another spark to her breast. Her whole body spasms and she gasps for a large breath.

"Whatever this is, you and Sabre will do what's right. I love you, *leannàn*, no matter what." I give her the truth of what's in my heart.

Paige clears her throat and does her best to explain in between gulps of air. "I'd tell you if I could… whatever happens… it's for us. Not being stubborn… please remember."

Curling her into my chest with my arm, I hold her as tight as I can. Telling her with this hug, I do understand, and I get that it will be the natural progression of how this must play out. "I'll remember. I won't like it, but I do trust you with all my heart."

She twists her neck at an awkward angle to try to meet my lips, and just before I lean in to meet them she whimpers, "I trust you'll give me the punishment I deserve."

As my beauty requests it, I giveth.

Sparking the flame one more time while burying my cock deep, I light her clit with a burning jolt so impactful, I feel it in my own balls. Like a violent explosion, she blows apart.

"God, yes, Zander," she screams as the wave of lust pours out.

There's no need for me to speed my thrust, I've been

holding this release off long enough. Once the heat of her eruption coats my cock, my balls retract and I pump her full of my sin. As it ends, there is no telling who's coating who. We are a mess. A beautiful, fucking mess.

Paige shakes her head when she glances at her dress, then turns in my arm with a giggle, as she joyfully exclaims, "That was the best killing of thirty minutes, ever."

"You're welcome, but it's going to take another thirty to clean you up." I kiss her forehead before I wander off to the cabinet behind her desk, in search of a towel.

"Totally worth it." She's beaming like she's charged with renewed energy.

It fills me with worry, and I stop my search to face her. I might have just fucked her like she was unbreakable, but it doesn't mean I don't want to protect her like she's a delicate piece of glass.

"Please be careful today, Paige. For me, okay?"

Her beaming smile falters a bit, enough for me to see she has reservations, too. She takes a breath, and with it, she adjusts her stance. Straightening her shoulders, lifting her chin, to show me that determined drive and confidence she often wears proudly. Like September, Paige is a force of power, and I wouldn't wish to feel her wrath either.

Her eye roll is so dramatic, she could very well roll herself into another damn dimension with this one. But, it's so her, and with her attitude-laced comment, it's exactly what I need to feel reassured.

"Fine. For you, I'll keep the dumb-fuckery to a minimum."

CHAPTER 23

The royals, the court, and the Queen's supporters spill out of the old hinged doors at the back of the barn into what had once been a barren pasture, but is now a magically transformed, vibrant, growing meadow. Phenomenon for non-believers of the occult, and hard to explain to an average human. For us supernatural, it's becoming an everyday occurrence to see forests grow from sand, an average human crowned our Queen, secret legends becoming truths, and an entire group of supernatural become so powerful that the divine beings above throw challenges down to try to destroy them.

A fitting backdrop for what awaits today, tomorrow, and for our future.

We stand in unison, facing west, utterly silent. The last hour had gone by without a hitch. All but one in our party made the trip to the barn undetected. Lazarus remains at the bar holding Bear's followers in his spell until the last of the orange hues fade into darkness, signaling sundown. Our eyes are fixed upon that line where the heavens meet the Earth, waiting for the glowing orb's collision to happen. With each sliver the sun drops, and each hue darkens, the air buzzes with an exhilarating rush of energy.

We have a plan. We are prepared. We are more than pumped. We are ready.

"Fifteen more minutes," Sabre calls out from the mouth of the door, a position he took when we arrived.

As King, it seems right for him to be up front protecting September, while the others stay with her inside the barn. And like a true warrior, he's willing to be the first sacrificed to protect his mate. He knows Magennis is vulnerable in his coffin and Chris, though strong for a human, couldn't defend himself against most of the supernatural, so Gage is standing on guard inside with them.

Sabre and Gage are equal, but in this case, Sabre's loyal stance is saying he's put Gage ahead of himself. He's willing to die so Gage can go on as King and father of the young. Once the fight starts, Gage has instructed Sabre to stay with September. This is Gage's version of sacrifice. If Gage is killed, he wants Sabre to go on in his place, as King and father-figure to the young. They admire each other with the highest form of respect. This is what I hope to create with my mate, an equal partnership built on respect and love. One I will defend to my last breath to keep.

As though she has read my mind, Paige's long fingers link with mine to connect us. I assume she senses my thoughts until she gives my hand a tug, then I realize it is to get my attention. She's been facing east with her eyes fixed on the swinging steel barrier in front of the MC compound. It appears to have opened. Her grip on my fingers tightens as a lone biker rolls out from behind the wall of crushed cars, heading south, behind the brothel.

Mac Tire whistles to get my ear. I have to turn south towards him and Shax. They have been covering the back side of the barn. Once we are facing each other, the wolf speaks in a normal conversational tone. This far away, most would have trouble hearing. For us, it is as though we are a mere foot apart.

"Th'ee gate to th'ee cunt farm has opened, mate, won't be long now."

I snort at his crude candor, he has always been a shoot-from-the-hip kind of guy.

"A scout?" I ask.

He holds up a finger to tell me to wait, before disappearing down the side of the building. He's not gone long before he's jogging towards me, stopping only an arm's width away to make our conversation more private.

"Bikes gone past th'ee Pearl, bet he'd be th'ee messenger."

"And so, it begins," I comment.

"Aye," he answers. "What now, then?"

"Are the hills covered?"

"Aye," he says, nodding toward the concrete barrier in the distance. "Shax sent some boys to keep an eye on that entrance. Not one of them fuckers be getting past them now. The rest of th'ee Warlocks be spread out with eyes on us."

"You sure there's only five of Bear's guys in the hills?"

"Aye, piss poor planning, that," he says with a chuckle.

"It is, but to our favor." I clap my hand on his shoulder as I share in his chuckle over Bear's mistake. "Okay my friend, you know what to do."

He rubs his hands together with vigor then cracks his knuckles. He's warming his fingers before reaching behind his neck to stroke the handle of his axe.

"This be bringing back memories, me brother. Tis going to be a great day, indeed."

"Don't get excited, yet. We need Bear here first, and once he is, your eyes better be on Paige." I warn.

"Awk," he grunts at me, but turns to give Paige a wink. "Of all the wild beasts in this realm, Pea be the wildest. She doesn't need saving, she bloody well be doing it herself, but I'll happily stand beside her and kill a few just to shut ye up."

I roll my eyes at the wolf. "Just go get into position, you bloodthirsty bastard."

He coughs a laugh while he walks off. "Says th'ee serpent of death."

I hear Paige snickering behind me. "He's got you there."

"Don't start," I warn, turning to give her an impatient glare.

She's smiling sweetly. "I would never," she says, with a put on innocence.

"Yeah, right," I mock her right back. "Just go with him, and don't fuck shit up."

She slowly wets her lips with her tongue; this time she's being obvious in her seduction. "And if I do?"

Her purr gives me chills, but I react the only way I know she'll listen. Turning her in the direction Mac Tìre has gone, I smack her ass with my palm to get her going.

"You already know the answer to that, *leannàn*," I grunt.

Her moan gets drowned out by the fleshy sound of the slap against the leather one-piece short-set she put on, in her office before we left. This outfit is marginally better than the last, in that it's a short-set and not a dress. It still amazes me how little it covers.

"Oh, beat me, my sexy beast," she giggles as she walks away, swaying her hips with provocative purpose.

I'm shifting my hips to adjust my boner, mumbling under my breath as I watch the beautiful sway that's turning me on. "Be happy to paddle that ass red, later."

She stops at the corner of the barn, turning to address me with a teasing wink. "Trust the Canadian to know paddles aren't just for canoes."

I bark a laugh and shake my head as she disappears down the side of the barn with Mac Tìre. Once again, my vixen has turned an otherwise tense situation around, and it has me rejuvenated with energy. My beast roars to life, equally as keyed-up as he charges forward in my conscious mind, letting me know he is ready for battle.

My skin begins to prickle and my blood boils from the churning heat within, bringing a reddening shade to the surface of my skin. My scaled armor ripples beneath my flesh, locking into place. My sight shifts and the world around me is viewed on a nocturnal level. I register the heat of life rather than the setting before me.

My hearing becomes so crisp, I can make out the catch of breaths from the trees. My sense of smell is so sensitive, I can detect the differences of who or what is around me with just a sniff. As man and beast connect, becoming one united being of strength and power, I embrace the change.

Sky above, Earth below, fire within, I am Ruadan.

Sabre lets lose two quick whistles so shrill in pitch they practically blow my eardrums. I cover my ears and turn to the King with a harsh glare. He's not paying me any attention, his gaze is set on the gate, and the figures crowding before it. Bear is readying his troops.

"Showtime," I announce to those in the pasture.

The remaining members of Shax's MC and Brigid's coven have been waiting with us, and now begin to run off towards hiding spots downwind, amongst the trees. I glance up at the front of the barn, over the doorway, and check the spot where a board has fallen free. It appears to be just a dark hole on the side of the aging building, but hidden somewhere in the hayloft inside, is Ducky keeps watch. The only sign of his presence is the barrel of his gun sticking out a knothole in the board below the opening.

It isn't the only one, either. As my eyes flicker over the weathered wall, I spot a few more guns aimed directly at the fence line around the pasture. To anyone else, this could resemble a showdown scene from an old western movie, with Doc Holliday or Billy the Kid. To me, it's a flashback to my past, and the days I ran with those very men, and Shax, in a wilder time in history.

Knowing the warlock like I do, I'm betting one of those guns is his prized six-shooter. He's probably dancing on his feet, draped in that leather duster of his, eagerly waiting for a great gun battle to begin. The mere thought of it has me smiling from ear to ear, as I make my way to Sabre at the door.

"They are heading over," he states, his eyes fixed on Bear's compound.

"Gage, you're up," I call to the Alpha, then turn at the door to stand on guard with Sabre.

We are silent while waiting for Gage. I assume the Alpha is taking his time because he's soothing his mate. It's the right thing to do before battle. Whether you think you'll win or not, you always kiss the girl goodbye. This makes me frown with concern, though. For our parting, Paige and I shared only a smartass exchange. There was no kiss. I didn't tell her I loved her. As thoughts of the missed opportunity swirl in my head, Sabre places his large hand on my shoulder to give it a squeeze.

"Don't worry, she knows what's in your heart."

He's saying this like he's read my mind. I cock my head to give a questioning look, though I'm too shocked at his words to say my own.

He reads my face and laughs it off. "I wasn't in your head. I've just been to many a battle, with men who held the same worry in their eyes. I, too, worry. We wouldn't be respectable men if we didn't. But, in my many years and experience with war, there has never been a maiden who didn't know, deep down, that her male loved her. So, if you die on this day, Paige will know how you felt about her. Hell, we all know what you feel for her. It is why we decided to stand with you, in the beginning. You are an honorable male, Zander Paine, and it is my privilege to fight with you."

I bow with gratitude. "Thank you, my King."

He grunts uncomfortably, like he still isn't used to the title. "There's no need for thanks, just don't die. Paige has one hell of a temper, and I hate to say it, but none of us would wish to deal with her wrath if that happens."

I swear the guy actually shudders at the thought. To know my beauty has put the fear of god into this great warrior, is beyond amusing, and has me laughing.

He cuts my laughter short when he adds, "I also know we don't have any hope of restraining you if you lose control. Be mindful of that as we progress. If a change brings forth a different outcome, and you need to place blame, place it on me and leave the others out of it. I will be just as honored to fight with you as I am to die at your hand. Remember that."

He doesn't allow me any time to comment. He just turns away to head inside the barn. I'm left standing alone with my thoughts and his words, not liking the way either are forming in my head. He's hinting at something not going according to our plan just as Paige had done earlier. It proves my suspicions, these two have a completely different agenda. One Sabre is fearful of me losing control over.

A cold sensation washes over me, just as the rumbles, of many motorcycle engines firing up at once echo across the landscape. Trepidation sinks deep into my bones, causing me to shiver. There's no time to figure out what Sabre means or what Paige is about to do. I can't stop Bear's advance, even though I know, deep in my gut, it means certain danger for my beauty and possibly for the Kingdom. This pivotal moment is now in the hands of fate. For us all, and for our future, whether I wish it to be or not, I must live with the outcome, whatever it ends up being.

A flicker of my past comes back to me. I've been at this crossroads before. I had been betrayed by my father, then judged by the highest court for my unspeakable acts. They deemed me unworthy and banished me to the bowels of the Underworld. Last time, I was blessed with the opportunity to start again. Only it was part of Livia's game and left me wandering alone. As a lost, anonymous figure from the shadows, shrouded in the secrecy and lies of our history.

Is this redolent of my past?

Is this more betrayal? From the only woman I have ever truly loved?

An ache of torment grips my heart, a strangling hold of despair. I can see Bear and his minions drawing near. Gage has suddenly appeared at my side. If he has said a word, I have not heard it. I'm tangled up in my emotions, my thoughts, and on the idea that I am dangling on the precipice of something bigger than I can possibly imagine. Whatever is about to happen is going to change the course of our world, and will impact mine tenfold. I can see it brewing. I can smell it thick in the air around us, wrapping me in its web, trying to choke the last breath from my lungs.

As the panic tries to overtake me, my eyes dart over to the horizon. The sun is but a faded memory of the past, and the sky is as black and bleak as my future.

The bikes roll into the pasture in a single formation, weaving around to line the front of the broken fence as they park. The rumbling of the engines can be felt through my boots from the earth below my feet. The earth itself travels with the breeze to form a giant dust cloud. It resembles an ocean wave, crashing in and over us, covering our bodies with a thin layer of grit. In a slow receding motion, the sandy haze shrinks back and dissolves into the desert floor as the thundering roars of bike motors still, leaving the sound of the sand pellets dropping to the ground like a gentle rain.

My eyes swing back and forth across the group of men on the bikes and on foot, finally entering the opening in the pasture. Like in the bar earlier, I recognize some of the faces from passages in time, but the two I seek now are Bear and Garo.

Bear has been the first to dismount, while Garo is one of the last to arrive. It tells a little about each male, that one is confident in his battle plan, while the other stays back from the fire in hopes of getting a scrap or two after the fight.

The traits of these men remind me of my father, Bres. Like Bear, he was also a great fighter. However, much like Garo, if he could scheme his way around a fight and still manage to come out on top, he would. My father was not a well-liked King. He was harsh and lazy, as well as a self-absorbed narcissist. Looking at both Bear and Garo, I see those same flaws in them.

It also reminds me that the pain my father inflicted upon me taught me to appreciate the things that do not hurt. I thought this situation was mirroring the one from my past, but there is one big difference.

Love.

Those that hurt me in my past, did it for their own agenda. Whether it be greed or higher purpose, they did it for themselves. Paige is different. Sure, her plan might bring her some gain, but like me, she too has been taught the lessons of pain. It is from our similar life lessons I know her heart is pure, and today she fights for us.

For our love.

Watching Bear take his confident stance in front of his crew, I recall my father, my past, and the path I had to take to get here. Bres thought he broke a part of me when he taught me his lesson. He took away my wings, thinking it would make me a lesser man. Bear thinks he can take away my heart to destroy me. But what both men have failed to understand is, I still have claws.

And I will use them to keep what's mine.

"Alpha, good of you to join us for the hand-over ceremony." Bear's greeting sounds supercilious, but there is an inflection in his tone suggesting he has been taken by surprise.

Gage snorts in disgust. "You can cut the bullshit, we both know that's not what this is about."

Bear puts on a shocked expression. "I'm not sure what you're getting at, Alpha. My pack and I are only here, to perform the ritual as I renounce my title as the Nevada Alpha." His expression quickly switches to something smugger as he gloats over his next words. "I'm assuming you came to support my successor. He is, after all, your second-in-command."

My eyes dart to Garo, and his equally conceited expression. They both think they have us by the balls.

"Interesting," Gage ponders out loud, holding his hand up to tell me to stay.

He slowly distances himself from the barn, walking with that confident swagger of his, to the middle of the pasture. He's playing coy, putting himself in this vulnerable position. Bear could easily attack at this moment, and Gage would be without back-up. It's a brave move, and I respect the male for his choice.

"You see, Bear, I have never officially claimed a second." He stops to pivot, looking at the pack leaders and Bear's crew, then back at the empty space behind him, to me. "Until now."

Bear crosses his large arms over his chest, and eyes up Gage. "It seems your cornbread ain't cooked in the middle. Garo has always been the pack liaison to the crown."

Gage grins at me, knowing Bear has taken his bait. He gives me a wink then spins to face the confused crowd. "It's true, my brother has been the acting pack mediator. In fact, it was your pack advisory board who gave him the title as my second, not I."

"If it looks like a duck, quacks like a duck, it must be a duck," Bear proudly states, and the childish dig gets received with chuckles from his side.

Gage snorts. "I'm not denying he's been fulfilling the duties of a second. It took the pressure off me while I shopped around for someone more worthy of the role, without having you all kissing my ass for the position."

"I really wish I could understand you, but I don't quack," Bear snaps with frustration. "None of your gibberish matters, anyway. Garo is your second and has been given the claim I hold on my daughter, making him the heir to my title and her estate. He now has more territory than any of us, including you. It makes him the head of the advisory board and gives him the power to make the laws for the pack, even above you. It weakens your status as King, not like any of us thought you were strong enough to rule in the first place."

He stops to join the others in another laugh. They think they have Gage over a barrel, it's evident in their faces and the superior smirks upon their lips.

"By the end of this night, we will find out exactly who is the rightful male of the title, True Alpha," Bear takes great pleasure in announcing. "It's just sad that you showed up alone. I had wished your misfit crew and pregnant whore would be here, to witness your fall."

From the corner of my eye, I see a flash of light and Lazarus materializes out of thin air. Following his appearance, Lilith emerges beside him, as though she has been there all along. Perhaps she has, she does possess that power. But when the girls from Avenging Angles emerge from the darkness behind them, I wonder if my sister has had them under a cloaking spell. When Sam and his human friends walk out from the side of the barn, and I realize these two girls have some serious powers of their own.

There is no time to chew it over, as September does her own materializing only a few feet away from Bear. This has Sabre, Magennis, and Chris rushing out the door, and Gage moving forward towards her. She holds up her hand to stop her men in the center of the pasture.

Paige and Mac Tire inch out behind them, to stand with me. Under her breath, Paige murmurs, "Oh, hey, look at all the village idiots. Too bad we have so few dragons."

Mac Tire coughs on a laugh just as Bear gets verbally offensive with the Queen. "If it isn't the human whore in question. Did you all know; her birth certificate is an apology letter from the condom factory?"

More laughter rings in the air on the one side of the desert, while deep growls from every one of us fill the space around our side. I move forward to be closer to September as the tensions mount. I don't trust Bear or the other leaders not to try something.

Again, September lifts her hand to stop us, from growling or advancing, I'm sure from both. She stands straight, head tilted up, and unleashes her own smack-talk. "I wear bigger heals than your dick, Bear, but unlike you, I know how to use something that big. So, if you don't want my size seven planted in your balls hard enough to make your grandfather feel it, I suggest you shut up."

This brings a stunned silence to the riding ring and has everyone paying the fire-tongued Queen the attention she deserves. "You, and the rest of the leaders here, can strike as many deals as you wish. They will never be recognized by the OSU or by me. And in case you forgot, I am the ruler of this Kingdom, so what I say, goes."

Bear isn't looking as smug as he once was, and his shoulders have dropped a little from the kick September just gave him. I will give him credit, he doesn't give up easily. I can see his hamster wheel turning.

"You do not rule everything and you don't know pack law," Bear snaps back.

Gage inches closer to his mate, and I follow to cover the Queen's back, while he counters Bear. "No, but I do."

"Then you know I have every right to pass my title to an heir of my choosing, and I chose your second," Bear slips this out with fury.

Gage snickers. "If that is how you worded it, there won't be any issue."

Gage walks ahead of September and I take my post beside her. He stands in front of the community leaders and makes his announcement so loud, it ricochets off the landscape. "I declare, by right of pack law," he states, turning in the open field to step before me.

The grin he gives me is full of pride. Then he nods for me to take a knee. "As True Alpha and King, I proclaim this before our Queen and all of you as witnesses, Zander Paine, will hereby be Commander to the Queen's court, and the second-in-command of my position as Alpha of all packs. From this day on, he will uphold the laws, and rule my territories, and be responsible for legal claims and the rights of our people, for me or in my absence. So it shall be."

"So mote it be," I hear the chant behind me from the court.

In front of me, Bear is blasting his refusal to accept Gage's rule. "By putting a mutt, with no pack, in charge, he shows how unfit for the throne he is."

September's feet shuffle before me and she puts her hands on my shoulders to place a soft kiss to my forehead.

"Bí mo Cheannasaí in ainm ár déithe, Zander Paine, déanaim beannacht ort."

September has been doing her research and has become better at royal statements. Be thou my Commander in the name of our gods is the perfect phrasing for a magical blessing, and makes what she just did, completely legitimate in the eyes of the high courts.

But, it's the last bit after my name, I bless thee, that brings a well of tears to my eyes. Not because it reminds me of the second chance Livia gave me. Though, it does tug my heartstrings that September is also granting me another chance. I feel it in the air, she has lifted the remainder of the curse her Mother left on me.

The tears I shed are from the remaining curse leaving me, bringing about an excruciating stab of pain in my spine. It's an echo of a nightmare I once had, that I thought would never resurface.

Oh, how I wish not to relive this.

I screech from the pain, and it comes out as the call of my beast, high enough in pitch to have everyone covering their ears. My body convulses and flips back at an odd angle. I can see September standing before me with her mouth hanging open. I open my mouth to tell her to run, to tell Gage to get her out of the way, but the only sound leaving my throat is similar to a prehistoric creature.

There is a blurring flash of light before the Queen disappears. I thank the heavens Lazarus knows to take her away, and that Gage has enough sense to follow them on foot. I hope the rest take the same route and get the hell back, for I can't save them if they get in the way of what's about to happen.

My body twists again, this time I land on my face in the dirt. My jacket is pulled off my back, my gun harness is peeled down to my hips, and my shirt rips open from behind. I wonder how I am able to perform such a task when I am withering in pain, seemingly paralyzed by a transformation

I never believed would come again. Until cool delicate fingers are placed upon my shoulders.

I recognize Paige's connection in an instant, but it is not her touch that makes me know it is her behind me. It is the bond of our mating, and her deep connection to her shaman magic, calling out to me. I hear her energy singing in my soul, the lingering hints of her blood running through my veins. She is my mate, my purpose, my calm and peace.

"Consider what I'm about to do as a form of foreplay."

Her whispers tickle at my brain, but make zero sense. It's those well-manicured talons of hers that do, as they dig into my hide, piercing both flesh and scale. In a move, resembling a band-aid being ripped off, she rakes her nails down my back in a quick and fluid motion. The warmth of my own blood oozes from the deep cuts she makes in the scars. Although I bleed, I do not feel pain. Instead, the blood is cleansing me, washing the wounds of my past and making me whole.

"You are free, ollphéist dána. I release you from the burden you carry, regain yourself and fly. Fly high, to the heavens and have your peace."

Her words are filled with sorrow this time. A sadness I feel deep in my heart, though I do not understand it. My brain is not functioning as a man. I am no longer caged. I am free to be my true self.

I am dragon, and I must soar.

CHAPTER 24

"You better come back to me, cowboy. Do you hear me?"

The velvet croon comes to my ears from the breeze. I do not understand the language, but I do appreciate the tone. It mixes well with the energy I gain from the Earth below and heavens above, gifting me my god-strength as I begin to shift.

I welcome the shift. I greet it like the old friend I have been missing, for so long.

Soon I will be whole and can return home.

Home?

Such a foreign word. It seems hollow, it doesn't translate. Perhaps the meaning isn't what I thought it was. That veil of magic just beyond, hidden in the clouds, enticing me back. It was once the birthplace I pined for, ached for. My world. Not this wasteland I've been imprisoned in by the betrayal of a goddess.

I shake off the anger with a snarl as I try to understand. The transformation is tumultuous, I forgot that. There was a time I could change as quickly as the thought, and spend days in my true form. But now, I can't seem to sort through the uncontrolled turbulence occurring inside of me. It's disorderly, confusing, a rollercoaster of emotions and pain. So much mental anguish.

My head is spinning from it, making the meadow and desert blend together into a blur of colors and shapes. There are people around me, but not really with me. I don't see them, anyway. I sense their emotions, though. A mix of excitement and terror, happiness, and outrage. It confuses me further. There is no reason for anyone to fear me, and yet, I know they should. I am kind and sensitive, but I was also once a powerful and feared beast amongst the gods.

Except, I have not been this for a long while, and since that time, no one has pined for me. No one has thought to worship me. Hell, no one has even mentioned my name. If they had, it wouldn't have taken me this long to regain myself. If someone had missed me, my powers would have returned sooner. It's how the gods stay powerful, in prayer or passing. They remain as long as someone whispers their name.

I roar out a loud screech of my suffering, to be heard in the heavens, for what they have done. They have given me the biggest kick of rejection to the balls. They left me here, a prisoner, fighting to exist amongst the humans. They discarded me. I remember now. I remember I already mourned this loss and rebuilt from those ashes.

A fire beast can never truly burn, though.

I try to get up, to stand and run from this, again. Something is wrong, though. There is a heaviness pressing down on me, pinning me to the dirt.

My past, perhaps, weighing in on me.

I kick and buck. I'm struggling against this weight, knowing the only way out is to deal with the torment in my mind. I must speak my secrets and spill my lies. Confess my greatest sins, to be forgiven, so I can return to my glory.

I laugh, for this is a part of the joke. They do not want me back. The sound of the laugh rumbles up, coming out my throat with fire. A spray of hot flames shoots from my mouth, melting the tiny sprigs of grass growing before me.

"No, stop it," someone growls out. "Control yourself. Don't make me have to bust your balls, cowboy."

I recognize the deep reverberation more than the words of warning. Its sound is inviting to my ears, soothing to my soul, and reminds me of something beautiful. Someone beautiful.

Paige.

A vision of my tattooed, smartass, and strong beauty comes to mind. And with this vision, I realize she is the weight pressing me down, along with a few others. The court is holding me to the dirt, trying to control me as I shift.

I sense their familiar signatures around me. They are acting like a real family. They have helped guide me to this point. In fact, it was September's magic that started this transition, when she blessed me as her Commander.

But it was Paige who bravely cut the ties, Livia put on me, that kept me bound to this realm. Paige is the one who set me free. She willingly granted me freedom by digging out my missing wings so I could finally have my peace.

Except, she is my peace.

She is my home.

Here I am, selfishly grieving for something that was never real. I thought all the years of hiding in shadows had taught me the lessons I needed to know. But my greatest lesson, is what has been realized today. The heavens never wanted me, they were the ones who orchestrated my downfall in the first place. Livia said she wanted me, but only because she knew she could use me.

Paige is the one. The only reason for me to go on.

She worships me, praises me, and loves me. It is because of her love the curse lifted, and I'm able to return to my true form. By gifting me my wings, she's given me the chance to go home. I'd be a fool to go back, though. Heaven isn't my paradise, not if she can't come with me.

No, this is my home. Here, with her, and with these people.

My family, blood of my blood.

I have felt more love in this world, and from these people, than any other. The proof is around me, as they work together to keep me tethered. There is magic involved, but mostly I sense their love as they-- September, Lazarus, Lilith, Samuel, Chris, Magennis, Sabre, Gage, Brigid, Shax, Ducky, Mac Tìre, even the two girls and the humans, my sister's friend Jamie, Bean and Kingsley, and of course, my beauty-- all lay upon me to keep me with them.

They care enough to protect me when I am so vulnerable, even though there is a threat to them. That is love, that is family, and this is everything I have always wanted. Now I must repay this kindness so we can do what we came here to do.

No more outbursts. No more shifting. It is time to get serious and win this fight with Bear so we can rebuild. Together. And to do that, I must reverse my shift. Turn the scale armored beast back into human flesh.

Easier to think than to do.

My massive body, pinned beneath numerous people, is bigger than the barn itself. It's difficult to turn a semi-truck into a child's tricycle, but it is what I must do.

I fill my mind with thoughts of their concern, and the acts of their kindness. It helps to tame the beastly part of me, to calm his wild nature so I can begin to shrink.

I'm a deflating balloon, shriveling in size. My tail whips up and back. It might have even hit someone in the process, but like a snake slithering back into a hole, my tail wilts and withers until it is just part of my spine.

My tree trunk arms, and even larger legs, give up the fight. Slowly contracting, softening as they become more human muscle and less dragon ripped. I'm still chiseled, with a well-defined muscularity that might be considered overdone for a human, but for a supernatural, I rival the likes of Sabre and Lazarus.

My form is shrinking at such a fast pace, the elasticity of my skin has to catch up. For a few moments, until my dermis snaps back over my skeleton, I resemble an old gnarly prune, complete with bright red coloring.

The red tint doesn't leave my skin, nor do the scales of armor just below the surface. It's for my own protection. We still have a fight before us, and though I fight as a male of worth, I have no issues with using my beastly advantages to cross the finish line, undefeated.

"I think he's…" Someone starts to speak.

"Eww, he's melting," shrieks a girl I do not recognize.

"He's not melting, Jamie, he's reversing his change," September states with impatience at her friend.

"No wolf can reverse a change," Bear calls out. "Cale was right, this court is full of abominations."

There is a reduction of the weight on me, a little less off my right leg and a lot more off my back. I must not be a flight risk anymore, if people are getting off of me. A set of bare feet cross in front of my face, small in size with dainty toes. I don't know whose feet these are until September begins to speak.

"I can tell you, from experience, a shift can be reversed. It is not easy, and only those of great power can make it happen. Zander is that powerful."

Bear barks a laugh. "He's a mutt, and mutts don't have power."

September's impatience for Bear's stupidity comes out in a sigh. "Zander is no mutt, if you were paying attention you would have noticed he isn't a wolf. He is the first shifter of this realm, a god amongst us, and whether he is in his true dragon form or not, he has more powers in his little finger, than all of you, put together."

"A god my ass," Bear snaps back. "This is what I warned you all of. Cale said this would happen. This human is a liar. She spouts these tales to make us think she is an all-powerful Queen. She is no Queen. Livia was our true Queen, she fought brutally and bravely for our kind. This girl is nothing more than a trickster of the dark arts. This one plays games, tries to fool us with make-believe creatures."

"Jesus Christ, you're an idiot," Paige's anger vibrates against my back as she speaks with passion. "Zander isn't some made up figment of the imagination. He is from the old world, of the great gods and goddesses. He came from a time before we even existed, before your precious Livia came to us. You would know this if you picked up a history book. You never seemed to have a problem believing in the

Goddess Livia when she created our world. Why do you not
believe in her daughter?"

"Quiet child," Bear scolds her. "You sound like your
father spewing this nonsense. He was just as gullible. Except
he believed in those Indian spirits, and look where that
landed him."

Bear stops to laugh and a few on his side join him. Paige
jumps off my back, her steel heels land in the dirt inches
from my face.

Since I am no longer the danger, having returned to my
human form, the rest of the court, and our friends, also leave
me to join Paige, beside September. I roll to my side to stand,
and realize I am completely naked. The shift destroyed what
clothing I had on, in tattered shreds, leaving me with nothing
to wear.

Lazarus suddenly appears at my side and stuffs a ball of
cloth in my hand. I look down at the pair of colorful surfing
shorts in my hand, then at him with annoyed displeasure.

He shrugs his shoulder as he chuckles. "What? It's not
like I had time to get you something designer. Just be
grateful I brought you something at all."

His smirk sings of sweet revenge. Through his gift of
sight, he knew I would be needing clothing today. He also
knew I would choose these people over the homeland. So, as
a form of punishment, Lazarus is getting back at me, for my
brief consideration of leaving him and the court.

"Fucker," I mumble, the sound garbles out as though I
have a mouth full of stones.

My motor skills aren't quite up to par, either. I'm slow
and clumsy trying to get my leg in the shorts. When I almost
wobble over, Lazarus catches me before I fall, and helps me
pull the garment on.

I offer a nod of thanks and he grins back. "I'll always be
here for you, my brother."

With shorts tied tight to my waist, Lazarus and I join
Paige and the others. The verbal mud-slinging is in full

swing, with Paige leading the charge.

"My father was loved by his people, a better Alpha than you."

Bear laughs. "An Alpha, to who? The humans who believed he was the great wolf spirit or to the woman he bit to become one of us? Your father wasn't an Alpha, my dear, he didn't even have a pack. He was too weak to lead one, just like this Queen is too weak to lead us. The only thing your father did that was worth anything, was have you, and you have served me well. But the time has come for history to repeat. I got rid of your father, now I will rid us of the True Alpha."

Paige steps forward, stands defiantly, in front of her adopted father. Her voice drops a degree as she spits out her question. "What do you mean you got rid of my father?"

My heart speeds up, knowing what Bear will say is going to break my beauty. I step closer to her, to be at her back when the truth comes.

Bear's grin is dripping with malicious intent. "Sweet Pea, you wear almost the same look of surprise your mother did, before I gutted the wench. And your father, well, he was so stricken with grief, he didn't even put up a fight."

I'm standing behind her when she hears this devastating news. I wait for her to drop, to faint, to react somehow. There's nothing, no tremble in her shoulders, no wobbling on her feet. She's holding strong. Her only movement is the clenching of her fists.

"You lie," Paige's accusation cracks in her voice.

"Yes, but not about this, and you know it's true," he states. "I saw what your father had built in these untouched lands. There was an opportunity here for our kind, and I took it, then I took you and became Alpha. I told you then I would take care of you, but you had to defy me every chance you got. Normally, to find a prince you need to kiss the frog. You took it upon yourself to fuck the whole pond, and ended up the whore of a serpent."

He shakes his head at her, curling his lip in disgust. My own fists curl from the deep urge I have to punch him in the face. A growl rips from my throat as I lunge forward to get at the man.

"No, Zander, don't," Paige pleads with me, turning to hold me back.

"It seems I've upset the snake," Bear calls back to his crew.

I don't hear as many laughing with him, this time.

"What's done is done," Paige whispers to me. "His insults are just words, and he'll get what's coming to him for the rest. I swear on my father's name, he will pay for what he's done."

"And what are you going to do, child, turn your monsters on me? You know they can't attack if I've done nothing wrong, and according to our laws, I haven't. I challenged your father and won. By right, I could take you as my kin, and today, I am giving you to Alpha Garo, to do with as he sees fit."

September wedges herself in the middle of the conversation. "A woman's body is her own private property, and only she has the right to pick her trespasser. That is the law of the Kingdom. Paige has picked Zander, and they have been mated, she wears his mark. Garo can have your lands, but he has no ownership of her."

"Kingdom law is not pack law, our Alpha advisory board made sure of that, after Livia left. We are not ruled by the old laws and you cannot enforce them on us," Bear spews back.

"No, but I can," Gage booms out, pushing Bear back from the Queen.

Bear's face starts to turn red from anger, he appears to be at his breaking point. "You also have no say. You are the True Alpha in title only. You belong to the Blackwood pack, led by your brother. He rules the lands, not you, and as we discussed, he holds all the wealth, which makes him our leader."

Gage towers over Bear, staring down at the man with a glint of challenge in his eye, daring the wolf on. "I belong to the Blackwood pack because it was me, not Garo, who killed my father. It was me who started the Calgary pack. It was me who killed Leland Kline and took Kelowna, and it is me, not my brother, who leads the pack in Toronto. If you need proof of this, Cody and Taylor, who came with Garo today, are from my pack, and they are marked by the royal crest, my crest."

Gage snaps his fingers; Cody and Taylor, the two mystery travelers Ducky spoke of earlier, appear from the crowd. Our heated grouping makes room for them to come into the fold. The two men take a knee and whip off their shirts, bowing their heads for everyone to see the paw mark on their necks. It has the Blackwood swirl at the bottom of the mark, in the middle are two swords crossing, and at the top sits the crown.

Sabre comes to stand beside the wolves. He unbuttons his flannel shirt and drops it from his shoulders. "Many of you know me as the hybrid, and you know I had never been given a mark. When Gage Blackwood became the True Alpha, he marked me and our Queen with his crest."

Sabre takes a knee beside the other two men, and again, we all gaze upon the same mark as he continues to speak. "If you still aren't satisfied, then look at Zander's neck. Today, you witnessed the True Alpha naming Zander as his Commander. You saw the Queen bless him, and his shift to dragon beast. Never in our time has there been a shifter, never has one been marked, until today."

I hear Paige gasp from my side. When I swivel my head her way, she has her hand cupping her mouth with tears gleaming in her eyes.

"It'd be true, the paw be more of a clawed foot, but it'd sure be the same crest," Mac Tire announces behind me.

My hand instantly goes to my neck and I run my fingers

across the spot between my shoulder blades. I can't feel anything different on the surface, but somehow I know it's there. The Queen didn't just bless me she had also kissed me. It was through her touch that she magically placed her mark on me. The marking of the crown, the symbol of belonging to this group. I had once been angry with Gage for never giving me this. He has righted that wrong and officially made me his Commander. More importantly, he made me his brother. And like the other men, I too, take a knee to proudly show the world I have a family.

"They are brothers, Gage and Garo, so of course they will have the same mark. This is not proof," Bear urges the crowd. "The title, land, and money, it's all Garo's."

Gage snort. "He wishes."

"I run it," Garo pipes up from the back of the crowd.

Gage turns toward the voice as the crowd parts open to reveal Garo out in the pasture, alone.

"Sure, only because there was a time when none of it mattered to me. You always seemed to like dealing with the financial shit, so I let you."

Garo is smug as he explains to his brother. "Right, and I still have control of it. I made sure, before I left home, to consolidate the whole Blackwood fortune into one off-shore account. You now have nothing."

A wave of shock rolls through the crowd, on both sides. Gage, however, starts to laugh. It's loud and echoes around us. "No, you didn't. Tell him, Samuel."

My sister's mate stands off to the side with his human friends. A smug grin sits on his face, as well. "Last week, Sabre and I had a conversation about securing files. He talked with Gage, and they asked me to build a computer program, just for the court. Yesterday, my system warned me of the breach Garo was making. Gage was able to stop the transfer and move his entire fortune, titles, and land, into a numbered account under his name. The only one with access is him. According to my system, Gage still has billions. Garo, has about half a million."

I'm watching Garo as Samuel makes this fundamental announcement. Garo's face drains of color, leaving him looking ghostly white. "No, that can't be. I watched the money transfer."

Sam shrugs his shoulders. "That's what the program does, and it seems to be working, really well."

"Wait, so Garo has nothing," Paige blurts then addresses Bear, "Aren't you supposed to sell me off to an Alpha of worth? This guy has less than I do. This can't be a legal trade in pack law."

"The arrangements have already been made," a wolf from the crowd, the Alpha from the California pack, speaks out. "The Alphas have already decided, Garo will take over Nevada and Paige Sky will become his mate. Money had no part in the deal, but it is part of the deal we made for Garo to be the head of our board. Only an Alpha of great wealth can lead us, and it would seem..."

Gage cuts the man off, "That I am your leader. Your plan is crumbling, Bear."

"Only if I lose the challenge, and I don't feel much like dying today." Bear sounds like a man ready for a fight.

The hint of the dare has been put out in the air, and the crowd backs away to allow for what will come next. I'm on my feet and taking my place at Gage's side. The rest of the court files in behind us, readying themselves for the moment Bear throws down the gauntlet.

Bear's crew has distanced themselves from him, allowing a few of the supernatural leaders to stand at his back. There are only a handful, fewer men willing to fight with Bear than the numbers he arrived with at sundown. It's a curious turn of events, more so, when I notice Paige is still standing her ground, at the center of the circle. She has taken up a fighting stance, as though she will be taking the challenge, instead of Gage. I'm about to go to her, to pull her back, when Sabre slams his large arm across my chest, stopping me from moving forward.

I don't get a chance to question his actions as Paige begins to speak. "You shouldn't commit to a promise you can't keep."

Bear glares at his daughter, there is hatred in his eyes. "You have no say in this, Pea. Get out of the way or I swear…"

"You'll what?" Paige interrupts him. "You'll strike me? I hope you do, but unlike the times before, this time I get to punch back. And when I start, I won't stop until you are dead."

I watch Bear's face go through a transition, it's the visual version of what's going through my own head. The confusion turns to question, ending with understanding and a loud cackle.

"Are you challenging me, child?"

Another wave of shock runs through the crowd, mostly on Bear's side, and I realize our side isn't surprised by this because they already knew Paige would do this. It's the hint Paige and Sabre gave me earlier, and I still don't understand what is being said.

I'm not the only one, as the Alpha from Texas, standing behind Bear, voices his distaste. "Girl, you are off your rocker. Females can't be Alpha, it's the law. You're wasting your breath even speaking the words."

Paige straightens her posture, from fighting crouch to the bitch boss she is so good at being. "Perhaps you should all reread your regulations again, before you deny me of my rights."

"Rights? You have none. Pack law states it," Bear angrily spews, spittle flying from his lips.

"Ah, but you are wrong," she proudly announces, turning back briefly to offer Sabre a wink. "A friend of mine pointed out that after Livia disappeared, the pack was in such a hurry to distance themselves from the rest of the supernatural, they didn't catch their own mistakes when they put new rules in place."

"There are no mistakes," spouts the Alpha from California.

"Yes, there are several," Sabre breaks into the conversation. "In the laws, it states, an Alpha with no sons can use his oldest blood daughter to gain an heir. There is nothing about an adopted daughter because none of you thought of providing orphans new possibilities. Therefore, in this case, Bear's oldest blood daughter is Jillian, not Paige, so the trade is not legal by pack laws."

"Don't forget the best part, Sabre. The part they forgot to mention, probably because they thought a female would never be smart enough or strong enough to consider the matter," Paige is gloating and I don't blame her.

This news is everything we hoped for and more. She is not Bear's blood, and as such, he cannot use her as an heir. This whole thing could have been avoided, and I'm wondering why she's not taking this win to get out of here. A wave of unease washes over me when the light goes on inside my head.

"Paige, what are you doing?" I gasp out my question.

"I'm doing what I have every right to do. I, Paige Sky, hereby put forth my challenge to Bear for the title of Alpha of the state of Nevada."

"You can't challenge me," Bear shouts.

Sabre snorts, "Oh, but she can, and she did."

"How can this be?" The Texas Alpha sputters out, seeming shocked by this outcome.

Sabre begins another teaching lesson. "Again, the laws have holes. In the event of a challenge it states, an Alpha can only challenge another Alpha. No one considered a female could be Alpha, but once Paige's father had died, his title was passed to her. She is marked by her family crest, a Viking troll cross of protection, and she is not the only one."

"Aye, tis the mark I wear with pride," Mac Tire calls out over the crowd.

Ducky seconds the claim, "I, too, wear the mark of Pea's pack."

"Paige is my sire, and I'm proud to wear her mark," Samuel also shouts out.

"And I wear Pea's mark." Kingsley steps forward, swinging her red locks over her shoulder to expose her neck symbol for us to see, the horseshoe with double curly-Qs.

"That's an official four members, enough for a pack with Paige as their Alpha, and gives her the status to bring forth a challenge to Bear," Gage announces. "By my authority as True Alpha, I declare this legal and a challenge must take place."

Bear jerks forward towards Gage, shouting as he moves, "I didn't come here to fight my daughter, I came to fight you."

I hold my breath as Paige steps in front of his path, blocking him from reaching Gage. "You want to get to him, you go through me, first."

Bear stops, barking a laugh inches from her face. "You will not win, little girl. This is a man's game, we have the power and strength. You were nothing when I took you, and you are still nothing."

I watch Paige shrug her shoulders at the insult, her left hand disappears in front of her. I envision her smiling, and wearing it like a loaded gun while she curls her fist to make the first strike, but she surprises me with her rebuttal instead. "Whenever you put me down, I hold my vagina just like this because holding this much power always cheers me up. Admit it, I outsmarted you, and it didn't take a set of balls to do it."

God, I love her bravado, but she picks the worse times to show it. I know what she's doing, she's poking the Bear, literally, and it works.

"You whore," Bear snarls in her face, a warning before he makes his move. I watch his right fist cock back as he throws the first punch.

Paige is quick, dancing on her feet and ducking off to her right. Bear's body goes forward with his momentum, and Paige comes out of her duck, with a flying fist of her own. Swinging her right arm in, she nails Bear in the gut. It takes him by surprise and buckles him over, but she's waiting with her left fist and clocks him square in the jaw.

I'm rooting for my beauty, she fights with as much passion as she fucks, and proving to be equally talented at both. She has the grace of a champion ring fighter and is as dirty as a back-alley brawler. She isn't afraid to use what she has, those sharp talons, the spikes of her heels, she even pulls a blade and cuts Bear across the ribs. It isn't deep enough to create damage, but it's enough to send a wave of fear through him. I see it clearly in his eyes, he underestimated the strength and skill of his opponent, and he's starting to realize this is one fight he will not win.

The rest of Bear's crew is starting to see the same result, their leader is falling. They must make the decision to either join the winning side or gamble with a losing hand. People tend to lash out when they are out of options, and with nothing to lose they will fight to the death.

"Defend the Queen," I shout to prepare the court, as the first wave of Alphas charge across the pasture.

With wings out on full display, Lilith and Lazarus, as well as the Avenging Angel girls, take the lead to guard the Queen, with magical balls of light they fire at the wolves. Like bowling pins, the half-dozen men go down in a fit of screams as their flesh bubbles from the magical burn. The girls rush forward with blue crystal daggers in hand, attacking the weakened men by cutting off their heads.

I haven't seen daggers like theirs since the war with the gods. The magic in the blade is said to be powerful enough to kill a god. Only one race has ever been strong enough to wield these blades, one race that was said to be extinct.

"Did ya see that kill, mate? They'd be girls after me own heart. I think I'm in love," Mac Tìre gushes with admiration.

Turning my head to the wolf, I notice his eyes have a glassy glaze to them, he's mesmerized by what he's witnessed. He's attracted to the girls, maybe even turned on by them. The Viking has always loved a good battle and if the two females have an equally fierce spirit, Mac Tìre might have just found his love connection. I'm not sure I have the heart to tell him what they are. I'm not sure I even believe it myself.

The wolf runs off, and I swear there's a skip in his step as he makes his way to the girls. I brush off the whole exchange. This is not the time to dwell on ghosts or Mac Tìre's love life, not when there's an enemy wolf coming at me with gun drawn.

The sight of the weapon sends me charging forward. The shot rings out as the wolf pulls the trigger. The bullet hits my chest with an audible ping then bounces off me, hitting the wolf in the throat. The jolt knocks the man to his back, blood sprays from the hole with burping bubbles as he tries to take a breath. He withers on the ground, trying to crawl away, but he's slowed by lack of breath.

I stand over the man, he is not familiar to me. It is his colored patch that informs me he is from the Wicked Ones. He's only a prospect, not yet a full member. I imagine he thought if he killed me, he could get patched in. I smirk at the wolf as I kneel between his legs, grasping a chunk of his hair in my hand to hold back his head. His eyes grow the size of oranges as he watches my claws grow out from my fingers.

"Karma's a bitch, and then you die," I whisper as I slice his head clean off his shoulders with my nails.

I stand quickly to do a survey. I turn left to check on Paige, she's still holding her own and Bear isn't looking good. I want to finish the fucker off, but this is her fight. Her revenge for a lifetime of suffering. I'm proud of her, she is making history and I know she is going to be an inspirational, first female, Alpha.

I leave her to her history-making, continuing to take stock. I turn a little further left, to see Gage has his hands full with the California Alpha, while Sabre fights at his back against the Texas Alpha. The Kings both appear bloody, but not battle worn. The blood is from the Alpha dogs they are beating to a pulp. By the looks of this match, it will soon be over. Another win for the warriors.

Behind the Kings, the Queen fights with my sister. They are using their magic to hold back some of the vamps, while Magennis spars with the ancient New Orleans leader. The Queen's human and my sister's wolf mate, are guarding their females' backs. They are honorable men for defending their women, even though they are the weakest beings here. They have courage for being a part of our world, for mating who they did, knowing there will always be a threat. The first time I met these men, I thought them foolish, but I now understand the love they hold in their hearts. These men aren't foolish, they are brave.

Someone grabs me from behind, and the large male body slams into my back. His forearm comes around my throat into a choke hold while his hand grips the hair on my head. He squeezes tight, trying to crush my windpipe while pulling my head as far back as possible in an attempt to pull it from my neck.

A wolf or a vampire can be decapitated in this manner by another wolf or vampire. I suspect the vampires don't have much use for me so this is probably a wolf. There are only two wolves who would gain from my death. Since Paige is currently in front of me, with Bear at her feet and her blade at his throat, I know this has to be Garo.

Just as I figure this out, he begins to speak. "She is still betrothed to me, and when I kill you, she will be my mate and with her wealth, I will gain back my position in the court. Once I do, I will find another way to bring Gage down, and you won't be here to stop me."

I snort a laugh and he squeezes my throat tighter. "Give

it your best shot, wolf," I gasp out.

He yanks on my hair hard enough for the strands to rip out. My beast roars out a battle cry, filling the air with a high-pitched shriek. With Garo on top of me, his ear is right beside my mouth. He screams and jumps off me, hands to his head. I realize, once I see his blood dripping between his fingers, that my shrill cry has burst his eardrum.

"Serves you right for trying to play a game you won't win," I taunt him.

He's a tough fucker, though, as he shrugs off the pain he reaches inside his suit jacket for a dagger. It's a thick steel blade he pulls out, curved in the shape of a crescent moon, and has a bone handle. The chieftain dagger has aged longer than the man holding it, and probably seen more battles than him, too.

He secures it in his hand, holding it with the handle tip up so the blade runs the length of his arm. "I'm not playing, and this isn't a game. My plan is still the same, I will be the Queen's Alpha. Gage took it from me, but I am a patient man. Once I get you out of the way, I'll climb back up to take my rightful place beside her."

He waves the blade out in a striking motion, aiming high for my head. I arch my body back and over, weaving away from his strikes. His fingers dance, twisting the handle around in his hand so the blade is away from his body. Then he lunges forward to stab me low in the stomach. The blade tip sinks into my skin less than a half of an inch and stops, or rather it gets blocked by hard scale.

Garo's eyes flicker down and he frowns at my bare belly with the end of the knife sticking into my flesh. He steps forward to put his weight behind the push, trying to get the knife in deeper. Between his wolf strength and my armor, the blade actually bows out, causing Garo's arm to extend. The knife tip skips across the bumpy ridges of the scales below my skin's surface, and slices a gash from bellybutton to ribcage before the knife flies from his hand.

The force he put behind himself, has him coming straight for me in a fall, landing face first into my bloody laceration. I step back to let him fall into the dirt. The armor protected me from the knife, and the possibility of Garo gutting me open, but the cut still stings like a bitch.

From the irritation of the prickle, not to mention the mess of blood oozing down my side, I hiss. It causes a plume of smoke to swirl out from between my teeth. I breathe deep to try to calm the anger growing within. The more air I take in, the darker the smoke is coming out. If I continue, it will turn to fire. As much as I want to end this, Garo is still Gage's brother.

This is why I have been holding back. I respect Gage. I remember how he grieved after he killed his father. I don't want him to go through that again. I don't want him to be reminded of it every time he looks at me. This isn't a judgment I can make, for him, for Garo, even for the crown.

I kick Garo's leg to make him roll over. "Get up."

He's cradling his dagger hand, there's blood coming out the slash across his palm. The knife didn't fling out from his hand, his hand wasn't strong enough to hold on and went across the blade.

"That's going to leave a mark," Gage vocalizes the same thought floating around my head.

"He won't be wielding his dagger at me anytime soon, and technically I'm taking this as my win," I answer with a laugh.

"I meant you," he says with a sincere tone. "Someone get a towel or something, Zander's cut up."

I twist my head, to look at him and end up scanning the field around us. "The fight's over?"

He snorts at me, grabbing Garo by the scruff to push him towards the Queen. "Don't sound so shocked, it's not like we had strong competition."

I grumble out some sort of noise as a reply, more concerned with finding Paige than finishing this conversation. I turn to the east and scan towards the barn, across to the west and back down. When I don't see her standing, panic sets in, and I push myself to look down at the many headless bodies littering the ground. It's difficult to make out who they are, so I concentrate on the bodies themselves, to find any covered in tattoos.

My heart is pounding in my chest, a trickle of sweat starts to bead across my hairline as my eyes jump from mangled body to mutilated body parts.

"Paige," I whisper, unable to speak any louder. "Oh, God, Paige, please be alive."

"Relax cowboy, I don't have the energy to tackle you if you get beastly again."

Paige's voice sounds drained, the rasp is missing, but I'm not complaining. I'm relieved to just hear she is alive, but I need to feel her in my arms. I turn to greet her with a smile, it fades once I see she's covered in blood.

"Jesus, you're hurt."

She shakes her head. "Not my blood," she tells me, then touches my side with her fingers. "But this is yours. We have to get you patched up."

I pull her into my arms and hold her as tight as possible. "I'll sew it later when we get home. Right now, I need to hug you."

I hear her soft moan of happiness in my ear as her arms hug me back. "I won, by the way."

"I'm not surprised, I never doubted you for a moment," I tell her back. "Congratulations, Alpha."

Our reunion is brief as the movement in the pasture starts to draw a crowd. Paige and I both turn to watch the commotion as Garo is put on trial.

"Garo Blackwood," September announces from her position in the pasture. "You have been charged with treason, for the act of conspiring to overthrow the Kingdom, and for the role you took in the attempt to kill the True Alpha. As Queen of the supernatural Kingdom, I act as your judge and jury when I sentence you to death for your crime. Have you anything to say before I serve justice?"

Garo looks up at September from his kneeling position in the sparse grass. His eyes have softened, they plead for her forgiveness. "I ask for mercy, my Queen. My actions were made for the security of the crown, for your protection. No harm was to ever become of you. My brother is not worthy, and he can't be trusted. I beg of you to reconsider your punishment. I will show you my support, and do whatever you ask to regain your trust."

"There are so many problems with what you just said," September sighs out. "Killing Gage would have hurt me deeply, but it would have done more harm to the child growing in my belly. The future King or Queen of our Kingdom. You didn't try to protect the crown, you tried to take it for yourself. There is no way I could ever trust that you wouldn't try to do again, and for the safety of my family, and this Kingdom, you must be condemned."

Lazarus approaches the Queen carrying his own specially crafted, two-handed, angel steel, battle sword. The blade is as long as the male's leg, the handle as long as his forearm, but even with this massive size, Lazarus can wield the weapon as though it weighs less than a twig. I have seen him in action with it, and it is more than impressive.

He bows his head to September, then steps beside Garo to take his position as executioner. Garo takes his final look at the Queen, at the court standing around September, to Paige and me, then finally at his brother.

"The better brother has won," he says and bows his head.

September glances at Lazarus for the nod. Once the signal is made, Lazarus swings the blade over his left shoulder straight above his head. He then pulls it directly down to slice off Garo's head. As soon as the cut is made, and Garo's blood hits the steel on the sword, a cold blue flame engulfs the blade. It sears the head, burning the open wound, and taking away any chance for a supernatural or even a god, to come back from the dead.

"Return to the fade, my brother, for your time here is done," Gage starts to pray. "May your sins be forgiven and the gods welcome you into the fold. Until we meet again."

"Blessed Be," we chant with him.

On Paige's orders, Ducky begins to organize the pack and remaining members of the MC. Shax has his crew chip in, and the bodies start to disappear inside the barn. Once the dead have all been taken inside, Lilith throws up a protection spell around the pasture, to hide the flames as I light the barn on fire. The traditional dragon way.

We stand, watching the flame slowly burn, until the whole barn catches. The heat becomes too much for most, especially the vampires, and our group starts to dwindle in numbers.

There are handshakes and hugs as we say thanks to our allies, and warn those that took a knee as they switched to our side. Then it's just the court, standing at the fence line in silence.

Lazarus and Sam hold Lilith between them. Gage and Sabre hold September, with Magennis and Chris close behind them. Shax stands with Ducky and my mother, whispering quietly between them. While I hold Paige close, with my mind racing through thoughts.

Only a few days ago, I stood outside this barn thinking about moments that mark our lives. How those moments are divided into two parts, before this, and after this moment in time. Here I am again, at another moment, but unlike the last time, I now know I can never go back to change my beginning. I can, however, start where I am in this moment and change my ending.

With everything I have been through, in my long and difficult life, I realize I can't feel sorry for myself. What has happened to me has given me the opportunity to grow, and obstacles to grow from. I chose this path and I consider it my gift. I have more than any man could ever ask for, a family, a home, and someone who I adore with all my heart. I look forward to more moments with them, as I shape my ending, if and when it may come. And the only thing that matters to me now, are the memories I get to make with these people in our future moments.

"We should head back and get packed. I'll call to have the plane ready for a flight out before dawn." I hear Gage tell the court.

"I'll be glad to get back to something normal, like planning the wedding. This trip has been exhausting," Lilith comments.

The group starts to head off, but September remains. She tilts her head to look at me and I can see she's chewing on something. "What if we get married here?" She asks, although, I'm not sure if she's directing the question to anyone in particular.

"What are you talking about, baby?" Gage comes back to ask his bride.

Her grin spreads across her lips. "I'm saying, we are in Las Vegas, and it's the wedding capital of the world. Right? So, why not do it here."

"Ye can't mean ye want to get some shotgun wedding in a chapel, on the strip, in front of some bloody Elvis impersonator, love," Magennis blurts.

"Oh, my, Goddess, please tell me you do not want that," Lilith screeches.

"No, God, no, not like that," September blurts then takes a breath and explains. "I just thought, a lot happened here, on Paige's property. We gained some family and lost some family. I don't want to wait until we pick the perfect date, and plan some big affair. I want to have a celebration with the people that mean the most to me, all of you right here. And, if Paige would be willing, I'd like to do the ceremony on her land, so that when we do leave, it's after something happy, and not all of this sadness."

Paige frowns then looks up at me with a shrug. "I don't know, what you do think?"

I'm touched she asked and I give her a squeeze. "I'm good with it if you are, *leannàn*, and the bonus part is, we don't have to do it in the snow."

Paige rolls her eyes and laughs. "In that case, I'd be happy to host your wedding, my Queen."

My sister squeals with joy and the conversation bursts open. Paige and I stand back with wide eyes, trying to avoid the craziness. I can see some fear in my beauty's eyes, but I don't know if it is from the idea of getting married or Lilith's over-the-top enthusiasm for it.

I shake her shoulder to get her to look away from the train wreck of matrimonial mayhem. "You scared you might catch the marriage bug?"

She chuckles, "Not at all. I'm looking forward to the day we tie the knot because I'm certain there will be bedposts involved."

"I fucking love you."

She grins and leans forward for the kiss, but before our lips meet she whispers, "And when the dragon falls in love with the desert princess, she is truly the one that's blessed."

ACKNOWLEDGMENTS

I first must give my immense gratitude to all the Legacy Series readers. Thank you, from the bottom of my big mushy heart for all of your wonderful support, encouragement, and growing friendships over the last few years. I love getting to meet you and see how much my world excites you. There is no greater gift for an author, than to know, someone enjoys their world as much as they do. Thank you!

A book just doesn't happen, it doesn't just appear out of thin air after you wave the magic wand...Trust me, I've tried. A book is created, nurtured and grown with immense love from all the following people. To Tanya, my wonderful editor, thank you for taking a chance on this series and for falling in love with it, so much that you came onboard to help make it even better. It's no secret I studied to be a chef not Shakespeare, and I needed all the help I could get with the technical parts of writing. You showed me the way and I will never be able to thank you enough for that. My life for you, my Queen!

To Cora, the best damn cover artist EVER! It truly amazes me how you can take my wish-list of ideas and pictures, and turn it into absolute brilliance. Thank you, for making my world look so damn good!

To my eager beta readers, who chew through these books like they are chocolate covered crack! Theresa, Ajay and Petra, your feedback, comments and many questions are why I keep finding new plot-lines, and those creative twists and turns...Just to keep you on your toes! Your dedication is fuel for my fire. You make me want to write a million more books just to hear your screams of excitement. Thank you, for every review, word of encouragement, and especially, your lust for more- Melt off the page, hotness! I aim to please, I just hope I can keep the heat warning at extreme, where you all seem to like it!

To my dear friend Eniko, four years ago you gave this newbie author a chance by opening my first book, I thank you for taking that chance, but I am honored you joined me on the journey. I love how our friendship has grown through this common love for books. I love how you listen on the edge of your seat as I run ideas by you. I, especially, love how you claim my hero's as your own with such fierceness...Back away ladies, Eniko has claimed Zander, Lazarus, Sabre, and Gage, and I have no doubt, she will win any challenges you set forth to her. Thank you, for being you, and for being a true friend.

And last, but certainly never least, to my wonderful partner, friend, lover, Mister, and awesome husband, Scott. None of this would even be possible if it wasn't for your continued support and encouragement. Thank you, for ALWAYS listening to my crazy ideas, and for pushing me to make them become written words. Thank you, for missing our 2018 New Year's tradition so I could finish this book. Thank you, for those drill-sergeant pep-talks when my self-doubt threatens to take over. Thank you, for ALWAYS being there, through the good times and bad, the happy and sad, the exciting highs and devastating lows- you will ALWAYS be my rock, my strength and my heart; today, tomorrow and forevermore!

ABOUT THE AUTHOR

Marianne Maguire is your sister in sin, and the bestselling Paranormal Erotic Romance author of the Legacy Series. She lives outside of Toronto, Ontario, Canada on her critter ranch with her husband and four-legged fur-kids. When not entertaining you with her devious mind, you can find Marianne beautifying family pets, helping the bereaved in her community, or out in her backyard jungle taming the wild landscape and saving the woodland critters.

Learn more about Marianne's books and where to follow her at:

www.mamaguire